"Where do you think your little boy is now, Mrs. Mellon?"

When there was no response from the woman in front of her, Detective Jackie Kaminsky repeated her question. "Do you know where Michael is?"

"Why are you asking me that? How would I know? I told you—I turned my back on him at the store for a few seconds, and he disappeared."

Jackie took a deep breath. She chose her words carefully. "Ms. Mellon, in my opinion, you seem upset, but not distraught the way a mother might be expected to feel if her child were in the hands of strangers. I think it's entirely possible you have some knowledge about where Michael is."

Leigh's voice was barely loud enough for Jackie to hear. "I think my ex-husband has him."

"Why? I thought he won his visitation rights in court."

"He did, but it wasn't enough. He wants to win everything—he wants to take Michael away from me forever. He's a monster." Leigh's face was white with emotion; her eyes blazed.

For the first time Jackie began to wonder if Leigh Mellon was entirely sane. She thought of the smiling little boy wearing his jaunty vest and bow tie.

A chill of fear went through her.

"Margot Dalton's a writer who always delivers: probing characterization, ingenious plotting, riveting pace and impeccable craft."
—Bethany Campbell, bestselling author of
See How They Run and *Don't Talk to Strangers*

Also available from MIRA Books and
MARGOT DALTON

TANGLED LIVES

Watch for Detective Jackie Kaminsky's
return in

SECOND THOUGHTS
March 1998

MARGOT DALTON

First Impression

MIRA BOOKS

MIRA

ISBN 1-55166-265-5

FIRST IMPRESSION

Copyright © 1997 by Margot Dalton.

MIRA and the star colophon are trademarks of MIRA Books.

Printed in U.S.A.

For Barb, Donna, Lila and Marilyn, who
liked this story as soon as they heard it.
And for Ross, who helped so much.

AUTHOR'S NOTE

This is entirely a work of fiction. There is no Northwest Substation presently associated with the Spokane Police Department; nor are any of the characters in this book based on real people.
Apart from a basic effort to portray the work of an investigating officer with some accuracy, a number of liberties (mostly related to administrative and procedural matters) have been taken for the sake of the story.

Many thanks to Sergeant James Earle of the Spokane Police Department, and to Sergeant L. K. Eddy (retired) of the RCMP for their generous assistance. Any errors or discrepancies in this work are not theirs, but the author's.

1

Jackie Kaminsky was in the shower, shaving her legs and making a poor job of it. For one thing, the blade was dull and needed to be replaced. But even with a new blade, she usually lacked the patience to shave properly.

"Damn!" she muttered as she nicked the skin over one of the protruding bones of her ankle. Blood mingled with the spray from the showerhead, flowing in a thin stream onto the wet tiles.

She leaned out of the shower, tore off a strip of toilet paper and jammed it against the cut in a messy wad, then stepped onto the bath mat and began to dry her slender, well-muscled body.

At thirty-two, she had the sort of looks that made truck drivers and construction workers whistle—at least when she wasn't in uniform.

Jackie glanced at her reflection in the mirror, half-obscured by steam, and tried to remember how long it had been since a man had seen her naked. These days she was far too busy for that kind of adventure, and usually too exhausted.

She switched on the blow-dryer and aimed it at her short glossy black locks, wondering idly if she should let her hair grow. Still short enough to meet the regulations for female police officers, her hair lay casually around her face just clear of the collar of her blouse. It looked neat and presentable, but it didn't have much style.

Two years ago she'd finally made detective and started wearing street clothes to work. She could probably let her hair grow if she wanted, but twelve years of habit died hard. Besides, she wasn't sufficiently interested in her appearance to give it more than a few minutes of passing consideration.

Blood had seeped through the clump of wet paper on her ankle, staining it bright red. She finished her hair, then dug out a bandage. After securing it over the cut, she pulled on furry white socks, a pair of gray jogging pants and a matching sweatshirt emblazoned with the crest of the Spokane Police Department. Finally, she collected a mystery novel, a half-written letter to a friend back in Oakland and a copy of the month-end report she was working on.

After a moment's thought, she took a banana and a couple of apples from the fridge and dropped the fruit into a plastic grocery sack. Carmen, she'd learned from experience, didn't tend to keep her fruit bowl well-stocked.

Still in her stocking feet, Jackie let herself out of her apartment, padded across the hall and knocked.

"Jackie?" a voice called from behind the door. "That you?"

"It's me."

The door swung open. The pretty brunette pulled her neighbor inside and hugged her. "This is so sweet of you, Jackie," she said. "Really. Giving up your Friday night to baby-sit for me, just so I can have an evening out…"

"No big deal," Jackie said mildly. "Friday night means nothing to me. I'm working weekends all summer. Besides, what else would I be doing?"

Carmen shook her head. "Well, Tiffany's asleep already. You don't have to do a single thing. She won't wake up again."

While Carmen stepped back into her bedroom to finish getting ready, Jackie set her fruit, book and paperwork on a sagging green couch. Then she took out an apple and crossed the living room to peer into the other bedroom, where Carmen's four-year-old daughter slept in a bed covered with a pink ruffled quilt and mounds of stuffed toys.

Turning toward Carmen's open door, she said, "I was hoping Tiffany and I would have enough time to play a few rounds of Old Maid before bedtime."

"Why?" Carmen asked. "She always beats you."

"Hey, I'm getting better." Jackie grinned. "Nowadays, I even win sometimes. So, when does Prince Charming arrive?"

"In about ten minutes. You'll like him, Jackie," Carmen said earnestly. "Tony's not all that great-looking and he could probably stand to lose a few pounds, but he's really nice to me and Tiffany. He runs his own bakery."

"Hell, if he's gainfully employed and he's nice to you," Jackie said, munching on her apple, "I like him already."

She moved back into the living room and flopped onto the couch. The TV was on, and she found herself distracted by the image on the screen. A uniformed police officer was saying something to the camera.

"Hey, Carmen," Jackie called. "What's Kent Paxton doing on TV in the middle of a Friday evening?"

Carmen came back into the room, fastening a dangling silver earring and holding a high-heeled shoe in her other hand. "Wow. He's cute," she said, looking at the earnest young policeman. "Do you know him?"

"Sure. I work with him down at the substation. What's going on?"

"He must be talking about that little boy who was abducted from Northtown Mall," Carmen replied. "The mother's going to make a public appeal to the kidnappers in a few minutes. Haven't you been watching TV?''

"I hate watching television when I'm home alone," Jackie said absently, still staring at the screen. "I was listening to a flute concerto on my stereo."

"A flute concerto!" Carmen echoed in disbelief. "My God, Jackie, anybody would think you were some kind of highbrow."

"Yeah, right. A real highbrow, that's me. How old is this missing kid?" She watched as Kent Paxton moved around near the front entry of the mall, followed by a throng of cameras and reporters.

"Three. Apparently the mother turned her back for only a few seconds to look at something, and when she turned around he was gone, vanished into thin air. They've already put out a statewide bulletin and made an appeal to the public for anybody who knows or saw anything related to the kidnapping to come forward. God," Carmen whispered, "how can she stand it, the poor woman? If that were Tiffany, I'd just die."

Jackie continued to watch the screen as her young colleague indicated the various mall entrances and recounted the police procedures that were being implemented. Carmen, meanwhile, slipped on her other shoe and turned to examine her face in the mirror above the couch.

"Do I look okay?" she asked.

"You look great." Jackie smiled at her friend.

Carmen was a hairdresser at a shop near the police substation. She and Tiffany were the nearest thing to a loving family that Jackie had in this city.

Or anywhere else, for that matter, she thought with a touch of bitterness.

"Oh!" Carmen's attention had returned to the television. "There's the mother. Poor thing, she looks terrified."

Jackie agreed. The woman appeared to be in her late twenties, tall and slender in a white shirt, cardigan and faded jeans. She had blue eyes, long dark blond hair pulled back from her fine-boned face, and her mouth was trembling visibly. She cast the policeman a glance of nervous appeal. He gave her an encouraging nod and she turned to face the cameras again.

"I'm Leigh Mellon," she murmured. "My son...my son's name is Michael Panesivic. He's only three years old." The camera zoomed in for a close-up. "Please, if anybody knows where he is, could you just..." She choked and looked down at her feet.

The young policeman put an arm around the woman's shoulders. She nodded tightly, collected herself and went on.

"Please," she repeated, blinking rapidly to hold back the tears. "Please, don't hurt my baby. If you have him or know where he is, just take him to the nearest police station. You can drop him off and drive away, and nobody will even know who you are. You'll be safe."

The camera stayed mercilessly on Leigh Mellon's face as she finished her appeal. At last she turned aside, replaced on the screen by a local news announcer who held up a small picture of the missing child, along with a further plea for any information on his whereabouts.

Carmen and Jackie were both sitting now, watching the screen. Carmen was crying openly, smudging her careful makeup.

"Oh, Jackie," she said, "do you think they'll ever find him?"

Jackie took a couple of tissues from a box on the coffee table, handed one to Carmen, then wrapped her apple core in the other. She thought about Leigh Mellon, her tearful blue eyes and heartfelt appeal to viewers.

"Sure, Carmen," she said at last. "I think they'll find him."

After Tony had arrived to pick up Carmen, and the pair had set out for the evening, Jackie watched television in brooding silence, wishing she hadn't promised to sit with Tiffany. Though she was off duty, she would have liked to drive over to Northtown and volunteer her services. She knew that the police and security personnel at the mall were going to be putting in a long frantic night.

Leigh Mellon stood near the mall entrance, watching as the television crew moved their van around to the side, following a police handler with a dog. The big German shepherd moved among the parked cars, whining eagerly and straining at his harness. It was the last day of June and the evening sun still smoldered above the horizon, flooding the parking lot in a wash of dull gold. The wind began to freshen and picked up scattered bits of debris, whirling them across the dirty pavement.

Leigh shivered, hugging her arms. She turned to the young police officer beside her. "Was that…was I all right?"

He gave her an encouraging smile. "You did fine. Like I told you, the main thing in a public appeal is to alert people so they're watching for anything unusual, but not to pressure or spook the possible abductor. If somebody's got your boy, we want them to feel as safe as possible about returning him."

"And you think I said the right thing?" Leigh's hands were shaking. She clenched them into fists, then jammed them into the pockets of her cardigan.

"I think you did just fine. Come inside." Kent Paxton put an arm around her shoulders. "We can talk in the mall office."

Michael's stroller stood nearby, with his little coat lying on the seat. Leigh crossed to it and picked the coat up, turning it aimlessly in her hands.

The coat was so small. It was made of red satin with knitted cuffs and collar, and had a decal of Mickey Mouse on the back.

"We bought it for him in Disneyland last summer," she murmured. "Just before we…"

At that moment, one of the other policemen came over and whispered something to Paxton. Leigh waited tensely while they conferred in low tones.

"What is it?" she asked when the policeman hurried away.

"Nothing for you to worry about," Paxton told her. "We have to open the mall again, but it's okay. We have officers in place to monitor all the exits."

"Open the mall? What do you mean? The mall doesn't close until nine."

"Nobody's been allowed in or out for the past half-hour, Ms. Mellon. We're hoping your son's still somewhere inside, and we'll spot him if somebody tries to leave with him."

"Oh, God," she whispered, holding the coat to her face. The terry-cloth lining still smelled like Michael, a sweet combination of baby powder, sunshine and active little boy.

"Please," she said to the police officer. "Please find him. Michael's so small. And he hates being separated from me. He always cries when I leave him with the sitter in the morning and go to work, even though he knows I'm going to be coming back soon. I don't know how he'll—"

"It's all right, Ms. Mellon. We'll find him. Come inside, okay? We'll go to the mall office and I'll take down your statement. The best way you can help Michael right now is to stay calm."

Leigh nodded and went inside with him. People began to file toward the mall's entry doors. When they saw her pushing the empty stroller, they whispered to one another and cast her looks of sympathy.

She knew their concern was genuine, but she felt naked and violated, her agony exposed to hundreds of prying eyes. Lowering her head, she followed Paxton's dark blue uniform blindly, and felt a surge of relief when he escorted her into an empty room and closed the door.

The young officer spoke briefly into his portable radio, giving their location, then replaced the unit at his belt. "This is the mall security office," he said. "We can stay here for now. Would you like a cup of coffee or anything?"

She shook her head and sank into a chair, pulling the stroller close to her. Again she picked up Michael's little red coat, holding it to her face.

Her longing for her child was all-consuming. She couldn't think clearly anymore, and she felt breathless and panicky.

Kent Paxton seated himself behind the desk and flipped open his notebook. "I'll need quite a bit of general information from you," he said, "but let's start with your home address, then the events leading to Michael's disappearance, all right?"

Leigh nodded jerkily and struggled to find her voice. "All right," she said at last.

"First, then, are you a resident of Spokane?"

"All my life. My family's been here in Washington for…more than a hundred years."

The officer looked up, suddenly alert. "Is your father Alden Mellon by any chance?"

"Yes," she said listlessly, toying with the zipper fastening on Michael's jacket.

"I see." He studied her with interest for a moment, then

jotted something in his book. "Your parents live over in the South Hill area, right?"

She nodded again.

"How about you, Leigh? Where's your home?"

"Not far from the mall. I live here on the north side, by Loma Vista Park." Leigh gave the street address and watched while he wrote it down.

"All right." Paxton looked up again. "What time did you and Michael come to the mall?"

"About six o'clock. We had a sandwich in the food court, then window-shopped for a while."

"And what time did you go to the toy store?"

"Just before seven. Michael had..." Leigh stopped and swallowed hard. "It was his third birthday last week. A fair amount of money had been given to him by his grandparents, and I promised he could spend some of it on a toy. Whatever he wanted."

"You were letting him pick out the toy by himself, then?"

"Michael seems to want to do everything by himself. I...I sometimes let him."

"If I left my kids alone to pick out their own toys, they'd all want electric trains and Nintendo games," the officer said with a rueful smile.

Leigh clutched the little coat and rocked in the chair, trying not to cry. "If...if only I hadn't gone away and left him..."

"It's okay, Ms. Mellon. Try to stay calm. What happened after you took him to the toy store?"

"I showed him a bank of toys that weren't too expensive and said he could have anything he liked from that section and...and that I'd take him out of the stroller and leave him all alone to make the choice, like a big boy. I went out into the mall with the stroller and started looking at clothes in the shop window next door. There was a summer dress I liked, and I went inside to see what it cost. I was right near the window, keeping an eye on the front of the toy store every minute to make sure he didn't wander out into the mall. But when I went back into the toy store, Michael was…'' She shuddered and gulped, swallowing hard. "He was gone," she said finally. "I couldn't find him anywhere."

"How long did you look for him before you told somebody?"

"I don't know…" Leigh closed her eyes and took a deep shuddering breath. "Probably five or ten minutes. I looked all through the store, then out in the play area at the front, and up and down the mall in both directions."

"After that, you went back and spoke to the clerk in the toy store?"

"Yes. She helped me look for a few more minutes, checked the storeroom and office at the back of the store, then notified mall security. They made an announcement over the loudspeaker and we waited about fifteen minutes to see if anybody had found him. I guess after that, they called the police."

Leigh put the coat in her lap and smoothed the bright satin decal with shaking fingers.

"Did you notice anything unusual in the toy store when you and your son were there?"

Leigh frowned, trying to remember. "Just…there was some kind of disturbance near the front. A bunch of boys about ten years old were fooling around and roughhousing with some plastic swords from a wire bin by the entry. I remember that the clerk was trying to stop them, and they were being quite rude. She seemed really upset. Everybody was watching her while she dealt with them."

"But this disturbance wasn't anywhere close to where you left Michael?"

Leigh shook her head. "When I noticed the boys, I got a little worried and went back to check on Michael, but he wasn't even aware of them. He was squatting in the middle of the aisle, looking at some little plastic warriors or something on one of the bottom shelves."

"And we've got an accurate description of his clothes?" Paxton consulted the notebook. "Denim overalls, red-and-white-striped T-shirt and red canvas running shoes?"

"With blue laces," Leigh said automatically. "Did I tell you the laces were blue?"

The policeman's eyes softened with sympathy. "Yes. You told me about the laces."

Leigh bit her lip and stared at the pale gray wall above the officer's head.

Maybe it was just a nightmare, she told herself desperately. Maybe she was dreaming all this, and when she woke up, Michael would be safe in his bed just down the hall.

2

Leigh sat in the police car next to Kent Paxton, feeling small and frightened. The summer night was warm, the sky rich with stars. A delicate new moon drifted above the horizon.

Two cars followed them as they drove the few blocks from the mall to her house. One was Leigh's car, being driven by a police officer, and the other was a cruiser deployed to take the second officer back to the mall.

The radio crackled at frequent intervals, delivering bits of information that sounded garbled and terrifying. Paxton replied in monosyllables and gave Leigh an occasional worried glance.

Before they reached the house, he radioed police headquarters. "Could you find me an off-duty female officer to spend the night with Ms. Mellon?" he asked the dispatcher. "Maybe you could track down Detective Kaminsky. She lives not too far from here."

Leigh stiffened in alarm. "No," she protested as he replaced the radio. "Really, I don't need somebody to stay with me."

"If this is a kidnapping for ransom," he said gently, "there might be some kind of contact during the night. I don't want you to be at the house alone."

"But my sister... I'm sure Adrienne will come over.

She's at a charity fund-raiser tonight, but she'll be home soon."

"If we can get hold of her, that'll be fine. If not, we'll get somebody to stay with you."

Leigh subsided, realizing the futility of arguing with him. They reached her house and Paxton got out to open the garage for the officer who was driving Leigh's car. They exchanged a few words before the cruiser sped off into the darkness. Some media people clustered near the curb but Paxton hustled Leigh inside before they could get close to her.

"You said you wanted a bigger picture of Michael?" she asked, pausing in the foyer.

"Please. And some of yourself and other close family members, if it's not too much trouble. Especially your husband. Which way's the kitchen?" Paxton asked. "I'll make a pot of coffee for us while you're getting those pictures."

Leigh took him down the hallway to the kitchen, got out a tin of ground coffee and a filter, then went upstairs to look for the photographs.

She returned to find Paxton sitting at the table, his patrol jacket hanging over the back of another chair, making notes in his book while the coffee dripped into the pot. It was a warm reassuring sound in the evening stillness.

"Where do you work, Ms. Mellon?" he asked as she put mugs, cream and sugar on the table, then got out a tin of oatmeal cookies. She moved automatically, her mind numb with fear.

"Ms. Mellon?" he prompted gently.

She sank into a chair and pulled herself together with an effort. "I'm sorry. Please call me Leigh. I work at Southwood Elementary. I teach third and fourth grade, but we've been on summer vacation for more than two weeks."

"And Michael's father?"

"He teaches political science at Gonzaga University here in Spokane. His name is Stefan Panesivic."

Leigh handed over a family portrait, showing Stefan and her with Michael when their son was about a year old.

Paxton studied the photograph. "You said you were divorced?"

"Yes." Leigh got up to fetch the coffeepot, then poured the steaming liquid into their mugs.

"How long?"

"We separated last year in August, and the divorce was finalized about six months ago, in January."

"We haven't been able to get hold of your ex-husband. Do you have any idea where he might be?"

She shook her head.

"Well, maybe he's just out for the evening." Paxton made a couple of notes. "How often does Mr. Panesivic see Michael?"

Leigh sank into her chair and gripped her mug with shaking hands. The officer looked at her, suddenly alert.

"Leigh?" he said again. "What are your custody arrangements?"

"He's... Stefan is supposed to have Michael every Saturday from ten in the morning until bedtime. That's what was stipulated in our divorce agreement. But for the past few months..."

"He hasn't bothered to pick him up? Is that what you're saying?"

Leigh shook her head and swallowed hard. "He wants to, but I haven't...I don't let him have Michael alone. So Stefan hasn't actually taken Michael out since April. He's seen him two or three times when...when I've allowed him to come here to the house for a few hours."

"Why? Has there been some kind of problem with abuse or mistreatment of the child?"

"No, no, nothing like that. At first, while we were separated and then right after the divorce, Stefan took Michael every week. They usually went out to spend the day with Stefan's parents."

"Where?"

"Stefan's family has a place near Painted Hills Golf Course. It's actually like a little farm, with animals and chickens and a big garden. Michael loves going there."

"So what happened in April? Why did you change your mind about visitation?"

"I was…afraid," Leigh murmured.

"Of what?"

"I'm…" Leigh's voice caught. She cleared her throat nervously. "I'm afraid that if Stefan's allowed to have Michael without supervision, he'll take my son back to Croatia and I'll never see him again."

Paxton's eyebrows shot up in astonishment. "Isn't your ex-husband an American citizen?"

"His citizenship is pending. He's been teaching at Gonzaga for the past five years on a lecturer's visa and having the visa renewed annually."

"Does your son have dual citizenship?"

Leigh shook her head. "Stefan wanted to apply for Croatian citizenship for Michael, in addition to his American citizenship. He kept pressing me about it all the time but I…I wouldn't agree to it. That's one of the things that frightened me." She stared into her coffee mug. "The way Stefan kept insisting we should get Michael's dual citizenship established. Stefan wants him to have a passport, too."

"Doesn't Michael have a passport now?"

"No, he's able to travel on mine."

Paxton made some more notes in his book. "So Michael wouldn't be able to travel on his father's passport, because your ex-husband doesn't have his American citizenship yet and Michael doesn't have Croatian."

"That's right."

"In that case," Paxton said, "wouldn't it be pretty difficult right now for your ex-husband to take Michael out of the country?"

"I think Stefan could do anything he set his mind to. He's a...very powerful man."

"But has he made any specific threats, besides all this talk of dual citizenship? Has he done anything else to make you suspect he might be planning to abduct Michael?"

Leigh twisted her hands in her lap, feeling helpless. How could she explain the force of Stefan's personality, his coldness and power, the fearful strength of his family ties?

And how could she possibly make this young American policeman understand what a firstborn son meant to a man like Stefan Panesivic?

"I just...believe it's likely to happen," she said at last. "In fact, I'm certain of it. Sometimes when Stefan gets angry, he says things that really frighten me."

"Such as?"

"Oh, all kinds of things. He... Oh, I'm sorry. I'm having a really hard time thinking straight, remembering things..."

"All right. Let's just focus on what happened in April to change things." Paxton rubbed his forefinger thoughtfully over his upper lip. "You were allowing access without any problem until then. Why did you suddenly start being so afraid?"

"Stefan's teaching contract expired in mid-April," Leigh said. "He wouldn't go away in the middle of a term, but now there's nothing to hold him in Spokane anymore. And there's certainly nothing in the world he wants more than Michael."

"I wish you'd told me all this earlier." The policeman frowned at his notes.

"There...there's something else I have to tell you," Leigh said.

"What's that?"

"We had a court hearing yesterday. Stefan took me to court to enforce his visitation rights."

"Family court?"

"Yes. He filed a complaint that he wasn't being allowed to have Michael on Saturdays anymore."

Paxton gave her a keen glance. "And this hearing was held yesterday?"

"Yes. Early in the afternoon."

"What happened in court?"

"The judge ruled..." Leigh paused and took a deep breath. "He said I had to obey the order. He said..."

Her voice broke, and she held back the tears with an effort.

"What?" the young officer asked. "What did the judge say?"

"He said Stefan could come over on...on Saturday mornings, and take Michael. He said that if I didn't comply, Stefan could bring a policeman here with him to enforce the order."

"How did you feel about that, Leigh?"

"I was devastated. I absolutely don't want him to have Michael without supervision. I'm certain that Stefan is capable of stealing Michael away from me. Stefan is...a very ruthless man."

Paxton looked at the smiling family group in the photograph. "Do you think he has your son now?"

"I don't know."

"Is there a chance you could have been followed to the mall tonight?"

"I…I suppose so. The mall was really crowded, and I wasn't watching to see if there was anybody behind me."

"How many people knew that you and Michael were going to be at Northtown?"

Leigh frowned, thinking. "I told my mother when we spoke on the phone yesterday. She called to find out what happened at the court hearing."

"Anybody else?"

"There was Helen, of course…"

"Who's Helen?"

"Helen Philps," Leigh said. "She's my regular baby-sitter. I've known her all my life. She lives in the South Hill, just a few blocks from my parents'. I don't need her much during the summer, but I did leave Michael with her yesterday when I was in court."

"Address?"

Leigh recited the address and phone number.

"What can you tell me about Helen?"

"Well…I guess she must be almost fifty by now. She lives in the old family home and looks after her mother. The mother's name is Grace Philps."

"Helen's not married?"

"Years ago, she was engaged to a young soldier from Portland who was killed in Vietnam." Leigh gave the policeman a brief strained smile. "My sister and I were just kids at the time, and Helen was our neighbor. We found the whole story so sad and romantic."

"Why does Helen baby-sit for you? Considering her address, it's hard to believe she needs the money."

"Oh, no. I think there's still a fair amount of family wealth. I believe she just really loves Michael. He adds a lot of brightness to her life."

"And she's a good baby-sitter?"

"She's wonderful," Leigh said. "I couldn't ask for a better person to look after Michael."

Paxton studied his notes. "We were talking about all the people who knew you were going to the mall. Is there anybody else?"

"Stefan knew. I spoke to him on the phone on Wednesday, the day before our court hearing. In fact, we had quite an unpleasant argument."

"What about?"

"The money Stefan's family had given Michael for his birthday. Stefan demanded to know how I planned to spend it."

"What did you tell him?"

"I said Michael and I were going to the mall on Friday night, and Michael would be allowed to pick out a toy for himself. I told Stefan that if he was so worried about this gift from his parents, I'd call Miroslav and Ivana the next day and tell them exactly what Michael bought with their money."

"Miroslav and...?"

"Miroslav and Ivana Panesivic. They're Stefan's parents. I told you," Leigh said patiently, "that they have a small farm southeast of town."

Paxton flipped back through his notes. "They're the ones who live near Painted Hills Golf Course?"

"That's right."

"Leigh, I'm not sure I'm getting all this straight. How does it happen that your ex-husband is a Croatian citizen, but his parents live here in Spokane?"

"Miroslav and Ivana emigrated from Croatia about twenty years ago. They brought Stefan's younger brother with them, but Stefan stayed in Croatia along with another older brother who still lives there."

"Younger brother's name?"

"Zan Panesivic. He was fifteen when the family came. Now he's in his thirties, lives in Spokane and works for the city as a landscape engineer."

"Is Zan married?"

Leigh sipped her coffee. "Yes. To a woman named Mila. She's an interior decorator. They have one child, a little girl, Deborah, who's about eight months older than Michael."

"Do you get along well with these people?"

"Well, Michael and Deborah are best friends, and I've always liked Zan. He's a big, easygoing kind of man. A real teddy bear. But Mila is different. I think she...hates me."

"Why?"

Leigh shrugged. "Just for being what I am."

"And what's that?"

"American, I guess." Leigh sighed. "And from a fairly privileged background. Mila's got a passionate social conscience and disapproves of American politics and culture. She can be quite an uncomfortable person to be around."

"What about Stefan's parents? Do they hate you, too?"

Leigh's face softened. "Oh, no. They're wonderful. Miroslav and Ivana are truly good people. They've been so nice to me ever since I met Stefan."

"Why didn't he move to America back in the seventies when the rest of the family did?"

"Stefan's forty-three now. He was well over twenty when the family emigrated, already finished a couple of college degrees and teaching at the university in Zagreb while he worked on his doctorate. They didn't manage to entice him to America until much later. By that time, of course, the situation in Croatia was starting to look pretty grim."

"And that's when you met him?"

"Soon after he arrived. We met through mutual friends at a college faculty party."

"And fell in love?" Paxton asked.

Leigh smiled a little sadly in reminiscence. "Immediately. Like a ton of bricks. Stefan was the most attractive man I'd ever met, so suave and cosmopolitan. And I loved his family, too. I was certain that all my dreams had finally come true."

The telephone rang, shrilling though the quiet house. Leigh's eyes widened and her hands began to shake as she stared at the police officer.

"You'd better get it," he said. "Hand me that portable, okay?"

She gave him the portable phone, then moved to the wall phone on the other side of the kitchen. She watched while Paxton switched on the Talk button and prepared to monitor the call.

"Hello?" she said when Paxton gave her an urgent nod.

"Leigh! What the hell's going on? We just got home, and the whole city's in an uproar."

"Oh, Rennie." Leigh sagged in relief when she heard her sister Adrienne's voice. "Can you...can you possibly come over here and stay with me tonight? I know it's a lot to ask, but—"

"I'm on my way. I'll pull off these dammed sequins and be there in twenty minutes."

There was a brisk click and the line went dead.

Paxton returned to the table and flipped open his notebook while Leigh wandered into the living room to peer out the window at the darkness.

After a moment, Paxton came to the doorway. "As soon as your sister comes," he said, "I'll get back to the station and start recording all this. Give us a call if you need something or if you think of anything else, all right?"

"About that policewoman you asked to come over…"

"I'll make sure that gets canceled."

Leigh moved back into the kitchen and poured herself another cup of coffee, took a couple of sips and dumped the rest into the sink. She watched for a few moments as Paxton upgraded his notes, wondering what he was writing. At last, restless, she returned to the living room.

"Here's my sister," she said as a sports car pulled up to the curb with a noisy screech of brakes. "She must have driven even faster than usual."

Paxton appeared in the hallway, shrugging into his patrol jacket. "Thanks for all your cooperation, Leigh." He smiled and put a hand on her shoulder. "Don't worry. We'll find him," he repeated.

His kindness was too much for Leigh. Her composure snapped and tears began to flow down her face. The policeman gave her an awkward hug, patted her back a couple of times and headed for the door.

Leigh stood in the open doorway, watching as Kent Paxton met Adrienne in the driveway and they conversed in quiet voices.

She was still crying, and her arms ached for Michael's small warm body. She went back inside and upstairs to his room, looking among the stuffed toys for something to hold.

It was then she realized that Michael's stuffed duck was missing, too.

The whole evening was becoming a confused blur in Leigh's mind, but she was certain Michael had taken Dixie Duck to the mall. The soft toy was made of bright yellow plush, with floppy orange feet, big flirty eyelashes and a broad yellow bill. Michael never went anywhere without it, couldn't fall asleep without it. If Dixie ever went missing, there was a frantic search until she was found again.

I hope you still have Dixie Duck with you now, my darling, Leigh thought silently, looking out through the dark square of window. *I hope you're holding on to her tight, and you're not scared of anything.*

Trees rustled in a cold breeze and stars glittered above the hills, cold and impossibly distant. Leigh sank onto Michael's little bed, surrounded by his toys, and began to sob.

3

Just before eleven o'clock, Carmen and Tony returned from their dinner date. Both of them looked flushed and happy. Carmen carried a bouquet of flowers, which she ran to put in water, pausing on the way to peek at her sleeping daughter.

Jackie sat cross-legged on the couch as the final credits rolled up on the movie she'd been watching. She switched off the television while Carmen arranged the flowers.

"Hey, Carmen. Did you have a nice time?"

"We had such a fabulous meal." Carmen sparkled like a love-struck teenager. "Steak and lobster, no less. Tony even bought a bottle of champagne."

Jackie looked from one to the other, feeling a touch of alarm. "So what's the occasion?"

"It was our first special date," Tony said, leaning against the door frame with his jacket slung over his shoulders.

Jackie wondered if Carmen's new boyfriend was waiting for her to leave. She'd been introduced to him earlier, when he'd come to collect Carmen, but the meeting had been so brief she hadn't formed any opinion about him. Now she looked at him appraisingly, trying to see all the way into his soul.

Tony Bechtmann was medium height, with a comfortable roll of fat around his middle and light brown hair that was thinning at the temples and crown. His blue eyes were mild, his gaze steady as he returned Jackie's scrutiny.

A dozen years on the police force had made her cynical, slow to trust newcomers no matter how nice they seemed. She had seen dreadful gruesome things during her service, many of them things men had done to women.

What a hell of a world to live in, Jackie thought wearily, when your first reaction was always suspicion. Not that she'd ever had a lot of trust in strangers, even as a small child. The mean streets of Los Angeles weren't exactly the place to inspire confidence in fellow human beings...

Tony gave her a beaming smile that broke the slight tension between them.

"Well, I have to go mix up a big batch of dough," he said with a laugh, shrugging into his jacket. "Otherwise, the police force won't have their doughnuts in the morning and this whole city will grind to a halt."

Jackie laughed with him and felt a grudging relief. Maybe Tony was going to be all right. Besides, Carmen looked so happy.

"Jackie, what happened about the poor little boy at the mall?" Carmen crossed the room to stand next to her date, smiling up at him. "Tony and I were talking so much all evening we didn't even listen to the news on the way home in the car."

"No sign of him yet. They called me twice from the radio room," Jackie said. "The first time, they wanted me to go over and spend the night with Leigh Mellon so she wouldn't be alone."

"They called you here?" Carmen asked in surprise.

"If I'm not carrying my cell phone, I always leave a number with the dispatchers in the radio room letting them know where I can be reached, just in case they need me."

Carmen fussed over a bit of lint on Tony's shoulder,

smoothing it away. Jackie recognized her friend's small gesture as an excuse to touch the man. She suddenly felt lonely and excluded.

"And then they called back just a few minutes ago to cancel," she continued. "Apparently, Mellon's sister arrived to look after her."

"Oh, the poor thing," Carmen said. "I'm going to be praying all night long for her and her little boy."

Tony gave Carmen a look of tenderness and touched her hair.

"Well, I don't know about you guys, but I have to be getting home," Jackie said. "I'm supposed to be at work by eight in the morning."

She gathered up her book and notepaper and moved toward the door, pausing to shake Tony's hand before she left.

The baker smiled at her, his eyes creasing with humor. "So, will I do, Detective?" he asked in a whisper.

Jackie smiled back. "Nobody's good enough for Carmen, but you seem to be okay. Now, don't be hanging around till all hours," she added with mock severity. "Go and make those doughnuts. A lot of my colleagues are depending on you."

Her loneliness deepened as she left Carmen's bright cluttered apartment and crossed the hall.

Her own apartment was much sparser, clean and bare, with a few pieces of good artwork on the walls and the mismatched but comfortable furniture she'd picked up over the years.

She tried not to think too much about decorating. Despite the squalor she'd grown up in, Jackie had an instinctive feeling for what she liked, and for lines and colors that made a pleasing balance. But until she could afford the look she wanted, she preferred to make do with practical simple things like a bookcase in the living room made of weathered bricks and stained wooden planks, and a pair of plain oak side tables she'd built a few years ago when she took a woodworking course at the local junior college.

The only bright color in her living room was provided by a couple of afghans in garish tones of orange, magenta and lime green. The afghans didn't match anything else in the apartment and were truly ugly. But they'd been knitted by her grandmother years before, during a happier time in the old lady's life. Jackie couldn't bear to part with them.

While she was brooding over the afghans, the telephone rang. Jackie moved automatically to pick up the receiver.

"Hello, Jackie," a querulous voice said. "Is that you?"

Jackie tensed. "Hello, Gram. Why are you calling so late? You're supposed to be sound asleep by now."

"They're here again," her grandmother whispered hoarsely. "They're in the other room hiding behind the couch. Thousands of them."

"The spiders?" Jackie asked.

"Come and get rid of them, Jackie. They're as big as washtubs, and they have yellow fangs. Their eyes shine in the dark."

"How much have you been drinking, Gram?"

"I'm not drinking," the old woman said. "You know I don't drink anymore, Jackie."

You don't drink any less, either, Jackie thought without humor. *You damned, stubborn old woman.*

Her eyes stung with tears. "Please, Gram," she urged, recognizing the futility of her plea as soon as she spoke. "Why won't you come out here and live with me? I can find a bigger place, maybe even a house, and we'll have such a nice time together."

"Oh, sure. Until you find a boyfriend and start pushing me out the door."

"It's been at least three years since I've had a boyfriend. I don't have time to fall in love, Gram. I work all the time."

"Well, I don't want to be alone all day. I want to stay right here in my own neighborhood where I know everybody."

"For God's sake, Gram. Your neighborhood is a war zone."

Jackie was wearied by the familiar argument. She frowned, thinking about the squalid apartment in Los Angeles where she and her cousins had passed their scrappy growing-up years.

"Tell me, Gram, how many times has a window been shot out in that place? Twice, at least."

"I'm not moving," her grandmother said with drunken stubbornness. "You can't make me."

"Well, I can't do anything about the spiders. I'm more than a thousand miles away. Where's Carmelo? Aren't he and Joey still living with you?"

"Your cousins? They come and go. I think Carmelo's in jail. There's nobody here now but the spiders. They're coming after me, Jackie. They're trying to get under the door of my room."

Jackie sighed and struggled for patience. "Are you in bed?"

"Yes. I'm in bed with the covers pulled up."

"Well, stay there. Try to sleep, Gram. In the morning you'll feel better."

"When are you going to send me some money? I don't have any money."

"We talked about this last week." Jackie was suddenly cautious. "I told you I wasn't going to send money for you to spend on liquor, Gram. If you stop drinking, I'll send more money."

"I don't drink." The old woman's fretful tone changed

abruptly. She sounded crafty and alert. "I told you, I don't drink at all anymore. Send me some money, Jackie. I can't even get food stamps this week. There's nothing to eat in this place. I've been eating dog food for two days, Jackie."

"I'll call your social worker tomorrow," Jackie promised. "If she confirms that you're not drinking, I'll send some money."

"But she'll lie!" her grandmother shouted. "They're all liars. And *you!* You're the worst of all." The degree of venom in her tone still shocked and hurt Jackie, even after all these years. "When I think how I sacrificed to raise you and your cousins, working my fingers to the bone, and now you won't even lift a hand to help me. You nasty ungrateful little bitch."

Jackie endured the onslaught stoically, thinking about the kind of upbringing her grandmother had provided after Jackie's mother had abandoned her. Most days, Irene Kaminsky had been too drunk to know what her ragged brood of grandchildren was doing. By the time Jackie was ten, she was the caregiver and her grandmother had become the dependent one.

"Just a selfish nasty girl," the old lady was mumbling. She began to cry. Jackie heard a loud gurgle of liquid over the phone.

"Gram," she said sharply. "Stop that! Put the bottle down now."

"Just a...just a nasty girl, don't even care about these damn spiders, these spiders..."

The voice trailed off, and the next thing Jackie heard was a ragged breath and a click. Her grandmother had hung up.

Jackie sat gripping the phone, feeling desolate. The old lady would drink herself to sleep now, and by morning the spiders would be gone. But the delirium would return, and then there would be another midnight call, and another....

"Oh, shit," she muttered, then got up and crossed the room to the stereo. She turned it on, flung herself onto the couch and pulled one of the afghans over her body, staring at the ceiling while the mellow tones of a flute concerto began to fill the room.

Jackie arrived at work the next morning just after eight. She pulled her old Subaru into the parking lot behind the substation, gathered up her files and leather handbag and sprinted toward the door.

The northwest substation was a civic experiment, part of Spokane's ongoing commitment to community-based policing. But unlike the half-dozen storefront police stations scattered throughout the city and manned primarily by civilian volunteers, the northwest substation was a fully operational unit. Its staff comprised eighteen uniformed patrol officers, six detectives and a couple of sergeants who worked closely with the police bureaucracy at the downtown station a few miles to the south.

Jackie hurried through the small reception area and headed for the squad room where her partner was already seated at his desk.

Brian Wardlow greeted her with a cherubic smile. "Hey, nice outfit. Is that new?"

Jackie looked down at her brown gabardine slacks and her old tan blazer. "Very funny. Why are you so chipper this morning?"

"It's Saturday. One more workday after this and we get some time off. Why don't you ever wear a dress, Kaminsky?"

"Because it's not easy to carry handcuffs and a gun under a dress, that's why. What's happening?"

With his freckled face and crinkly red hair, Wardlow looked like an impudent child. Though he was three years older than Jackie, he'd just passed his detective examination ten months earlier after several failed attempts. That made her the senior member of their investigative team.

He jerked his thumb at a new file in the basket on her desk. "See for yourself."

She glanced at him, surprised by his tone, and opened the file. Her eyes widened. "What the hell?"

"Briefing in Michelson's office," Wardlow said, getting up and slouching along behind her as she headed for the glass-fronted office. "Better get yourself some coffee."

Sergeant Lew Michelson was a big heavy man with tired blue eyes, an expression of benign cynicism and a peptic ulcer that absorbed much of his attention. He sat behind a littered desk, the buttons of his dark blue uniform shirt straining over his belly.

"Hello, Kaminsky," he said mildly as Jackie and her partner appeared in the doorway with their coffee mugs. "About time you decided to show up for work."

"It's four minutes past eight," Jackie said, unruffled, settling into a vinyl chair next to her partner. "Sarge, how come we've got the Michael Panesivic file?"

"Why not?" He leaned back in his chair. "It happened in our district. And the mother and kid live just a few blocks away from here, up near Loma Vista."

"But it's a child abduction." Jackie frowned at the file. "Why wouldn't it be handled downtown by the guys in Major Crimes?"

Michelson leaned forward and folded his hands on his desk. "There are some concerns about this case," he said at last.

"Like what?"

"It's all there in the file, as much as the patrol officers

were able to find out last night. Apparently, the mother and father are divorced, and there's a custody dispute over the kid. The mother's been holding out on access, afraid her ex was going to steal the kid and take him overseas. The family-court hearing was on Thursday.''

"The day before the snatch," Jackie said, her interest sharpening.

"That's right. It seems the mother decided a few months ago that she didn't want the father to have the kid for his weekend visits anymore."

"What happened in court?" Wardlow asked.

"The judge ruled that the mother was to obey their order."

Jackie leafed through the brief notations on the file. They outlined the police search of the mall, the questioning of nearby merchants and shoppers, and Kent Paxton's interview with the little boy's mother.

A brown envelope was attached to the file with a paper clip. She opened the envelope and took out one of the photographs, a studio portrait of a bronze-haired child with big brown eyes. He wore a yellow shirt, blue vest and bow tie, and smiled shyly for the camera.

"Cute kid." She looked up at the sergeant. "So you think maybe the father has something to do with this kidnapping?"

Michelson shifted uneasily in his chair. "Nobody wants to say that out loud. We'll try to put as many officers at your disposal as you need. But when a kid's disappearance follows so closely on a custody dispute, there's always some official reluctance to commit the kind of manpower the public might demand."

"What if you're wrong?" Wardlow asked. "What if he really was snatched by some weirdo?"

The sergeant shifted his blue gaze to Jackie's partner. "How long you been a cop, Wardlow?"

"Twelve years."

"And in that time, how many cases do you know of personally where a preschool kid was abducted by a stranger?"

The detective frowned, thinking. "None I can remember offhand," he said at last.

"Exactly. How about you, Kaminsky? During those wild and woolly years you spent with the LAPD, did you folks ever work on a case where a toddler or an infant was grabbed by a stranger?"

Jackie shook her head after a moment's concentration. "Not personally. It's one of those odd things, right? Sort of like an urban myth. You always hear about it from other people, but you don't seem to run into it yourself."

The sergeant put on a pair of reading glasses and consulted a file on his desk. "I looked up some figures this morning while I was waiting for Detective Kaminsky to honor us with her presence."

Jackie smiled placidly and sipped her coffee.

"Less than one percent of all missing children in the United States are abducted by strangers," Michelson said. "According to police reports, it works out to about a hundred kids each year for the entire population, and almost all of those are over the age of nine. There's been only a handful of reported cases involving random abductions of children under four, mostly babies taken from hospital nurseries."

He gave them a bitter glance over the rims of his glasses.

"Even though the media loves to scare people," he said, "by reporting all the time that the figure runs into the thousands."

"And how many kids are abducted by their own parents?" Jackie asked.

The sergeant consulted his files again. "That's a tougher one to call, because the crime often isn't reported or else goes straight to family court. The best estimates I got were between twenty-five thousand and a hundred thousand kids."

"Annually?" she asked in astonishment.

"That's right."

Jackie looked down at the sketchy police file again.

The patrol officers making the first response weren't required to do an in-depth investigation on a serious case like this. They simply recorded time, place, addresses and names, along with the results of their initial questioning of witnesses, and handed it all to the detectives. Still, Paxton's notes were detailed and competent.

"So it's our call?" she said at last.

Michelson nodded. "We've got some patrols out there checking around the mall. You might want to get Wardlow to follow up on that. Kaminsky, I want you to talk with all the family members as soon as you can and let me know your impressions."

"How about rounding up known pedophiles to check their alibis, that sort of thing?"

"It's up to you. I'll want a full debriefing by the end of your shift."

Jackie got to her feet, followed by Wardlow. She continued to examine the file as they moved toward the door, then paused, thinking about Leigh Mellon's tense face on the television screen.

"Can I order a polygraph for the mother?"

The sergeant looked uneasy. "Do you know who this woman is?"

Jackie shook her head.

"Very famous people in this town," Wardlow told her succinctly. "Her father's Alden Mellon."

"Never heard of him."

"He's a retired judge," the sergeant said. "Also did a couple of terms as state attorney general. The Mellons have represented money and power in this city for at least a hundred years."

She smiled sweetly. "Does that mean we can't run a polygraph?"

Michelson sighed and took a couple of antacid tablets from a roll in his shirt pocket. "Just don't go charging into this thing like a bull in a china shop, Kaminsky. Okay? And if you're going to requisition a test, be sure you follow all the rules. Twenty-four hours' advance notice, full disclaimer, the whole nine yards."

"I always follow all the rules," Jackie said.

Her partner grinned amiably. Their superior officer shook his head in despair, closed the file and reached for his telephone.

"Get out of here," he told them. "Hit the streets and keep me posted. I'll want some regular updates."

4

Most of the addresses in the police file were a lot more upscale than the places where Jackie was accustomed to spending her day.

Leigh Mellon's parents and baby-sitter lived on the South Hill, her sister had an address in the southeast corner of the city, Stefan Panesivic occupied an apartment on the grounds of Gonzaga University, and *his* parents owned some land out in the Valley.

But Jackie's first stop was Leigh Mellon's house, which wasn't pretentious at all. It was a small two-story with modest grounds, painted white with dark green trim, and looked much the same as all the other homes lining the street.

Jackie parked the unmarked police cruiser behind a sporty green Porsche, which, unlike Leigh's house, definitely looked out-of-place in the modest neighborhood.

She made a couple of notes in her book, then stashed the ring binder away in her handbag along with her cell phone, locked the car and walked up to the front door.

A young woman answered the doorbell, looking tired and annoyed. "Who are you?"

Jackie took a small leather folder from her pocket and displayed her badge. "Detective Kaminsky," she said. "Spokane P.D."

The woman's eyes widened. "No kidding. You're in charge of the case?" she asked, sounding amused.

Jackie studied the woman closely, struck by how her fine-boned face resembled Leigh Mellon's. This woman had dark hair clipped very short, almost butch. But the mannish cut served only to accentuate her intense femaleness. She was very thin, with hollow cheeks, huge dark eyes and a complexion like soft pearls.

Briefly, Jackie wondered how rich people always managed to have skin like that. Was it a potion they bought in little stone jars, smuggled in from some exotic country? Or was it merely a testimony to the gallons of orange juice and bushels of healthy vegetables they consumed from infancy?

"I'm Adrienne Calder," the woman said. "Leigh's sister." She moved into the house, motioning Jackie to follow. "The police suggested I spend the night with my sister because she was so upset, and there was a possibility the kidnapper might call with a ransom demand."

"Did you have any calls?"

Again the woman looked sardonic. "I'm afraid not."

She was barefoot, wearing skintight brown jeans and a long beige tunic fashioned from some kind of silky velour.

"How's your sister feeling?" Jackie asked.

"That's a terrific question. How would *you* be feeling if your three-year-old kid had just been stolen from under your nose?"

"I'd be very upset," Jackie said neutrally. "Do you think she's able to talk to me? I'd like to learn as much as I can about the incident."

"She talked to the police last night, and she's sleeping now. Can't you leave the poor woman alone for a few hours?"

"Those were patrol officers who questioned her at the mall," Jackie said, accustomed to this kind of rudeness.

"I'm part of the detective team that's been assigned to the case. We'll be doing a more in-depth investigation."

"More duplication of services, you mean." The woman took a mandarin orange a fruit bowl on the antique hall console. She began to peel it daintily with long painted fingernails, her eyes fixed on Jackie with a look of detached insolence. "My tax dollars at work, right?"

Jackie was getting a little tired of all this. She took out her notebook, flipped to a fresh page and uncapped her pen.

"Your name is Adrienne Calder?" she said, writing busily.

"Yes." The woman seemed taken aback.

"And what were you doing last night between the hours of 6:00 and 9:00 p.m.?"

"You don't mean to imply... Oh, for God's sake. This is ridiculous."

Jackie waited, her face impassive.

"I was at a fund-raiser for the local ballet company," Adrienne said coldly. "In the ballroom at the Sheraton. I was with my husband, Harlan Calder. We were a part of the organizing committee, so we sat at the head table. I would say there were at least five hundred people who saw me during those hours."

"Thank you." Jackie finished her notes, then looked around at the house.

The modest exterior was certainly not reflected inside. Leigh Mellon might be living on a budget these days, but she'd obviously collected some beautiful and expensive things during her lifetime and they were all on display—tastefully, however, not ostentatiously. Jackie found herself admiring the elegant simplicity.

She peered into an alcove where a length of stark white tapestry was thrown casually over a bentwood rocking chair. On the windowsill behind it was a collection of costly blue glass that shimmered in the morning sun. A pair of Boston ferns on antique stands, richly green, trailed their fronds almost to the polished hardwood floor.

The tapestry, the glass and plants were the only ornamentation in that part of the room, and yet the look was perfect.

Jackie thought of her own shabby apartment with its mismatched chairs and couch, its homemade tables and garish afghans.

She always felt intimidated and a little baffled by the sort of room she now confronted, afraid that she could never, in a hundred years of effort, achieve the kind of spartan, cool look that seemed to come instinctively to a woman like Leigh Mellon.

The rich were different, she thought gloomily. They really were. She wondered what Leigh's *mother's* house was going to be like.

Adrienne vanished into an adjoining room and Leigh came down the stairs at that moment, wearing navy jogging pants and a plain white sweatshirt, looking tired and uncertain.

"Adrienne," she called, "did I hear the doorbell ring? Oh," she said when she saw Jackie standing near the entrance to the living room. "I'm sorry. I didn't notice you over there."

Again Jackie displayed her badge. "I'd like to ask you a few questions, Ms. Mellon, if you don't mind."

"Of course," Leigh said.

Adrienne came back into the foyer, shuffling along in a pair of leather sandals, a big suede bag slung over her shoulder.

"Are you going?" Leigh asked.

"Duty calls." Adrienne gave her sister a brief kiss on

the cheek. "You'll be okay now, won't you? After all, you've got half of Cagney and Lacey here to protect you."

"Thanks, Rennie," Leigh murmured. "It was really sweet of you to stay with me."

"No problem." Adrienne turned to Jackie with an insolent wink. "But now I have to rush home and coordinate alibis with my husband. God forbid our stories shouldn't match, right?"

Jackie was on the verge of making a sharp reply, but controlled herself. It was clear the woman was trying to needle her. Adrienne Calder seemed to enjoy being obnoxious.

Instead, Jackie gave her a benign smile. "We're always happy if the alibis match," she said pleasantly. "And it also saves you all those hours down at the police station, going through brutal interrogations."

Adrienne looked at her sharply, then chuckled with genuine amusement. She hurried out the door.

"Don't let Rennie bother you," Leigh said from the foot of the stairs. "She's always like that. It's mostly bluff and bravado, you know. Underneath, she's a really good person."

Jackie turned to get her first good look at the mother of Michael Panesivic.

Leigh Mellon seemed even more appealing in person than she had on television. Though red-eyed and pale from lack of sleep, she had an air of gentleness that was absent in her sister.

"Come into the kitchen," Leigh said. "I hope Rennie left us some coffee. Oh, good, there's almost a whole pot."

Jackie sat at the table and accepted a Staffordshire mug filled with aromatic coffee. Some sort of designer blend, she thought, French dark roast and Brazilian maybe. In the window behind them, a big crystal teardrop rotated slowly between white muslin curtains, smearing the walls with soft broken rainbows.

"Cream and sugar?" Leigh asked.

"Just black, please."

Jackie opened her notebook on the table while Leigh settled across from her, gazing moodily into the depths of her own cup.

"Now, Ms. Mellon—"

"What should I call you?" Leigh interrupted.

"I beg your pardon?"

"Your name. I just glanced at your...your badge, or whatever you call it, but I didn't catch the rank or anything."

"Detective Kaminsky. You can call me Jackie, if you prefer."

"All right." Leigh turned and looked out the window at a neatly tended flower and herb garden in the backyard. "Thank you."

Jackie studied the woman's fine profile, the dark smudges under her eyes, the look of contained sorrow. Leigh Mellon, she decided, appeared to be a woman who was very unhappy.

But she didn't look frantic.

Jackie sipped the coffee, which was hot and tasted wonderful. "If we could just begin last night at the mall," she suggested.

Leigh sighed and launched into a recitation of her movements the previous evening while Jackie followed along with the notes in her file. The story matched almost word-for-word with what the woman had already said to Officer Paxton.

"So you were looking at the summer dresses," Jackie said at last.

"Just right next door. And I was only gone for a few

minutes at the most. When I came back, he was... Michael was gone.''

Tears sparkled in the woman's eyes. She wiped at them with the back of her hand and took another sip of coffee, her lips trembling.

"I can't believe I was so horribly careless, leaving him alone like that. Michael is so little," she whispered. "And he's a...such a gentle child. I can't bear to think...''

Jackie cleared her throat and gripped the pen tightly in her hand. "Ms. Mellon," she began.

"Yes?"

"In order to facilitate our investigation, I wonder if you would agree to a polygraph."

"What's that?"

Jackie forced herself to meet the woman's troubled blue gaze. "It's generally known as a lie-detector test."

Leigh's face cleared. "Of course," she said without hesitation. "I wouldn't mind at all, if it would help you find Michael. When can we do it?"

Jackie remembered the sergeant's warnings about Leigh Mellon's family. "There are certain technicalities that have to be observed first. I need to inform you that the results, though often quite accurate, are not admissible in any court. You'll be given twenty-four hours' notice to prepare for the test. I'll supply you with a list of the questions you'll be asked, and go over them with you ahead of time."

"Twenty-four hours," Leigh said. "So we could do it tomorrow? That's...Sunday, right?'' She shook her head and rubbed her temples wearily. "I can't even remember what day it is anymore."

"I'll try to schedule a test for Sunday afternoon, if the polygraph officer is available."

Jackie made a note in her book and frowned at it, troubled by Leigh Mellon's apparent readiness to undergo the test. She'd expected some resistance.

"Where do you believe your son is now, Ms. Mellon?" she asked.

"Why are you asking me that? How would I know?"

"Because of your reaction." Jackie took a deep breath and went on, choosing her words carefully. "In my opinion, you seem upset, but not deeply distraught and terrified the way a mother might be expected to feel if her child were in the hands of strangers. I think it's possible that you have some belief or knowledge about where Michael is."

Leigh wrung her hands and muttered something unintelligible, her head lowered.

"I beg your pardon?" Jackie leaned forward tensely.

"I think Stefan has him."

Jackie glanced at her notes. "Why do you say that now? Last night—"

"I've been thinking and thinking all night long," Leigh interrupted. "At first I thought it might be a stranger, like the other policeman suggested. But now I'm sure it was Stefan. He must have been following me all evening, keeping out of sight somehow, and seized the first opportunity to grab Michael."

"As far as we know," Jackie said, "none of the people in or around the toy store noticed anything suspicious."

"What's suspicious about a father walking away with his son? It would be the most natural thing in the world."

Jackie made a couple of notes in her book. "Doesn't the timing seem a little odd to you, Leigh?" she asked, slipping deliberately into the use of Leigh's first name to establish some closeness between them.

"Why?"

"Well, there'd just been this family court hearing the day before, right?"

Leigh gave a jerky nod, her eyes brimming with tears again.

"And your ex-husband won his case. You might even say he got everything he wanted. So why would he choose this particular moment to abduct his son?"

"You don't understand." Leigh gripped her coffee mug with both hands, as if to warm herself. "Stefan didn't get everything he wanted in court. He only got an enforcement of the Saturday visitation, that's all."

"And what does he want?"

"He wants Michael." The woman's fine golden features were strained and harsh, suddenly making her look much older. "He wants to take Michael away from me forever. He wants to win."

"You mean, he looks on this as some kind of contest? He's being deliberately cruel?"

"Yes." Leigh's face was white with emotion, her eyes blazing. "Stefan is a monster. He's demonic."

For the first time, Jackie began to wonder if Leigh Mellon was entirely sane. She thought of the smiling little boy in his jaunty vest and bow tie, and felt a chill of fear.

"You seem awfully certain."

"I am." Leigh settled back in her chair, looking cold and tired. "He is. He'd do anything to get his own way. I keep telling people, over and over, but nobody ever believes me."

The sun was high and warm by the time Jackie left Leigh's house and headed south toward the downtown park that fronted the Spokane River. She turned east near the river and drove onto the grounds of Gonzaga University, slowing to admire the lush grounds, the huge spreading trees and massive brick buildings with their graceful spires and columns.

Gonzaga, the alma mater of Bing Crosby, was an old Jesuit college and one of the loveliest places in the city. Summer students walked among the buildings with books under their arms or sprawled on the grass in small groups, talking and laughing. Jackie looked at them wistfully, wondering how it would feel to be young and carefree, spending the summer in this beautiful place with nothing to do but study and socialize.

She parked near a tall brick apartment building which appeared to be part of the campus, checked the address and made a few notes. Finally she got out of the police car and approached the doorman, displayed her badge and was admitted. She rode up silently in the elevator, still thinking about Leigh Mellon.

A man answered the door and gave her a look of inquiry.

"Detective Kaminsky," Jackie said. "Spokane P.D. Are you Stefan Panesivic?"

He nodded. "Please come in. I've been expecting you." He stood aside courteously to admit her to the foyer, then moved past her into the living room. Jackie saw that he wasn't alone. Half a dozen young people lounged on couches and chairs in the sunny room, watching her in silence.

"That's all for today," he said to the group. "I need to have a chat with this lady. Maybe we can reschedule for tomorrow, all right?"

They gathered their books and prepared to leave, speaking to their host with obvious respect and affection as they passed through the foyer. Jackie took advantage of the distraction to make a quick assessment of Stefan Panesivic and his home.

He was, she guessed, in his early forties, with almost

breathtaking good looks. He had crisp dark hair silvered with gray at the temples, piercing brown eyes and finely molded aquiline features. Tall and well-built, he was dressed in jeans and a long-sleeved polo shirt open at the throat.

His voice was deep and caressing, and accented only slightly. The slurring of consonants and broadening of vowels gave his speech such an appealing musical sound that Jackie found herself looking forward to hearing him say something else.

Stefan's apartment was more casually decorated than his ex-wife's house, and a lot warmer. The living room was furnished with scuffed leather chairs and couches, Oriental rugs and dark hunting prints. Books were everywhere, in glass-fronted cases, on shelves and tables, even in stacks on the floor.

"Sorry for the mess," he said. "I never seem to find the time to clean this place up."

"Were you having some kind of study group?" Jackie followed him into the room and seated herself in one of the leather chairs. "Our reports indicate you aren't teaching at the moment."

"It's sort of an impromptu thing. They're summer students doing a practicum on political science. I help them out by having a discussion group on the weekends and directing them toward research material, that kind of thing."

"Just out of the goodness of your heart?"

He leaned back and smiled, clearly unruffled by the dryness of her tone. "You might say that, I suppose. But I enjoy the exchange, so it's not entirely unselfish."

Stefan's face was charming when he smiled. The fine eyes crinkled with warmth, and his white teeth flashed against tanned skin.

"They seem like quite a mixed group," Jackie said casually.

"In what way?" He gave her a keen glance.

"Oh, I just find it interesting that out of seven students, I noticed there were two African-Americans, two Orientals and one who looked Hispanic."

"So? Is the police department really all that interested in one's ethnic background, Detective?"

"Of course not. We're just trained to be observant. It's a part of the job."

"I see." Panesivic gave her a thoughtful measuring glance. "Well, we like to think our student body reflects the changing face of America." Again he examined her with that penetrating dark gaze, then smiled. "You're a bit of a mix yourself, aren't you?"

She was startled for a moment, but his manner was so warm and engaging she couldn't take offense. "You might say that."

"Native American?"

"Cherokee. But only partly."

"Irish?"

"You're very good, Mr. Panesivic. Or should I call you Doctor?"

He waved his hand. "My doctorate is in political science. To me, it's always seemed terribly pretentious to use the title on an everyday basis. Besides, I really don't want to be called on to deliver babies on airplanes."

Jackie laughed, then resumed her serious demeanor and looked down at her notebook.

Panesivic continued to study her face. "African-American?" he suggested.

"A little."

"And West Russian." He leaned back in triumph.

"That's easy," she protested. "You already knew my name was Kaminsky."

"Not at all. It's those beautiful Slavic cheekbones." He sobered. "Any news, Detective?"

"Nothing concrete, I'm afraid." Jackie hesitated, as puzzled by his behavior as she'd been at Leigh Mellon's lack of emotion. "You don't seem exactly devastated by all this, Mr. Panesivic."

"You mean, because my son's been abducted by some stranger?"

"Yes. That's what I mean."

He got to his feet and began to prowl around the room, picking up books and setting them down again, then pausing to look out the window at the college grounds.

"Michael isn't in the hands of a stranger," he said.

"Where is he?"

"Leigh has him. I'm sure he's quite safe. Physically, at least," he added bitterly.

"That's odd." Jackie watched him closely. "She said exactly the same thing about you."

"She did?"

"Yes. She believes you have the boy."

He gave a mirthless laugh and waved his hand at the small apartment. "Now, that's really funny. Where would I hide a three-year-old child? Downstairs in my storage locker?"

"Where would Leigh hide him?"

He came back across the room and sank into his chair again. "Obviously you haven't met the rest of the Mellon clan as yet."

"What do you mean?"

"I mean," Stefan said coldly, "that they have resources you can't imagine. Houses all over the place, staff at their disposal, extended family with loads of money. Michael could be anywhere by now."

"Out of the state?"

"Perhaps."

"Out of the country?"

"That's entirely possible. In Mexico or Canada, at least."

"If she did take him, and then lied to the police about it, she's committing a serious offense. What would her motive be?" Jackie asked.

Stefan lifted a heavy reference book from the coffee table, then put it down again. "I should have realized this was inevitable after what happened at the court hearing on Thursday. The Mellons don't tend to lose gracefully. After all, it's not something they have much practice at."

Jackie thought about Leigh Mellon's pale face and tortured eyes, and wondered if the woman was really driven only by a compulsion to win at all costs.

"Leigh believes you abducted Michael and are going to take him back to Croatia with you, and she'll never see him again. What do you say about that, Mr. Panesivic?"

"Simply that it's ridiculous. My family and job, my whole life is in America now. My parents are here, my brother and his wife and child, my son... Why would I go back to Croatia?"

"So you plan to make Spokane your permanent home?" Jackie asked.

"My citizenship will be finalized before the end of the year. By the way, I don't suppose Leigh mentioned, in the midst of her hysterical accusations, that Michael doesn't even have a passport and can't travel with me on mine?"

"I noticed that detail in the preliminary report. Would it be possible to take him out of the country without a passport? I thought children didn't need them if they were under a certain age.''

"Well, you're wrong," Stefan told her calmly. "Nobody travels to Europe without a passport, not even a babe in arms, unless he's the same nationality as the traveling parent.''

"I see." Jackie made a note in her book while Stefan watched her.

"Look," he said at last. "I know that your jurisdiction is limited, and so is your manpower. I assume that budget constraints are a fact of life for modern police departments, aren't they?''

"Yes, they are."

"Well, I think I'll let your search continue for a few days and see what happens. If you don't turn anything up, I plan to hire a private investigator and begin looking on my own. But whatever happens—" Stefan's eyes fixed on Jackie with cold intensity "—you can be very, very sure, Detective, that I intend to find my son."

Jackie nodded and glanced at her notes. "You married Leigh Mellon…four years ago?''

"That's right. We had a June wedding."

"She became pregnant quite soon afterward."

"We didn't see any reason to wait. I was nearly forty by then, and Leigh claimed she was ready to be a mother. Michael was born almost a year to the day after our marriage.''

"And you were happy together?"

"At first." He looked out the window again, his face tight with pain.

"What happened?"

Stefan made an abrupt gesture. "Who knows what happens in a relationship? It was a combination of many things.''

"Could you tell me some of them?"

He sighed heavily. "For one thing, Leigh wasn't as mature as I'd been led to believe. In fact, she was quite an insecure person, despite her privileged upbringing. And she was almost pathologically jealous. But the main problem was her family."

"What about them?"

"They couldn't accept the fact that Leigh had married a foreigner, as they would no doubt express it. They're not very cosmopolitan, those people, despite their wealth and power. Barbara Mellon, in particular, is a terrible snob. You haven't met her?"

Jackie shook her head. "I'm going over there this afternoon."

"Watch your back," Stefan said with a grim smile.

Jackie made a further note in her book. "What about your family?" she asked. "How did they feel about the marriage?"

"They were very happy. My parents adored Leigh from the beginning, and she loved them, too. My mother still feels as if she's lost a daughter."

"What were you doing last night between the hours of six and nine?" Jackie asked.

"I was at a small faculty dinner with some friends. We wanted to get together one last time before dispersing for our summer vacations."

"Can you give me the names of a few other people who were there?"

He listed some names and addresses. Jackie noted them in her book, then spent about fifteen minutes asking Panesivic about his academic training and background, his teaching job and the status of his citizenship, mostly confirming the notes that were already in her file. At last she got to her feet and moved toward the door.

"I'd like to be able to get in touch with you if I need more information," she said. "You won't be going anywhere, will you?"

"Not until I know where my son is."

Jackie paused by the door. "Mr. Panesivic…"

"Yes?"

"Your ex-wife has agreed to undergo a polygraph test regarding the details of her son's disappearance."

"And?"

"Doesn't that surprise you?" she asked. "I mean, considering your accusations against her, don't you think Leigh would be unwilling to subject herself to that kind of procedure?"

"Not at all."

"Why not?"

He leaned in the doorway and looked at Jackie steadily. "Because," he said, "I understand it's quite easy for a mentally unbalanced person to fool a lie detector."

Jackie felt a little chill of alarm, an icy prickling of the hair on the nape of her neck. "Do you think your ex-wife is mentally unbalanced?"

"It's going to be your job to determine that, isn't it?" he said, holding the door open for her. "Please keep me posted, Detective Kaminsky. I want to know the minute you find out anything about my son."

5

By the time Jackie confirmed Stefan's alibi and headed back across town, it was close to noon. She was hungry and the car was getting low on gas, so she swung east out of the downtown area to one of the service stations used regularly by the police.

While the attendant was cleaning the windshield, Jackie noticed a girl standing on the street corner nearby. Her blond hair was tousled, her face pale and sullen. She looked young and awkward in her leather miniskirt, spike heels and tight leopard-patterned halter top.

Jackie grimaced, wondering where the "working girls" found their outlandish clothes. Maybe there was a thrift shop somewhere out on East Sprague that specialized in supplying tacky outfits to hookers.

Suddenly she leaned forward for a better look.

This girl seemed suspiciously young. There was something almost touching about her, an air of unsureness and timidity that was at odds with the seductive outfit.

Any other time, Jackie would probably have drifted by and picked the kid up for questioning to see if she was a runaway. But the Panesivic case was top priority, and left no time for anything else.

Still, she made a mental note of the girl's location, resolving to come back and check her out later if she had time. She left the service station, pulled into a drive-through to order a cheeseburger, fries and milk shake, then parked in the lot at the substation and carried her lunch and her notebook inside.

Wardlow was at his desk making computer entries. When Jackie arrived, he shrugged out of his sport jacket, hung it over the chair and looked hungrily at the sack of food.

"You could have brought something for me," he complained.

"I thought you were meeting your wife for lunch at the mall."

"Sarah had to cancel."

Jackie glanced at him quickly but he was concentrating on a sheaf of papers next to the computer. His face, usually so cheerful, looked drawn and miserable.

She dug a couple of French fries from the sack, took a calling card from her wallet and placed a long-distance call, munching on the fries while the phone rang at the other end.

"Hi, Joey," she said when her cousin answered.

"Hey, Jackie! How ya doin'?"

"I'm fine."

Jackie smiled into the phone, happy to hear his voice. Joe was ten years younger than she was, and probably her favorite among the rowdy gang of cousins.

"But I'm a little worried about Gram," Jackie went on. "She called me late last night and sounded pretty rough."

"God, Jackie, I'm sorry. She got hold of a bottle somewhere. You know what she's like."

"I know. Is she okay now, Joey?"

"She's fine. I'd let you talk to her, but she went down the street to have lunch with Maria."

"That's okay, as long as she's all right." Jackie hesitated. "Gram wanted me to send money. She said there was nothing to eat in the apartment. She told me she was all alone, eating dog food.''

"That's a goddamn lie!" Joey said indignantly. "She just wants money for booze, that's all. I brought home a whole pile of stuff just a couple days ago."

"Are you working, Joey?"

"I got a little something going," he said evasively.

Jackie grinned. "Don't tell me, okay?"

"Hey, count on it."

There was a brief silence while Jackie twisted the phone cord around her fingers. "Gram said Carmelo was in jail."

"It's nothing, Jackie. A parking ticket."

"He went to jail for a parking ticket?"

"Carmelo took a stand on principle," Joey said loftily. "You never heard of principle?"

Jackie sighed. "You guys are going to be the death of me someday." She hesitated again. "I was thinking I should maybe call Lorna after the weekend, get her to stop by and see how things are."

"Hey, I don't like no social workers hanging around, but I guess Lorna's okay. Maybe she can even talk some sense into Gram."

"You're sure everything's all right, Joey?"

"Everything's fine. Don't worry."

"Try to keep the liquor away from her, will you?"

"I'll try," he said gloomily. "I try all the time."

"I know you do. 'Bye, honey."

"'Bye, Jackie. See ya."

Jackie hung up the phone and took a sip of her milk shake, then craned her neck to look at Wardlow's papers.

"Did you turn up anything?" she asked.

"Not much. The girl in the food court remembers serving Mellon and the little kid, and thinking how cute they looked sitting at the table together."

"What time?"

"About six o'clock, just like Mellon told the patrol officer."

"Okay. Anything else?"

He looked at the computer screen. "A clerk at the toy store saw them come in together. She actually noticed the little guy's blue shoelaces and thought he was a really cute kid."

"But she didn't see them leave?"

"She didn't see much of anything. Apparently, there was a bunch of kids in the store last night giving her a hard time. They were fooling around with the toys and generally acting up, and she had to throw them out. Soon afterward, Mellon came to her and reported the kid missing."

"And none of the neighboring merchants noticed anything?"

"I guess the mall was really crowded last night. I watched some of the tape from the security cameras and there were wall-to-wall people at every station."

"Any cameras near the toy store?"

"No such luck. The nearest is halfway down the aisle, close to the entry door, and it wasn't working last night. They have it on their service list, but the technician hasn't been around yet."

"Great," Jackie said gloomily. "The security camera wasn't working."

"There's one thing," Wardlow added, "but it doesn't amount to much."

"What's that?" She opened her burger to rearrange the sliced pickles.

"Why do you always do that?"

"What?"

"Mess with the pickles?"

"I like them to be neatly distributed so I get some pickle with every bite of my hamburger. Does it bother you?"

"Everything bothers me when I'm hungry."

Jackie suspected that it wasn't hunger making her partner so irritable. It was the broken date with his wife. But she kept her thoughts to herself, chewing on the burger and nibbling a couple more fries.

"There's a little computer shop right across from the toy store," Wardlow said. "The manager noticed a girl hanging around at about seven o'clock, playing with the display model at the front of the store. He said she looked 'suspicious.' That's a direct quote."

"What kind of girl? How old?"

"He thought maybe high school or college age. He said now that he's over fifty, they all look the same."

"College age?" Jackie thought of the group of students in Stefan's apartment that morning, and their worshipful expressions as they left with their arms full of books.

"There's more. Listen, can I have some of the fries at least?"

Jackie handed him the little carton.

"The lady at the toy store noticed a girl, too, but their descriptions don't really match." Wardlow munched fries as he consulted his notes. "The computer guy thought she had red hair cut short and slicked straight back. The toy-store lady figured maybe it was dark hair in a ponytail or a bun."

"Do they agree on anything about this girl?"

"Jeans and a dark green shirt, but not enough of her face to do a composite. They both just got a fleeting glimpse, and they were busy with other customers."

"But she was hanging around in the toy store, too?"

"Briefly. The clerk noticed her at the same time she was dealing with the noisy kids. The girl seemed to be wandering through the aisles, looking for somebody. When the clerk approached her, she practically ran out of the store.''

"Alone?"

"Yeah. Right afterward, Mellon came back and said her kid was gone. The clerk helped her look for a few minutes, then notified mall security. They did a search of the immediate area, and the police were called at eight o'clock.''

Jackie rubbed her temples. "This is making me crazy. I talked to both of them this morning. The little boy's parents, I mean. Each of them claims the other one has the kid.''

Wardlow gave her a curious glance. "So what do you think?''

"It scares the hell out of me," Jackie said bluntly. "One of them has to be wrong. And if one of them is wrong, it's possible they both are.''

"Which means he still could have been picked up by a stranger.''

She nodded and looked at the picture of the smiling dark-eyed child in his vest and bow tie.

"Do you think we should ask for more help?" Wardlow asked.

"And do what?''

"I don't know. We could do a sweep of the neighborhood around the mall, go door-to-door, that kind of stuff.''

"Michelson doesn't think the manpower is warranted, and he's probably right. The odds are still in favor of this being some kind of family squabble. It just really bothers me that she...''

"What?''

"Leigh Mellon's agreed to do a polygraph," Jackie said. "Didn't hesitate for an instant. I already called Sergeant Kravitz and set up an appointment for tomorrow afternoon.''

Wardlow leaned back in his chair, looking troubled. "So maybe it was the father. What's he like?"

"He seems very nice, and extremely concerned about his little boy. And he's got an iron-clad alibi. I checked it before I left the university."

"He could have hired somebody to do the snatch. Maybe this girl who was hanging around."

"But the clerk saw her leave the store alone, right? She could hardly be hiding a three-year-old kid in her pocket or her shoulder bag. Besides, Panesivic just won his court case the day before. Why get involved with a kidnapping at that point?"

Wardlow handed Jackie the carton of fries. She shook her head.

"You can finish them. I'm not hungry anymore." She looked at the boy's picture again. "The police manuals cite three reasons to abduct a little child, right? Ransom, nurture or abuse."

Wardlow dug the last of the fries from the carton. "The Mellon family's wealthy enough for ransom to be a possible motive. But we can probably rule it out if Leigh Mellon hasn't had a call by now."

"She hasn't. And there was somebody there all night to answer the phone. Leigh's sister stayed with her at the house. A real charmer, that sister, by the way."

"Not nuts about her, huh?" Wardlow frowned thoughtfully. "Okay. If he's been taken for nurture, it's probably a family member, right? Somebody who knows him."

"Not necessarily. It could just be somebody who's mentally unbalanced and wants a little kid to love."

"So maybe we should check with the social-service agencies and see if anybody there knows of somebody who's been trying hard to adopt and hasn't been able to get a kid."

"It's a pretty long shot, don't you think? Let's make a note of it for later if we exhaust our other leads."

"Okay." Wardlow jotted a memo on his notepad. "How about abuse?"

"That's a more likely motive. Have you got a list of local child molesters?"

"They're running one for me now at the downtown station, and I've got three patrol officers assigned to help me, more on standby if needed. Should we start checking alibis on the convicted pedophiles?"

"I think so." Jackie handed him an envelope. "But I don't want to overlook the family thing, either. I've collected pictures of the immediate family members from Mellon and Panesivic, both their parents and siblings." She gestured at the envelope. "I think you should take them back to the mall while memories are still fresh and see if any of these people were spotted around there last night."

"We're not going to get any days off at all this week, are we?"

"We will if we find the kid," Jackie said. "Otherwise, it's not looking good."

"Great," Wardlow muttered. "Just great. That's all I need right now—to tell my wife I'm going to be working through another holiday."

"What holiday?"

"It's the Fourth of July on Tuesday," he told her. "We're supposed to have three days off this week, remember?"

Jackie stole a glance at his unhappy face. "Brian..."

He waved his hand and leaned back, tugging wearily at the knot on his tie. "Never mind. I shouldn't complain, because it goes with the territory. It's just that Sarah's been getting a little..." He didn't finish.

Jackie opened her notebook and began to transcribe data

onto her computer, keeping her face averted so he wouldn't feel uncomfortable about talking.

Brian had a spectacular-looking wife. Sarah Wardlow was a brunette with a superb figure who worked at a dress shop downtown and made extra money modeling clothes for television commercials. She had a seductive flirtatious manner, and caused a stir among the policemen whenever she came in to the substation.

Wardlow loved his wife almost obsessively, but Jackie suspected that he worried about Sarah's commitment to their marriage. The demands of police work didn't help, especially the frequent long hours and disruptions of scheduled holidays. Lately, Wardlow seemed increasingly unhappy, and though he hinted occasionally at marital problems, he never came right out and said anything.

"Hey, Kaminsky," he began again, clearing his throat. "Did you ever…"

Just then, a woman appeared in the doorway to the squad room. She was plump and disheveled, and carried a handful of papers. "I hear you two are looking after the file on that poor kidnapped little boy," she said.

"We're trying," Jackie said. "Have you been getting lots of calls, Alice?"

The woman rolled her eyes. Alice Polson was one of the civilian staff who handled office duties at the substation. Alice had four adolescent children at home and she treated all the police officers, including the sergeants, like unruly youngsters who needed a firm hand and regular doses of discipline. Most of the men were a little intimidated by her, but Jackie liked the woman's efficiency and her cheerful forthright manner.

"Everybody in the city has seen this kid," Alice said, coming into the room and putting a couple of files on Brian's desk. "He's been spotted in restaurants, service stations and four playgrounds. Three people, in different parts of the city, mind you, claim they saw him at their neighbor's house this morning.''

Wardlow leafed through one of the files. ''That's the problem with these public appeals,'' he muttered. ''They bring in so much useless information. Here's somebody who saw the kid with a man on the Keller ferry this morning, crossing the river and heading north.''

''Still, we have to check them all out,'' Jackie said. ''One of them could be the break we're waiting for. Wardlow, you'd better tell Michelson right away if you think you're going to need extra help, and he'll pull some more officers off regular patrol. I'll do as much as I can, but I'm going to be interviewing the family members for at least another day or so, and witnessing Mellon's polygraph tomorrow afternoon.''

''She called, by the way,'' Alice said. ''Just a few minutes ago. She left a message for you, Jackie.''

''Leigh Mellon?''

Alice consulted one of the papers in her hand. ''She said she just remembered something. The little boy was carrying a special toy.''

''What kind of toy?''

''A stuffed duck made of yellow plush, with floppy orange feet.''

Jackie wrote the information in her notebook. ''I don't think she told this to the patrol officers, either.''

''She says she forgot about it completely until just now, when she was trying to think of anything that might help you.''

Jackie exchanged a glance with her partner, then looked at Alice. ''Let's keep this detail confidential, all right? Don't release it to the press or to anybody else. Then we'll have something we can use for confirmation if we get a confession."

"I've already taken two confessions." Alice looked at her notes again. "One guy says he strangled the boy and dumped him in the river. And a woman says he's locked in an empty church, waiting to be used as part of a satanic ritual. Neither of them left a number."

"God," Wardlow muttered in disgust. "People are sick, aren't they?"

"Any other calls?" Jackie asked the secretary.

"Five calls from psychics who have strong feelings about where to find Michael."

"I hate psychics the most," Jackie said. "They're always using somebody's personal tragedy to grab the spotlight."

"A few of them are on the level," her partner argued. "Every cop knows of at least one time when a psychic helped to solve a case."

"Well, I'd have to be damned desperate before I'd use one of them," Jackie said. "And even then, I'd want to be the one making the call. All this stuff they phone in and volunteer is just garbage. If you let them distract you, they take up a lot of manpower and don't accomplish a bloody thing."

Alice stood by the desk, looking troubled. "One of them came to the station this morning," she said at last.

"A psychic?" Wardlow asked.

The secretary nodded. "I thought you might like to know about him."

"Why?"

"Well...he wasn't what you'd expect. For one thing, he was a young guy about your age, Brian. And he was a carpenter or something, wearing work boots and jeans. He said he was on his way to work."

Jackie looked up, suddenly tense and alert. "A young working-class guy, claiming to know something about this case? And he came here in person?"

Alice nodded again. "Apparently he had some kind of psychic flash last night about where the little boy was being hidden. Something about a pit in the ground."

Jackie frowned. "Alice, I hope you got a name and address from this guy."

"All the morning calls are logged on the computer and printed out in the file." Alice handed Jackie a sheet of paper. "I also wrote down the address where the carpenter said he'd be working today."

"Perfect." Jackie studied the paper, then looked at her partner. "This is over in the South Hill. In fact, it's less than two blocks from Leigh Mellon's parents' place. I've got an appointment with them after lunch."

"Better get over there right away," Wardlow told her. "Do you want me to come along?"

Jackie considered, then shook her head. "I'll call if I need you. I'll be going directly to the Mellon house after I talk to this guy. What's his name?" she asked, squinting at the paper. "I can't make out your handwriting, Alice."

"Paul Arnussen," the secretary said. "Not the kind of man you'd expect to be having psychic flashes," she added thoughtfully, heading for the door. "Definitely not."

6

When Jackie got her first look at Paul Arnussen, she understood exactly what the secretary meant. He was a most unlikely-looking psychic.

He was working on one of the so-called heritage homes in the old South Hill district, apparently replacing a sagging veranda. Jackie parked the police car behind a dark blue four-wheel-drive truck with a white canopy covering the back. Through the Plexiglas windows of the canopy, she could see a tidy assortment of tools.

She took the notebook from her shoulder bag and made a record of the license plate, then went up the path to the veranda where a big man in faded jeans, baseball cap and a yellow T-shirt was prying up floorboards with a crowbar.

Jackie watched the man's broad back, his lean hips and the rippling muscles in his tanned arms as he strained on the bar. A section of rotting boards came loose with a crash and he staggered briefly to regain his balance, then began lifting the boards and tossing them onto the grass.

"Paul Arnussen?" Jackie asked.

He whirled to face her, the crowbar dangling from his hand. She had a confused impression of handsome maleness, of a strong jaw and sweaty chest and dark eyes shadowed under the peak of the cap.

"That's me," he said mildly. "Can I help you?"

He had a small flesh-colored bandage on one cheek,

Jackie noticed, just below his left ear on the edge of his jaw. He was well over six feet, and his body had a prowling, athletic look, like a man poised and ready for some kind of violent action.

She took the small leather folder from her pocket and displayed her badge. "Detective Kaminsky," she said. "Spokane P.D. I understand you came to the station this morning with some information about Michael Panesivic."

He took off his cap and reached out to shake her hand. Jackie was briefly taken aback by the courtliness of the gesture.

Arnussen had smooth blond hair that glistened in the sunlight. Though he was even more attractive without the cap, his golden hair seemed strikingly at odds with the dark eyes and high blunt cheekbones.

His ancestry must be almost as diverse as her own, Jackie thought, watching him closely. It was impossible to determine the man's background, but if she had to guess, she'd venture something like Apache and Swedish.

He shifted his weight from one foot to the other and looked uncomfortable as he replaced his cap. "I don't suppose you could call it information. It was just…sort of a feeling. But it was strong enough that it disturbed me quite a bit. I thought I should tell somebody."

Did you really? Jackie thought cynically. *Or did you just commit a brutal crime, Mr. Arnussen, and then decide you could get a little more of a thrill by jerking the police around?*

"Would you describe this…feeling of yours?" she said aloud.

"I was out in my truck last night and I heard the report about this missing kid on the radio. A few hours later, when I was in bed and half-asleep, I saw a dark pit underground. I saw the little boy in this pit."

"Buried alive, you mean?"

He shook his head and looked at the crowbar. "Not buried. It was more like a little house underground." Arnussen glanced at her. Jackie was conscious of the almost mesmerizing directness of his eyes. "You know the storybooks about Peter Rabbit, where he lives in a burrow in the dirt but it has little furniture and quilts and pictures on the wall?"

She nodded.

"Well, it was more like that," he said.

Jackie flipped open her notebook and jotted down a couple of notes. "Anything else?"

"There was some kind of chicken."

She looked at him sharply, wondering if he was making fun of her. But his face was completely sober.

"A chicken," she repeated.

"That part of it was pretty hazy. I'm not sure if the chicken was real or some kind of sculpture or artwork. I had the impression it was kind of...fancy. Really ornate, you know?"

"I'm not an expert on chickens," Jackie said dryly. "To me, a chicken is something under plastic wrap at the meat counter."

He grinned. "A real city girl, right?"

"You could say that."

"Well, I'm pretty sure this chicken had feathers."

"So you think the boy might have been in a rural location? A place where there's livestock?"

"I don't know. I never really saw the chicken. I just had a flash of it, mostly through the little kid's eyes, I think. I...sort of felt him seeing it."

"Can you tell me anything else about this...psychic impression?"

Arnussen looked at the rotting boards on the ground by

his feet. "He was really upset. That's what bothered me, the way I could feel how terrified the poor little guy was. He kept crying and calling for his mother."

"I see." Jackie pictured the child's terror and began to feel an active hatred for Paul Arnussen.

"He was sitting on the floor, sort of rocking back and forth," the man went on. "He had on blue overalls and a red shirt."

Those details had been contained in all the radio and television broadcasts. Jackie kept her face impassive as she wrote.

"And he was holding something. A yellow stuffed toy. I couldn't tell what it was."

The hair prickled on Jackie's scalp. She glanced sharply at Arnussen's powerful body, his muscular tanned arms and callused hands.

"Where were you last night?" she asked with forced casualness. "When you heard the radio broadcast, I mean."

"I was out in the country north of town."

"Anywhere near the mall?"

"No, a few miles farther out. There's a sort of canyon west of the highway. I like to hike out there when the weather's nice."

"So you were just out for walk in the country?"

"I grew up in the country," he said quietly. "I get homesick sometimes. I hate living in the city."

"You didn't happen to have anybody with you?"

"Last night? No, I was alone."

"All evening?"

"I finished work at five, went home and showered and made myself some supper. Then I—"

"Where's home?" Jackie interrupted.

He gave the address and Jackie noted it matched the one Alice had given her from the computer printout.

"That's over in Cannon Hill, isn't it?" she said. "Just a couple of miles west of here."

"But not nearly as fancy a neighborhood. I live in a basement suite, and spend most of my time doing renovations on these old houses in the South Hill."

Jackie made a note. "Please go on, Mr. Arnussen. You made yourself some supper…"

"Then I went out about six, drove north of town and hiked around in the canyon until it started to get dark. On my way home, I heard the news broadcast about the little boy."

"How did you get that cut on your face?" Jackie asked abruptly.

He lifted his hand to the plastic strip on his jaw, looking surprised. "This, you mean? I'd forgotten all about it."

"What's it from?"

"I cut myself shaving this morning."

"You don't use an electric razor?"

Arnussen gave her a steady look. "You make it sound like some kind of crime. Listen," he said, "do you mind if I work while we talk? I want to get this done before sunset."

"Aren't you working tomorrow?"

"It's Sunday. I'm taking the day off and driving over to Kalispell to visit a friend." He lifted an armful of rotted boards and stacked them neatly near the driveway, then went back to work with his crowbar.

Jackie sat on the steps with her notebook and watched him. "About the cut on your face…"

Arnussen straightened and lifted his cap to swipe an arm across his forehead. "I can't use an electric razor," he said calmly. "I have a very heavy beard, and if I don't use a blade, I need to shave again by the middle of the afternoon."

She looked at his face. Golden stubble shimmered on his jaw in the warm July sunlight.

"Besides," he went on, breathing hard as he heaved on the bar, "I'm not a real careful shaver. Seems I'm always in too much of a hurry. Next thing I know, there's blood running down my face and I'm rushing around looking for the bandages."

Jackie was surprised by a sudden feeling of empathy. The same thing happened to her all the time.

But there was a good chance Paul Arnussen wasn't telling the truth.

The bandage that currently graced her ankle under her socks and loafers was an innocent thing, the result of carelessness and preoccupation. But the cut on this man's jaw could have been made by the fingernails of a terrified little boy, trying to fight off his abductor...

"So when you got home last night after your walk, it was about nine?" she said.

"Closer to ten-thirty, I'd reckon. Maybe even eleven."

"But you said you were just a few miles north of town. You hiked till the daylight started to fade, then came home. What took so long?"

"I had a few problems along the way. How old are you, Detective Kaminsky?"

Jackie looked up, startled. "Why?"

He gestured at her notebook. "I admire a woman who goes out and does a hard job like yours. You must have been pretty good to make detective when you're still so young."

"I'm not all that young," Jackie said curtly, wondering if he was trying to unsettle her. "I'm over thirty. Any patrol officer can apply for detective rank after four years on the force."

"But most of them don't make it the first time, right?"

Arnussen heaved another load of boards onto the grass. "You have to be really good at your work, and pass the tests, too."

"How do you know all that?"

"I have a friend who's a policeman back in Montana. He's been working in Great Falls for quite a few years. Name's Clint Paget. I think he's a lieutenant by now."

Jackie wrote down the name for future reference. She suspected that she and Wardlow were probably going to be spending quite a lot of time researching the life and background of Paul Arnussen.

"So have you always worked in Spokane?" Arnussen asked.

By now he'd pried off the last of the floorboards and laid bare the underpinnings of the veranda. He took a flashlight from his toolbox, climbed inside and bent down to examine the foundation.

"No," Jackie replied. "I started my police career in Los Angeles as a patrol officer, then moved up here when I began to burn out on gang violence and street warfare."

Arnussen stood erect and looked at her over the skeleton of the veranda floor. "Don't you have to start over at the bottom again anytime you switch police forces?"

"That's right. But a cop tends to know a lot more the second time around, so it doesn't take as long to climb back into a good position."

"Still, you can't have been a detective very long, right?"

"Two years," Jackie said coldly, annoyed with herself for allowing the man to draw her into this kind of personal conversation. She should have known better. Many sexual predators were notoriously charming and manipulative, both with their victims and with the police. In fact, they were highly skilled at all the things Arnussen was doing now. They liked to get themselves actively involved in a

case, then cloud the issue by moving conversations onto a
personal rather than a professional footing, controlling both
the interview and the investigator.

"Do you mind if I have a look at your truck?" she asked.

"Why? Are you interested in trucks, Detective Kaminsky? It's a pretty ordinary model."

Jackie was conscious again of the intensity of those dark
eyes. She felt as if Paul Arnussen could look right inside
her head and read her innermost thoughts, and was amused
by what he saw.

She forced herself to meet his gaze. "I'd like to have a
look inside."

"What if I said I wasn't happy about you looking inside
my truck?"

Jackie shrugged. "Then I'd have to go back and get a
warrant. But I'd also have to wonder quite seriously about
your reluctance."

He vaulted lightly over the edge of the foundation and
moved to the steps where Jackie was sitting. He stood so
near she could smell the hot dampness of his cotton shirt,
the musty dirt from under the veranda and the bits of rotting
wood that clung to his jeans and boots.

"Am I a suspect in this case, Detective Kaminsky?" he
asked.

Jackie looked up at him steadily. "Are you a genuine
psychic, Mr. Arnussen? Because if you aren't, then I think
you're definitely a suspect."

He straightened, and leaned on a broken column near the
steps, slapping the crowbar lightly against the palm of his
hand. "I've had these experiences a few times in the past,"
he said at last. "I don't like to talk about them. They started
when I was a kid."

"Psychic episodes, you mean?"

"Just flashes. The first I can remember was when I was

seven years old. I saw an image of a horse tangled in some barbed wire, thrashing around on the prairie. I told my father and we drove out to check. There she was, almost five miles from the ranch. Not much doubt she'd have bled to death if we hadn't come when we did.''

"And as an adult?'' Jackie kept her voice carefully neutral. ''These flashes, as you describe them, have they continued?''

"I don't encourage them, if that's what you mean. I haven't had one for a long time, and never as strongly as I felt it last night. God, it was horrible,'' he said moodily. ''That poor little kid...''

"Did you know him? Have you ever met Michael Panesivic?''

"How could I know him?''

"I thought you might have seen him around the neighborhood, if you work over here all the time. Some of his family lives here, as well as his regular baby-sitter.''

"Hey, that's right. His grandparents are just around the corner from here, right? They have that monster house made of old brick.''

"That's right,'' Jackie replied. In truth, she didn't know what the house looked like, not yet, but a monster house fit her image. She thought about Michael Panesivic and his parents and grandparents. She was beginning to feel a deep concern for the boy's safety. For the first time, she had an uneasy certainty that Michael could be in serious danger, if not already dead.

"The truck,'' she said briefly, her face cold. ''May I have a look, Mr. Arnussen?''

He shrugged and tossed the crowbar down on the grass. ''Why not?''

Jackie followed him down to the curb, then waited while

he unlocked the cab and stood back so she could look inside.

Arnussen's truck was neat and sparse, very clean. The storage area behind the seats contained coils of rope, an emergency lantern and a metal case full of tools. The glove compartment held nothing but a few folded road maps, an invoice book and the truck's registration.

"You're a tidy housekeeper, Mr. Arnussen." She followed him around to the back as he lifted the foldout door on the canopy.

The truck box was half filled by a homemade toolbox near the front. Other tools were neatly arranged on racks alongside the box, and the rear of the truck contained a wheelbarrow and a folded tarpaulin. Jackie leaned in to examine the tools, looking for anything out of order.

Idly she lifted a corner of the loose tarpaulin, then froze when she saw a dried brownish stain on the metal floorboards. The underside of the tarpaulin was similarly stained.

"What's this?" she asked sharply.

Arnussen lounged nearby, waiting. He'd taken a small jackknife from his pocket and was whittling on a piece of oak.

"What?" he asked.

"This stain on the floor and the tarp," Jackie said. "What is it?"

Arnussen moved closer. Again Jackie could smell his warm maleness and feel the contact of his hard body. "I reckon that's blood," he said, looking down at her with an enigmatic expression. "Dried blood. Are you going to arrest me?"

Jackie folded the tarp back over the stain, her heart pounding. "Where did it come from?"

"I hit a dog on the highway last night when I was coming home in the dark. It was just out past the Newport Highway cutoff. I loaded him into the truck and took him down the road to the nearest house, where I figured his owners probably lived. But he was dead by the time I got there.''

''So that's the dog's blood in there?''

''Of course. What else would it be?'' Arnussen looked annoyed.

Jackie wavered, wondering what to do. Maybe she had enough circumstantial evidence to book Paul Arnussen on suspicion. But his story about the dog could check out, and then he'd walk. Besides, if he had Michael and the boy was still alive, the police probably had a better chance of success if they let Arnussen go about his business. In custody, he'd just clam up to protect himself.

''Do you mind if I take this tarp with me for a while?''

''You need a tarp, Detective?''

She ignored the sarcasm. ''I'll get it back to you as soon as I can.''

''No problem.'' He lifted out the bundle of waterproof fabric and handed it to her.

Jackie rested it carefully on the hood of the police car, then flipped her notebook open again and jotted down a few words.

''Could you sign this for me, please?'' She handed the book to Arnussen.

''What is it?''

''Just a formality. It's a release form, stating that you're giving me this material of your own free will in the absence of a warrant.''

''Sure. Can I borrow your pen?''

Jackie handed him the pen and watched while he signed. His signature was surprisingly fluid and graceful, with well-formed letters and strong downstrokes.

"Anything else?" he asked, returning her notebook and pen.

"One thing. Could you direct me to the farm where you took the dog?"

"I can do better than that. I can give you the lady's name, address and phone number." He took a wallet from the back pocket of his jeans, opened it and handed Jackie a slip of paper.

"Why do you have this woman's name?" she asked, recording the information in her notebook.

"She was real sad about her dog. He was a cattle dog, an Australian blue heeler, and my friend in Kalispell raises them. One of his bitches just had a litter a few weeks ago. That's why I'm driving over there tomorrow. I hope to get a pup for this lady to replace the one I killed."

"How nice of you," Jackie muttered. "Driving all the way to Montana—more than two hundred miles—just to do a favor for a stranger."

"I'm a nice guy." Arnussen gave her another of those direct looks, so dark and probing it was almost an invasion of privacy.

Her composure snapped. "Look, Arnussen," she said, her voice low and tense, "I don't know for sure what your game is. But if there's anything else you want to tell me, you might as well do it now and save everybody a lot of trouble."

He looked startled, then withdrawn and cold.

"I've got nothing to tell you, Detective," he said, heading back to his job. "Except that I hope you find this little kid before something bad happens to him. There are monsters out there, you know. Real monsters."

Jackie put the tarp in the trunk of her car, then climbed behind the wheel. Arnussen strode back up to the old house and began stacking the rotted lumber in a neat pile. She radioed the substation and was relieved to find that Wardlow was still at his desk, going over the masses of telephone tips and leads with one of the patrol officers.

"I need some help," she said when he came to the radio.

"Sure thing. What's the problem?"

Jackie gave the name and address copied from Arnussen's slip of paper. "I need to know if this woman's dog was killed on the highway last night. I want somebody to talk to her in person."

"Okay."

She waited as her partner wrote down the information.

"I'll do it myself. I'm heading out that way, anyhow," Wardlow said. "I have to go back to the mall this afternoon, and this address is just a few miles farther north, right?"

"If it exists. Look, it's kind of urgent," Jackie said. "I have a vehicle under surveillance, and I don't want to leave the scene until this checks out, but I have another appointment this afternoon. Okay?"

"I'm on my way. I should get back to you within half an hour, depending on traffic."

"If possible, I'd like you to see the dog's body. I want to know for sure."

Wardlow didn't ask for details over the radio, just confirmed and signed off. Jackie replaced the mike and settled back to wait, studying her notes and watching Paul Arnussen.

He was clearly aware of her scrutiny, but he continued to work impassively. A truck arrived with a pile of new boards strapped to a flatbed. Arnussen helped the driver unload and stack the fresh-cut lumber, then went back to his job. When the last of the old wood was cleared away, he sat on the edge of the foundation to take a long drink from a silver thermos flask, opened a lunch box and un-wrapped a couple of sandwiches and an apple. After he finished eating, he strolled across the grass to her car.

"I've got to pick up some supplies," he said, bending near the open window on the driver's side. "Are you planning to follow me to the hardware store?"

"I will if you leave right away," Jackie said. "I'm having somebody check on that dog you ran over. But if you can give me a few more minutes, you'll be free to go wherever you want."

The radio crackled and she picked it up, identifying herself. Wardlow's voice filled the car.

"Does it check?" Jackie asked tensely.

"I saw the body. Little gray spotted dog, pretty badly mangled. The woman at the farm looked like she'd been crying all night."

"Okay," Jackie said. "Thanks." She signed off and re-placed the mike, then looked up at Paul Arnussen, who watched her quietly.

"Now you can go," she said.

He nodded without a word and walked toward his truck. Jackie watched him get in and pull away from the curb. She put her car in gear and followed him to the corner, then turned and headed for the Mellon house on the next block.

7

Leigh Mellon's parents lived in one of the most imposing private homes Jackie had ever visited. The three-story building was made entirely of weathered brick with a deep veranda, fronted by columns and curved upper balconies. It was gracefully constructed despite its bulk, without the ornate Tudor half-timbering that adorned many of the large neighboring homes.

Jackie was admitted through an electronic gate set in a hedge backed with wrought iron. She drove up to the house and parked in the front driveway, wondering what the interior was like.

When she rang the front doorbell, she was admitted by a uniformed maid to a lofty white foyer that was floored in beige marble streaked with chocolate and gold. The furnishings were a few pieces of polished teak, almost stark in their simplicity.

Above a long console in the foyer, she saw a huge stylized painting of two fighting cocks. They danced as they faced each other, long feathers drooping around their bodies in a flare of dull orange and green.

Immediately Jackie recalled Paul Arnussen's confusing story about a chicken and an underground pit. She glanced at the painting with a little chill of uneasiness as she reached for her identification.

The woman examined the badge and nodded gravely.

"Mrs. Mellon is expecting you. Would you come with me, please?"

The Mellons' housekeeper was middle-aged, neat and plump in a gray uniform and white athletic shoes. She was probably Filipino, Jackie guessed from the accent, with dark hair cut short, a smooth complexion and brown eyes.

Jackie followed the woman through a series of rooms that left her breathless with admiration. The decor continued to surprise her. The carpets were mushroom-colored, acres of thick plush that flowed from one room to the next. All the furniture was that same unadorned teak, glowing softly in the muted light. Chairs and couches were constructed of soft leather in shades ranging from cream to dark taupe.

The only color came from masses of plants and fresh flowers, and from wall hangings, afghans and throw cushions woven in rich earth tones. The whole impression was one of costly austere loveliness.

If I ever win fifty million dollars in the lottery, Jackie thought, *I want a house exactly like this.*

The housekeeper ushered her into a room with tall windows flanking a set of French doors that overlooked the grounds at the rear of the house. The room was obviously a place where family members spent a lot of time. It was comfortably furnished with couches, chairs and a couple of desks, and lined with shelves full of books and bundled yarn. Near one of the windows, a woman sat working the treadles on a loom, holding a shuttle as a piece of fabric took shape under her hands.

Jackie recognized the colors and realized to her astonishment that this loom was probably the source of most of the decorative accents in the house.

"Ma'am, this is Detective Kaminsky."

Barbara Mellon looked up from her work. She was tall

and slender like her daughters. Her silver hair, pageboy length, was tied back casually at her neck, and she had wide blue eyes that were free of makeup. She wore faded jeans, a pale blue sweatshirt and a pair of heavy leather sandals over white socks.

"Hello, Detective," she said to Jackie, indicating a chair nearby. "Please sit down. Monica, don't go. I need you for a minute."

The housekeeper paused in the doorway, then came back into the room. Jackie remembered Stefan Panesivic's comment that his former mother-in-law was a terrible snob. She watched to see how the woman treated her household help and was surprised again.

"I tried that shade of orange we picked out," Barbara said. "But now I'm not so sure. What do you think, Monica?"

The housekeeper moved closer to the loom, soundless in her white Reeboks. "It's too bright," she said at last, studying the pattern on the loom. "It needs to have more brown, or it's going to clash with that mossy green, right?"

"That's what I'm thinking." Barbara scowled. "Damn, damn, *damn*. Now I have to pull it out and do it all over. Oh, well."

The housekeeper turned to leave. "Would you like coffee, ma'am?"

"Please," Barbara said. "Or do you prefer tea, Detective Kaminsky?"

"Coffee would be fine," Jackie said. She cleared her throat, trying not to be intimidated by the luxury of the place and the easy confidence of her hostess. "But really, you don't need to bother on my behalf. I don't have much time this afternoon."

"It's certainly not on your behalf," Barbara said, sounding amused. "The fact is, I missed my lunch and I'm going to fall asleep if I don't have a caffeine fix pretty soon. Monica, please bring some fruit and cheese, too."

The housekeeper nodded and vanished. Jackie looked at the wooden loom. "I've never actually seen somebody weaving," she said. "Is it hard to learn?"

"It's like anything else," Barbara said curtly. "There's a vast difference between learning how to do it and doing it well."

"Are you self-taught, or did you take classes?"

Her hostess smiled without humor. "You didn't come here to make small talk about my hobbies, Detective. Let's get to the point, shall we?"

"All right." Jackie took her notebook from her bag and flipped it open. "Your grandson disappeared from the mall last night between seven and eight o'clock. Do you have any idea where he could be, Mrs. Mellon?"

"I expect that his father has him." Barbara fingered idly though a box of wool at her feet. "The rotten bastard," she added.

"You don't like your son-in-law?"

"*Ex*-son-in-law. They've been divorced since January, thank God."

"That's right."

Jackie waited in silence, sensing that Barbara Mellon was the sort of person who would talk more freely if she felt herself in control of the conversation.

"You know, I wish I'd thought of it," the woman said gloomily.

"Of what?"

"Stealing Michael. If I'd been the one to grab him, he'd be safe now. Instead, God knows where he is. I should have done it long ago and saved Leigh all this misery."

"Child abduction is a very serious crime."

Jackie was conscious of the hollowness of her words

even as she spoke. People like Barbara Mellon weren't afraid to break the law. They tended to look on their money as a sort of cushion, something that not only gave them great power, but also shielded them from the consequences of their actions.

"Mrs. Mellon, could you tell me why you dislike Stefan Panesivic?"

Barbara shrugged and stretched her arms over her head, then glanced at her watch. "I wish Monica would hurry. I'm dying of thirst." She met Jackie's gaze. "I disliked him from the beginning. I considered the man an adventurer, if you'll excuse my use of an old-fashioned term."

"You didn't think he was sincere in his feelings for Leigh?"

The older woman gave a short bark of laughter. "Stefan? I doubt that he has a sincere bone in his body. I think he was an opportunistic immigrant who met a rich American girl and decided he could feather his nest by marrying her. A person of that class is always looking for somebody who can advance his own cause."

Jackie was liking this woman less and less. The phrase "a person of that class" she found particularly offensive. But she continued to make notes, keeping her face carefully expressionless.

"Do you think he loves his son?"

"I think he *wants* his son. The two things are entirely different."

"Do you love your grandson, Mrs. Mellon?"

"Michael? Of course I do. He's my only grandchild, and probably always will be. When I think of him being taken away…"

She turned aside and moved the loom's shuttle aimlessly, staring out the window.

"You imply you won't have other grandchildren. Why not?"

"I doubt that Leigh will want to marry again after the trauma of this experience. And Adrienne isn't able to have children."

"Why not?"

Barbara shrugged again. "Some sort of medical condition, I assume. I'm not entirely sure of the details. I only know that she and Harlan have been trying to conceive for years and haven't. Adrienne is very unhappy about it."

Jackie recalled Leigh's brittle dark-haired sister, surprised and a little unsettled to hear about Adrienne Calder's frustrated longing for a child. She made a note and placed an asterisk in the margin next to it.

"I'm finding it rather puzzling the way everybody seems to assume that Michael is safe with another family member," she said, choosing her words carefully. "In fact, Stefan believes *your* family has hidden the boy somewhere."

"Yes?" Barbara said. "So what's your point, Detective?"

"It just surprises me that nobody's particularly frantic about Michael's safety. Everybody I've talked to seems to express more annoyance than worry."

"Do the police have any reason to believe he's been abducted by a stranger?"

Jackie thought about Paul Arnussen's callused hands and piercing dark eyes, the smears of blood in his truck, the confusing talk of psychic flashes, of an underground pit and a chicken.

"Nothing definitive," she said. "I assume nobody's called you with any kind of threats or demands?"

Barbara shook her head. "Of course not. I would have told you immediately."

"Has there been somebody around to take calls? If a

ransom demand were to come here, would you be sure to receive it?"

"We know all about ransom demands," Barbara said, looking grim. "This wouldn't be the first time it's happened to us."

Jackie's interest sharpened. "You've had somebody in the family abducted for ransom?"

The woman leaned back in her chair, smiling gratefully as her housekeeper appeared with a laden tray and placed it on a coffee table nearby. Monica set out plates of fruit, cheese and cake, then left the room as silently as she'd arrived.

Barbara leaned forward to pour, offering sugar and cream, which Jackie declined. The coffee service and mugs were made of a delicate brown ceramic streaked with rust and green.

"Another of my hobbies," Barbara said when she saw Jackie studying the mugs. "I have a wheel and a kiln out in one of the sheds."

"They're very beautiful."

"Thank you. Have some fruit."

Jackie helped herself to a cluster of seedless grapes and looked at her notebook. "You said there's been a kidnapping in the family previously?"

"It was a long time ago." Barbara sipped her coffee reflectively. "Probably almost twenty years, because Adrienne was in her early teens. She was attending a private school in California, and she disappeared from the dormitory. Soon afterward, we got a ransom call demanding two hundred thousand dollars in cash for her safe return."

"What happened?"

Once again Barbara gave one of her expressive shrugs. "Alden was still working on getting the money together when Adrienne turned up at the school three days later, completely unharmed.'' She nibbled on a piece of cheese, then speared a section of honeydew melon with a little silver fork.

Jackie was puzzled by the woman's offhand manner as she recounted this story. ''Where had your daughter been? Who abducted her?''

''We never did find out. Adrienne refused to talk about where she'd been or tell anybody what had happened to her.''

''But you must have been frantic with worry. Didn't you make some attempt to force her to tell you?''

Barbara laughed without humor, showing a set of strong square teeth. ''Nobody could ever force Adrienne to do anything.'' She stared into her coffee mug, frowning thoughtfully. ''Besides,'' she said at last, ''there was so much going on in our lives at the time. Alden was in the midst of a campaign for public office. At any rate, Adrienne was safe and we were too busy to spend a lot of time worrying about her escapades.''

Jackie made another note in her book, troubled by the resemblance to her own childhood. She, too, had been able to disappear for days at a time when she was a young teenager, and nobody ever made a fuss about it. In fact, her family, like Adrienne Mellon's, hardly even noticed she was gone.

Maybe there were similarities, after all, between the very rich and the very poor, attitudes setting them both apart from what her hostess would probably call the working classes.

Barbara was watching her intently, apparently reading some of her thoughts. ''Did Stefan tell you I was a snob, Detective?''

Jackie gave the woman a level glance. ''As a matter of fact, he did.''

Barbara's lip curled with contempt. She began to speak, then looked around as a man in baggy corduroy pants and an old brown cardigan crossed the lawn and entered the room through the French doors.

He was tall and erect, with thinning silver hair, a lean frame and a handsome finely molded face. Jackie saw immediately his strong resemblance to Leigh.

"Barbie?" he said. "Come look at my new cymbidium. It's just begun to bloom."

"That's nice, dear." Barbara cast Jackie a quick glance. "My husband," she murmured, crossing the room to put her hand on the man's arm and whisper something in his ear.

Jackie watched with interest, noting the tension in the woman's shoulders and the way her husband's mild blue gaze began to look troubled and confused.

"A policeman?" he asked.

"She's a detective, Alden. Detective Kaminsky. She's just dropped in to talk with me for a minute. Won't you join us for some coffee?"

He shook his head, still glancing at Jackie with that unhappy expression. "I wanted you to see my flower," he said to his wife.

"I'll come right away, dear. As soon as the policewoman leaves."

"Why is she here?"

"We're having a little visit," Barbara said. "She's interested in my weaving."

"Will Michael be coming out this afternoon?" the man asked, plunging his hands into his pockets.

Jackie looked sharply at her hostess, who resumed her seat and picked up her coffee mug with deliberate composure. "Not today, dear."

The old man's face crumpled with disappointment. "You

promised me Michael would be here this afternoon, Barbie. You said he'd help me fill the pots.''

"Maybe tomorrow," Barbara said in a soothing tone. "Run along now and finish watering the orchids. I'll come out in a few minutes to see your cymbidium."

"And you'll bring Michael?"

"Not today," she repeated patiently. "Maybe tomorrow."

The man closed the French doors behind him and shambled across the yard, leaving Jackie and her hostess in silence.

"Alden had a severe nervous breakdown a few years ago," Barbara said at last. "He was hospitalized for several months, then allowed to come home, but he's never fully recovered and probably never will. Still, he keeps busy with his orchids and other hobbies, and I think he's happy."

"He seems to think that he's going to see Michael soon."

"Alden adores Michael. Helen brings him over for a visit almost every afternoon, so Alden's grown accustomed to seeing the boy around this time."

"Helen?"

"Helen Philps. She's a neighborhood girl who looks after Michael while Leigh teaches. I suppose I shouldn't call her a girl," Barbara said with a brief smile. "Helen must be almost fifty by now, but I've known her all her life."

"Oh, yes. Now I remember reading her name in the file. She lives nearby, doesn't she?"

"Just down the street. Poor Helen," Barbara added reflectively. "She's probably frantic. She really loves Michael."

Privately Jackie thought it would be gratifying to meet somebody in this group who was frantic over Michael's whereabouts. But she kept her face impassive as she made notes.

"I haven't had the heart to tell Alden what's going on," Barbara said. "He wouldn't understand, and he'd be terribly upset."

"I see." Jackie hesitated. "Just for the record, Mrs. Mellon, can you tell me what you were doing last night between six and nine o'clock?"

Barbara seemed unruffled by the question. "I was right here, working at my loom."

"Alone?"

"Alden was with me for most of that time. He has a new paint-by-number he's working on."

"What time did you eat dinner?"

"We don't dine formally in this hot weather. Last night I believe Monica brought us soup and sandwiches at about seven o'clock."

"Did she stay in the room for any length of time afterward?"

"Of course," Barbara said, looking surprised by the question. "She ate with us, then came back after clearing the dishes to help Alden with his painting and chat with me about the colors I was using for my weaving. She was here all evening."

"You seem very fond of your housekeeper."

"Monica is one of my best friends," Barbara said simply. "No matter what Stefan may have told you about me."

"Is there anything else you can think of, Mrs. Mellon? Something that might help us to find Michael?"

"Like what?"

"Anything more about Stefan, for instance, since you feel he's responsible for Michael's disappearance."

Barbara looked down at her mug. "Perhaps you should talk with Adrienne," she said at last.

"Adrienne?" Jackie asked. "Why?"

"Because I think Adrienne was probably closer to Stefan than anybody else in the family. Except for Leigh, of course."

Jackie considered this information, startled and puzzled. Her hostess gave her a smile of cool withdrawal and got to her feet.

"If you'll excuse me, Detective, I really should be going. Alden will be waiting for me in the greenhouse. Please let us know as soon as you learn anything about my grandson."

Back in the car, Jackie settled behind the wheel, then noticed her Polaroid camera and the snapshot of Paul Arnussen she'd taken while waiting for Wardlow to call. She considered going back into the house to show the photo to Barbara Mellon, but decided against it.

The photograph would give her an excuse to come back, and Jackie was certain she'd be returning to this house very soon.

8

On a sudden impulse, Jackie consulted the address list in her file, then drove down the tree-lined street to the home of Helen Philps and her mother.

She hadn't yet made an appointment for an interview with Helen, since the baby-sitter wasn't employed by Leigh during the summer. But Helen Philps had been mentioned by Leigh and now her mother, and Jackie was becoming increasingly curious about the woman. Maybe Helen had become too attached to the little boy she cared for and decided she wanted him all to herself. Similar things had been known to happen.

The Philps property was set well back from the street, accessed by a circular driveway bordered with flowers and shrubs. It was a large older home, not as lavish as the Mellon residence but still impressive. The house itself was white clapboard with a steeply pitched roof broken by dormers and gables, surrounded by a wide yard full of trees and well-tended flower beds.

A woman worked among the peonies near the fence. She wore a long cotton dress, white ankle socks and running shoes, and a wide-brimmed straw hat.

Jackie walked across the lawn and displayed her badge. "My name is Detective Kaminsky, Spokane P.D.," she said. "I'd like to speak with Helen Philps."

"I'm Helen Philps."

The baby-sitter was a small slender woman with soft blue eyes and a mass of light reddish brown hair, shot with gray, which she wore in a long plait down her back. Her face and arms were lightly freckled, and her expression was pleasant but anxious.

Despite the graying hair there was a touchingly shy girlish air about Helen Philps, as if she'd been preserved in a bell jar and the years had brushed past but not marked her.

Jackie recalled Kent Paxton's notes about Helen, how her young lover had been killed in Vietnam and then Helen had simply stayed here in this house where she'd been born, looking after an aging mother. Perhaps the gracious old house really had served as a sort of preserving jar, keeping the weight of life and years from pressing too heavily.

At the moment, though, it was clear that Helen was very upset. Her lips were trembling, and she gripped the handle of her trowel so tightly her knuckles were white.

"Have you…do you know where Michael is?" she asked.

"Not yet, I'm afraid."

Tears began to spill down the woman's freckled cheeks. "I'm so frightened," she whispered. "Michael's such a dear sweet little boy. I can't imagine why anyone would…"

Jackie put a hand on the woman's shoulder. "We don't need to assume the worst at this point," she said gently. "It's quite possible that Michael is safe."

Helen looked at her blankly. "Safe? But you…you said you hadn't found him yet."

"I know, but he might well be with a family member, in which case there's no cause to be alarmed about his physical safety."

Jackie waited for this information to sink in.

Helen's eyes widened. "Do you think the Mellons

have—'' The woman fell abruptly silent and shifted awkwardly on her feet.

Jackie looked at her, intrigued. ''Would you be able to spare a few minutes to talk with me, Helen? I'd really like your impressions of the two families involved in all this.''

''I don't know much about anything.'' Helen gripped her trowel. ''I'm only the baby-sitter.''

''But you've know the Mellon family all your life, haven't you?''

''I've been acquainted with Alden and Barbara for almost as long as I can remember. But the girls were so much younger than I was, and they both grew up and moved away years ago.''

''Still, you've been looking after Michael for quite a long time, haven't you?''

''About a year and a half.''

''And how did that come about?''

''Leigh went back to work last year after Christmas when one of the other teachers quit her job. She didn't have a sitter when she started work, so she left Michael at her mother's place. But it got to be too much for Monica, so I—''

''Monica—that's the Mellon's housekeeper?''

''That's right. I often go over in the afternoon to visit with them. When I saw how much of a strain taking care of Michael was getting to be for Monica and Barbara, it just seemed like a good idea for me to take him. He's a darling little boy. Mama loves him, and he brings so much happiness into my life, too.''

Helen's lips began to tremble again. She knelt on the ground to lift one of the heavy white peony blossoms, tucking it inside a wire cage for support. A few ants crawled from the flower onto her hands. Helen brushed them away, her head lowered so that all Jackie could see was the wide brim of the woman's straw hat.

She reached into her notebook and took out the snapshot of Paul Arnussen.

"Have you ever seen this man, Ms. Philps?"

Helen got to her feet and studied the photograph, then frowned in concentration.

"You know, I think maybe I have. But I can't seem to recall where it was."

Jackie waited, not giving any prompting.

At last Helen shook her head in defeat. "I'm sorry."

"That's all right." Jackie put the photograph away. "If you could just spare me a few minutes…"

"Of course. I'm being so rude. Please, won't you come inside?"

Jackie followed while Helen gathered up the trowel and rake, then went around the corner of the big house to put away her tools in a garden shed. Jackie looked at the gracious, flower-starred privacy of the big yard, where willows trailed their branches onto the grass and roses grew in profusion over a white trellis against the fence.

"This is lovely," she said. "You must really enjoy gardening."

"I don't do it all by myself." Helen latched the shed door and came back to join her. "We have a gardener who comes in to help me a couple of days a week. He's a cousin of Monica's, actually. He shovels snow in the winter, rakes leaves, digs the garden and does all the heavy work."

"But you look after the flowers?"

Helen gave her a shy smile. "My father inherited this house from his parents and brought my mother here as a young bride more than sixty years ago. She planted a lot of the flowers, so I feel a strong responsibility to take care of them."

There were several other outbuildings behind the big house, including a small greenhouse and a long garage with mullioned windows.

"That used to be the stable," Helen said, following Jackie's gaze. "Around the turn of the century, my great-grandfather kept as many as four teams of horses in there."

Bees hummed sleepily among the flowers, nesting birds chirped in the trees overhead and a weather vane of tarnished brass rotated sleepily on the peaked roof of the old stable.

"It's all so beautiful," Jackie said wistfully. "Leigh must have been very happy to have a place like this to leave her son while she worked."

Again Helen began to look agitated. She took off her straw hat and walked quickly toward the house with Jackie at her side.

They went in through a back door to a pleasant old-fashioned kitchen, warm with the smell of baking. Helen washed her hands at the sink while Jackie sat in one of the ladder-back wooden chairs and took out her notebook.

"Michael was here on Thursday afternoon, right? Just two days ago?"

"Yes. Leigh had an...an appointment, so I looked after him. It was so nice to see him again." Helen took a jug of iced tea from the fridge. "I really miss him in the summertime."

"Thank you." Jackie accepted a glass of iced tea and sipped it gratefully. "Leigh's appointment on Thursday was at the family court, wasn't it? She had to go and hear the ruling about the custody dispute with her ex-husband."

"Yes, that's right." Helen arranged some date squares on a Wedgwood platter and put them on the table along with matching plates and blue linen napkins, then sat in the opposite chair.

"How did she seem when she came here to get him?" Jackie asked.

"You mean, after the hearing?"

"Yes."

"Poor Leigh," Helen murmured. "She was...terribly upset."

"Did she say anything to you about it or tell you what the judge said?"

"Not really. I knew it hadn't gone well, though."

"How?"

"Well, I mentioned being surprised that she was back so soon. I remember telling her that I'd just put Michael and Mama both down for their naps, because I thought Leigh would be gone all afternoon. She said it hadn't taken any time at all. She sounded so unhappy. Very sad and bitter."

"But she didn't tell you any details?"

Helen shook her head. "The Mellons just aren't like that."

"Like what?"

"They aren't...friendly and confiding about things. If they have some kind of family problem, they tend to band together and keep it to themselves."

"Can you give me an example?" Jackie asked.

"Well, like when Alden got sick a few years ago. It was a long time before anybody in the neighborhood even knew he was in the hospital. And to this day, Leigh has never mentioned her father's condition to me."

"So you wouldn't describe Leigh Mellon as a close friend?"

"Not close, but definitely a friend. After all, she's here every weekday while she's teaching. And her school isn't very far from here, so she often comes over to have lunch with Michael on days when she can get away. We actually spend quite a lot of time together."

"But you didn't talk with Leigh about her marriage or her relationship with her ex-husband?"

"I doubt that Leigh discusses things like that with anybody, except possibly her mother or sister."

"What about Stefan? Do you ever see him?"

"Not anymore. When they were still living together, he used to come by and pick Michael up sometimes if Leigh was going to be working late."

"What did you think of him?" Jackie asked.

"He always seemed like a nice man. He was very polite, and wonderful with Michael."

"But you haven't seen him at all since their divorce?"

Helen was silent, crumbling a date square onto her plate. Her pleasant face began to look increasingly strained.

"Ms. Philps?" Jackie prompted gently.

"He came here one afternoon a couple of months ago," Helen murmured. "I think it was in early May, just before Mother's Day."

"What did he want?"

"He wanted me to let him visit with Michael and not tell Leigh about it. He said she wasn't allowing him his regular weekend visits, and he couldn't bear not to be with his son. He asked if he could come by occasionally and take Michael to a playground or something for a few hours."

"I see," Jackie said thoughtfully.

"I remember that he especially wanted Michael to see his grandmother—Stefan's mother, I mean—sometime close to Mother's Day."

"What did you say?"

Helen's wide blue eyes filled with pain as she remembered. "I felt just terrible. He really loves that little boy, you know. And Michael was so happy to see his father. But I had to refuse."

"Why?"

"Because Leigh was paying me, and I felt it would be wrong to deceive her like that. I told Stefan that if he wanted to visit with his son, he had to work it out with Leigh. I said I didn't want to be involved in something that was…shady."

"How did Stefan react?"

"He seemed very disappointed. I still remember how terribly sad he looked when he was walking away."

"Did he ever come back again and try to see Michael?"

"No, he didn't. Just that one time."

"You did the right thing," Jackie said firmly when the woman's lips resumed their trembling.

"Do you think so?" Helen gave her a pleading glance. "I just hated being caught in the middle of all their problems like that. And I had nobody I could talk to about it…"

An old woman shuffled into the kitchen while they talked. She wore a fleecy jogging suit and bedroom slippers, and had a blue thermal blanket wrapped around her shoulders. A bulky old-fashioned hearing aid was attached to her left ear.

"This is my mother, Grace Philps," Helen murmured. "Mama, this is Detective Kaminsky."

"Detective?" The old woman's skin was wrinkled and papery, and her head was like a fluffy white dandelion. But her eyes were alert as she studied Jackie. "You're a policewoman?"

"Yes," Jackie said.

Grace Philps examined her carefully, then turned to her daughter. "Helen, it's cold in here. I want the furnace on."

"There's no filter in the furnace right now, Mama," Helen said patiently. "I'm having it serviced while the weather's so nice."

"I'm cold." The old woman's face took on a petulant

expression, and she moved aggressively toward her daughter. "I want the furnace turned on."

Helen cast Jackie an awkward glance. "Please, Mama," she murmured. "As soon as our guest leaves, I'll go downstairs and see if I can find one of the electric heaters for your room."

"Well, hurry it up. I'm freezing." Grace poked thoughtfully at one of the date squares, then picked it up and stuffed it into her mouth. Crumbs spilled onto her chin. "Do you have a gun?" she asked Jackie.

"Yes, I do."

"What? Speak up, girl."

"Yes, I have a gun!" Jackie shouted, feeling ridiculous.

"Good. Maybe you'll have to use it pretty soon," Grace told her darkly. She turned and wandered out of the room, trailing her blanket.

Helen's face was pink with embarrassment under the drift of freckles. "You'll have to excuse Mama," she whispered. "There are times when she—"

"Never mind," Jackie said. "I have a grandmother who can be pretty difficult when she wants to. I know exactly what it's like."

Helen smiled gratefully, watching as Jackie got to her feet and put away her notebook. "I'm sorry I couldn't help you more."

"You've been very helpful." Jackie handed her one of her cards. "If you think of anything else, feel free to call me."

"Of course. Detective…"

"Yes?"

"I hope you find Michael soon. I won't be able to eat or sleep until you find him. I'm so frightened."

Jackie patted the woman's shoulder. "Don't worry, Ms.

Philps,'' she said with considerably more confidence than she felt, ''we're going to find him.''

Leigh made herself an egg-salad sandwich and heated a bowl of soup in the microwave. She put a single place mat on the kitchen table and sat down to eat her meal, looking at Michael's empty place across from her.

Her son had graduated from his high chair to a booster seat a few months earlier. It seemed so strange to be eating without his vigorous chatty presence. The silence pressed against her, making her feel tired and lost.

She felt tears gathering behind her eyelids and blinked furiously to hold them at bay. Instead, she imagined his face, his big dark eyes and golden curls, the way he always clutched the fork so solemnly in his plump little hand and tried hard to copy all her movements.

''Where are you, Michael?'' she whispered, looking at the crystal prism as it rotated slowly in the breeze from the window. ''Are you all right, darling? Are you frightened? I miss you so much—''

The doorbell rang. Leigh stared, her eyes widening in alarm. She put down the spoon, got up and hurried out to the foyer, leaning forward to look through the peephole.

Detective Kaminsky stood on the porch, her big leather bag over her shoulder. Leigh opened the door and stood aside to admit the policewoman, feeling tense and nervous.

There was something intimidating about Jackie Kaminsky. She was so composed and noncommittal, with her air of cool professionalism and her keen measuring glance.

When the detective had reached into her shoulder bag during their morning interview, her blazer had fallen open to reveal a black side holster strapped to her belt. Leigh shivered, remembering. She could hardly imagine how it would feel to be a woman like Jackie, who carried a gun and knew how to use it.

But there was nothing masculine or repellent about the woman. In fact, Jackie Kaminsky was very attractive, in a dark exotic kind of way. She had glossy black hair, golden skin and clear hazel eyes, flecked with green. Her body was slim and graceful, and on the rare occasions when she smiled, her face sparkled and her wide mouth curved sweetly, making her look much younger and more vulnerable.

Yet her attractiveness was even more frightening to Leigh than if Jackie had been tough and surly. It was important not to yield to the detective's personality. Leigh couldn't afford to like Jackie, couldn't let herself confide in her.

In fact, this policewoman was a real threat. Leigh had to be on her guard all the time....

"I was just having a bite to eat in the kitchen," she said. "Would you care to join me?"

Jackie shook her head. "Thanks, but I've already eaten. A few of the guys brought Chinese takeout to the office."

"It's past six," Leigh said. "Aren't you off duty by now? You were here so early this morning."

"I still have a few things to check out before I go home." Jackie followed Leigh into the kitchen.

"Won't you at least have a cup of tea?" Leigh asked while the policewoman sat at the table and took her notebook out of her bag. "I was going to make a pot for myself anyhow."

"All right. Thanks, Leigh." Jackie looked at her directly.

Again Leigh was conscious of how probing those hazel eyes were. She forced herself to meet the woman's gaze. "Have you found out anything more about where Michael is?"

"Nothing definite." Jackie took out a snapshot and handed it across the table. "Do you know this man?"

Leigh took the photograph and studied the image of a handsome young man in jeans, work boots and baseball cap, holding an armful of lumber. "I don't think so," she said at last, puzzled. "Should I?"

"He's working on some renovations to a house in your parents' neighborhood. I just wondered if you'd ever seen him before."

Leigh shook her head and poured boiling water over the tea leaves in a ceramic pot.

"Did your mother make that teapot and cups?" Jackie asked.

Leigh turned in surprise. "How did you know that?"

"I thought I recognized her work. Thank you," Jackie said as she accepted a cup of tea.

Leigh seated herself and began to eat her soup. "That's Michael's place," Leigh said, indicating the red plastic booster chair. "Before you came, I was sitting here thinking how lonely it is without him. I hardly know what to do with myself."

Jackie reached into her bag again and removed a manila folder. "We have to go over the questions for your polygraph," she said.

"What will it be like?" Leigh put the spoon down and clenched her hands in her lap, out of sight beneath the table.

"Don't worry, it won't be anything scary," Jackie said. "We'll go over the questions now and I'll record your responses. Then tomorrow afternoon, down at the main police station, you'll be hooked up to some monitoring devices and Sergeant Kravitz will ask you the same questions. She's specially trained to administer polygraphs."

"Will you be there when she does it?"

"Not in the same room. I'll be next door, watching

through a two-way mirror, in a room equipped with a microphone so I can interrupt if I'm not clear about any of the responses."

"And all I have to do is tell the truth?"

Jackie looked at her soberly. "That's all you have to do."

Leigh took a deep breath. "So I have nothing to worry about, do I?"

She was aware of Jackie's eyes resting on her as she took another spoonful of soup, then picked up the sandwich and tried to eat.

They ran through the list of prepared questions, and Leigh was relieved to find that there was nothing difficult or tricky about them. The questions covered all the same ground they'd been over before. Jackie asked when Leigh had arrived at the mall, what time she and Michael had eaten, how Michael had vanished from the toy store and what she'd done immediately afterward.

Patiently Leigh gave the same answers while Jackie made note of her responses.

"Okay," the detective said at last, putting the file away. "That's it. I guess I'd better get home." She hesitated. "Nothing else has happened today? No unusual calls or anything?"

"Not really. A lot of media people are hanging around and I've noticed a few more people driving by the house than usual, but I think they were just curious."

"We always get some of those. It's amazing how many people take an active interest in the misfortunes of others. By the way, Leigh..."

"Yes?"

"I live in an apartment building not far from here. It's north of the mall, just off Francis Street."

"Yes?" Leigh tensed again, her instincts alerted by something in the detective's casual tone.

"I have a neighbor who lives in the apartment across the hall," Jackie went on. "Her name's Carmen. She's a single mother with a four-year-old daughter called Tiffany. I baby-sit for her sometimes."

"I see," Leigh said, wondering what the detective was getting at. She forced herself to spoon up the last of the soup.

"I called her tonight just before I came over here," Jackie said. "I wanted to ask her about a couple of things."

"Like what?"

"Well, I wondered about how you happened to leave Michael in the toy store and go next door to look at dresses. Tiffany's a year older than Michael, but Carmen says she'd never leave her daughter alone in a store for thirty seconds without checking on her."

Leigh tensed and her heart began to pound. "Are you implying that I'm a careless mother, Detective?"

"No, I'm not. By all accounts, you've always been a very careful mother. That's why I can't help wondering why you'd leave your son alone for five minutes in a crowded mall."

"He was busy looking at toys," Leigh said, concentrating on her plate. "And the time just…got away from me. I checked on him, then went next door for a minute and started looking at the dresses. I was near the front, watching the entrance to the toy store all the time to make sure he didn't wander out into the mall."

"But you didn't go back to check on him?"

"Not for a few minutes," Leigh said quietly. "I know it's my fault. I'll be sorry about it for the rest of my life, but that's the way it happened."

"And you still believe that your husband has Michael now?"

Leigh took a deep breath. "Yes," she said. "Of course Stefan has him. Where else would he be?"

"I saw Stefan's apartment this morning. He hardly has room to hide a three-year-old."

"But there's the whole farm to hide him. Miroslav and Ivana probably have Michael out at their place. Have you been to the farm yet?"

"I'm going out there first thing tomorrow morning." Jackie got to her feet and gathered up her bag and notebook. "That's another thing I asked Carmen about, by the way," she said in the same casual tone.

"About what?" Leigh got up, as well, and followed the detective to the door.

"About how she'd feel if her ex-husband abducted Tiffany and she didn't know where he was."

Leigh held the doorknob tensely, waiting for the woman to leave.

"Carmen said she'd be absolutely frantic. In fact, she got upset and almost started to cry just talking to me on the phone about it."

"I don't see any sense in getting hysterical," Leigh said coolly. "That can't possibly do Michael any good."

"No, but it's probably a natural reaction, don't you think?"

"I suppose it depends how you're raised," Leigh said. "My mother taught us that we should always keep our emotions to ourselves in a crisis no matter how upset we feel, and try to present a calm face to the world. She always said it was the responsibility of people in our position."

She regretted the words as soon as she spoke them and heard how pompous they sounded. The young policewoman's eyes widened in surprise, then flickered and went cold with dislike, as if a shutter had been dropped over her face.

She thinks I'm passing judgment on her friend, Leigh thought in agony. *She probably thinks I'm just like my mother.*

But she couldn't say anything. For Michael's sake, she had to keep her distance from this woman.

"I'll see you tomorrow afternoon at one at the downtown police station," Jackie said, moving outside into the summer evening. "Call me right away if anything happens. You still have my card, don't you?"

"Yes," Leigh murmured.

She watched as Jackie started down the walkway to her car. Then she closed the door and went inside, wandering down the hall to the kitchen as the silence of the empty house came flooding back.

9

The following morning, Jackie drove through town and headed south toward the Painted Hills area. It was Sunday morning, and traffic was sparse under a warm midsummer sky.

She passed the wildlife refuge, then the golf course, enjoying the way the light shimmered on hills covered with evergreens and poplars. The residential areas thinned and gave way to a valley filled with small acreages and farms where horses grazed behind white rail fences. Through the open window she could smell fresh-cut hay and hear the occasional lowing of cattle.

She checked the address in her notebook, then pulled off the highway and down a side road toward a place set on a small rise of land. Surrounded by a well-kept yard and a stand of trees, with corrals and hay meadows in the distance, the house was a white-stuccoed sprawling bungalow, with a deep pillared veranda, tall windows and a red-tile roof. Jackie was surprised by its size and opulence; it made her think of a castle positioned at the center of a small kingdom. From all the Mellon family's references to the "farm" and to Stefan's social standing, she'd rather expected his parents to be living in an old frame house with a couple of shabby outbuildings.

God help me, she thought. *I'm getting as snobbish as the rest of them. It must be catching.*

As she pulled around in the driveway, Jackie had a commanding view of the entire valley. At the back she could see a swimming pool next to an emerald green lawn and masses of shrubbery and groomed flower beds. All the pens and outbuildings seemed to be freshly painted, and the grounds were impeccable.

A half-dozen shaggy ponies capered along a fence at the base of the hill, tossing their manes and kicking up their heels in the warm sunlight. Nearby, a few chickens scratched and clucked in the gravel by a small white shed. The chickens were some kind of ornamental breed with showy plumage that glistened in iridescent shades of brown and green.

Jackie parked, then got out of the car and examined the chickens in gloomy silence.

There were getting to be entirely too many barnyard fowl in this case, all the way from Michael's yellow stuffed duck to Paul Arnussen's weird account of "some kind of chicken."

Too many, that is, if you believed Arnussen's psychic flash, which Jackie, of course, did not...

She shook her head and started up the walk toward the house, then paused.

A group of people were outside in a garden area behind and to the side of the big house, about a hundred yards from where she'd parked. She could hear voices, both male and female, and also the high-pitched chatter of a child.

She hitched her bag up on her shoulder and headed for the garden, letting herself in through a white gate set in a picket fence.

Four adults worked in the neat rows of vegetables. Two men plied hoes and rakes among the potatoes, while a couple of women stooped to pick runner beans and put them into wide baskets. The child was playing somewhere among the tall lush corn, invisible but easily heard.

One of the men looked up as Jackie approached, wiping a gnarled hand across his forehead. He was tall and broad-shouldered, with an impressive mustache and longish silver hair swept back from a face tanned dark by the sun. The younger man, also in jeans and a cotton shirt, was fair-haired and cheerful, with the same strong features and pleasant expression.

Jackie extended her hand to the older man. "I'm Detective Kaminsky," she said. "And you must be Miroslav Panesivic."

He shook her head with a firmness she liked. "We've been expecting you, Detective. My son, Zan," he said in a heavily accented voice, indicating the younger man who leaned on his hoe and watched.

"Hi there," Zan said, grinning at her. "The Spokane Police Department is getting better-looking all the time."

The two women approached, and Miroslav introduced them, as well. "My wife, Ivana, and my daughter-in-law, Mila."

A small child came bursting out of the rows of pale green corn and stood looking curiously at the stranger.

"And this," the old man said fondly, touching her hair, "is Deborah, my granddaughter."

"Hi, Deborah," Jackie said, smiling.

The little girl was about three years old, wearing red shorts and a white T-shirt. A black kitten was cradled snugly in her arms. The child had light brown hair and big brown eyes, and looked like her mother, a small slim woman with delicate features and a wary expression.

Ivana Panesivic, Stefan's mother, was tall and regal, her gray hair braided and piled on top of her head like a crown. With her aquiline features and piercing dark eyes, she looked a lot like Stefan, Jackie realized. But where his smile was confident, hers was tentative, almost shy.

"Are you a real policeman?" Deborah asked, breaking the silence.

Jackie nodded solemnly.

"Do you have a gun?"

"Yes, I do." Jackie pulled her blazer aside to reveal the holster containing the snub-nosed pistol at her waist.

The little girl's eyes widened with awe. She hugged the kitten and shifted from foot to foot.

"What's your kitty's name?" Jackie asked.

"Star. 'Cause he has a little white star on his forehead." Deborah held her kitten up for inspection. "He lives in the barn."

Jackie touched the kitten's fragile skull, scratching gently behind the soft ears. "He's a very nice kitten."

"Star should go back to the barn now, Deborah," Miroslav told his granddaughter. "The lady wants to talk with us."

Miroslav was clearly in charge of the situation. He turned to Jackie while the women waited in silence and Zan picked up the gardening tools. Deborah followed her father, still clutching Star.

"Do you want to speak with us alone or all together?" Miroslav asked.

"Individually, if you don't mind," Jackie said. "And perhaps I could start with you, Mr. Panesivic. Is there someplace we could sit?"

"On the veranda." Miroslav glanced at his wife. "Is that all right, Mama?"

Ivana nodded. "I'll make a pot of iced tea," she said, giving Jackie a gentle smile. "Come, Mila, and help me."

The two women headed off toward the house while Zan started for the barn with his daughter and her kitten.

A leafy trumpet vine that grew up the side of the porch provided shade for a grouping of cushioned rattan furniture on the veranda. Jackie seated herself in one of the armchairs, took out her notebook and gazed at the sweep of the valley, bounded by tree-covered hills. "This is beautiful. Such a lovely view."

"We are very happy here," Miroslav said quietly. "We bought this property twenty years ago when it was nothing but a bare hill, and we have worked hard ever since to make it nice."

"Did you build the house and all those outbuildings?"

"Every stick. And mostly with these two hands." He held up a pair of brown and callused hands for Jackie's inspection. "We had some money when we came here," he went on. "My family owned a big winery near Zagreb, which I inherited when my parents died. Ivana and I could see the trouble coming in Yugoslavia, so we sold the property and took our money out of the country. Zan was just a boy of fifteen at the time. He came with us, but Stefan stayed behind."

Jackie calculated rapidly. "Stefan must have been twenty-three when you left the country."

"Yes. He was teaching by then. We thought he might have wanted to marry one of the young women he was seeing, but none of them turned out to be quite what Stefan wanted. He had very clear and noble ideas about what he was looking for in a wife."

"Barbara Mellon thinks he was just looking for a rich wife."

Miroslav's face hardened. "Barbara Mellon is a foolish old woman. It breaks my heart to think that my grandson—"

He stopped abruptly, his gaze fixed on the cloudless sky beyond the trees.

"What were you saying?" Jackie prompted. "It was something about your grandson."

Miroslav tensed his big shoulders. "I hate to think of Michael being exposed to such influences. Selfish and shallow behavior, and unkindness to one's fellow man, if not controlled, can become poisonous to the soul."

Jackie knew this to be true, but it wasn't her place to agree. She wrote impassively in her notebook, then looked up at the old man again. "Do you know where your grandson is, Mr. Panesivic?"

"I do not," he said firmly. "But I think the Mellons have stolen him away. She always hated to share him with us. She thinks we are beneath her, and we will contaminate the boy somehow with our 'common' ways."

"Leigh, you mean?"

The old man's face softened. "Not Leigh. She is a sweet girl. I loved her like a daughter, right from the first. She used to come out here and follow me around the farm, asking questions like little Deborah and helping me with everything. Even in the rain and the mud, Leigh would put on rubber boots and come outside with me to feed the chickens and gather the eggs."

Jackie considered this information, startled and confused. Again, she was forced to readjust her mental image of Leigh Mellon.

"So," she said at last, "it was Barbara who didn't approve of your family?"

"Yes." His face hardened again. "She is the true power in that family, and she is a bad person. Very unkind."

"Do you think she has Michael?"

"I think I would not be surprised by anything she did."

They continued to talk, with Jackie asking routine questions and Miroslav giving firm unhesitating responses. She also showed him, without comment, the snapshot of Paul

Arnussen. Miroslav put on a pair of reading glasses to study the picture, but couldn't recognize the man.

After about ten minutes Ivana came out with a pot of iced tea and lemon slices, followed by Mila, who carried a tray of tumblers and hot oatcakes.

The two women set the refreshments on a wicker table nearby, then turned to leave.

"Mrs. Panesivic," Jackie said, "could I speak with you next, do you think? Your husband's already answered most of my questions, so it'll only take a minute."

Ivana cast a nervous glance at her husband, who gave her an encouraging nod.

"She is a very nice lady, this young police detective," he told his wife. "If the police are like this nowadays, maybe I should try to get more speeding tickets."

The little joke helped to lighten the tension among them, as Miroslav had obviously intended. He led Mila from the veranda, leaving Jackie alone with Ivana, who poured two glasses of iced tea, then folded her hands tightly in her lap and stared at the table.

"Mrs. Panesivic," Jackie said gently, "where do you think your grandson is now?"

"I don't know." Tears filled Ivana's eyes and began to trickle down her cheeks. "I am so afraid for him," she whispered, giving Jackie a look of naked appeal. "Michael is a tender little boy. He is timid and easily frightened, and very afraid of the dark and of monsters. If he…"

The older woman's distress was clearly genuine. Jackie reached out impulsively and covered Ivana's hands with her own.

"We'll find him," she promised with considerably more confidence than she felt. "We're looking at every possibility, following up on every lead, and we're going to find him."

"If Michael is hurt or…or…" Ivana choked and rummaged blindly for a handkerchief in her apron pocket. "I love him so much, Detective. I don't think I could go on living."

At last, Jackie thought grimly, somebody in the family was finally expressing real sorrow and concern about the fate of Michael Panesivic.

"Mrs. Panesivic, I want to ask you one more thing. About Leigh Mellon… What kind of person is she? Would you call her a good mother?"

Ivana looked up. "Oh, yes. A very good mother. Leigh was such a sweet girl. I still cry, all these months later, because we lost her."

"What do you mean, you lost her?" Jackie said.

"A divorce is a terrible thing. Not just a matter between a man and a woman," Ivana said in a low voice. "There are others who lose the ones they love when a divorce happens. I cared for Leigh like my own daughter. I loved her and I still do, but I never see her anymore. And I only see Michael when Stefan brings him to the farm for his visit on Saturdays."

"But in the last few months, Leigh hasn't allowed those visits."

"No, she hasn't. Leigh is…afraid."

"Afraid of what?"

"I suppose it is our family, so different from her own, and our ties to another country. She is afraid for her son, but Leigh has no reason to fear us. We would never, never hurt our grandson by taking him away from his mother."

"Thank you, Mrs. Panesivic. That's all I need for now," Jackie said.

Ivana got up and moved toward the door, then hesitated. "If you talk to Leigh, Detective…"

"Yes?" Jackie said.

"Tell her that I love her and I miss her. Tell her that I'm sorry for her worry, and that I pray all the time Michael will be found safely. Could you please tell her that?"

Jackie felt a lump forming in her throat, along with a sense of increasing bewilderment. "I'll do that" she said. "Would you send your daughter-in-law out next, please?"

Mila Panesivic's feelings for her former sister-in-law were not nearly as tender.

"Leigh was a haughty bitch," she said, perched tensely on the wicker chair across from Jackie. She refused an offer of iced tea and seemed anxious to be gone.

Jackie studied the woman, finding her unexpectedly interesting. Mila Panesivic spoke flawless, unaccented English. Her face was pale and composed, and her brown hair sleek. Jackie could see she had the trim body and graceful carriage of a ballerina, despite the concealing loose shorts and shirt.

"Are you a dancer?" Jackie couldn't help asking.

"Hardly." Mila gave her a cold smile. "I hold an arts degree with a specialty in interior design. I have my own decorating business, primarily serving corporate clients."

"I see. Here in the city?"

"Mostly. I also travel quite a bit doing consulting work out of state on referral."

Jackie asked the same question she'd asked the others. "Mila, where do you think your nephew is right now?"

"I think the Mellons have him," Mila said without hesitation. "They're such a power-mad arrogant group of profiteers. They simply can't endure not having things their own way, and any notion of sharing is beyond their ability to understand."

"Even Leigh?"

Mila's lip curled. "I see that the American beauty has fooled you, too. She fools everybody."

"You really don't like her, do you?"

"I hate her. In my opinion, Leigh Mellon is a symbol of all that's wrong with America."

"What's wrong with America?" Jackie asked mildly.

"Everything," Mila said, her eyes blazing. "Hypocrisy, apathy, wallowing in hollow sentiment, brutality, moral laxity and utter indifference to the suffering of others."

"That's a pretty extensive list of sins. I take it you're not an American citizen?"

"You're wrong. I'm a first-generation American. My parents came here from Croatia after the war, in the early fifties, to make a fine new life for themselves."

"And did they?"

"Oh, yes," Mila said bitterly. "They became very successful Americans."

"So what's your beef with the United States?"

"For one thing, the criminal lack of a decisive policy when the war in Yugoslavia first began to escalate. Americans blundered around the edges of the conflict, putting up arms embargoes to keep the citizens from defending themselves, providing illegal partisan support, looking the other way while people were being slaughtered... All that time trying to keep their skirts clean as they slept with all sides in the conflict. It was a truly horrible disgusting spectacle. And people like the Mellon family were the worst offenders."

Zan Panesivic strolled though the kitchen door with an amiable smile, but his eyes were tense as he glanced at his wife.

"Is Mila talking your ear off?" he asked Jackie, dropping a hand on the smaller woman's shoulder. "You really shouldn't get her started on politics."

Jackie smiled. "She holds some strong opinions, true, but I always admire people with enough passion to take a stand on an issue, no matter what it is. As Mila says, most people in this country are far too apathetic.''

Mila shot her a look that was both startled and grateful. Jackie told her she had no more questions, and Mila got up and went inside.

''I guess I'm next,'' Zan Panesivic said cheerfully.

''I won't keep you long.'' Jackie watched as he seated himself in the opposite chair. ''You don't look at all like Stefan.''

''I know. We're probably about as different as two brothers can be. Stefan takes after our mother's side of the family, and I'm more like Dad.''

''You also seem much more American.''

Zan shrugged. ''I was here for most of my adolescence, went to high school in Spokane, played football... I don't really have many ties with Croatia.''

''Do you ever go back to visit?''

''I haven't. Not once. It's an expensive trip.'' Zan gave Jackie a boyish smile. ''Mila's been nagging me for years to go and visit. She still has a lot of relatives living around Dubrovnik. So we've finally booked a flight. We're leaving in just over a week and planning to spend almost a month over there, showing off Deborah to all the aunts and uncles. Mila's wild with excitement.''

Jackie tried without success to picture Mila Panesivic wild with excitement about anything other than politics. But maybe, like many people, the woman was different within the privacy of her marriage.

''Will any other family members be going? How about your parents?'' she asked.

''No. Mama would love to come with us, but she won't travel without Dad, and my father has no desire to see the old country again. He's disgusted by what's been happening there. He can't even stand to watch television anymore.''

''And Stefan?''

Zan's face tightened with concern. ''He was thinking about a trip this summer, but he's far too worried about Michael to make any travel plans right now. He's just going to sit tight until he knows his son is safe.''

''So you agree with the rest of your family? You think Stefan's ex-wife and her family are responsible for Michael's disappearance?''

''I have to think that,'' Zan said quietly. ''Anything else is unthinkable.''

His eyes were blue and direct, utterly sincere. Jackie nodded, then looked down at her notebook. ''What's your occupation, Zan?''

''I'm a landscape engineer, employed by the city.''

''I see. What were you doing on Friday evening between six and nine?''

''I was here at the farm along with everyone else for the whole evening. I arrived just after five, as soon as I got off work. It was Mila's birthday, and Mama had baked a big lemon cake. Mama was so happy on Friday night,'' Zan added with a sad faraway look.

''Why?''

''Because of the court order. She knew Stefan was going to have Michael the next day and would be bringing him to the farm. Mama hadn't seen the little boy for so long. It was all she could talk about, how wonderful it was going to be to have Michael for the whole day.''

Deborah came out of the house and climbed into her father's lap, nestling against his chest.

He cuddled the little girl and rested his chin on her smooth head. ''Anything else, Detective?'' he asked.

Jackie took the photograph of Paul Arnussen from her

notebook and displayed it, but Zan showed no signs of recognition.

"Mama!" he called. "Mila, come out here."

The women came onto the veranda and took turns in examining the photo. They shook their heads.

"Sorry," Zan said at last, returning the picture to Jackie. "Can we do anything else to help?"

"I don't think so. Not at the moment, anyway." Jackie got up and put away the notebook. "Thank you for your time, and let me know if you think of anything that might be helpful," she said to the family.

Zan followed her to the edge of the veranda, carrying his daughter.

Jackie smiled back at the group briefly and headed for her car, where two of the brightly feathered chickens were scratching and clucking by one of the rear wheels.

She stared at the birds, thinking about Paul Arnussen, his strange "vision" and the smears of blood in his truck. At last she got in and drove away, while Zan stood watching from the shadow of the trumpet vine.

10

By Monday morning, there were so many police officers working on the Michael Panesivic case that it was no longer possible to hold the daily briefing in Lew Michelson's office. Besides Michelson and Brian Wardlow, the group included a lieutenant and a captain from the downtown office, two other detectives, and a number of uniformed officers. They spilled into the squad room, sitting in chairs and at desks, while Jackie sat behind her own desk with the file open in front of her and outlined the information gathered so far.

"First," she said, "I have to tell you all that Leigh Mellon passed her polygraph yesterday afternoon."

Most of the faces registered surprise. "That's exactly the way I felt," Jackie said. "I was certain her story wouldn't check out, but she sailed right through the test with no discrepancies at all. Sergeant Kravitz is planning to run another test in a couple of days, but she thinks the woman is telling the truth."

"So where does that leave us?" Sergeant Michelson asked.

Jackie looked at her notes. "With two other possibilities, I guess. If Michael's mother didn't take him, then it was either another family member or a stranger."

Michelson looked at her partner. "You've been checking out the pedophiles, Wardlow?"

"A few of them. We got the list yesterday, but it's hard to get hold of people on the weekend. Especially," Wardlow added bitterly, "when it's supposed to be a holiday."

"Anything more about that girl at the mall?"

Wardlow shook his head. "When I went back a second time, both witnesses were even vaguer about the girl. Nothing concrete at all."

"And you showed them the family photographs?"

"Yes. Nobody in the neighboring stores saw any of the immediate family members at the mall on Friday night. A complete zero on that one."

"How about other leads?"

"Nothing so far," Wardlow said. "Just a ton of dead ends and wasted time."

Jackie glanced at her partner in concern. He looked tired and out-of-sorts, and there were dark circles under his eyes. Probably he was fighting with his wife, in addition to working long hours and missing his days off.

"How about this so-called psychic?" Michelson asked, turning back to Jackie.

"The lab says the blood on the tarp isn't human. I didn't expect it would be. The man seems too smart to leave evidence like that lying around."

"So you believe his story about killing the dog on the highway?"

"Brian saw the dog's carcass and spoke to the owner," Jackie said. "But I still don't know what to think. Arnussen could have run over the dog deliberately to mask some other kind of evidence. We're hanging on to the tarp, though. We want to be able to check it thoroughly for trace evidence if it turns out he's involved somehow in the abduction."

"Don't you think he'll object?"

"I don't particularly care if he objects," she said grimly.

"Let him go to court to get his damned tarp back if he wants it."

The sergeant gave her a long thoughtful glance, then turned from her to Wardlow. "What do you two think about this guy? What's your gut reaction?"

Jackie looked at the Polaroid snapshot clipped to her file. Again she thought how this man, standing in the sunshine in boots and cap, holding an armful of lumber, did not look like a psychic.

"I'm not sure what to think, Sarge," Wardlow said. "But I do believe that either he took the kid or else he's a genuine psychic and we should probably be looking around for chickens."

"Why?" the lieutenant asked.

"Because he knew about the kid's toy duck. We didn't give that detail to anyone. The mother remembered it Saturday morning and called it in to Jackie while we were here for lunch."

"You know, I've been thinking about that," Jackie said. "He could easily have seen the little kid in the neighborhood, carrying that stuffed duck. Arnussen works up there in the South Hill all the time, and the baby-sitter often walks Michael over to visit his grandparents."

"So there's also a possibility he's not a psychic and he's not mixed up in the case? Just a weirdo wanting to get involved?"

Jackie hesitated, then nodded. "I guess that's a possibility."

Michelson looked at her partner again. "What do we know about this Arnussen guy? Were you able to get anything on him?"

Wardlow consulted his notes. "No criminal record in this state. Clean driving record, no indication of any kind of trouble. He's been living in a basement suite in Cannon

Hill for almost six years, and the landlady knows a bit about his history. She's a widow in her late seventies, by the way, and she thinks Arnussen's just a hell of a guy.''

"Sometimes even serial killers are terrific guys," the sergeant said grimly. "They can charm the birds right out of the trees. The same goes for kidnappers and other psychos. Did you get a look around the landlady's house?"

"Most of it. She was very agreeable about showing me the upstairs and the rest of the basement, though she reminded me that she couldn't legally let me into Arnussen's suite."

"Is it worth trying for a warrant to get in there?" Michelson asked.

Wardlow shook his head. "I doubt it. When I commented how nice and bright everything was, the old lady told me she cleans her whole house every single week. On Friday she does the upstairs, and on Saturday she does all the lower floor, including Arnussen's rooms. Apparently, it's part of their rental agreement."

"So she cleaned his apartment the day after the kidnapping?" one of the detectives asked.

"That's what she told me."

"You said she's fond of him. Would she cover for him?"

"Not on something like this," Wardlow said firmly. "Not if it involved a child's safety. This lady loves her grandchildren, Sarge. She spent about an hour showing me pictures."

"Okay." Michelson sighed and rubbed his stomach. "What else do you have on the guy?"

Wardlow continued to read from his notes. "He grew up on a ranch in Montana. His mother died when he was five, and his father raised him. Seems the old man was pretty reckless. He gambled the ranch away and died in a bar fight when Arnussen was eighteen."

"So our guy went to work as a carpenter?" The question came from Shelly Williams, one of the patrol officers assigned to the case.

"He's worked at a lot of things. Oil rigger, ranch hand, general laborer. He's got quite a profitable little business going now, doing renovations on heritage houses. He's been working up on Summit Drive and in the South Hill area for almost five years."

"And he still lives in a basement suite?"

"Apparently he's saving money to buy a ranch. The landlady says that's his only goal in life."

A few of the officers exchanged glances. "There's been no ransom call?" one of them asked. "It wouldn't be hard for the Mellons to cough up the down payment on a nice little ranch."

Jackie shook her head. "Michael was abducted Friday night. It's now Monday morning. If ransom was the motive, somebody would have been contacted by now."

Captain Alvarez made his first contribution to the briefing. He was a thin man in his early fifties, neat and spruce in his dark blue uniform. "It could be," he said, "that the family's had a ransom call and been warned not to tell the police about it or the boy will be killed. That's been known to happen. People can be closemouthed when they believe their child's life is at risk."

Jackie considered the various members of the Mellon family. "I'm not sure Leigh would be able to carry something like that off without arousing my suspicion," she said at last. "But I'll bet her mother could."

Michelson frowned. "I'm still concerned about the timing of this court order on Thursday, requiring the mother to give up the kid for regular visitation. I'd like to get back to the family angle for a minute. Jackie, you said Leigh Mellon was clean on her polygraph?"

"Completely."

"Do you think the Mellons could have lifted the kid without her knowing about it?"

"I don't know. I still have to talk with her sister. There's something…" She hesitated.

"What?" Michelson asked.

"Leigh's older sister, Adrienne, was abducted for ransom about twenty years ago, when she was a young teenager."

"What happened?"

"She disappeared from a private school in California, and the parents got a ransom call demanding two hundred thousand dollars. A few days later, while they were getting the cash together, Adrienne turned up at the school again. Mrs. Mellon told me they never did find out who was responsible. Adrienne didn't want to talk about it, and they were too busy to press her. Apparently," Jackie added without expression, "the father was running for public office. It was an inconvenient time to be kidnapped."

"Jesus," one of the detectives muttered, shaking his head. "Can you believe it?"

"It may be a little strange, but it doesn't signify a whole lot," the sergeant argued. "People with that kind of money are much more likely to be the target of kidnappers. It doesn't mean there's any kind of connection."

"I know," Jackie said. "But I'd still like to get the whole story from Adrienne, if I can. I'm seeing her this afternoon."

"Good idea." Michelson turned back to Wardlow. "Anything else about Arnussen? Friends, hobbies, activities?"

"Nothing much. The guy seems to spend most of his

time working. When he has evenings or days off, he likes to go for walks in the country.''

"Girlfriends?"

"Not that anybody knows of. He seems to be pretty much of a loner."

"That's consistent with the profiles of psychos, too. Wardlow, we're already coordinating with the FBI on this. Get them to run a complete check on Arnussen's previous locations, okay? See if there are any unsolved child disappearances in other places he's lived."

Wardlow nodded and made a note.

"So how does this carpenter spend his free time, besides going for long walks in the country?" Captain Alvarez asked.

"He putters around the landlady's house, keeping everything fixed up and in good repair. In return, she gives him a better deal on the rent. And that's about all I could find out about the guy."

"Let's come back to the family, Kaminsky," Michelson said. "What's the father's side like?"

"The Panesivics all seem to be really nice wholesome people." Jackie told the group about Stefan, then about his family out working in the garden. "The sister-in-law seems a little crazy," she added, "but it's got nothing to do with Michael. My guess is that she's too obsessed with politics to pay much attention to anything else."

She was silent a moment, toying with a pen.

"Kaminsky?" the sergeant asked. "What are you thinking?"

Jackie looked up at him. "Something's bothered me right from the beginning," she said at last.

"What's that?"

"The mother's family isn't upset enough. They all really love the little boy, but they don't seem to be frantic about his disappearance. I can't understand it, Sarge. I just can't understand these people.''

Leigh awoke early on Monday morning after a couple of hours of fitful sleep. She hadn't been able to sleep more than a few hours at a time since Michael's disappearance, and when she did manage to drift off, her dreams were terrifying.

But today was different. After an endless anguished weekend, she could finally make her telephone call and be given some reassurance.

She climbed out of bed, stripped off her cotton night-gown and dressed rapidly in shorts, T-shirt and sandals, then hurried downstairs to make herself some breakfast. But the toast and poached eggs tasted like dust. She looked at the clock above the table, willing the hands to move faster.

Ten o'clock, she thought. *They said I couldn't call until ten o'clock.*

She tidied the kitchen and wandered through the house, plucking dead leaves from plants, aimlessly rearranging books and ornaments.

When the empty rooms became too stifling, she went outside into the clear morning sunlight and worked for an hour or so among the flowers, pulling weeds by hand and using a round-mouthed shovel to loosen the soil around the daisies.

Finally she went inside, washed her hands and took her handbag from the shelf in the closet, then locked the house and headed for her car.

They'd told her to use a pay phone, and she was anxious not to disobey any of their instructions, no matter how small. The nearest pay phone was at the mall, where the parking lot was still almost empty on this Monday morning.

Leigh looked around in surprise at the deserted streets,

then realized that tomorrow was the Fourth of July. Everybody who didn't have to be at work was probably away on holidays or taking the day off to relax at home.

She parked near the mall entrance, hurried inside and found a telephone.

Memorize the number, they'd instructed her. Don't write anything down.

Trembling with nervous excitement, she dialed the number from memory and waited while it rang hollowly at the other end.

"Yes?" a woman's voice said, sounding harried and impatient. "Who is calling? Please identify yourself."

Leigh's throat tightened with emotion and she forget everything she'd been told. "This is...this is Leigh Mellon," she whispered. "I wanted to know if—"

"Don't use names!" the woman snapped. "Use the identification number you were given."

Leigh twisted the metal cord in her fingers and recited the number. "Please," she said. "I just want to know if he's all right."

There was a long silence. "We don't have him," the woman said at last.

"*What?*" Leigh said.

"Look, I don't know what kind of game you're playing, but this certainly isn't funny. We don't appreciate being used like this."

"But," Leigh floundered, drowning in horror. "But...I don't understand. I did everything you said. I left him in the—"

"No details over the phone!" the woman said angrily. "We had our person on the scene as arranged. She went to the site to make the pickup, but the target wasn't available. She waited as long as she could without arousing suspicion, then left empty-handed."

"The target wasn't... What are you saying?" Leigh gasped.

"As I told you, we don't appreciate this kind of treatment. Our group takes a considerable risk, without any profit for ourselves, to ensure the welfare of others."

"But I did everything I was told," Leigh pleaded. "I dressed him exactly the way—"

"We don't have him," the woman repeated. "We have no idea where he is, and we request that you not try to contact us again. If you do, we'll deny all knowledge of you."

"Wait!" Leigh shouted. "Don't hang up! Just tell me if—"

The phone clicked in her ear. She stood gripping the receiver, her hand shaking. Finally, numb with terror, she hung up and fumbled her way out through the door into the sunshine, heading for her car.

The only thing she could think of was getting home, back inside the safety of her house, and calling Detective Kaminsky. Somehow, Leigh didn't feel able to call the policewoman from the phone in the mall. She wanted to be at home where Michael's room was, with all his toys and clothes.

She drove erratically through the quiet streets, whimpering and clutching the wheel, her face streaming with tears.

"Michael," she said aloud. "Darling, where are you? *Where are you?*"

11

The police briefing was about to wrap up, when Alice poked her head into the squad room. "Jackie?" she said. "Can you take a call? I don't like to bother you during a meeting, but it sounds kind of urgent."

Jackie nodded and reached for her desk telephone while the sergeant continued to run through work assignments for the day.

"Detective Kaminsky," she said into the receiver, then listened in growing alarm.

"Hold on, Leigh," she said at last. "I can't understand what you're saying."

"He's *gone!*" Leigh wailed. "He's not there. I called and he's not there!"

"What are you talking about?"

Leigh was sobbing breathlessly as she struggled for words. "Michael. He's not there. They said for me to call on Monday morning and they'd let me know where he was and that he was all right. But now they say they don't have him."

Jackie stared blankly at the other police staff in the room. "They? Who did you call, Leigh?"

"The people who were supposed to have him! Please, you have to find him. I don't know if they're lying to me or if something terrible has happened. Please, Jackie, you have to find him. I don't know what to do. I just don't know what to—"

"Leigh, calm down," Jackie interrupted. "Take a couple of deep breaths before you try to say anything. *Do it*," she commanded when Leigh's sobbing continued.

The others in the room had stopped talking and were listening tensely.

Leigh finally seemed to pull herself together. When she spoke again, her voice was still shaky and uncertain, but no longer hysterical. "Can you…can you come over here right away?" she asked. "Please?"

"I'm on my way."

Jackie hung up and gathered her files, then looked around at the others in the room.

"I don't know what the hell's going on," she said grimly. "But I can tell you, the woman's finally sounding frantic."

She parked in front of Leigh's house and hurried up the walk. Leigh met her at the door, her long blond hair in disarray and her face pale and streaked with tears. She was trembling visibly, hugging herself and leaning against the door frame for support.

Jackie took the woman's arm and led her inside, down the hall to the kitchen.

Leigh sank into a chair and stared at the window with wide vacant eyes.

"You need a cup of tea."

Jackie switched on the heat under the kettle and took a tea bag from a copper canister. She found the ceramic pot, then looked over at Leigh.

"Now, what's this all about? Have you had a ransom call?"

Leigh took a deep breath and twisted her hands together

on the table. "I made arrangements to have Michael kidnapped," she said.

Jackie stared at her.

"These people..." Leigh faltered and stopped talking for a moment, then went on, "I saw a printed circular on a bulletin board at church a couple of months ago. It said something about children at risk and gave a number to call. They told me about a group I could contact. The people in this group help mothers whose children are at risk of parental abduction. They smuggle the children into Canada."

"So you arranged to have them kidnap your own child?" Jackie asked in disbelief. "A bunch of strangers?"

"It was all very well-organized," Leigh said in a low tone. "I met with them several times."

"Where?"

"They came here to the house. It was a man and woman. They told me how to leave Michael in some public place for them to pick up. That way, when I reported his disappearance to the police, I could tell the truth and even pass a lie-detector test if there was any suspicion."

"Did you ever meet with these people anywhere besides your house?"

"Not the man and woman. But I took Michael to a park in the Valley a few times, where a young woman was waiting for us. She played a lot with Michael and brought him gifts."

"Why?"

"So that when she came to...to pick him up, it would be somebody he knew and he wouldn't be frightened of her."

Jackie began to feel a growing outrage. She turned away quickly when the kettle boiled, and poured hot water into the pot. "Why did you go to all this trouble?" she asked, struggling to keep her voice calm.

"So Stefan couldn't take Michael away to Europe. After the judge said I had to give him up on Saturday mornings again, I knew the risk was too great."

"Why not just take him yourself and vanish? Why all the complication?"

"I didn't want Stefan to know what I'd done. I didn't want him looking for us. The whole idea was to make him think Michael was gone, or…or dead," Leigh concluded in a whisper, her voice breaking, "so he'd go away and leave us alone."

"You made all these arrangements after the court hearing? In one day?" Jackie put the teapot and cups on the table.

Leigh shook her head. "It was planned in advance. The arrangement was that if I lost the court hearing, I was going to contact these people so they could pick up Michael before Saturday morning, when I had to give him to Stefan."

"So you called them on Thursday?"

Leigh gave another jerky nod, staring down at the gleaming wooden table.

"And when you said you'd lost in court, what did they tell you?"

"Not much. I never knew anybody's name. They're very secretive. They used an identification number for the case. I called and made arrangements to leave Michael alone in the toy store at seven-fifteen. I did everything I was supposed to. I took Michael to the toy store and left him alone for five minutes, and when I came back he was gone."

Gradually Jackie was beginning to grasp this incredible story. "So then you reported him to the police as a missing child?"

"That's right. The group said I could call on Monday morning to make sure he was safe in Canada."

"And how were you going to find him again?"

"About two or three weeks after the kidnapping, when everybody had started to give up looking for Michael, and Stefan wasn't suspicious of me or my family anymore, I was supposed to drive north to British Columbia and call the number again. Then they'd give me an address where I could pick Michael up. We were going to stay in Canada for a while until I decided what to do next."

Jackie was appalled. But she kept her feelings to herself, asking calmly, "Did your family know about any of this?"

Leigh shook her head. "I couldn't tell anybody. Not even my mother. I had to let everybody think he'd been kidnapped."

"So what happened? Why don't they have him?"

"The woman said they sent somebody to pick him up, but he wasn't there. She said he wasn't in the toy store!"

Leigh began to sob again. Jackie poured her a cup of tea and urged her to take a sip. Leigh blew her nose and complied, then Jackie said, "And you didn't leave him alone for more than five minutes?"

"Somebody else...must have grabbed him as soon as I turned my back. Oh, God, *Michael...*"

Jackie frowned, thinking. "These people you were working with—have you given them any money?"

"No," Leigh said. "They don't do it for money. They're just really concerned about the welfare of children. The plan was that I'd reimburse them for their expenses after Michael was safe and we were together again."

"They might still have him, but be holding out for a little more reimbursement. Did they make arrangements for further contact with you?"

"I told you, they don't have him! The woman I talked to this morning..." Leigh's voice broke. She gripped the teacup until her knuckles turned white. "She told me not to bother them again. She thought I hadn't been serious about the arrangements we made. The woman was…she was really angry with me.''

''Well let me tell you, she's not the only one,'' Jackie said bitterly.

Leigh gave her a bleak puzzled look.

''You've been lying to the police. It's a very serious offense. I could probably charge you with half a dozen things.''

''I don't care what you do to me!'' Leigh shouted. ''Don't you understand? Charge me with anything you like. Just *find my baby!*''

Jackie paced the floor of Lew Michelson's office while he and Wardlow watched in silence.

''Jesus,'' she muttered. ''I was so furious with the damned woman I could hardly stand to look at her. I just scribbled down some notes and got out of there as fast as I could.''

''I've never known you to get so emotionally involved in a case,'' Wardlow said. ''What's your problem, Kaminsky?''

She turned to him in disbelief. ''What's my *problem?* Brian, the woman engineered this whole thing. She was trying so hard to beat her husband in their little emotional warfare that she was willing to let her son be carted off by a bunch of strangers! And she didn't give a damn who else got involved in her game, either. She's been manipulating the police, her family, the sympathies of the entire community—''

''So what?'' the sergeant said. ''Brian's right. You need to get a grip on yourself. This doesn't change anything.''

''What do you mean?'' Jackie demanded, still furious. ''It changes the whole goddamn investigation!''

But she stopped pacing and sank into one of the vinyl chairs.

"It doesn't change a thing," Michelson repeated firmly. "Right from the beginning, we've been looking for an abducted child. And we still are, except that now we can probably rule out the mother as a suspect, that's all."

"How can we be so sure?" Jackie muttered. "If she lied before, maybe she's lying now. Maybe she really is insane, and this whole scam is even more complex and twisted than we realize."

"Wardlow doesn't think she's lying," the sergeant said.

Jackie looked at her partner. "Why not?"

"Because two witnesses at the mall corroborate her story," Wardlow said. "Remember? Both the computer-store manager and the clerk in the toy store saw a young woman hanging around at the time the kid disappeared. The woman in the toy store even said the girl seemed to be looking for somebody, but confirms that she left the store by herself."

"So you think your mystery girl was the person sent by Leigh's child-save agency to pick Michael up?"

"I think so. She got there a little too late, that's all. Leigh Mellon left her kid alone in the store and the other woman was on hand to pick him up, all according to plan. But somebody else snatched him before the woman could get to him."

Jackie looked down at the file in her hands, still battling her feelings of outrage and betrayal. The two men waited.

"It's the way they behave that really gets to me," she muttered at last. "People like the Mellons. When Leigh was busy making all her little plans, she didn't have the slightest hesitation about lying to the police and jerking us around to suit her purposes. Now that her kid seems to be actually gone, she's demanding we hurry up and find him right away. It's just so...so bloody arrogant."

"Maybe not," Michelson said quietly. "Maybe it's just a normal parental reaction. There's nothing stronger than a mother's love, you know. If a mother really believes her child is threatened, she'll do anything to protect him."

Jackie shook her head. "I met the Panesivic family. I honestly don't think they pose a threat to anybody. Leigh Mellon had to know that, too. She just doesn't want to share the kid with her ex-husband, that's all."

"Look, Jackie," the sergeant said, "you're too good a cop to be reacting like this. I want you to pull yourself together and be objective. If you can't, I want you to let me know right away so I can give the file to somebody else."

Jackie took a deep breath. "I'm sorry," she said. "You're right, Sarge. I'm letting this get to me, and I know I shouldn't. I want to keep the file. I'll do my best to keep my feelings under control."

"Good." Michelson smiled briefly over the rims of his glasses, then consulted a sheaf of papers on his desk. "What's next?"

"We have to check out these child-save people and see what we can learn about them," Jackie said. "It sounds like a pretty well-organized operation."

"Did she give you the name of her contact?"

"They don't use names. They just gave Leigh a case number to use when she called them."

"I've run into people like these before." Michelson grimaced. "They're all fanatics, totally committed to their cause. They'd rather go to jail than give any information to the police."

"That's what Leigh says, too. She's convinced they're

really dedicated to saving children from potential abduction.''

''So how do they save these kids? By abducting them,'' Wardlow said dryly. ''God, what a screwed-up world we live in, where innocent little kids get shuffled around like chess pieces.''

''Leigh gave you the phone numbers she was using?'' Michelson asked.

Jackie handed him a sheet of paper.

The sergeant glanced at it, then gave it to Wardlow. ''Run a check on these, Brian. Find out everything you can about these people before you go in, okay? We might need to lean on them a little bit to see if they know anything more about the Panesivic kid.''

''Brian's probably right,'' Jackie said. ''Now that I've calmed down, I think it's true that Leigh Mellon honestly doesn't know where her son is. And I doubt that these child-save people have him, either.''

''I agree,'' the sergeant said. ''We won't spend too much time on them now except to check out their involvement in this case, but somebody's going to have to go after them later. They're committing a serious crime every time they aid and abet a parental abduction, no matter how pure their motives.''

''I'll find out whatever I can and turn the information over to Juvenile and Family Services.'' Wardlow looked at his partner. ''How about you, Kaminsky? What's next?''

''I have a whole list of people to see for a second interview. I guess I'll start with Stefan Panesivic, since the father becomes the number-one suspect now that we've eliminated the mother, right?''

''Are you going to tell him about her plan to abduct the kid?'' the sergeant asked.

''I don't know. I think I'll play it by ear once I'm with

him. Knowing what she was planning might make him mad
enough to jolt some information from him."

"On the other hand," Michelson said, "if he's involved
in the little guy's disappearance, he might decide to clam
up even more and let her take the heat."

"I know. Like I said, I'll play it by ear. I also want to
talk to our friend, Paul Arnussen." She turned to her part-
ners. "Did he really go to Kalispell yesterday, Brian?"

Wardlow consulted his notebook. "Arnussen's truck left
the landlady's place at seven o'clock yesterday morning
and headed east on the freeway, out of state. Montana highway patrol spotted him near Kalispell and kept an eye on
him, then followed him back to the state line. He got home
about midnight."

"Why did he go to Montana?" Michelson asked.

"He said he was going over to see a friend and get a
new puppy for the woman whose dog he killed on the highway," she told him.

"Just a real nice guy, isn't he?" the sergeant said.

"He's a sweetheart," Jackie said coldly. "A kindhearted
carpenter with amazing psychic powers."

"Let's keep some heat on him, too," Michelson said.
"Is he working today?"

Wardlow nodded. "He's back at the same place on the
South Hill. The patrol officer said he's finished the veranda
decking and started on the new columns and railings."

"I'll talk to him later in the afternoon," Jackie said, "or
maybe this evening. I also want to see Adrienne Calder."

"Leigh's sister?" Wardlow asked.

"That's right. She was really flippant and rude the morning after the abduction. Her behavior was completely in-
appropriate, given the circumstances. At the time, I chalked
it up to a nasty personality, but now I wonder if there
wasn't something more to it."

"Her alibi checks?" Michelson asked.

"Oh, sure," Jackie said gloomily. "Everybody's alibi checks. But this woman…"

"What about her?" Wardlow prompted.

"Her mother told me that Adrienne and her husband have been trying for years to conceive, and Adrienne's really upset about not having children."

Wardlow snorted. "Come on, Kaminsky. She'd hardly go out and snatch her *sister's* kid to satisfy her frustrated maternal instincts, would she?"

"In this family, anything's possible. The Mellons might be filthy rich, but they're also pretty weird."

"Anything else about the Calder woman?" Michelson asked.

"That story about Adrienne being abducted and held for ransom. It bothers me. I want to ask her about it."

"But that was twenty years ago," Wardlow said mildly.

"Jackie's right," the sergeant said. "It's still an angle that's worth looking at. What else?"

Jackie shook her head. "I'm not sure." She glanced from one man to the other. "I have this feeling…"

"What?"

"Like somebody's told me something really important in the last couple of days, but I can't remember what it was."

"Did you check all your notes?"

"I checked everything. I keep going over the whole file until my head aches, but I can't find anything. Still, I keep thinking there's something one of these people said that holds the key to the whole case."

She frowned, thinking, while the two men waited. Finally, she shook her head again in defeat and got up, heading for the door with Wardlow ambling behind her.

12

It was early afternoon by the time Jackie drove onto the tree-shaded grounds of Gonzaga University. She hadn't been able to reach Stefan by phone since Leigh's startling revelation this morning, but she'd left a couple of messages and was taking a chance that the professor had just been out for lunch.

The parking lot by his building was awash in sunshine, and so quiet she could hear the trill of birds in the trees nearby. Most of the campus seemed to be deserted for the long weekend. Only three cars were parked in the lot. Jackie studied them, wondering if one belonged to Panesivic.

She didn't even know what kind of car he drove. She gripped the shoulder strap of her bag and sighed with frustration.

Police work was such a hell of a job. They were expected to work miracles on a daily basis, risk their lives to protect the public, catch the bad guys and solve all the crimes. But every year, all over the country, they also had to deal with the grim reality of budget cuts and fewer officers to service a booming urban population.

To make it worse, the criminals were much better armed than the police, and most of the laws and constitutional protections were slanted in the criminal's favor.

"Police work is like a big game," Captain Alvarez explained to the young recruits who entered the academy every year. "The good guys fight the bad guys. We're the good guys. But there's one little problem, kids. There's a long list of rules for this game, and your side has to follow all of them. The bad guys get to ignore them."

In the course of an investigation like the one Jackie was conducting, even with a small child possibly at mortal risk, she could only learn what people were willing to tell her. If she wanted to know anything more about their homes or private lives, she had to obtain a warrant to search and seize.

To get the warrant, she first needed to establish probable cause. But this, too, was a risky procedure, open to all kinds of different legal interpretations and challenges in court that could get an unlucky investigating officer into real trouble.

The only other recourse was to mobilize a massive investigative team who could circle the perimeter of the case and keep a constant watch, while digging into every bit of information about the suspects that was legally available.

But, unlike the cop shows on television, no police department in the country had access to the kind of funding such an investigation would entail. Other crimes kept happening all the time, and officers were needed to work on them, too. There was never enough manpower to go around at the best of times.

On this child-abduction case, for instance, there was just their little investigative team, and as much auxiliary manpower as Michelson could scratch together from other departments to assist them. As a result, it appeared that nobody had yet found the time to determine even what kind of car Stefan Panesivic drove.

While Jackie was brooding over the frustrating limitations of her job, the man himself appeared through a gate at the far side of the parking lot, set into a tall hedge of lilacs.

Stefan wore white shorts and T-shirt with a red towel draped around his neck, and carried a duffel bag from which protruded the handles of a couple of tennis rackets. His face, neck and arms glistened faintly with perspiration. He looked even more handsome in the daylight, tall and vigorous, his dark hair gleaming with bronze highlights. His legs were tanned and well-shaped, bulging with muscle.

Jackie met his glance as he approached and realized that he'd noticed her frank appraisal of his body.

"Not bad for an old guy," he said with a brief smile. "Is that what you were thinking, Detective?"

Jackie gave him a level look. "Actually I was wondering which of these vehicles is yours."

"I don't park my car out here except for short periods. I leave it in a covered storage facility near the campus."

"What is it?"

"A gray Mercedes SL. I can show you the registration if you like."

He lowered his duffel bag onto the pavement and scrubbed the towel over his arms and neck.

"Teaching must pay really well," Jackie observed. "That's an expensive car."

"I also have some business interests in Europe," Stefan said casually. "They've become surprisingly profitable in recent years."

She took out her book and made a couple of notes while he watched in amusement.

"Do you ever dress up, Detective? With your coloring and those great cheekbones, you'd look like a million dollars in a slinky little black dress and high heels."

"Thanks for the fashion tip," Jackie said. "But I've never been the dressing-up type, I'm afraid. Do you have a few minutes to talk with me, Mr. Panesivic?"

"Is it about Michael?"

"I'm afraid so."

His face paled and she could see the spasmodic jerk of his throat as he swallowed. "What?" he whispered. "Have you... Is there any news?"

"If we could just go inside..."

He nodded, all the teasing and humor gone from his face. They walked into the building and rode in silence on the elevator. Jackie could smell the sun-warmed cotton of his tennis clothes, and the scent of some kind of men's cologne or after-shave mingled faintly with perspiration.

"Is Michael..."

She shook her head as a couple of elderly people entered the elevator, dragging a cranky poodle on a leash between them.

At Stefan's floor they got out and entered the apartment. He hesitated in the foyer, his handsome face twisted with pain.

"Do you have some terrible news to give me, Detective?"

"No," Jackie said gently.

It must be hell to have your child go missing, she thought. The real agony would be not knowing what was happening to him or even if he was alive.

"It's not really terrible," she added. "Just a little confusing, I guess."

Stefan exhaled in a sigh of relief. "Then do you mind if I have a quick shower before we talk? I had a pretty heavy workout this morning. It won't take more than five minutes, I promise."

"Sure."

Stefan took her elbow to lead her into the living room. It looked cluttered and comfortable, much the same as the last time Jackie visited.

"Is it all right if I look around at some of your books while I wait?" she asked.

"No problem," he called over his shoulder, vanishing down the hallway. "If you see anything that interests you, feel free to borrow it."

She moved around the room, examining the titles of the books stacked on tables and shelves. Many of them were scholarly reference works on topics she'd never heard of. But there was also a good selection of contemporary fiction, and quite a well-stocked poetry section.

On a shelf near the floor, Jackie found a row of well-thumbed children's books. She pictured Michael visiting here, being cuddled in those strong arms while Stefan read stories to his son.

One of the books was an illustrated edition of *Peter Rabbit*. She pulled it out and studied the winsome illustrations.

Michael was in a pit under the ground, Paul Arnussen had said. There were furniture and quilts and pictures on the wall....

Jackie's skin crawled and she felt a touch of nausea. She leaned back on her heels, frowning at the books.

It still haunted her, the feeling that somebody she'd talked with in the past few days had told her something vitally important to the fate of Michael Panesivic.

Maybe if she could go home tonight and lie still in her bed, make the room completely dark and empty her mind of everything, the thought would come to her. That sometimes worked, but not always.

"Sorry for the delay." Stefan appeared in the doorway, wearing khaki shorts, leather sandals and a white cotton shirt, neatly ironed. "I see you've found Michael's picture books."

Jackie took the snapshot of Paul Arnussen from her notebook and handed it to Stefan. "Have you ever seen this man?"

He studied the photograph, his eyebrows raised. "Yes," he said at last. "I've seen him."

Jackie's interest quickened. "Where?"

Stefan continued to study the image on the Polaroid. "I don't know. It's one of those… Damn! I can't remember. I know I've seen this man, and not that long ago, either. But I can't remember where. Doesn't it make you crazy when that happens?"

"Yes," Jackie said dryly. "It really makes me crazy." She took the picture from him and replaced it, then sat in a chair nearby. "I learned something a little upsetting from Leigh this morning," she said.

"Upsetting?" He leaned forward, cautious and alert. "In what way?"

Jackie recounted the events of the past couple of days. She told him how Leigh had passed her polygraph, then called Jackie in hysterics and confessed to arranging the complex plan to have Michael abducted and removed from the country.

Stefan's face settled into a cold mask as he listened.

"Why?" he said at last. "Why would she go to so much trouble?"

"So she could tell a credible story and fool the police and the polygraph. But mostly it was you she wanted to deceive. She didn't want you searching for her. She wanted you to believe your son was dead, or at least had hopelessly vanished, and that she knew nothing about it."

His mouth twisted with anger. "The bitch!" he muttered. "The goddamn little bitch. God, I'd like to…"

Jackie looked down at his clenched hands, feeling a certain sympathy. Her own reaction hadn't been much different when she first heard Leigh's story.

But she kept her face and voice deliberately expressionless. "Hey, take it easy," she murmured. "That kind of response isn't going to get us anywhere, you know."

"What kind of response?"

She indicated his hands, still clenched into fists. "I hope you aren't thinking about going out there and hitting somebody, Professor. It's not going to help Michael."

He glared at her, and Jackie sensed the hard edge of violence in the man. For a moment she was shaken, almost frightened.

Leigh Mellon said her ex-husband was a monster. Jackie wondered if Leigh had ever felt the grim force of the rage that now darkened his face.

But Stefan Panesivic was also a man who gave up his free time to help his students, who kept books about Peter Rabbit in his bookcase and sat in an armchair to read them to his little son...

"Sorry," he muttered, flexing his fingers and staring at them moodily. "I know I have to keep my emotions under control. It's just that the damned woman drives me wild, and I've been so worried about Michael I can't sleep."

He looked up, his dark eyes sparkling with tears, and dashed an awkward hand across his face.

Jackie turned aside tactfully while he struggled to compose himself. She hadn't been surprised by the rage, but she was taken aback by his tears. It took an awful lot, Jackie suspected, to reduce Stefan Panesivic to tears.

"So, what happens now?" His voice was still rough with emotion.

"We carry on with our investigation," Jackie said, recalling Sergeant Michelson's words earlier in the day. "We were looking for an abducted child, and we still are. But now it seems we can be fairly certain that Leigh doesn't know where he is."

"Her family might."

"What do you mean?"

He made an impatient gesture. "I assume you've met the gracious Lady Barbara?"

Jackie nodded.

"Well, does she strike you as the kind of woman who'd hesitate to break the law if it happened to suit her purpose?"

"I'm not sure," Jackie said honestly. "I try not to be overly influenced by first impressions. Do you think Barbara Mellon would have abducted Michael without letting his mother know?"

"Certainly she would. That family has always recognized Leigh as the weak link in their chain. Barbara and Adrienne are utterly ruthless, while Leigh is merely immature and ineffectual. If there were any plans afoot to steal Michael away from me, I think Leigh would probably be the last to know."

"But she claims that her family knew nothing about this scheme to have Michael smuggled into Canada. She says she didn't even tell her mother."

"And you believe her?" Stefan asked. "After all the lies she's told you, I would think that she wouldn't have a lot of credibility."

"You're right. It's hard to know what to believe anymore. But Leigh is completely frantic, and I don't think she's faking."

There was a brief silence while Jackie made some notes in her book and Stefan gazed out the window in brooding silence.

"How about these mysterious people Leigh was supposed to be dealing with?" he asked after a moment. "Is there any chance they actually do have Michael, in spite of what she's told you?"

"We're checking on them. I'll let you know as soon as I can." Jackie got to her feet and moved toward the door. "Could you be sure to call me if you think of anything else?"

"Like what?"

"Like, if you remember where you saw that man in the photograph."

"Is he important?"

"He could be."

Stefan gave her a long thoughtful look. "I'll try to remember. Where are you going now?"

"I'm paying a visit to Adrienne Calder."

Jackie watched his face closely and noted a brief tensing of muscles along his jawline.

"Mrs. Mellon suggested I speak with Adrienne about all this," she added casually. "In particular, Barbara mentioned that Adrienne seemed to have a closer relationship with you than most of the other family members."

Stefan's eyes widened slightly, but he said nothing.

"What do you think Leigh's mother meant by that?" Jackie asked.

He shrugged. "Just what she said, I suppose. Adrienne and I were quite good friends at one time. She's more intelligent than the rest of her family, although I realize that's not saying a whole lot. Still, I enjoyed talking with her."

"But you don't talk with her anymore?"

"You've never been married, Detective Kaminsky?"

Jackie shook her head.

"Then you still have all these pleasures ahead of you." Stefan gave her a humorless smile. "You'll find that a divorce is much like a civil war. Once the hostilities are under way, you tend to lose all your friends on the other side."

Jackie recalled Ivana Panesivic saying much the same thing about her daughter-in-law.

She said goodbye and left the apartment, hurrying down
to the parking lot where a couple of little girls were playing
a complicated game of hopscotch, drawn with chalk on the
smooth pavement near Jackie's car.

They were probably faculty children. One of them was
Chinese and had a smooth cap of dark hair, while the other
was blond and plump, her stubby little pigtails tied with
pink bows. Jackie leaned on the car and watched them for
a while, enjoying the sound of their laughter, the shimmer
of sunshine on their hair and the graceful ease of their
movements.

"Do you know how to play hopscotch?" the Chinese
girl asked with grave politeness.

Jackie shook her head in regret. "I never learned," she
said. "But it certainly looks like fun."

She wished she was on holiday like other people, and
could spend the rest of the afternoon in this peaceful place
watching the happy children. At last, reluctantly, she got
into her car and drove out of the college grounds, heading
south across the river.

13

Adrienne Calder's home was in stark contrast to the gracious mansion belonging to her parents. This house was sleek and modern, all sharp angles and big windows, finished in silver-gray cedar and nestled against a hillside in one of the new housing developments at the southeast corner of the city.

The yard featured dry landscaping of rock and shale, planted with juniper, cactus and small evergreen shrubs. Jackie walked up a flagstone path set into the shale toward the entry. The double doors were massive, made of washed oak and fitted with beautiful stained-glass panels that looked handmade. Jackie waited a few moments, then rang again, increasingly annoyed when there was no response.

She'd made an appointment with Adrienne Calder just a few hours earlier. But the woman seemed like the kind who'd break an appointment without notice and cause a busy person to drive all the way across the city for nothing.

While she was wondering what to do next, a teenage boy in baggy shorts and plaid shirt came lounging around the side of the house, carrying a pair of hedge clippers.

"Hi," he said when he saw Jackie. "Are you the fuzz?"

"Yes," she said curtly, controlling her temper with an effort. "Is the lady of the house around?"

"At the back." He waved his clippers at the corner of the house where the walkway disappeared through a tall cedar gate. "She's in the pool." The boy grinned lasciviously and began clipping the bank of juniper along the fence.

When Jackie went through the gate and rounded the house to the backyard, she could understand the reason for the grin. Adrienne Calder stood at the opposite side of the swimming pool, her tanned body dripping onto the red clay tiles. She wore a pale brown maillot, so scant and clinging that from this distance she appeared to be naked.

While Jackie watched, Adrienne ran her hands briskly down her body and over her legs, then bent and slipped back into the water. She crossed the pool with a powerful crawl, her head cleaving through the water, and stopped near Jackie's feet to cling to the side of the pool.

"Hello, Copper," she said cheerfully, her face and cropped dark hair glistening. "Why don't you throw off those hot old clothes and join me? The water's lovely."

"No, thanks. Do you have a few minutes to talk with me, Mrs. Calder?"

"I have all the time in the world. In fact, I have nothing but time. But I'm afraid you'll have to get over that pompous tendency to call me Mrs. Calder. My name is Adrienne."

She pulled herself out of the water and reached for a towel that lay across one of the dark green chaise longues, while Jackie seated herself in the shade of a big umbrella fixed into a glass-topped table.

"So what's up?" Adrienne asked, scrubbing the towel over her taut abdomen and down her legs. "You're looking especially grim today."

Jackie found a pen and took out her notebook.

"Do you always wear those stuffy blazers?" Adrienne asked. "My God, it must be ninety degrees out here. Aren't you roasting?"

Jackie pulled back the bottom of her white linen jacket to show the leather holster and handcuff pouch at her belt.

"I prefer to keep them covered," she said. "Otherwise they attract attention."

"Now, that's where you and I are different." Adrienne rubbed suntan oil on her legs and arms, then stretched out in the lounger nearby and closed her eyes. "I like doing things that attract attention. The more the better."

Jackie studied the woman with interest. Adrienne Calder had a lovely profile, and a slender athletic body. She and her sister were rather similar in looks, but they had utterly different personalities.

Like day and night, Jackie thought. Or rather, the dark side of the moon.

"Can't you carry that stuff in your bag?" Adrienne shifted lazily on the chair and raised her face to the sun.

"Some female officers do, but I don't think it's a very good idea."

"Why not?"

"It's too easy to get separated from your bag. Depending on who got hold of it and under what circumstances, an officer could find herself in big trouble."

Adrienne rolled her head on the green pillow and eyed Jackie with interest. "It's really serious shit, your job, right? Like, you could be killed if you made a mistake."

"That's true."

"I would have liked to be a cop." Adrienne closed her eyes again and turned away. "Back in the Dark Ages, when I was a girl and all my options weren't closed, I even got some information about the police force and considered applying."

Jackie gripped her pen in astonishment. "Really?"

"Yeah. Really."

"Why did you change your mind?"

Adrienne gave a short bark of laughter. "I didn't change my mind. My mother changed it for me. Can you imagine a Mellon working as a lowly cop? Barbara practically had heart failure when I told her."

"You don't strike me as the kind of person who'd be overly influenced by her mother's opinions, Adrienne."

"I'm not, usually. But my dear mother has always controlled the purse strings, and back in those days I never wanted anything badly enough to risk being cut out of my share of the family funds."

Jackie considered this in silence.

"God, it's such a trap." Adrienne shifted restlessly and drew one leg up into a graceful curve. "The whole money thing. You get addicted to it, and then you're tied up and nailed down for life. It's like a drug. They can control you forever by regulating the supply. You know?"

"Not really," Jackie said dryly. "I've never had a supplier."

Adrienne chuckled. "Lucky you. Made your own way in life, have you? Battled all the way up from humble beginnings to become a real live cop with a gun on your belt."

"Yes, I have," Jackie said, wondering why this conversation didn't annoy her.

It was the woman's attitude, she decided. Adrienne seemed as blunt and outspoken as she had on their first encounter, but Jackie sensed that her interest was genuine.

"Nobody controls you now, Adrienne," she said at last, waving her hand at the luxurious house and yard, and the sparkling pool ringed by chairs, chaise longues and beach umbrellas. "This is all your own property, right?"

"Hell, no. This is Harlan's property. If I left him, I'd get my share, but he's still the one who goes to work every day and provides the money that keeps it all going. I'm purely ornamental, Detective. I'm not productive in any way. I toil not, neither do I spin.''

"Stefan Panesivic just told me that in his opinion, you're probably the most intelligent person in your family.''

Adrienne's hands tensed on the arms of the lounger. "Did Stefan really say that?''

"Yes, he did.''

"Well, bless his little black heart,'' she said lightly.

"Your mother told me that you and Stefan were quite good friends.''

Adrienne took a pair of large horn-rimmed sunglasses from a bag near the chair, unfolded them and put them on. Instantly her face seemed to vanish, leaving her cold and remote. "My mother doesn't know nearly as much about me as she thinks she does.''

Jackie flipped back though her notebook and removed the snapshot of Paul Arnussen. "Have you ever seen this man, Adrienne?''

The other woman leaned forward and tipped her glasses upward to examine the photograph. "Oh, my,'' she said at last. "What a perfectly delicious creature. Is he your boyfriend?''

"Hardly,'' Jackie said.

"He looks like your type.'' Adrienne lay back and replaced the glasses.

"Why?''

Her hostess waved a casual hand. "He's got that same look you have, all wholesome and earnest about your job, and just a tiny bit scornful of the rest of us. I guess it's that whole working-class snobbery thing you've got going.''

Jackie was beginning to understand the woman a little better. "You're just trying to get a rise out of me, aren't you?'' she said calmly.

"I know, but I can't resist." Adrienne smiled without contrition, her teeth flashing in her tanned face. "You're such an easy target."

Jackie smiled back. "Well, cut it out, or I'll arrest you for obstruction of justice. Have you ever seen this man?" she repeated.

Adrienne shook her head lazily. "Never. If I saw a man like that, I'd probably bring him home and keep him. Wouldn't you?"

Jackie wondered what kind of man Harlan Calder was. She knew that he and Adrienne had been married for almost twelve years, but apart from the fact that he was a successful lawyer, she had no idea what Adrienne's husband was like. She made a mental note to contact him after the holiday.

"Have you talked to Leigh today?" she asked.

Adrienne rolled her head on the pillow. "No, I haven't. Is she all right?"

"Not really. She's had some pretty upsetting news."

Adrienne whipped off the glasses and turned to stare at Jackie, turning pale beneath the tan. "Jesus," she whispered. "Is it something about Michael? Why didn't you tell me right away?"

"It's nothing definitive." Again Jackie told the story about Leigh's planned abduction, and her shocking discovery that the little boy wasn't where he was supposed to be.

Adrienne clutched the sunglasses tightly in her hands, looking shaken. "I never would have thought Leigh had so much gumption."

"Everybody seems to have underestimated Leigh."

"I know. It's probably because Stefan had her so completely overpowered. Maybe now that she's out of that goddamn farce of a marriage, she'll turn into a real person, after all."

"You still don't seem all that worried about Michael's fate," Jackie said.

"What's that supposed to mean?"

"Aren't you concerned about where he might be or what's happened to him?"

"Of course I'm concerned," Adrienne said. "But I doubt that he's in any danger. He's probably out at the farm with Grandma and Grandpa Panesivic right now, feeding the chickens."

"I've been to the farm. I didn't see him."

"They're a tight little group, that family." Adrienne gave Jackie a bleak smile. "Not that I'd know much about family togetherness. But I think they'd pull together to hide the kid if they needed to."

Jackie consulted her notebook. "Your mother told me that you were kidnapped from your school and held for ransom when you were a girl. Can you tell me something about that?"

Adrienne swore fiercely under her breath, then got out of the chair and walked away. "Come inside," she called over her shoulder. "It's too hot out here, and I'm dying for a drink."

Jackie closed her notebook and got up, intrigued to see she'd apparently struck a nerve. She waited while Adrienne paused in the entry to the house, took a short terry-cloth robe from a hook and belted it around her slim waist, then scuffed her feet into a pair of sandals and started up a flight of stairs.

Following her, Jackie glanced around and was surprised again, this time by the interior of Adrienne Calder's house.

She'd expected a kind of silvery elegance, a cool mixture of chrome and glass and pastel colors. But Adrienne obviously preferred antiques and a warm decor. The big house was expensively furnished but casual, almost cluttered. It was also filled with lush plants.

"You must have a green thumb," Jackie observed.

"I like plants. They let me do whatever I want and don't talk back."

Jackie peered into a room that appeared to be a man's den, decorated in warm plaids and wood paneling. A faded red cardigan lay across one of the chairs. A leather golf bag leaned against the desk, and a flock of model airplanes dangled from the ceiling on slender wires.

"See this?" Adrienne paused next to a massive wooden sideboard in the upper foyer. It was finished in golden oak with beveled mirrors, wide drawers and much ornamental carving.

"It's lovely." Jackie caught up to Adrienne and ran her hand over the gleaming surface.

"I bought that last summer at a farm auction in Idaho. It was in terrible repair, had been kept out in a granary for years. I restored it myself with my own fair hands."

"Really?"

Adrienne chuckled. "Don't look so astounded, Detective, I'm not completely useless, you know. I'm just lazy. Come into the kitchen."

Her kitchen, like the rest of the house, was comfortable and warm, with oak cabinets fronted in glass, creamy wall tiles and butcher-block countertops. Like her sister, Adrienne had a big crystal prism hanging in the window. The fridge was adorned with a pair of ceramic magnets shaped like chickens.

Jackie sank into a chair at the table and looked at the brightly colored feathers and yellow beaks on the ceramic birds.

"My mother made them," Adrienne said. "She modeled them on that big painting in her foyer."

"I thought I'd seen them somewhere before. They're very beautiful."

Adrienne was holding the fridge door open, staring into the well-stocked interior. "I've got a pitcher of daiquiris in here," she muttered, "but I promised Harlan I wouldn't start drinking before four o'clock. What time is it?"

Jackie consulted her watch. "Three forty-five."

"Close enough." Adrienne reached for the pitcher. "Want a tall cool banana daiquiri, Officer? They're really delicious."

Jackie shook her head. "No thanks. I'm still on duty."

"God, you're so *stuffy*. Lemonade, then?"

"That would be nice." Jackie watched while Adrienne moved around the kitchen in her brief terry-cloth robe, taking out glasses and ice and pouring their drinks. "Do you look after the house all by yourself?"

"Jason—that's the boy you saw out front—wanders over on weekends and after school to do the outside work. And I have a woman who comes in three days a week to clean."

"But you do the cooking?"

"I like to cook." Adrienne seated herself at the table opposite Jackie and handed the detective a glass. "There aren't that many meals to prepare actually. Harlan eats downtown a lot of the time, so I just have to look after myself. It's not hard to make a peanut-butter sandwich."

She sounded bleak and lonely. Jackie remembered Barbara Mellon's comment that Adrienne and her husband had been trying for years to conceive a baby, and that her daughter was upset about their childlessness.

"Adrienne, I was asking you about the time you were abducted as a girl."

The other woman lowered her head and studied the etched pattern on her drinking glass. "I can't believe my mother still remembers that little bit of ancient history. At the time, she hardly seemed to notice.''

"She said you refused to tell her what happened to you."

"Damn right I refused. She would have killed me if she knew."

"Why?"

Adrienne got up and moved restlessly across the room to pick a couple of dead leaves from the geranium on the windowsill.

"It was all a scam. I had this enterprising boyfriend at the time, who should probably have been in jail. He dreamed up the whole plan of pretending I'd been kidnapped, then stiffing my parents for a bunch of ransom money. It seemed like a great idea. We were going to run away and live in Mexico on the proceeds."

"So you weren't abducted at all?"

"Hell, no. We spent the entire time holed up in a sleazy motel, humping away like animals."

"And you were…how old?"

"Fourteen." Adrienne turned to look coldly at her. "I had a rebellious childhood, all right? In fact, during my teenage years I had a few very unpleasant encounters with the police, which didn't exactly make me a big fan of the boys in blue."

Jackie recalled the woman's belligerent manner at their first meeting and nodded thoughtfully. "Why did you want to become a police officer yourself, then?"

"I don't know. Revenge, maybe. Does all this shock you, Detective?"

"Not a bit," Jackie replied. "I had a rebellious childhood, too. Why did you give up on your scam and go back to school?"

Adrienne made an impatient gesture, tossed the dead leaves into a wastebasket and returned to her chair. "Daddy was taking so long coming up with the money that we started getting nervous. I guess I had serious doubts whether they cared enough about me to pay actual money to get me back.''

Jackie made some notes in her book, thinking about kidnapping and ransom demands.

"You said you were rebellious, too," Adrienne said curiously. "What kind of childhood did you have?"

"I grew up in a slum in Los Angeles. My father disappeared before I was born. When I was a baby, my mother dumped me with a grandmother who raised me along with a crew of assorted cousins. My mother died of a drug overdose when I was four. By the time I was fourteen, I belonged to a street gang.''

"No kidding." Adrienne leaned forward, her eyes bright with interest. "What kind of gang?"

Jackie shrugged. "It was all pretty childish stuff. We ran packages around for the dealers, carried knives in our belts, harassed the cops and thought we were really cool. When I was sixteen I got involved in an armed robbery and spent two years in a juvenile detention facility.''

"Well, now, isn't that amazing? You were a bad kid just like me.''

Jackie looked around at the luxurious house. "I doubt we had very much in common, Adrienne. But when your mother told me about your kidnapping, it occurred to me that both of us probably had kind of a lonely and unsupervised childhood.''

"No shit," Adrienne said gloomily, staring down at her glass. "So how did you happen to turn from a baby gangster into a cop?''

"When I got out of detention, I had to do something or I knew I'd start to go downhill really fast. Besides, after two years in that place, I wanted to help keep other kids from going there.''

Adrienne was looking at her in astonishment. Jackie shifted on the chair, uncomfortable about the turn she'd allowed the conversation to take.

She cleared her throat and returned to the notebook. ''If I could just ask you a few more things about your family,'' she said formally.

Adrienne rolled her eyes toward the ceiling. ''The cop,'' she announced, ''is back on duty.''

But her smile was considerably warmer as she leaned back in the chair, drink in hand, and prepared to answer Jackie's questions.

14

Back at the substation, Jackie opened her file and switched on the computer. She took out her notebook and made a few entries, then leaned back in the chair and rubbed her temples wearily.

After a moment or two, she sat up again and rummaged through her bag to find her calling card and address book.

"Hi, Lorna," she said when the call was answered on the first ring. "It's Jackie, up in Spokane. I guess social workers don't get holiday weekends any more than cops do, right?"

"Holiday? What's that?"

The woman's voice was rich and warm. Jackie smiled, picturing Lorna McPhee at her desk. Lorna was a big woman with chocolate brown skin and laughing dark eyes, and a personality so engaging that people tended to overlook her awesome efficiency.

"How's the weather in L.A.?" Jackie asked.

"Hot and muggy, like always. What's the problem, honey?"

"Gram called me on Friday night. She was drinking again."

"Oh, no," Lorna said. "Did she sound bad, Jackie?"

"Pretty bad. She was seeing those big spiders with the fangs and the shining eyes."

Lorna sighed. "Where are the boys?"

"Joey's around. I called next day and talked to him. Apparently Carmelo's in jail."

"Oh, Lord. Anything serious?"

"Joey said it was a traffic violation and Carmelo's making a stand on principle."

Lorna laughed with genuine amusement. "I'll stop by and check on them, okay? If I find any serious problems, I'll call you back. If you don't hear from me, you'll know there's nothing to worry about."

"Thanks, Lorna," Jackie said gratefully. "I really appreciate it."

She hung up and looked at Wardlow, who had come in and was listening to her conversation.

"I don't know what to do," she told him.

"About what?"

"My grandmother. I don't know what my responsibility is. Sometimes I think I should move back there so I can look after her."

"You're crazy," he said. "The old lady doesn't even *like* you, Kaminsky. She just uses you. Why should you give up your career now and start over again as a patrol officer so your grandmother can swear at you when she's drunk?"

"Wow. You're pretty harsh," Jackie said.

"All this loving family stuff, it's just crap." Wardlow slammed his briefcase open. "People get sucked in and keep looking for something that's not there, and it breaks their hearts."

"Come on, Brian. You think there's no such thing as a loving happy family?"

"Have you ever seen one?"

Jackie smiled, trying to lighten his mood. "Maybe we've both just had a really deprived life. There must be some people in the world who love each other and don't feel lonely all the time.''

He switched on his computer and tossed a couple of files onto his desk, ending the conversation.

"Got anything?" Jackie ventured after a moment.

"One of our perverts was at the mall on Friday night." Wardlow consulted one of the files. "Waldemar Koziak, age fifty-seven, convicted seven times for exposing himself in public, fondling, committing lewd acts, and other non-violent sexual offenses involving small children. Living on welfare in a downtown flophouse. No particular alibi for Friday night, but a waitress places him in the food court around six o'clock.''

"Has anybody talked to him?"

"I went over there about an hour ago. He was still asleep. God," Wardlow said with a shudder, "what an ugly old bugger.''

"What did he say?"

"Started to blubber when he saw my badge, denied everything, then clammed up and refused to say any more until he was provided with a lawyer. I doubt he has anything to do with this. None of his previous crimes involved any kind of violence or abduction, and he's probably at least borderline retarded. Certainly not bright enough to hide anything from the cops.''

Jackie sighed. "So, what do you want to do about him?"

"Like I said, it's probably a waste of time, but I think we'll watch him for a couple of days just to get him spooked, then bring him in and lean on him a bit. You want to be there when we do it?''

"Sure. Anything else?"

"Information Services called from downtown while you were out. The media have all been bugging them for a progress report, so they're requesting some kind of press release. Michelson wants to know what you plan to tell them.''

''Just that our investigation is proceeding, that suspects are being questioned, and we welcome any information from the public. Also, we'll keep running Michael's picture and the number of the tip line until further notice.''

''Okay. What about Arnussen?''

''He's probably still our best shot,'' Jackie said. ''Don't you think?''

''Yeah. By the way, the FBI files show records of two unsolved child deaths in places he's lived before this.''

Jackie looked up, suddenly alert.

''During the time he was there?''

''The dates are a little uncertain. Best I can figure out, they seem to jibe.''

''Anything helpful?'' Jackie asked.

''There was a little girl in Billings who went missing from a trailer park and was found six months later in an old barn outside town.''

''Assaulted?''

''The body was too badly decomposed for them to determine time or manner of death.''

''What about the other one?''

''Arnussen was living in Boise when a four-year-old boy went missing. The kid was found in the city landfill two days later. He'd been sexually assaulted and strangled with his own shoelaces. That file has never been closed, either.''

Jackie brooded over her notebook. ''And Arnussen was in both those places when the kids disappeared?''

''It looks that way. But they're both pretty good-size cities, you know. It's still a long shot. Besides, the little girl's death could have been an accident. They still aren't calling it a murder unless they uncover more evidence. She could have wandered away, got lost and starved to death. The barn was abandoned, and in a pretty isolated location.''

"There was no indication in the police files that Arnussen tried to insert himself into either of the investigations?''

"If he did, it was just on the telephone, and he wasn't using his own name.''

"I'm going to drive over and see him later this afternoon.'' Jackie checked her watch and frowned in surprise. "Scratch that. I likely won't get there now until after supper.''

"What are you going to do with him?''

"Just see if I can get him talking and watch how he reacts. He's really a strange one, that guy,'' she said moodily. "I can't figure him out.''

"I think we should play him.'' Wardlow began to work at his keyboard.

Jackie glanced up in surprise. "You mean, go along with this psychic thing?''

"It can't hurt. Why not treat him like a real psychic? Take him around to a few of the locations involved in the case and tell him you want to know if he's picking up any impressions about what happened to the kid.''

"I've never actually watched how they handle a psychic in an investigation. Have you?''

"Once.'' Wardlow leaned back in his chair. "We had a missing girl a few years back. Nineteen years old. She left her job at a local bar and started to walk home. It was a cold winter night and she lived about seven blocks from the bar. The girl dropped off the face of the earth. No sign of her, no suspects. After a month, they brought up a psychic from Illinois, a woman who works with police all over the country.''

"And?''

"This woman looked like everybody's next-door neighbor. Nothing weird about her at all. Dumpy and middle-aged, wearing jeans, a real milk-and-cookies type. We took her to the bar and let her follow the girl's usual route when she walked home. While the psychic was walking, she gave us her impressions.''

"Impressions?"

"It came to her in scattered images. She saw the girl's body dismembered, all in pieces. She said it was in a kind of metal tub, and there was rock all around. She saw the colour gray."

"Big deal. Everything's gray up here in the wintertime,'' Jackie said scornfully. ''What happened?"

"About two weeks after the woman went back to Illinois, we found the body. The girl had been hacked to pieces with a chain saw and dumped into an abandoned cement mixer at a gravel pit. Two days later, we arrested the owner of the gravel pit."

Jackie replaced her long-distance calling card, listening to her partner in silence.

"It was spooky, let me tell you," Wardlow went on. "The whole thing pretty much made a believer out of me."

"So you think Arnussen's telling the truth?"

Wardlow considered, then shook his head. "I doubt it. Not this guy. I'm not sure what his game is, but I do think treating him as if he's on the level is the best way to find out what he knows."

"You're probably right. I guess we'll try it."

"Look, if you take him anywhere, Kaminsky, be sure I'm with you, okay? Don't take Arnussen alone in the car."

"Okay. It'll probably be tomorrow," Jackie said. "If I can get him to agree." She cast her partner a cautious glance.

"That's fine." Wardlow glared at his keyboard. "I wasn't exactly planning any Fourth of July picnics." He paused. "What else have you got? How about the other family members?"

"God, they're such a confusing group, Brian. Everybody still seems absolutely confident that the other side has the kid. But there are all kinds of undercurrents and some weird little connections between the two families. There even seem to be connections with Arnussen. At least two of the people I've interviewed think they recognize him—Michael's father and the baby-sitter, Helen Philps. I feel like I'm getting sucked deeper and deeper into quicksand."

"You were talking to the sister today, right?"

Jackie nodded.

"Anything interesting? I remember you saying she was a real tough cookie."

"Yeah, well, I'm beginning to think Adrienne Calder's not nearly as tough as she lets on. I think maybe she's just lonely. But I still wonder..." Jackie glanced at her partner. "That reminds me. Could you get one of your boys to check on something for me?"

"Sure." Wardlow flipped open his notebook. "What do you want?"

"See what they can sniff out about Harlan Calder's personal affairs. He's a local lawyer with a corporate practice. Try to find out if he's been having any money problems lately, and if he might need a big infusion of cash."

Wardlow raised his eyebrows and jotted down a note.

"What about the child-save people?" Jackie asked.

"We've tracked down the phone numbers you got from Leigh. I made an appointment for the two of us to talk with one of these rescuing angels on Wednesday, after the holiday. But Michelson's right, they're not going to tell us anything we don't already know."

"You're certain they don't have Michael?"

"Pretty certain. These people are really passionate about

what they do. Their methods may be off-color, but from all accounts they genuinely care about kids. Besides, they wouldn't have any motive except money, and Leigh's already ruled that out.''

''If we can believe her,'' Jackie said gloomily.

''I thought you believed her now.''

''Yeah, I guess I do. Since her little plot's fallen apart, she seems completely desperate. I think she's finally telling me the truth.''

There was a brief silence while the two detectives concentrated on their computers, typing up files and transcribing notes.

Suddenly, Wardlow groaned and buried his face in his hands.

Jackie looked at him in alarm. ''Brian? What's the matter?''

His shoulders began to quiver, but he made no response.

Jackie wheeled her chair across the narrow space between their desks and put a hand on his arm. ''Brian?''

Wardlow lifted his head and turned to her. His face was haggard, so pale that the freckles stood out in sharp relief. ''It's nothing,'' he muttered. ''Get back to work, Kaminsky.''

He lifted a file with shaking hands and turned his back on her.

''Brian, for God's sake—''

''I'm fine. Leave me alone.''

''Look, I tell you everything,'' Jackie said. ''You know all about my grandmother and my cousins, and even the problems I had with my landlord last year. The least you could do is tell me what's bothering you.''

He said something inaudible, his head still turned away.

''What?'' Jackie asked. ''I didn't hear you.''

''I said, I think Sarah's cheating on me.''

Jackie gripped his shoulder, at a loss for words.

"I've been checking through her purse lately," he said with obvious reluctance. "This morning there were some...some notes in there..." His voice broke.

"Oh, Brian..." Jackie put her arm around him and hugged him awkwardly. "Maybe it's not what you think."

"Things haven't been good between us for months. But I kept hoping I could pull some holiday time so we could go away for a couple of weeks and work it all out. I wanted to talk her into having a baby. Now I'm thinking it's probably too late."

"Why don't you take some holiday time?" Jackie suggested. "If you like, I'll go and talk to Michelson about it. Maybe we can even arrange some kind of compassionate leave."

"In the middle of a child-abduction case?"

"At least we could ask about—"

"I'm going to follow her," Wardlow said abruptly, staring at the computer screen. "I'm going to catch them together."

"And do what?"

"I don't know." He clenched his hands briefly into fists. "I don't know what the hell I'm going to do."

Involuntarily Jackie glanced at the gun in his shoulder holster.

He followed her gaze and gave a humorless burst of laughter. "What? Are you planning to lift my gun, Kaminsky? Do you intend to have me disarmed for my own good?"

"Of course not," she said with deliberate calm, but her heart was pounding. "You're far too smart to do anything that crazy."

He continued to stare at the computer screen.

"Aren't you?" Jackie said.

"Sure," Wardlow told her bitterly. "I'm far too smart to do anything that crazy."

He wheeled his chair back into position and began to type with grim determination.

A couple of hours later, Jackie juggled two loaded bags of groceries as she looked for her key.

The door to Carmen's apartment opened and a smooth dark head adorned with pink ribbons popped into the hall.

"Hi, Tiff." Jackie set her bags on the hall runner and began a serious search for the key.

Still hanging on to the door, Tiffany leaned out into the hallway. She wasn't allowed to leave the apartment by herself, so she usually retained contact with some part of the door when she made these little forays into the outside world.

"Tony's coming for supper," she announced.

Jackie found the key and looked up. "Do you like Tony, sweetheart?"

Tiffany nodded vigorously. "He's neat. He laughs like this." She held her small abdomen with one hand and imitated a deep jolly bellow of laughter.

Jackie smiled. "I like people who laugh that way. They make me laugh, too."

"He brings me treats from the bakery." Tiffany let go of the door and stood in the hallway, arms spread. "See, Jackie? I'm all dressed up." She wore a white cotton shirt printed with strawberries, and a pair of bright pink corduroy overalls.

"You look like a treat yourself." Jackie grinned fiercely and bared her teeth. "In fact, I'm going to come over there right this minute and take a big bite out of that strawberry on your shoulder."

The little girl squealed with delight and gripped the door

again, swinging it back and forth while Jackie approached. "Mommy said you can come and have supper with us, too. Will you come, Jackie?"

Jackie swept the child into her arms, nuzzling her soft cheek. "Not tonight, honey. I have to go back to work right after supper. Tell Mommy I'll see her later in the week."

"Maybe you can come with us to the picnic."

"Picnic?" Jackie asked, still holding the little girl, enjoying the warm feeling of the child in her arms.

"At the river. It's a For the July party," Tiffany said. "Tony's taking us to have a picnic tomorrow and see the fireworks. Mommy and Tony said you should come with us."

Jackie smiled. "Well, that's very nice of them. I really love the Fourth of July, especially picnics and fireworks. But I'll probably have to work tomorrow, too."

Tiffany leaned back in her arms and made a face. "You have to work all the time. It's yucky."

"It sure is. You better run back inside now, Tiff, before Mommy starts wondering where you are."

Jackie set the little girl on her feet and watched Tiffany scamper into her own apartment, a flash of pink and white.

Before Mommy starts wondering where you are.

The image of Michael Panesivic in his jaunty vest and bow tie, carrying his stuffed yellow duck, crept into Jackie's mind. Her smile faded.

She carried the groceries inside and stored them away, then went down the hall to her bedroom and pulled on her old gray jogging suit, sighing with relief to get out of her work clothes.

She remembered Adrienne Calder making fun of her slacks and blazer, and then how impressed the woman had been at the sight of Jackie's gun.

A lot of people in this group seem impressed by guns,

Jackie thought idly. Even Grace Philps, Helen's ancient mother, had asked about the gun.

She went back to the kitchen and made herself a mushroom omelette and a salad. Her hands worked automatically as she mulled over the details of the case, the interviews she'd done so far and the faces of the people involved.

Again she struggled with the vague feeling that she was overlooking something important. But the memory remained elusive, like the tag end of a dream that vanished into the mist when morning dawned.

Finally she set out a brown linen place mat and napkin, carried her plate of food to the table and sat down to eat. It was so quiet and lonely in her apartment that Jackie almost wished she'd accepted Tiffany's dinner invitation.

But Carmen and Tony were in the beginning stages of their relationship. They needed a lot of time alone, just the two of them and Tiffany, to start building a sense of family.

Family…

Jackie's mind brooded over the disturbing phone call from her grandmother, over Adrienne Calder with her beautiful home and her obvious loneliness, and the way Jackie's young cousins were wasting their lives, and the misery in her partner's face when he talked about his errant wife.

People were all searching desperately for somebody to connect with, but so often they started making each other miserable as soon as they got together.

She shook her head, recalling Wardlow's bitter opinion that nobody was happy, because all relationships were essentially dysfunctional.

Jackie tried to decide if she'd ever had a really warm loving relationship, something with the potential to last a lifetime.

Maybe Kirk Alveson, the young officer who'd been her partner during her rookie years on the Los Angeles force.

Gradually they'd become friends, then lovers. Jackie probably would have married him, but Kirk was killed in an uprising of gang violence on a hot summer night in the city.

That had been more than seven years ago. Nowadays she found she couldn't even remember Kirk's face. But their relationship, though warm and happy, had been based mostly on shared life-style and sexual attraction. If they had married they'd probably be fighting by now, or even divorced with a couple of unhappy kids getting jerked around between them.

Again she thought of Michael Panesivic and his parents. Leigh and Stefan were both intelligent, cultivated, well-educated people, but they couldn't agree on a way to share their parental responsibilities without open warfare.

And, as always, the child was the one who suffered the most.

Where are you, Michael? Are you all right? Are you even alive?

She pictured Paul Arnussen with his crowbar and the way his muscles strained as he ripped floorboards from the old veranda. Jackie frowned thoughtfully and scratched lines on the place mat with her fork.

Under different circumstances, the carpenter would probably have been attractive to her. She liked the look of mixed ethnicity in his face, so similar to her own, as if a lot of individuals from impossibly distant races and nations had come together to create this particular man. It made him seem special and mysterious. But Jackie's profession had taught her all too well that people could be sadly wrong in their judgments, especially women who tried to evaluate men.

And what about Arnussen's claims of psychic ability? Everything in Jackie's training argued against that possibility. She spent her life weighing and evaluating the things people told her, and she didn't believe for a minute that Paul Arnussen was a genuine psychic.

At the very least, he was a voyeur who got his kicks from involving himself in police investigations. And there was a distinct possibility he was also involved in a kind of savagery so heinous the mind could hardly encompass it— the deliberate torture and killing of innocent children.

Jackie thought about Tiffany's little body in her arms, her sweet fragrance, her laughter and shyness. She thought how terrified Tiffany would be if a man tried to…

"Oh, *God,*" she moaned, then got up and carried her plate to the sink.

She rinsed the plate and the frying pan, put them away and consulted her watch.

It was just after six o'clock, still too early to drive across town and try to catch Paul Arnussen at home. Better give him an hour to get himself cleaned up and fed after his workday.

She wandered over to the balcony door, opened it and pulled the screen into place, then sat cross-legged on an overstuffed ottoman situated in front of the door so she could look across the little balcony and down onto the green area behind the apartment building.

A group of teenage kids were out there in baggy shorts and T-shirts, playing a rowdy game of touch football.

Jackie watched them for a while, then opened a leather case at the foot of the ottoman and took out her flute. She assembled the instrument and began to play, easing into it, trying to remember the notes to "Greensleeves."

After a few efforts she gave up and retrieved the sheet music from the bottom of the case, balancing it on her knees as she played.

Her attempt was faltering and uneven, with just a few

notes that were pure enough to make her happy. She never had time to practice, that was the problem. She'd even had to quit taking lessons because she missed every other session and the instructor finally lost patience with her.

Now she tried to set aside a little time every few days to pick out tunes and teach herself the notes, but it was a hard discipline to maintain. Still, the music brought her pleasure. Playing the flute was a form of catharsis, as if the clear loveliness of the individual notes could somehow absorb her loneliness and worry, carrying them away into the blue sky beyond the window to leave her comforted and at peace.

Who do you think you are?

Jackie heard her grandmother's harsh voice in the evening stillness as she lifted the flute into position again.

You think Jackie Kaminsky is some high-class girl who can play the flute? You think learning to do this will make you like all those fancy women you been talking to, like Leigh Mellon and her mother and sister? Nothing in the world can make you any different from what you are. You're pitiful, Jackie. You're truly pitiful.

Jackie put the flute down in her lap and gazed at the blue sky beyond the balcony.

I can be whatever I want to be, she told the old woman silently. *You used to hurt me with your ridicule, Gram, but you can't do it anymore.*

She set her jaw, lifted the flute and began to play again, but the notes were feeble and uncertain.

Jackie practiced for a long time, until she'd exorcised her grandmother's scornful image and the music actually began to sound passable.

Finally, just before seven, she changed into blue jeans, a red plaid shirt and a light denim jacket, all worn and faded from many washings. She strapped the gun and handcuff pouch in position at her belt, made sure they were covered by her jacket, then left her apartment.

15

The woman who answered the door was small and plump, with a wrinkled face, alert blue eyes and hair dyed a shocking yellowish-orange. She wore a blue velour jogging suit and a pair of sandals decorated with plastic flowers.

"Mrs. Lederer?" Jackie displayed her identification folder. "My name is Detective Kaminsky, Spokane P.D. I'd like to speak with Mr. Arnussen."

The woman peered up at her with lively animosity. "Why do you people keep bothering the poor boy? He hasn't done anything."

"I know." Jackie gave the standard police response. "Mr. Arnussen has been helping us with our investigation."

Mrs. Lederer shifted from one foot to the other, gripping the door frame. "All right," she said at last, moving aside with obvious reluctance. "He's downstairs. He just got home a little while ago."

Jackie stepped into the foyer, which smelled of cooking and furniture polish. A door stood open to the upper suite, while another flight of stairs descended to the basement.

"Down there." Mrs. Lederer waved her hand at the stairs. "The first door on your right."

"What are the other two doors?" Jackie asked. "Do you have more than one tenant?"

The woman shook her head. "Just Paul. Those are doors to the bathroom and the laundry."

"Thank you." Jackie smiled automatically and went down the narrow flight of stairs. The old woman stood at the top and watched her.

In the dark basement, Jackie knocked and then waited, bracing herself. After a moment the door swung open and Paul Arnussen stood in the entry. He was barefoot, wearing jeans and a white singlet that displayed a hairy chest and a pair of well-muscled shoulders. The man had apparently showered recently. His blond hair was wet and showed the neat tracks of a comb.

His eyes widened when he saw Jackie. "Hello, Detective. Were you just in the neighborhood and decided to stop by?"

"Something like that. May I come in?"

"Do I have any choice?"

"Of course you do," she said evenly. "Let's not go through all this again, okay? I have a favor to ask of you, that's all."

He stood aside and gestured at the interior of the room. Jackie followed him inside and he closed the door. Immediately she was conscious of being alone with him, of his size and strength, and the hard-edged powerful look of the man.

Too late, she remembered Wardlow's injunction about not finding herself alone with Paul Arnussen.

But this was different, Jackie told herself. They weren't inside a car together. They were in a house with a witness just upstairs.

"Nervous?" he asked, watching her intently.

"Of course not." Jackie sat in one of the chairs and looked around.

Paul Arnussen's kitchen was as tidy as her own. A pot

of food bubbled on the stove, and there was a single place set at the table, complete with cutlery, water glass and folded paper napkin, even a matching bread-and-butter plate.

"You're very formal," she said, looking in surprise at the neat place setting.

"I think you have to be when you're alone all the time. Otherwise, you start living like a pig. Excuse me a minute."

He left the kitchen and Jackie could hear him moving around in the other room, opening and closing drawers. She took the opportunity to examine her surroundings more carefully.

The kitchen had a yellow linoleum floor, worn almost bare at the center, and white cabinets. It was austere, with no decoration or ornamentation of any kind except for a calendar pinned to the wall. The calendar displayed a photograph of a herd of wild horses running into a sunset sky, their manes and tails streaming.

"Great picture," Jackie said when Arnussen came back into the room, wearing work socks and a clean white shirt.

"Do you like horses?" He set another place mat on the table.

"Nothing for me, thanks," Jackie said. "I just ate."

"Coffee, then?"

"Thank you."

Jackie watched as he dished out some stew for himself and set a plate of sliced bread on the table, then filled a coffee mug for her and put out sugar and cream.

"I don't know much about horses," she said. "In fact, I don't think I've ever been close to one, except for a couple of times on riot duty in L.A. when they brought in the mounted patrol."

Arnussen gave her a thoughtful look. Again Jackie was

struck by those piercing dark eyes. Though she doubted the man's psychic abilities, she had the uncomfortable feeling that Paul Arnussen had the ability to look deep into her mind.

In fact, a number of the killers that Jackie had encountered had that same way of looking at you. It was probably a keen intelligence, coupled with the utter lack of a conscience, that made them able to give others such a cold searching appraisal.

Jackie touched her holstered weapon under the table, then folded her hands tightly in her lap, trying not to be unnerved by the man.

"How's your investigation going?" he asked, sitting at the table and beginning to eat the stew. Despite his rough working-class appearance, Arnussen's table manners were remarkably refined.

"Not too well," Jackie said, watching as he spread butter neatly on a slice of bread. "Everything we try seems to draw a blank."

Arnussen pushed the sugar bowl in her direction. Like the creamer, it was crafted of exquisite pale blue china, but had been cracked along one side and skillfully repaired with glue. "Sugar?"

"Just black, thanks. This is really beautiful china."

"It belonged to my mother. There are only a few pieces left. That tea set and a couple of plates."

"Your mother died when you were a little boy, didn't she?"

His face hardened. "You know a lot about me, don't you, Detective?"

"Quite a lot. Does that bother you?"

Arnussen got up and went to the fridge to take out a plate of sliced tomatoes covered with plastic. "Yeah," he said curtly. "It bothers me."

"Why?"

"Because I like my privacy. I don't appreciate having a bunch of strangers examining my personal history. Is that so surprising to you?"

Jackie watched while he speared a couple of tomato slices and put them onto his plate along with the stew. "I'm really interested in your psychic ability," she said, trying to sound casual. "I'd like to know how it works."

Arnussen's shoulders stiffened, and his jaw set. "Look, can't you forget about that?" he said. "I'm sorry I ever told you people anything. Let's just let it drop, okay?"

The bandage was gone from his jaw, Jackie noticed suddenly. Beneath where it had been, she could see a dark red scab almost an inch long.

"My goodness," she said. "That must have been some nasty shaving cut."

"It bled a lot at first. Made a real mess."

Jackie sipped her coffee while he got up and served himself another helping of the stew. "That looks delicious. Is it homemade?" she asked, trying to ease the sudden tension in the room.

"Cora made a big pot on the weekend and froze a few bowls of it for me. She's a great cook."

"Mrs. Lederer, you mean?"

"That's right."

"Is that part of your tenancy deal?" Jackie asked. "Do you get your meals, as well as the room?"

"Not formally. But I keep things fixed up around the place, and Cora cooks for me sometimes. It's a pretty good arrangement."

"Mrs. Lederer seems very fond of you."

"We're friends." Arnussen helped himself to another slice of bread.

Jackie cleared her throat. "About the psychic thing," she

said. "You have to understand that I need to ask you about it. I'd be remiss in my job if I didn't. We have to follow up on anything that can possibly help us find Michael."

"How's his mother?" Arnussen asked.

"What do you mean?"

"How's she coping? Is she really upset?"

Jackie felt a sudden hot flood of anger.

If Paul Arnussen was the person responsible for Michael's disappearance, she hated to give him the satisfaction of knowing about Leigh Mellon's anguish. But she had to think of Michael's welfare first, not her own emotions.

"Yes," she said. "The little boy's mother is very upset. I doubt if she's slept more than an hour or two since it happened, and she cries all the time. She looks terrible."

His face was remote, impossible to read. "I don't know how it works," he said abruptly. "The psychic thing, I mean. It only happens now and then."

"And you get these images? Flashes, I believe you called them?"

"Right," he said, sounding reluctant.

"Images involving strangers?"

"Sometimes. Look, I try not to think about it much. I only told them about the little kid because I was…it upset me. He seemed so scared."

"I wonder if you'd help me with something," Jackie said, tracing the crack on the sugar bowl with her forefinger.

"What?"

"I'm going out to a farm tomorrow just south of town. It's the farm where the little boy's grandparents live. I have their permission to search the place and see if we can turn anything up. I wondered if you'd mind coming along."

He looked up, startled. "Me? What for?"

She met his gaze steadily. "I thought you might pick up

some kind of…psychic impression that would be helpful to us.''

Again Arnussen's face took on that hard dangerous look. ''Are you by any chance jerking me around here, Detective? Because if you are, let me tell you that I don't appreciate it.''

Jackie looked at his strong callused hands, the dark scab on his jaw, the arm muscles bunched under his shirtsleeve.

''Lots of police departments use psychics in their investigations nowadays,'' she said with forced calm. ''In fact, it's a fairly routine procedure. I thought you might be able to help us because…''

He watched her intently, gripping the butter knife in his hand.

''Well, for one thing,'' Jackie went on, feeling increasingly foolish, ''you told me there was some kind of a…a chicken associated with the place where Michael was taken that first night. And there are actual chickens at this farm, you see.''

''You're driving me into the country to look at chickens?''

Jackie decided to take a chance. ''Look, I have to solve this case if I want to get anywhere in my career,'' she told him. ''It's the first really important thing I've worked on since I made detective. Mostly I spend my time checking on teenage runaways and stolen cars. And if there's any way you can help me, I'd appreciate it.''

Clearly this was the right approach. The man probably enjoyed being important and having power over the lives of other people.

Another thing consistent with the profile of a sexual predator, Jackie thought.

At any rate, he nodded agreement and went on eating.

"Okay," he said after swallowing a mouthful of stew. "What time?"

"We'll pick you up in the morning around nine o'clock, if that's all right."

"We?"

"My partner will be coming, too, to help with the search. His name is Detective Wardlow."

"I see," Arnussen said, his face inscrutable. "Don't you and Detective Wardlow ever get a holiday? Tomorrow's the Fourth of July."

"We're in the middle of a major investigation involving an abducted child. It's hardly the time to be demanding our statutory holidays."

"I guess not."

Jackie got to her feet and pushed in the chair. Arnussen immediately stood up, as well, pausing by the table with the same old-fashioned politeness she'd noticed when she first met him.

"Well, I should be leaving," she said. "I've got a lot to do."

"What?" he asked.

She looked at him.

"What are you doing now?" he said. "What does a lady cop do at eight o'clock on a summer evening?"

"She goes back to the office," Jackie said. "She types notes, fills in forms and updates her continuation file."

He stared at her, his eyes dark and slanted above the high blunt cheekbones. Again she had the feeling he was looking straight into her soul, and she had to suppress a childish urge to squirm and fidget.

His face softened.

"You're as lonely as I am, aren't you, Detective Kaminsky?" he murmured. "You don't have anybody in all the world to be close to."

"That's not true," Jackie said calmly. "I have some very good friends, both at work and in my private life. And my family…"

Her voice trailed off when she saw his look of amusement. She grabbed her bag and headed out of the kitchen, muttering something about their appointment the next day, then closed his door behind her and escaped up the stairs and into the evening sunlight.

It was intolerable, she thought as she slammed the car into gear and drove away. She couldn't endure a man like Paul Arnussen, with his cold uncanny insight. But the worst thing of all, she had to admit, wasn't Arnussen's scorn or his air of menace. What she'd found utterly unbearable was that look of surprise and sympathy on the man's face when he realized how empty her life was.

The city lacked funds to fully staff the northwest substation around the clock, so after-hours police calls were still answered from downtown. As a result, the substation was a pleasant place to work in the evening. Jackie had the entire squad room to herself, without any distracting bits of conversation or teasing macho come-ons from male officers.

She brewed a fresh pot of coffee in the lunchroom, rummaged through the cupboards and found a pack of stale cookies, then settled at her desk and began to transcribe the day's interviews onto computer.

It seemed incredible that Michael Panesivic had been missing for only three days. Even more astonishing, it was just this morning that Leigh Mellon had called with her hysterical story about the botched abduction of her son.

Every day seemed about a week long, Jackie thought miserably. And every detail had to be recorded so that if the officer in charge of the investigation fell victim to some kind of accident or illness, the police work would carry on without any interruption.

As she typed, she struggled again to capture that wayward bit of information, the one thing she felt sure would hold the answer to all the riddles. But it remained as maddeningly elusive as ever.

Finally, when the sky was dark beyond the windows and the coffeepot was empty, Jackie tidied her desk, leaned back and stretched her cramped muscles, then gathered up her bag and jacket and left the station, locking all the security doors carefully behind her.

She climbed into her own car, leaving the police vehicle in the lot, but she wasn't ready to go home. Instead, she drove around the city for a couple of hours, circling north past the mall where Michael Panesivic had last been seen holding his stuffed yellow duck and out to the little farming area on the edge of town where Paul Arnussen claimed to have run over the dog.

Then she went back down through the silent grounds of Gonzaga University and across the river to the South Hill where the Mellon house sprawled on its half acre, with lights gleaming discreetly behind expensive draperies.

At last she headed out on East Sprague to the turnoff they'd be taking the next day when they drove Paul Arnussen to the Panesivic farm.

She was a little nervous about the prospect of the coming day. Even though Wardlow would be with them and so Arnussen would pose no threat to her, it was going to feel strange having him lounging in the back seat of their police car like some big predatory animal.

Jackie didn't know how Miroslav Panesivic would react to Arnussen, either, especially if he suspected that this man had anything to do with the disappearance of his grandson.

But they had to do something. Standard investigative

procedures obviously weren't getting them anywhere. Everyone agreed that they had to stir the pot a bit and see what might come boiling to the top.

Jackie finally turned around and headed into the core of the city. She gripped the wheel and kept an eye on the traffic as she made mental notes about what still needed to be done.

Barbara Mellon had to be interviewed again. There was something about the woman, especially her relationship with her housemaid, Monica, that Jackie wanted to explore.

Maybe she should talk with Monica, too, and see if the woman might speak more freely in the absence of her employer.

Perhaps even Alden Mellon, that poor wreck of a man, would have something revealing to say if Barbara could be persuaded to let him be interviewed on his own.

Jackie also wanted to talk with both Leigh and Stefan again to go over the whole story with each of them and see if she could catch either one in some kind of discrepancy.

And on Wednesday she and Wardlow were going together to shake down the people from Leigh's child-save agency, though both agreed that the trip probably wasn't going to yield very much.

Then there was Adrienne Calder in her beautiful home, with her checkered past and a wealthy husband who was thus far invisible. Harlan Calder definitely needed to be interviewed, as well.

And Stefan's brother, Zan, and his passionately political wife with her obvious hatred for Leigh Mellon....

Jackie stopped for a red light and looked out the window, suddenly alert.

She was in a rough section of the city, peppered with strip clubs, porno parlors and seedy bars. It was fully dark by now, and the cracked sidewalks were lit by a wash of garish neon signs.

A woman stood for a moment under a streetlight on the corner near Jackie's car, then ducked into the darkened entry of an abandoned store.

Intrigued, Jackie pulled into the next block, parked and pretended to be adjusting her makeup while she watched in the rearview mirror.

The woman ventured out again after Jackie passed, and stood under the streetlight once more. Jackie studied her from a distance, confirming her first guess. It was the same girl she'd seen a couple of days ago at the service station.

And despite the tight black leather miniskirt, the scant jersey halter top and high heels, this wasn't a woman at all. It was just a girl, probably not more than fifteen or sixteen.

The young hooker had a mop of dark blond hair, teased into a tousled bouffant. The bodice of her halter top was tucked back to reveal a pair of swelling young breasts. The whole effect was sultry and provocative, but the girl also had the wide sulky mouth of a child, and her movements seemed jerky and awkward.

Jackie watched from the darkness of her car as the girl posed under the streetlight, then dived back into the shadows when a car slowed down.

She's scared, Jackie thought with a wrench of sympathy. *She's trying to score, but every time a car stops she runs and hides.*

Deliberately Jackie cruised the block a couple of times and observed the girl's behavior, the faltering approach to the streetlight, followed by a frantic dive for cover.

Finally she parked again, got out and walked toward the darkened alcove.

"What's your name?" she asked.

All she could see was a mass of hair and a pair of frightened eyes, gleaming in the shadows.

"Fuck off."

"That's not a very nice way to talk," Jackie said mildly. "Come on, get in the car."

"Like hell," the other muttered. "What are you, some kind of queer?"

"I'm a cop." Jackie displayed her badge "Now, get in the car."

"Oh, shit," the girl said wearily, tottering out onto the street in her ridiculously high heels. She swayed on her feet and would have fallen if Jackie hadn't clutched her arm.

"Are you high?" Jackie asked.

"No. And I haven't done anything wrong, either. You can't arrest me." The young hooker pulled her halter top back in place, hiding the exposed breasts, and tugged nervously at the bottom of her skirt.

"I'm not arresting you. I just want to talk to you for a minute."

She held the door and the girl got into the car, glaring sullenly through the windshield.

Jackie went around and got into the driver's seat, then switched on the interior light and turned to look at her passenger.

"Jesus," she whispered. "How old are you?"

"I'm nineteen."

Jackie felt a sudden hot flood of rage against men, against the system in general and a world that put children on the streets to sell their bodies. She gripped the slim bare arm so tightly that the youngster squirmed and yelped in surprise.

"I *said*—" Jackie spoke through clenched teeth "— how old are you?"

The girl wrenched her arm away, covered her face and started to cry, the gulping sobs of a hurt child.

Jackie turned off the overhead light and sat in silence for a while, letting her cry.

"Let's start over again, shall we?" she said more gently. "Now, how old are you, honey?"

"I'm f-fourteen," the girl whispered.

16

"What's your name?" Jackie asked.

Again she was met by stony silence. The girl glared through the windshield, her delicate profile lit by pulsing waves of red and green neon.

Jackie sighed. "Look, you don't have to tell me your real name, okay? Just make it up. Give me something I can call you."

"Sandy," the girl muttered without turning her head.

"There now, was that so hard? And my name's Jackie. What are you doing out here on the street?"

There was no response.

"You can't work this corner," Jackie said.

"I wasn't doing anything."

"Lucky for you. All this area is allocated, you know. It's staked out for the professionals. Do you have a pimp?"

The girl turned quickly. Jackie caught the flash of surprise and fear in her eyes. They were wide and blue, heavily ringed with makeup.

"I didn't think so. Look, Sandy, what I'm saying is that you can't free-lance around here. You'll get yourself beaten up."

"Free-lance?"

Jackie sighed. "You need a pimp if you want to work the street out here, honey. You need some big tough guy who'll take all your earnings and pay you an allowance. If you're on your own, the other girls will beat you up. And if they don't hurt you bad enough, their pimps will finish the job.''

Sandy huddled against the passenger door and turned her head away.

Jackie saw the bare shoulders trembling. She peeled off her denim jacket and tossed it across the space between them.

"Put this on," she said. "You're freezing."

Sandy hesitated, then picked up the jacket and held it under her chin, settling gratefully into its warmth. "I'm not a...a hooker," she muttered at last. "I just did it..." She paused and grimaced, then swallowed hard, clutching the jacket. "Just a couple of times. I started last week."

"Why?"

"I was hungry. I didn't know what else to do."

Jackie slammed the car into gear and started driving.

"Where are you going?" Sandy asked in alarm.

"To my place."

"What for?"

"God knows. Did you run away?"

There was no answer, but she could see the girl's mouth set and her hands clench on the jacket again.

"Don't worry," Jackie said. "We won't talk about it unless you want to."

"What are you going to do with me? You can't make me go back home. I'd rather die."

"You probably will die, if you keep doing what you were doing tonight."

"I don't care," the girl muttered.

"Of course you care. You want to live, Sandy. In fact, right now you want to eat badly enough that you'll let some creep pay money to paw you."

Sandy began to cry again, her gulping sobs wrenching

her body. The mascara ran freely, staining her cheeks and dripping off her chin.

Jackie took a small pack of tissues from a side compartment and handed it across the seat. "Clean your face," she said. "Don't drip that junk all over my coat."

Sandy gulped and coughed, then reached blindly for the tissues and began to mop her face. "It was awful," she muttered at last. "Those men—they were just awful."

"Of course they were," Jackie said. "What kind of man pays to have sex with a child? They'd have to be pigs. But," she added gently while the girl blew her nose and continued to rub at her face, "not all men are like that, Sandy. The world is full of nice men who'd rather die than hurt you. You're just not in the right place to find them, that's all."

She turned north on Division and headed for her apartment while the girl huddled beside her in silence.

Jackie cast a couple of concerned glances at her passenger and realized Sandy was so tired she could barely keep her eyes open. The girl drooped against the door, breathing heavily, her mouth slack with weariness.

"Where have you been sleeping?"

"Wherever I could find a place. I spent last night in an alley under some cardboard, but I was too scared to sleep. I still had a bunch of money from the…from the last time I…"

"Okay," Jackie said. "What happened to your money?"

"There was a man with a knife. He said he'd kill me if I didn't give him the money, so I had to…" The girl's mouth began to tremble again.

"Stop. No more crying." Jackie pulled off the street and into the covered parking lot beneath her apartment building. "This is my place. We're going to give you a hot meal and a bath, and then you're going to fall asleep. And after that, we'll decide what to do with you.''

Sandy was apparently too weary to argue. She followed Jackie through the lobby to the elevator, taking off the high heels and padding along in her bare feet with the denim coat draped over her shoulders.

"I'll cook something for you," Jackie said when they were in the apartment. "While I'm doing that, you can have a bath and put on some of my clothes. They'll be too long for you, but otherwise they should fit okay."

Chatting to ease the girl's tension, she moved down the hall to the bathroom and started running hot water into the tub, adding a liberal dash of strawberry-scented bubble bath. She set out towels and hurried into her bedroom, coming back with a jogging suit, cotton panties and a pair of socks, which she placed on the bathroom hamper.

Sandy stood by the tub, dazed and swaying on her feet, looking down at the swirling hot water and the fragrant mass of bubbles.

"That smells so nice," she whispered.

The overhead light was merciless, displaying the sticky teased hair, the young face with its absurd makeup, the sadly provocative outfit.

Jackie thought of how the child must have suffered. Yet somehow she'd managed to keep herself away from the pimps and dealers, and maintained a brave feisty defiance in spite of everything.

She was painfully reminded of herself at the same age, and was so moved that it was all she could do not to gather the girl into her arms and hold her.

"Get the rest of that makeup off your face," she said briskly. "You still look like a raccoon. And don't wipe it all over my towels, either."

She put out shampoo, hand lotion and a hair dryer, then

went into the kitchen and rummaged through the fridge to find some leftover chili, along with a macaroni dinner and a salad. When she was placing the food on the table, Sandy came shyly into the kitchen, looking utterly transformed.

The teased hair had been washed, dried and combed smooth, then parted on one side to hang in a shining golden mass onto the girl's shoulders. Her face was scrubbed clean, and Jackie's navy sweat suit puddled around her wrists and ankles. She looked like a junior-high-school kid wearing her big brother's clothes.

Jackie felt another hot wave of fury at the world in general.

"Sit down and eat," she said without expression. "I'll make up a bed for you on the couch."

She hurried out of the room so the girl could eat without feeling she was being watched. She opened the folding couch and made it up with blankets and pillows, then went back into the kitchen and began to tidy away the dishes.

Sandy's plate was already empty, wiped so clean that it shone, and she was finishing her glass of milk.

"Thank you very much," she said like a polite child, setting the glass down. "That was really good."

"I guess anything tastes good when you're that hungry."

The girl dropped her head and looked at the table, her thick hair falling like a curtain across her face. "Are you really a cop?" she asked.

"I really am."

"But you don't wear a uniform."

"I'm a detective. I wear street clothes to work. In fact," Jackie added with forced casualness, "I have to be at work early tomorrow morning. You'll probably still be sleeping, and I don't know how late I'll be getting home. I'll leave a key on the table for you so you can get back inside if you go out for a walk or something."

In spite of her obvious fatigue, Sandy's eyes widened and she stared at Jackie in blank astonishment.

"You'll go away and leave me here all alone? Aren't you afraid?"

"Of what?"

"That I...I might steal something, or let a bunch of bad people in here to trash the place, or—"

"Of course you won't," Jackie said. "Come on, get to sleep. You're practically dead on your feet."

Sandy followed her into the living room and looked at the couch with its clean bedding and soft pillows. Her eyes brimmed with tears. "I don't...I don't know what to say." She gave Jackie a helpless pleading glance. "This is just...so nice."

"You don't have to say anything." Jackie pulled the covers back and pushed the girl gently onto the sofa. "Curl up and get a good sleep. The remote for the television is on the coffee table. There's lots of food in the fridge, and I have some books there in the bookcase that might interest you. I'll leave more clothes for you when I go out, and try to be home at suppertime."

"If I run away again, will you come and look for me?"

The girl was in bed with the covers pulled to her chin. Her blond hair rayed out on the pillow, and her face was pale with exhaustion.

"No," Jackie told her. "If you run away again, honey, you'll be all on your own."

"If I stay here, what will you do with me?"

"I don't know. We'll have to talk about it, and find a place for you to live if you don't want to go home."

"I can't go back!" Sandy's face contorted with panic. "I can't ever go back. My stepfather—"

"Okay," Jackie said softly, smoothing the girl's hair back from her forehead. "We won't talk about that. And I promise I won't make any arrangements without talking them over with you. All right?"

Sandy nodded and her eyes dropped shut. Her eyelids were pale and delicate, veined with blue like a child's.

Jackie continued to stroke the thick golden hair. "Sleep tight, little girl," she whispered.

After a moment she got up and switched off the lights, then tiptoed down the hall to her own room.

"So the kid was still asleep when you left this morning?" Wardlow stared at her in disbelief.

Jackie nodded and gripped the wheel, watching the traffic as she passed under the freeway and headed for the area where Paul Arnussen lived. "Like a log. I don't think she'd moved in the past eight hours."

"You're crazy," he said flatly, settling back and resting his head against the seat. "You're really crazy, Kaminsky."

"Why?"

"Because you left her alone in your apartment and you don't know a goddamn thing about this kid. You don't even know her name, do you?"

"Just what she told me. But I checked through all the missing-children files this morning when I got to work and there's no sign of her under any name."

"See? Nobody's even reported her missing. She's probably a professional thief."

"Well, I'm not too worried," Jackie said cheerfully. "There's not all that much in my apartment that's worth stealing."

Wardlow slumped lower in the passenger seat and drummed his fingers on the armrest, tense with annoyance.

Jackie glanced at him thoughtfully, then concentrated on her driving.

They were traveling in bright morning sunlight, followed by a patrol car with a couple of uniformed officers who were ostensibly coming along to help with the search of the Panesivic farm. In fact, the extra officers had been assigned to make Paul Arnussen less conspicuous when they arrived at the farm.

Jackie parked in front of Cora Lederer's house and glanced at her watch. "He said he'd be ready," she told Wardlow, who was still scowling.

Her partner pulled himself together with an obvious effort. "I'll go in and get him."

"Let's just..." While Jackie was speaking, the door opened and Arnussen came striding down the walk. He wore blue jeans and boots, a plaid shirt and a baseball cap pulled low over his eyes.

"Hi," Jackie said when he opened the door and climbed into the back seat. "Paul Arnussen, this is Detective Wardlow."

He gave them a level glance and settled back, then looked over his shoulder at the patrol car parked behind them.

Jackie put the car in gear and turned the corner, heading up onto the freeway. Arnussen lounged in the back seat while Wardlow retreated into his stony silence, staring out the window at the passing scenery.

Jackie glanced in the rearview mirror and found Arnussen looking at her. His eyes met hers, dark and unreadable under the brim of the cap. She held his gaze for a long moment, then turned away without speaking, shaken and a little frightened.

The scene at the farm when they arrived was much the same as on Jackie's last visit. This holiday morning the whole family again appeared to be out in the garden, the men working with hoes and rakes, the women picking vegetables.

Even Stefan Panesivic was there, laboring next to his brother and father. The professor wore jeans and a T-shirt. He was bareheaded, and his dark hair glistened in the morning sunlight. Deborah was in the garden, as well, near her mother and grandmother, pushing a doll carriage along the path leading to the gate.

"Hi," Jackie said as she approached the little girl. "How are you?"

"See my kitty?" Deborah stood aside proudly to display the occupant of the carriage.

The black-and-white kitten was crouched on a pad of blankets, wearing a doll's bonnet tied under his chin. He gave Jackie a look of baleful misery from beneath the lacy frill of the bonnet, and tried to climb out the carriage. Deborah held him down firmly with her small hand.

"Star's going for a ride," she said with a fond smile at the angry kitten. "He likes it."

Jackie chuckled, then looked up as Stefan came through the rows of potatoes.

"What's going on, Detective? My father told me you were coming out here today."

"We want to do a search of the farm," Jackie told him.

"Why?"

"We're just hoping we might turn up something helpful."

"Like what? Do you think my son's hidden in the barn?"

"If we thought that," Jackie said calmly, "we would have searched there already. We're just looking for anything that might benefit the investigation. Your father agreed to the search," she added.

"I know he did. But I don't understand your motive. It's the Mellons you should be harassing, not my parents."

"According to what you told me, that wouldn't be very helpful. You believe the Mellons have already smuggled Michael out of the area, so a search would just come up empty."

"I didn't say it would be helpful to search their house. But it certainly makes a lot more sense than wasting your time out here." Stefan jutted his chin. "Who's that man?" he asked.

Arnussen stood apart from the police officers, leaning against the fence. A couple of shaggy ponies had trotted up to him. He reached over the rails to pat their heads and stroke their ears, murmuring quietly.

"He's a psychic," Jackie said.

Stefan's eyes widened in disbelief. He tightened his grip on the hoe. "You're joking."

"I can assure you, Mr. Panesivic, that nothing we're doing in this investigation is any kind of a joke."

"What a damned ridiculous farce," he said angrily. "My son's been missing for four days and the police are running around escorting some cowboy who's supposed to be a psychic?"

Jackie turned to Miroslav, who approached them and removed his straw hat with a courtly air, bending over Jackie's hand. "Detective," he said, "good morning. How are you?"

"I'm fine, thanks." Jackie smiled at the older man, charmed again by his warmth and cordiality. "Could we get started, Mr. Panesivic?"

"Of course. You said you wanted to look at the basements and root cellars?"

"That's right. Anything that's underground."

Jackie ignored Stefan's sardonic look and his snort of

annoyance. The professor turned and strode back into the garden without another word, taking his place next to his brother and hacking angrily at the weeds among the potatoes.

With Miroslav as their guide, Jackie, Wardlow, Arnussen and the other police officers made their way through the Panesivic house and basement, then the barns and outbuildings. Outdoors, they crept down flights of steps into dark root cellars filled with stacks of vegetables and braided chains of onions that hung from the roof beams.

Arnussen kept to himself, looking around in grim silence as they moved from one building to another. Finally, back in the sunlight near the barn, he came over to Jackie, took her elbow and drew her away from the others.

"This is a waste of time," he said. "There's nothing here."

"Are you sure?"

"Positive. It's nothing like what I saw. The kid's still underground, but not here."

Jackie stiffened and looked up at him cautiously. "He's still underground?"

"Yeah." Arnussen turned to watch the horses run across the field.

Her heart began to pound. "Is he alive?"

"I think he is. If he wasn't, I wouldn't be getting anything from him."

"And you're still…getting something?"

"It's pretty faint, but there's still a connection. He's not here, though."

"Okay. Let's go and look at some of the other places."

She gestured to Wardlow, who came over and conferred with her briefly, then spoke to the other officers. The uniformed men got into their car and left the farm.

"Why are we losing our escort?" Arnussen asked, watching them.

"Because we don't have search permission for any more places. If we decide to check some of the other residences, I'll have to make the calls tonight. In the meantime, we'll just do a drive-by and see if you get anything, all right?"

Jackie thanked Miroslav for his cooperation, then got into the car. The Panesivic family, including little Deborah with her doll carriage, gathered at the entrance of the garden to watch them drive away.

Arnussen and Wardlow rode in silence as they headed toward the city, both looking out the window at the passing fields and animals.

Jackie stared at the road in front of the car and thought about Paul Arnussen. The man was impossible to read. She couldn't tell if he really had Michael Panesivic hidden away somewhere, or if he just enjoyed the attention he was gaining by misleading the police.

He certainly didn't appear to be enjoying himself at the moment. Arnussen sprawled in the back seat with his arms folded, frowning at the passing countryside. He looked as miserable as Wardlow, who was missing his holiday and seemed gloomier with each passing hour.

They spent the remainder of the morning doing a circuit of the city, driving past Adrienne Calder's house, then the elder Mellons', the baby-sitter's well-tended grounds and the apartment at the university where Stefan lived.

Jackie watched Arnussen closely in the mirror as they passed the last two places, since both Helen Philps and Stefan Panesivic had thought they recognized his picture. But he showed no recognition of either residence. His only flash of interest came when they drove slowly by Leigh Mellon's neat white house with its dark green trim, sad and deserted on this holiday morning.

"That's where the mother lives," Jackie told him. "In the white house."

"I know. I looked up the address. What's she doing today?" He sat up and peered through the window.

"She's spending a few days with her sister," Jackie said curtly. "She's in pretty bad shape, and the family doesn't want her to be alone."

He nodded and settled back in the seat.

"Does any of this ring a bell?" Jackie asked. "Any of these places I've shown you?"

Arnussen shook his head.

"Okay. I guess we'll take you home." She turned around and headed south, back toward Cannon Hill and Cora Lederer's house with its little basement suite.

Wardlow began to drum his fingers on the armrest again, looking impatient and angry.

Jackie gave him a sharp warning glance and he subsided, glaring out the window. They rode in silence while the midday sunlight poured down on the road ahead of them in shimmering waves.

17

After dropping Arnussen at his home, they picked up some deli sandwiches and tubs of salad and took them back to their desks at the police substation, which hummed with activity despite the holiday.

Wardlow slumped behind his desk, looking like a thundercloud.

"This sucks," he muttered. "It really sucks. We're not accomplishing a goddamn thing, Kaminsky. We're just spinning our wheels."

Jackie dug into the sack to hand him an egg-salad sandwich and a carton of coleslaw. "Do you want to talk about it?" she asked.

"What?"

"Whatever's eating you. Maybe it'll help to talk some more."

"Oh, great," he said sarcastically. "Another helpful session with the amateur shrink. Maybe we should talk about *your* problems, Kaminsky. Like all the great relationships you've got going, and how your grandmother only talks to you when she's drunk because then she can be as mean as she wants."

The attack was surprisingly hurtful, but Jackie forced herself not to make a sharp response. That was what he wanted, after all. The man was in such pain that he needed to provoke a fight, even at the cost of driving away the only person willing to give him a sympathetic ear.

"You're right," she said at last. "I'm probably not in a position to be doing any counseling. I've never had a truly close relationship with anybody. Hell, I don't even know what it feels like. But I'm willing to listen whenever you want to talk."

"I know you are." Wardlow slumped over the desk and put his head in his hands. "Sorry, Kaminsky. I'm being a prize ass. It's just that..."

Jackie dug a plastic fork into a carton of potato salad, waiting for him to continue.

But Wardlow was apparently unwilling to discuss any further details of his personal life. "That poor little kid," he said. "It's making me crazy. What if he's still alive? What if he's starving to death somewhere, or being tortured and molested, and we're not doing anything to find him?"

Jackie stared at her partner in disbelief. "For God's sake, Brian. How can you say we're not doing anything?"

"Oh, yeah," he said bitterly, "I forgot. We're giving up our holidays to take a psychic carpenter out of town for a visit with the chickens and a nice look at some dried onions."

"Come on, Brian. We're doing everything we can. Everything."

Jackie held up both hands and ticked items off on her fingers.

"We've logged hundreds of man hours already. Seventeen officers have been working full time through the weekend, following up on tips and leads. Thousands of flyers with Michael's picture have been posted all over the state and across the country. We're liaising with all sorts of other police agencies through the FBI. Leigh Mellon's done one polygraph and scheduled a second one, and Stefan Panesivic has also volunteered to do one."

"Has he? You didn't tell me that."

"I was going to report it at tomorrow's briefing. He called yesterday and volunteered. He's scheduled for a polygraph next week, as soon as Sergeant Kravitz gets back from her vacation."

Wardlow nodded, gazing thoughtfully at the computer screen.

Jackie paused to leaf through some notes, then went on, "We've had local police visiting the other two Mellon residences in Palm Beach and Cabo San Lucas, and questioning the neighbors about anything suspicious. You and your men have shown pictures of every suspect in this case to everybody who we know was in that mall on Friday night."

"And drawn a total blank," Wardlow said gloomily.

"At least we've been doing something. Furthermore, you and I are going out tomorrow to shake down Leigh's child-save people, and then I have other appointments booked right through the week and weekend. In fact, personally, I've spent at least fifty hours talking with the principals and doing paperwork on the case, and so have you. What else can we do?"

"I know," he muttered, picking up his sandwich and looking at it. "I know we're busy, but it still feels like we're just nibbling around the edges of the investigation. We're not doing any of the really important stuff."

"Like what?"

"For one thing," Wardlow said, "a search of the Mellon house. Everybody seems to think they've got the kid."

"Doing a search of that place is absolutely impossible. Barbara Mellon has made it clear she doesn't want us in there, and I could never get a warrant."

"Why not, if people are convinced he's there?"

"What people?" Jackie asked. "Stefan Panesivic, who hates his mother-in-law? And the feeling's apparently mutual, by the way. It's a matter of urgency," she added gently. "You know that as well as I do. Even if Michael is holed up somewhere in the Mellon mansion, we could never prove he's in imminent danger. Leigh could argue that she'd given her son to her parents to protect him. They'd be committing some kind of crime—obstruction of justice, maybe, but nothing serious enough to warrant turning their house upside down against their will, especially since their daughter has legal custody. What judge is going to grant us a warrant under those conditions?"

"You really don't think we could get a warrant?"

"To search the house of a former state attorney-general to see if he's got his little grandson in residence? I don't think so." Jackie looked curiously at her partner. "Are you just blowing smoke, Brian, or do you really think the kid is at the Mellon place?"

Wardlow put down his sandwich. "It's pretty hard to believe," he admitted. "If they snatched him, why not at least tell the mother about it? The poor woman's obviously going through hell. I don't think Leigh Mellon believes her little boy is safe with Grandma and Grandpa. If they had him, she wouldn't be so frantic."

"Not necessarily. I'd have to look in my notebook to see who it was, but somebody told me recently that Leigh was probably the weakest link in the family chain, and if the Mellons were planning something illegal, she'd be the last to know."

"God, what a group. They sound as tough as your family, Kaminsky."

"I suppose so," Jackie said with a wry smile. She was pleased to see him making jokes again, even at her own expense. "Except that the Mellons are very suave and use

money as their weapon. My family, on the other hand, tends
to grab whatever blunt object is lying around at the moment.''

She switched on the speakerphone and dialed her home
number, listening to the hollow ring at the other end, then
the sound of her recorded voice telling the caller to leave
a message after the beep.

''Sandy?'' she said with a brief stab of uneasiness. ''Are
you there? It's Jackie. Pick up the phone if you're around,
okay?''

There was a long silence while Wardlow watched her
from the opposite desk. Jackie ignored his sardonic glance.

''Okay, I guess you're still asleep or maybe out for a
walk or something,'' she said into the phone. ''I'll have to
catch you later. Just letting you know that I'll be away from
my desk for the afternoon, but I hope to be home around
six. See you.''

She switched off the phone and turned to Wardlow, who
was still obviously listening with interest.

''So she's not answering,'' he said.

''Now why does that cheer you up so much?''

He leaned back in his chair, fingers laced together, and
stretched his arms behind his head. ''I like it when you
screw up like other people. It proves you're human, after
all.''

''Well, that's pretty uncharitable, isn't it?'' Jackie glared
at him. ''Just for that, I'm not sharing this last bit of the
potato salad. I don't care how much you whine and plead.''

''You'd better take a little swing past your apartment,''
Wardlow suggested, ''and run a check on the flatware.''

''You mean all that solid-gold stuff embossed with the
family crest? Crossed baseball bats, rampant cockroaches
and a stylized K?''

He laughed, the only spontaneous burst of amusement

she'd heard from him in some time. "Yeah. That's what I mean."

"I always hated that table service. Besides, I've been entertaining so much that the oyster forks and demitasse spoons are practically worn-out. The kid's welcome to steal them."

But Jackie's banter could barely hide her worry. She'd really believed the girl wouldn't rip her off. Now, faced with the prospect of betrayal, she dreaded the thought of going home.

"I'm serious," Wardlow said more gently. "You'd better run by the apartment, Kaminsky. See what the kid's up to."

"I don't have time." Jackie gathered together her files and notebook.

"Where are you going this afternoon?"

"Back out to the Panesivic farm. Miroslav told me that Zan and Mila were staying most of the day. I think I'll ask a few more questions of them as a group. Then I'll stop by to see Zan and Mila at their own place later. I want to talk with them without the others."

"Where do they live?"

"It's a little condo in the Valley. The two officers who were there yesterday say the walls are paper thin, and it's hardly big enough to turn around in, but beautifully decorated. Mila's apparently very skilled at her job."

"She's the pretty little dark-haired woman, right? The mother of the kid with the cat."

Jackie chuckled. "Cat in a bonnet." She shook her head. "You know, he looked a lot like my cousin Angela's little boy. Cute, but real mean."

Wardlow chuckled in reply, then sobered. "Mila Panesivic didn't seem nearly as awful as you said she was.

In fact, I liked her. We chatted for a couple of minutes in the garden.''

Jackie thought about Stefan's beautiful sister-in-law. "She was a lot nicer today. For one thing, nobody was talking politics. Also, I think at first she was sort of enjoying the fact that Leigh was suffering. Now she seems to be getting more concerned about Michael's welfare, which is obviously another story.''

Wardlow switched on his computer and began to type while Jackie stood and watched him.

"Where will you be this afternoon?" she asked.

"Right here. After lunch, four of the uniformed guys are coming over from the downtown station with a bunch of new leads. We'll spend the day running license plates and descriptions, and making telephone calls to people who think they've seen something. Michelson figures we've got a better chance of catching people at home this afternoon.''

"It's so tedious, doing all that stuff, but we can't forget that the slightest detail could turn out to be the one we need.''

"I know. But I still…''

"What?" Jackie asked.

"Nothing.''

She checked her holster and put the notebook in her bag. "What were you going to say, Brian?''

"I think Arnussen did it.''

"Really?''

Wardlow nodded, staring at the window. "I think he snatched the kid and hid him somewhere. Now he's torn between saving his own skin and taking advantage of more chances to gloat over the crime.''

"What makes you so sure?''

"I don't know," Wardlow said, frowning. "There's just

something scary about the guy. Have you ever noticed his eyes, Kaminsky?''

Jackie thought about those slanting eyes above the blunt tanned cheekbones. ''I've noticed them,'' she said.

''Doesn't he scare you? Tell the truth.''

''Yes,'' she said at last. ''In fact, he scares me a lot. But I still don't know if he's guilty. And we certainly don't have enough evidence at the moment to pull him in.''

''Well, I don't think we should let him out of our sight. Not for a minute.''

''We're watching him,'' Jackie said. ''Every officer on patrol anywhere in the city or the Valley has been alerted to Arnussen's description and his vehicle. If he tries to make a move, somebody's going to be following him.''

''I know.'' Wardlow glanced up as she headed for the door. ''Kaminsky, seriously, do you want me to take a run by your place? I've got a few minutes before the guys get here.''

Jackie hesitated, then shook her head. ''Thanks, Brian, but I'm not worried, There's not going to be any problem at my apartment. I'm sure of it.''

By the time Jackie finished her interviews at the Panesivic farm and stopped for a visit with Zan and Mila at their small condo, it was close to six o'clock. There wasn't the slightest evidence that Michael was hidden at either place. Furthermore, the entire Panesivic family seemed genuinely worried about his whereabouts, convinced he'd been kidnapped by the Mellons. She dropped in at the station to check on Wardlow's progress, then headed for home a little after six, wondering what she was going to find.

On the outside of the building, everything looked just the same. The drapes in her living room appeared to be pulled wide-open, but from the street below she couldn't tell if anything was amiss.

She rode up in the elevator, found her key and hurried along the hallway, then opened the door silently and stepped into the foyer of her apartment. All she could see was a bit of the kitchen and one corner of the table, which appeared to be set neatly for two. Place mats, cutlery and water glasses were arranged with careful precision, and a basket held sliced bread wrapped in a red gingham napkin.

Jackie felt a flood of relief. She opened her mouth to call a greeting, then paused abruptly as strains of music came drifting from the other room.

She recognized one of the flute concertos she liked to play. It was a lilting piece by Vivaldi. Jackie stood listening to the music with pleasure, amazed that Sandy would choose a disk like that when she was alone.

More likely the girl had anticipated Jackie's arrival and put on some music she thought her hostess would enjoy.

But when Jackie closed the door and hung up her jacket, the music stopped abruptly. She entered the living room, where her stereo was silent in its corner and Sandy sat cross-legged on the ottoman, her hands folded tightly in her lap, looking flushed and guilty. Jackie's flute case was shoved partly out of sight beneath the ottoman.

"Well, hi," the girl said with forced brightness. "Did you have a good day?"

"Pretty good." Jackie watched her young guest thoughtfully, still disturbed by those haunting strains of music. "How about you?"

"It was great." Sandy jumped up from the ottoman and headed for the kitchen. "I made a salad," she said over her shoulder, "and microwaved some carrots, and thawed out these steaks I found in the freezer. Is that okay?"

"That's fine. Did you get my phone message?"

"Yeah, but I must have been outside when you called. I went for a walk. It felt so good," the girl added shyly, "to walk around and have a place to come back to."

Jackie felt a pang of sympathy. She turned away quickly and started down the hall. "I'll just change out of these clothes," she said. "Do you know how to put the steaks on under the broiler?"

"Of *course*," Sandy called from the kitchen.

Jackie grinned at the note of lofty scorn in the girl's voice. She locked her handgun away in the bedside cabinet, washed her face and hands and slipped on a pair of khaki shorts, then returned to the kitchen where Sandy was putting a tossed salad on the table along with the steaks.

"This is great." Jackie looked hungrily at the food. "I can't remember when I've come home to find a meal all ready for me."

Sandy sat opposite her and dished out the salad. "I talked to a nice lady who lives across the hall. She has a little girl called Tiffany."

"That's my friend Carmen. Did she wonder what you were doing in my apartment?"

Sandy's cheeks reddened. "I told her you were my cousin. Is that okay?"

"Carmen knows I've got lots of cousins. One more isn't going to make much difference, I guess."

Sandy nodded in relief and concentrated on her salad.

Jackie watched surreptitiously, astounded by the change in the girl. Less than twenty-four hours ago, she'd plucked a foulmouthed, painted woman off a street corner. Now she sat eating dinner with a wholesome, well-mannered child who apparently had all kinds of hidden talents.

"Carmen said she can use a baby-sitter lots of times," Sandy went on. "I thought maybe I could look after Tiffany and some other kids in the apartment, too, and use the money to pay you some rent. I don't want to be a free-loader.''

Jackie was both moved and distressed by the girl's proposal. "You can't live here with me, honey," she said gently.

"Why not?"

"Because I can't offer you any kind of home life. I work almost all the time. You need to be in a place where there's a stable environment, people around that you can talk to."

"I don't need all that stuff. I can look after myself."

"Like you were looking after yourself last night?"

The girl concentrated stubbornly on her meal.

"Tell me about your home," Jackie said. "Why can't you go back?"

All she could see was the curtain of hair and the way Sandy's fingers tightened on her fork.

"What does your father do?" Jackie watched her closely. "I assume your parents must be pretty well off if they can afford flute lessons."

Sandy's head jerked erect and her cheeks flushed scarlet. "Look, I'm really sorry," she whispered. "I know I shouldn't have touched it, but I saw it there and I couldn't—"

"That's okay," Jackie said, smiling. "Except that my poor old flute is probably still in shock. It doesn't often get played with that kind of skill."

Sandy's face brightened with pleasure. "Did you really like it?"

"I thought you were playing a CD. You're a very talented girl, Sandy. I've been trying for years to learn to play like that."

There was a brief awkward silence.

"So tell me about your father," Jackie said.

"He's not my father, he's my stepfather," the girl muttered, looking down at her plate again. "He's a doctor."

"Where's your father?"

"He died five years ago in an accident on his boat."

"I see. And you don't get along with your stepfather?"

There was no answer.

"Sandy?"

"I hate him!" the girl burst out, looking up in anguish. "I'd like to kill him. I wish I could take your gun and shoot him right in the face."

Jackie studied her thoughtfully. "What about your mother?" she said at last. "Don't you miss her? Wouldn't you like to—"

The girl got up and rushed from the room. Jackie heard the slam of the apartment door. She ran out into the hallway in time to see the door to the stairs close, then stood looking at the empty corridor.

Finally she went back inside and finished her meal in silence.

An hour passed, and Sandy didn't return. Jackie cleared the table and washed the dishes.

Methodically she began to search through all the wastebaskets in the apartment, then went downstairs and rummaged in the foul-smelling Dumpster in the parking lot below the building.

At last she found what she was looking for, a brown paper sack containing the miniskirt, halter top and high heels that Sandy had been wearing the night before. There was a red leather billfold in the pocket of the skirt, empty except for an identification card.

Jackie tossed the clothes back into the Dumpster and carried the card upstairs.

Her name was Alexandra Gerard, aged fourteen years five months, and she came from Seattle.

Jackie washed her hands, sat on the couch, took a deep breath and dialed the number on the card. A woman's voice answered.

"Mrs. Gerard?" Jackie asked.

"No, this is Mrs. Collins. May I help you?"

"Do you know a girl named Alexandra Gerard?"

There was a long strained silence. "Yes," the woman said at last. "Alex is my daughter, but she's not home at the moment. She's gone to visit some school friends for the summer."

"This is Detective Kaminsky from the Spokane Police Department. And your daughter isn't with school friends. In fact, she's been staying with me."

Jackie waited so long that she wondered if the other woman had hung up.

"Is she...all right?" the woman asked at last, sounding cautious and reluctant.

"Not really," Jackie said. "She's in pretty desperate straits, as a matter of fact. What's the situation, Mrs. Collins? Why did she leave home?"

"She's a bad girl," the woman said coldly. "Alex is completely out of control. I just can't handle her anymore."

Jackie twisted the phone cord around her fingers. "The girl doesn't seem all that bad," she said. "Don't you think your problems could be worked out if she were to come home and give it another chance?"

"She can't come back here!" the woman said in alarm. "I won't have her back!"

"Why not?"

"She's...trying to ruin my marriage," Mrs. Collins said. "She seduced my husband."

Jackie thought about Sandy's bitter outburst at the dinner table and her expressed wish to kill her stepfather.

"Look," the woman went on, a pleading note in her

voice. "We haven't been married very long. David and I need some time alone together. And the way Alex is now...the way she looks..."

"She can't help the way she looks," Jackie said quietly. "She's only fourteen years old, Mrs. Collins."

"But he...he looks at her. And one night last month I came home from my bridge club and found him in her room. Alex cried and pretended he was attacking her, but I know David would never, never do anything like that. She was...she kept coming on to him, being seductive, and he weakened the same as any man would. I don't want her back!" the woman said hysterically. "I don't want her in my house!"

Jackie gripped the telephone receiver, struggling to control her fury. "What do you suggest we do with your daughter, Mrs. Collins?"

"I don't know. Can't you...put her in a foster home or something? I'll send the money to pay for it. Money's no problem. But I don't want her in my house."

"Considering the way you feel," Jackie said, "I doubt that Sandy...that Alex wants to be with you, either."

"So you'll look after her? You'll find a place for her to live and not send her back here to Seattle?"

Jackie sighed. "I guess I'll have to, won't I?"

"Give me an address. Tell me where to send the money."

Jackie knew that if she talked to the woman any longer, she was going to say something she'd regret.

"I'll keep your home number on file. Somebody from our local Juvenile Division will be getting in touch with you later," she said curtly. "Goodbye, Mrs. Collins."

What chance did a child have with a mother like that? Jackie thought as she hung up.

After staring pensively at the gathering dusk beyond the

window, she left the apartment and went for a long walk around the neighborhood, looking for a flash of blond hair or a yellow shirt. But there was no sign of the girl.

Jackie trudged back home and considered taking the car out and driving around the streets, but she knew the effort would be futile. Instead, she had a bath and went to bed, trying to read. Long after midnight, she switched the light out and lay gazing at the shadows on the ceiling.

Shortly before two o'clock she heard a sound in the foyer and sat upright, reaching automatically for the key to the cabinet where she kept her gun.

Footsteps came down the hall. Jackie could see the shadowy outline of a slim body in her doorway, a silvered aureole of hair.

"Are you asleep?" the girl whispered.

"Not yet. Come in, Alex." Jackie switched on her bedside lamp.

The girl stared at her with wide, frightened eyes. "How do you know my name?"

"I looked through the Dumpster and found your billfold and ID card. I also called your mother."

Alexandra Gerard came in and huddled on the edge of the bed, her hands clenched tightly. "My mother? What did she say?"

"She said you seduced your stepfather."

The girl buried her face in her hands and started to cry. Jackie looked at the heaving shoulders, the long delicate fingers.

"Did you?" she asked.

Alex shook her head and turned away. "My mom's crazy about him, but he's such a jerk. He kept...you know, looking at me. I tried to tell Mom I was scared of him, but she wouldn't listen. She acted like it was all my fault. One night when Mom wasn't home, he came to my room and…and…''

"Okay," Jackie said gently, her heart aching. "So what happened next?"

"Mom came home and caught him. She freaked out and called me all kinds of names. It was awful."

"What did you do?"

"I took the money from my bank account and got on the bus. I thought when I got here I could find a job or something. But it was so hard…" Alex gulped and began to sob.

Jackie put her arms around the girl. "It's okay, honey," she whispered. "It's okay."

"I can't go home again," Alex wailed. "I just can't."

"I know you can't. We'll have to think of something else."

"What…what will you do?"

"I don't know." Jackie released her and stroked the tangled mass of hair. "Go to bed," she said at last. "We'll talk about it in the morning."

"And you won't make me go back home?"

"Not a chance." Jackie took the girl's face in her hands and looked straight into the tear-filled eyes. "You won't go back there. Those people don't deserve you, Alexandra Gerard. And don't you ever forget it. They don't deserve a girl as good as you."

Alex met her eyes for a long moment, then dashed a hand at her face, wiping away the tears. At last she got up and padded down the hall to the living room and her bed on the sofa.

18

Though it was still early in the morning, and the day after a major holiday, the fresh-produce plant was a busy place. Trucks arrived, loaded with vegetables, and backed up to ramps to unload. Workers labored in the shadow of a corrugated metal roof, sorting through mountains of onions and cucumbers and potatoes while supervisors carried clipboards and shouted instructions.

Jackie and Wardlow sat in the parked police car, watching a group of women in hair nets as they packed tomatoes into cardboard boxes. It was his turn to drive, and he drummed his fingers moodily on the steering wheel.

"Stop that," Jackie said, flipping through her notebook.

"Stop what?"

"That drumming thing you're always doing with your fingers. It makes me crazy."

"And you keep saying *I'm* irritable these days," he complained. "Besides, I'm entitled, don't you think? It's not like you're watching your whole world falling apart at your feet."

Jackie swiveled to face him. "What's—"

"Sarah didn't come home at all last night. I sat up in my chair until four o'clock, watching old movies on TV and waiting for her. She finally sneaked into the house just before dawn."

Jackie regarded his pale face and shadowed eyes in sympathy. "Did you confront her?"

"Of course. She said her friend Connie was going through a rough time, so she had to stay with her. They were at Connie's cabin by the lake and there was no phone."

"Do you believe her?"

He snorted and turned away to glare out the side window of the car.

"Actually," Jackie ventured, "that's sort of a good sign, Brian."

"What is?"

"The fact that she's still bothering to lie to you. It shows that no matter what she's doing, she's not ready for everything to be over."

Wardlow gave her a look of grim amusement. "You're really something, Kaminsky. Did you know that?"

"Why?"

"Because you can find something optimistic in everything, no matter how awful it is. You're just a regular little Pollyanna, with steel wheels and a handgun."

Jackie considered his words. "I had a pretty tough life," she said at last. "I guess Nietzsche was right. Whatever doesn't kill you makes you stronger."

"Nietzsche? Sounds like a sneeze."

Jackie grinned and punched his arm. "He was a German philosopher, and a very mellow dude. I should lend you the book. Shall we go in?" she added. "It's after eight-thirty."

He sighed. "Might as well. Time to waste our shift by pursuing the daily dead end."

"You know, I was thinking…"

Wardlow released the door handle and settled back in his seat. "What were you thinking, Kaminsky?"

"Arnussen keeps talking about the kid being underground. And this group…" She waved her hand at the vegetable-packing plant. "They run a kind of underground system, smuggling kids out of the country. So maybe they do have Michael."

Wardlow rolled his eyes. "Has that juvenile delinquent at your place been feeding you drugs? Now we're tracking down clues based on what the *psychic* says."

Jackie flushed with annoyance. "Look, quit acting that way. You're the one who said we should play Arnussen and see what happened."

"I said we should play him." Wardlow got out of the car and glared at a pile of cucumbers glistening in the morning sunlight. "I never said we should start believing him."

"Well, I really wish we could start believing somebody. Then maybe we could find Michael before it's too late."

They discovered their quarry in a cluttered office at the back of the plant. A stout middle-aged woman in a polyester pantsuit and metal-framed glasses, she had ragged graying hair that she probably cut herself.

Jackie displayed her shield and introduced herself and her partner. "May we sit down, Mrs. Albright?"

"I have nothing to say." The woman gestured at a couple of wooden chairs near the wall, then went on with her task, calmly entering rows of figures into a computer.

"We've traced the telephone numbers that Leigh Mellon gave us," Wardlow began. "She called you both here and at your home. We have no doubt you were the person she was in contact with."

Geraldine Albright looked up, the fluorescent light glittering on the lenses of her glasses. "I've never heard of Leigh Mellon," she said.

Jackie and her partner exchanged glances. "If you cooperate with us now," she said, "there'll be no further investigation of your personal involvement in this case."

"You're granting me immunity?"

"For this case. If you continue to smuggle kids out of the country illegally, we'll certainly have to get involved at some point in the future. But right now we're prepared to grant you immunity in the Michael Panesivic case if you can give us some information leading to his recovery."

"I can't give you any information. I don't know anything about it."

Jackie could sense Wardlow's impatience rising, the tensing of muscles in his jaw. She kicked his foot lightly and shot him a warning glance.

"I understand your motive, Mrs. Albright," she said. "Leigh Mellon has told me the philosophy of your group. You're committed to protecting parents from the agony of having a child abducted by the noncustodial parent. And you only deal with children you've determined to be at genuine risk of abduction."

"Stealing a child from the custodial parent is a cruel despicable crime," Mrs. Albright said. "My ex-husband did it to me a long time ago, depriving me of a lot of precious years with my daughter. I vowed that it would never happen to another woman if I could prevent it."

"So you make arrangements to grab the kids and take them to Canada, right? They don't need passports to enter Canada—just some kind of ID—and once they're out of the country, their custodial parent can rejoin them later and live in safety from the threatening parent."

"I don't do anything." The woman punched her keyboard. "I just work here at my job and live as a law-abiding citizen."

"Look, Mrs. Albright," Wardlow began angrily.

"I admire what you do," Jackie said in a soothing tone, giving her partner another warning glance.

He subsided, glowering, and flicked a ballpoint pen in his hand.

"I know you're motivated by an unselfish concern for custodial parents and their children. Leigh assures me that she believes you're absolutely sincere. But we're doing the investigation into this little boy's disappearance, and we need to know if there's any possibility he might still be with your group."

"I would never take a child and keep him without his parent's knowledge, Detective. I'd rather die. That's the very sort of pain I'm committed to ending."

Behind the thick glasses, Jackie could see the utter sincerity in the woman's eyes. Geraldine Albright was a fanatic, as Michelson had said, but completely devoted to the welfare of children.

"So it happened just the way you told Leigh? You had someone in position to snatch Michael from the toy store, but when your person went to pick him up, he was already gone. Is that true?"

The woman's face set. "We had nothing to do with this case."

"Okay," Jackie said. "Let's run through the scenario just for the sake of argument. What if you determined that Stefan Panesivic was an abduction risk, possibly even about to take his son to Europe against the mother's will. What if you made arrangements with Leigh Mellon to leave her child alone in the toy store at seven o'clock and you sent someone to pick him up. Let's just pretend all this happened, okay?"

The woman pounded steadily at her keyboard. A strand of hair fell over her eyes and she brushed it back, then went on typing.

"And then let's say Michael was there and the girl actually picked him up. Is there any reason in the world she'd keep him and not let his mother know where he is?"

Geraldine Albright dropped her hands onto her keyboard and looked at Jackie. She removed her glasses, revealing a pair of eyes that were large, brown and surprisingly soft.

"Detective Kaminsky," she said quietly, "look into my eyes. If I knew where Michael Panesivic was, I would tell his mother immediately. Nothing in the world could stop me from giving her that comfort, even if it meant that I myself would be charged with a crime and go to jail."

Jackie met the woman's gaze steadily.

"Do you believe me?" Mrs. Albright asked.

"Yes," Jackie said. "I believe that you don't know where he is. But do you have any suspicions? Could he possibly be with somebody else in your organization?"

"Not without my knowledge." Mrs. Albright gave them a wry smile. "I'm not saying it exists. But if it did, it would be a very, very small organization."

"So you don't—"

"I have nothing to say." The woman replaced her glasses and immediately took on a remote shuttered expression. "I know nothing whatever about the case you're working on, or any other case, and if asked I will deny that I said anything today."

She wheeled her chair around and began to look through a stack of files, deliberately ignoring the two police officers. They got up, murmured their goodbyes and left the office, walking back out through the mounds of fresh produce.

"*Do* you believe her?" Wardlow asked.

"I think so. You?"

He nodded. "She's telling the truth, all right. They don't have Michael. But I wonder…"

"What?" Jackie got into the passenger side of the police

cruiser and watched her partner settle himself behind the wheel.

"I wonder," Wardlow went on, "what made them so convinced that Stefan was a threat to abduct the kid. Did they just go on what Leigh said, or something they learned on their own?"

"Good point." Jackie made a note in her book. "But Mrs. Albright isn't about to confide in me, I'm afraid. I'll have to pay another visit to Leigh and to the professor as soon as I can make the appointments."

"You said Panesivic has agreed to a polygraph, right?"

"Absolutely. No problem at all. And no matter how often I check up on him, he always comes out as clean as a whistle."

"Shit," Wardlow said wearily. "You know, whatever we do, it all keeps leading back to your goddamn psychic. I wish we could arrest Paul Arnussen and torture him until he breaks."

"Unfortunately," Jackie said dryly, "those good old days of police work are over in this country."

"So you first saw the little boy in the mall?"

"Yes. In a store."

"Which store?"

"I forget. He was so beautiful. Such a beautiful little boy." Waldemar Koziak licked his lips and dashed a hand across his eyes.

Jackie and Wardlow exchanged glances, then returned their attention to the convicted pedophile who'd been at Northtown Mall the night Michael disappeared. While most of his crimes involved showing pornographic pictures to children and exposing himself at parks and playgrounds, a few involved actual fondling of little boys, and on one occasion he'd abducted a neighborhood boy of five. After several hours the child managed to escape and run home.

Koziak looked much older than his fifty-seven years. He had a jowly wrinkled face covered with gray stubble, flaccid lips and watery blue eyes, and smelled strongly of alcohol and a general lack of hygiene.

The patrol officers had delivered Koziak to the main police station for questioning after he broke down during an interview in a doughnut shop and confessed to the abduction of Michael Panesivic.

Jackie and her partner were alone with the man in a small interrogation room. The place was bare except for a wooden table and chairs and a closed-circuit television camera mounted in one corner near the ceiling.

"Would you like more coffee, Mr. Koziak?" Jackie moved her chair a little closer to him, trying to overcome her revulsion. "How about a cigarette?"

"I'd like a smoke."

Wardlow opened the pack on the table and shook out a cigarette, then pushed the ashtray closer.

Koziak lit the cigarette with trembling hands and flicked his eyes nervously around the room.

"Which store did you see him in?" Jackie asked.

"I can't remember. Somewhere in the mall."

"And you took him away with you?"

"Yes. He held my hand and walked away with me. He loved me."

"Where did you go?"

"To my place. We went to my place on the bus. He was such a sweet little boy."

"And then what happened?" Wardlow asked.

Koziak blew out a plume of smoke and stared at the ceiling, looking troubled. "I can't remember."

"Did you take him somewhere else?"

"I think he went away. I can't remember. I was sad when he left."

Jackie nodded at Wardlow, who opened a file on the table. "I've got some pictures here, Waldemar," he said. "I want you to look through them carefully and tell us which of these is the little boy who left the mall with you."

Wardlow took out eight photographs of children and arranged them on the table. One was the picture of Michael in his vest and bow tie.

Koziak lingered over the smiling faces, gazing at them hungrily. Finally he pointed to a boy of about eight, with blue eyes and a halo of blond curls.

"This one," he said. "This is the boy."

Jackie and Wardlow exchanged glances again. "You're positive?"

"I'm positive." Koziak touched the picture with a dirty forefinger, tracing the curve of the boy's cheek. "I'd know him anywhere. His eyes were as blue as the sky, and his hair was pale gold. It was so soft."

Wardlow gave Jackie a brief nod, then swept the photographs back into his file. "We have to leave now, Mr. Koziak. The officers will take you home."

"I'm not going to jail?"

"Not today. But you'd better stay away from little boys," Wardlow added, his voice suddenly icy and menacing. "If you ever touch another kid, we'll be on you so fast it'll make your head spin."

Koziak huddled in his chair and watched with frightened eyes as they left the room.

In the hallway, Jackie paused and gave her partner a worried look. "Are you sure he's lying?"

"He's not lying," Wardlow said grimly. "He's fantasizing. He really believes it happened just like he describes, but I've talked to him three times and there's no consistency to what he says. The man's a complete waste of time."

"You're probably right." Jackie shuddered. "But he's also a threat to society. I wish we could find some excuse to get him off the streets."

"Oh, but that's not how the system works, Detective Kaminsky. We have to let him roam around loose until he hurts or kills some little kid. Then we can put him away for a couple of years."

Jackie nodded, realizing the truth of her partner's words. "What are you doing next, Brian?"

He shrugged. "Back to the telephones, I guess. We've got at least three more of these creeps who don't have alibis and need to be checked out. And quite a few more tips came in over the holiday weekend after we ran the photograph again. How about you?"

"I'm going to drop in on Barbara Mellon without an appointment and see if I can surprise her into telling me anything. Then I'm going around to check on Arnussen at his job site. Do you need a ride?"

"No, thanks. I'll catch one of the patrol officers. Hey, Kaminsky..."

Jackie paused and looked over her shoulder. "What?"

"Watch your back, kid."

She smiled briefly and headed outside to her car, then drove across town to the tree-lined streets of the South Hill.

But there was nobody home at the Mellon residence. The big house basked silently in the afternoon sunlight, its brick facade lit with a rosy glow. Nobody answered the intercom at the front gate, and Jackie couldn't see any twitching of the drapes or shadows moving across the windows.

She got back into her car and stared at the mansion for a while, thinking. Finally she backed out of the driveway and headed down the street to the house where Paul Ar-

nussen appeared to be putting the finishing touches on the
new veranda.

Jackie parked at the curb and walked across the grass,
studying his handiwork. The fresh construction was
adorned with lacy gingerbread trim carved from yellow
pine, marching across the decorative woodwork on the
eaves of the house.

She assumed he'd done the fretwork somewhere else and
transported it here, because nobody could have finished this
intricate carving in such a few days. Except for the fact that
the new addition wasn't painted, there was no way to distinguish it from the rest of the house.

Arnussen was fitting dowels into the edge of the railing
and didn't see her approach.

"Very nice," Jackie said when he turned, clearly startled
to find her at his elbow. "Your carpentry, I mean."

"Thank you, Detective." He put his hammer into his
tool belt. "Just out for an afternoon drive, are you?"

"I came over to visit Mrs. Mellon, but she's not home."

"I see." He hefted a piece of doweling and squinted
down its length, then carried the wood up the porch stairs
to a small table saw. "Any progress in your investigation?"

"Not really. We've had another confession, but we get
one of those almost every day."

Arnussen cut lengths from the doweling, measuring carefully, and placed the little cylinders in a row on the railing.

"What are you doing next?" Jackie asked.

He glanced down at her from under the brim of his cap.
"What do you mean?"

She waved her hand at the veranda. "You're almost finished here, right? I just wondered if you had another job
lined up."

"I'm considering a few options. Maybe I'll take a holiday."

"That sounds nice."

He smiled without humor. "Does it?"

"Everybody likes holidays."

"How would you know, Detective? You work all weekend, all summer, all the time. What would you know about holidays?"

Jackie looked away briefly, troubled by the probing directness of his gaze. "I've heard that people enjoy them."

"You're not alone anymore," he said abruptly, still studying her face. "But you're still lonely."

She stiffened in alarm. "What are you talking about?"

"Somebody's living with you. There's somebody in your house right now."

"How do you know that?"

He shrugged and returned to his job. "I've always been able to see your loneliness. It's like a cloud around your head. But now you've got another person in your life, and you're not sure what to do. It's not a comfort, it's just a problem."

Jackie stared at him in outrage, feeling violated. "What's your game, Arnussen?" she demanded in a low shaking voice. "Have you been following me? Are you watching my apartment?"

"I don't have to follow you, Jackie," he said quietly. "I can tell all kinds of things about you just by looking at your face."

"I don't believe any of that crap!" she said furiously. "In fact, I don't think you're any more psychic than this post!" She slapped the palm of her hand against one of the fluted veranda columns. "And I'm warning you, Arnussen…"

His face hardened. "Don't warn me about anything, okay? You've been making a lot of threats, and I don't appreciate them. Just back off."

"I'll back off when we find Michael Panesivic. Until then, I'm going to be in your face every time you turn around."

He swept the lengths of wood into his hand and brushed past her as he headed for the side of the veranda. Jackie moved aside hastily to let him pass, conscious of the hard musculature of his body and the strange concentrated power of the man.

She walked away from the house, shaken. After a moment she moved down across the grass to her car while Paul Arnussen turned his back with calm deliberation and went on fitting dowels into the wooden railing.

19

Sunlight shimmered on the surface of the water, breaking into thousands of tiny diamonds. Leigh stared at the turquoise depths of the pool and thought wistfully about drowning.

It would be so easy to slip down...down...until those shining waters closed over her head forever. After a few seconds of panic, her thoughts and feelings would cease and all the pain would be gone.

The pain would be gone...

She curled in the chaise longue and whimpered, clutching a teddy bear in her arms. The bear was Michael's favorite toy next to Dixie Duck, and had been cuddled and played with so much over the years that two of its waistcoat buttons were missing and the plush was wearing thin in places.

Adrienne approached from the house, carrying glasses of lemonade and a plate of cookies. She placed the tray on the umbrella table.

"Why don't you come in for a swim?" she asked, taking off a wrap skirt and stepping out of her sandals. "The water's beautiful."

Leigh looked up at her sister's tanned body, poised at the edge of the pool. "What day is it, Rennie?"

"It's Thursday. Have some lemonade."

Leigh shook her head, squinting into the sunlight. "How long have I been here?"

"A couple of days. Are you all right, honey?"

"I can't remember anything. It feels like my head is made of cotton."

Adrienne moved closer and touched her forehead. "Hey, those pills they're giving you must be some pretty potent stuff," she said lightly. "Maybe I should make you share your drugs, kid."

"He's dead, isn't he? My baby's dead."

"Of course he isn't. He's just hidden somewhere. They'll find him."

Leigh ignored this. "If Michael's dead, I don't want to go on living. I don't know how anybody could ever live with this kind of suffering."

"Don't talk like that." Adrienne came to kneel by the lounge. "You have to be strong, Leigh. You have to be strong for Michael's sake. When the police find him and bring him home, he's going to be scared and confused. He's going to need you there to comfort him."

"I try to imagine them bringing him home." Again Leigh stared at the glistening pool. "I keep trying to picture what it would be like, but I can't. All I can see is emptiness."

"Oh, Leigh..." Adrienne put her arms around her sister.

Leigh burrowed into the embrace and began to cry, with gulping heartbroken sobs that racked her body and burned painfully in her throat.

Jackie rounded the corner of the house and found them together. When Adrienne saw the newcomer, she moved hastily away from the lounge and stood, glowering.

"Don't you call ahead, Detective?"

"Not always." Jackie looked down at Leigh, who was

still weeping, the teddy bear clutched in her arms. "Hello, Leigh," she said, touching the woman's shoulder.

Leigh wiped her eyes with her sleeve and pulled herself upright in the lounge. Jackie was shocked at the way she looked. Her beautiful finely drawn face was haggard, her eyes so red and swollen they were like wounds.

"Have you heard anything?" Leigh asked, reaching out to clutch Jackie's arm. "Has anything happened?"

"Not yet." Jackie sat in a chair next to Leigh. She let the warm sunlight fall on her face and dropped her notebook into her lap.

Adrienne had dived into the pool and was swimming furiously up and down its length. Jackie and Leigh watched the woman's sleek dark head and slender body cut through the water.

"Leigh," Jackie said after a couple of minutes, "do you know where your parents are today?"

Leigh rolled her head listlessly on the cushion. "My parents?"

Adrienne drew herself out of the pool and reached for a towel, crossing the tiles toward them.

"What's this?" she said. "What are you asking her?"

"About your parents. I just wondered where they've gone."

"Why?"

"Because I went to the house yesterday afternoon and there was nobody home. When I called your mother this morning, I got the recording, and when I stopped by on the way over here, there was still no answer at the intercom."

"They've gone away for a couple of days." Adrienne wiped herself down with the towel and settled into another of the deck chairs. "They left on Tuesday afternoon."

Jackie's eyebrows rose. "Kind of an odd time to take a holiday, isn't it?"

"Leigh, honey," Adrienne said with apparent noncha-
lance, "could you please go into the house and find my
sunglasses? I think I left them on the sideboard in the
foyer."

Leigh got up listlessly and trudged into the house.

"It's not necessarily an odd time," Adrienne said after
her sister was out of earshot. "Mother is always very pro-
tective of Daddy. He's used to having Michael around the
house, and he's been getting upset at not seeing him.
Mother thought a change of scene might help to distract
him."

"So where did they go?"

"Over to Kalispell. They're staying at a resort on Flat-
head Lake."

Jackie recalled Paul Arnussen's quick trip to Kalispell
just after Michael's disappearance. The hair prickled on her
neck.

"Do your parents own a property on the lake?"

"Not anymore. They used to, but it was too hard to
maintain after Daddy...after he got sick. So now they just
rent a condo when they want to get away."

"I see," Jackie said. "And when do you expect them
back?"

"Tonight. Mother's been calling twice a day, and she
can't stand to be away any longer. She's just too anxious
about Michael. So they're coming home."

"Is Monica with them?"

"Of course," Adrienne said. "Mother wouldn't go anywhere without Monica."

"I see." Jackie made a note in her book while Adrienne
watched.

Leigh came back with the sunglasses, still holding the
teddy bear under her arm. She handed Adrienne the glasses
and curled on the chaise longue again, gazing at the water.

"Leigh," Jackie said, "could I ask you something?"

Leigh was silent, rubbing her chin slowly on the teddy bear's head.

"The people you contacted about helping you smuggle Michael out of the country," Jackie said. "I was wondering what you told them about Stefan."

Adrienne cast Jackie a startled glance, but Leigh didn't respond at all.

"I mean," Jackie went on, "how did you convince them that Stefan was likely to abduct Michael? Did you tell them something you haven't told me? Did he make any kind of specific threat, or do anything that..."

Her voice trailed off. Leigh still made no response. She held the toy in her arms and stared vacantly at the water.

Adrienne glanced at Jackie again, then inclined her head toward the gate. Jackie got up and followed her around the corner of the house.

"Sorry about that," Adrienne muttered, pausing by a massive growth of silvery juniper. "But you have to understand what it's like for her. I'm afraid she's practically going out of her mind."

"I know. Try to keep her talking, Adrienne. It's better than letting her sink deeper into this kind of brooding. And if she says anything that might be helpful, let me know right away, okay?"

"What's this? Now I'm assisting the police in their investigation?" Adrienne gave her a humorless smile.

"I hope so." Jackie didn't return the smile. "In this case, we need all the help we can get."

She let herself out through the gate and walked down the front path, conscious of Adrienne watching her as she got into the car and drove away.

* * *

A couple of hours later, Jackie paid a visit to the offices of Thorne, Thorne, Blake and Calder, where Adrienne's husband was a partner and a specialist in corporate law.

She sat in the waiting room, wondering what the man would be like. It was a game she often played, trying to construct the image of a subject based on the other people in his life and the things she'd been told about him. She imagined him a rather stuffy man in the prime of life, probably beginning to show signs of too much food and too much alcohol.

But when she was ushered into his office, her picture turned out to be completely wrong.

Harlan Calder was tall and thin, with a bald head and a silver beard, neatly trimmed. His eyes were set in good-natured creases, but keen and alert, and his face was gentle. He wore a pair of khaki trousers, an open-necked white sport shirt and a baggy cardigan with leather elbow patches, and looked much more like Jackie's image of a college professor than Stefan Panesivic did.

He also appeared to be about fifteen years older than his wife. All in all, their pairing seemed so bizarre that Jackie was briefly at a loss for words.

"Sorry, Detective." He stood courteously to shake her hand and indicated one of the leather chairs opposite his desk. "I didn't mean to keep you waiting, but everybody's still running on holiday time. Three of my appointments have been late today."

"That's fine," Jackie told him. "I was only waiting for a few minutes."

He steepled his fingers and regarded her pleasantly.

"I was at your house this morning," Jackie began, searching for a way to start their interview and get a measure of the man behind the desk. "Leigh seems very upset."

"Poor Leigh. It must be hell, having a child go missing.

And she's not always emotionally strong at the best of times."

"I suppose Adrienne is the stronger sister of the two."

Calder looked up in mild surprise. "What makes you think so?"

"I don't know. She just seems like a confident woman, I suppose."

"Another of those instances where appearances can be deceiving."

Jackie studied him with interest. "You mean Adrienne isn't strong and confident?"

"My wife puts up a brave front, but her reality is somewhat different. She's a very complex woman."

Jackie considered his words, wondering how far to take the line of questioning. "Has Adrienne's relationship with her mother always been so strained?" she asked at last.

Calder leaned back and smiled, though his eyes remained watchful. "You're very perceptive."

"Not really. Talking to people is my job, most of the time."

"And separating lies from truth?"

Jackie looked at him levelly. "Yes. That's my job, too."

He glanced out the window at the city skyline. "Barbara has been deeply angry with Adrienne for as long as I've known them. She generally tries to hide her feelings and present an impression of family solidarity, but she's not always successful."

"Why is she angry?"

"Because she's a controller, and Adrienne refuses to be controlled. Leigh was always more...malleable."

"What made Adrienne so rebellious?"

The lawyer continued to gaze into the distance. "I think it's simply part of her personality. The dysfunctional aspect of their relationship started in her early childhood and developed into a truly vicious circle. Adrienne was the first child, and Barbara wanted to control and dominate her every move. When she couldn't, she withdrew and became cold. Then Adrienne was forced to act out in an attempt to get a little of her mother's attention, and the situation escalated from there.''

"Is it still going on? I mean, is Adrienne still acting out?''

"I don't think so. I hope she's begun to move past the pain of her mother's rejection.'' He turned to face Jackie again, and his voice was suddenly cool. "Is any of this relevant to Michael's situation, Detective?''

"That depends on whether any of the family members are involved in his disappearance.''

"Do you think that's a possibility?''

"Certainly I do. Statistics tell us that very, very few small children are ever abducted by strangers, Mr. Calder.''

"I know. I've spent some time the last few days consulting the data,'' he said, surprising her. "But why do you suspect Leigh's family? Wouldn't the father's side be the obvious abductors, since he's the noncustodial parent?''

Jackie thought about Leigh's futile attempt to have her little boy smuggled out of the country. "At this stage in an investigation,'' she said, "we have to go further than the obvious suspects. Every possibility has to be explored.''

Calder was silent for a moment, then he nodded and said, "I can only speak for Adrienne. I don't know about the others, but I can assure you that my wife hasn't done anything wrong.''

Jackie glanced briefly at her notes, then decided to take a wild shot and see what happened. "Mrs. Mellon suggested to me that Adrienne probably knows Stefan Panesivic better than any of the rest of the family.''

Harlan Calder picked up a pen. Jackie saw his knuckles whiten. "When did she say that?"

"Soon after Michael disappeared, when I went over to talk with her."

"Damn the woman!"

His outburst seemed so uncharacteristic that Jackie looked at him with interest.

He toyed with the pen in brooding silence, then met her eyes. "My wife had a brief affair with Stefan a few years ago," he said quietly. "But I didn't realize Barbara was aware of it."

Jackie's jaw dropped in astonishment. She recovered hastily. "Adrienne had an affair with her sister's husband?"

"Don't look so shocked, Detective. Sexual sins, even within families, aren't terribly unusual, you know."

"I suppose not. But your kind of tolerance is pretty unusual. You've forgiven her?"

"I love my wife."

The statement was simple, but it spoke volumes.

Jackie looked into his eyes and found herself deeply moved. The man's face spoke of suffering and forgiveness, and a love so enduring it went far beyond words.

"What happened?" she asked.

"It was around the time that Michael was born. I suppose Stefan was frustrated because his sexual relationship with Leigh had been curtailed by the pregnancy. And Adrienne was consumed with misery during most of Leigh's pregnancy."

"Because she wanted a child of her own?"

"She always has. When Leigh, who's five years younger, conceived so quickly after her marriage and bloomed throughout the pregnancy, Adrienne was very ambivalent about it. She was happy for her sister of course, but more upset than ever that we didn't have a child of our own.''

Jackie waited in silence while he stared out the window.

"I think,'' he went on, "that Adrienne became totally obsessed with Stefan during those months. She saw him as the potent male figure, the giver of life. I believe the combination of circumstances and emotions was just too explosive for either of them to contain.''

"How did you find out?''

"Adrienne told me. She was in agony, consumed with guilt. She suggested that I would probably want a divorce, and she wouldn't stand in my way.''

"But you didn't want a divorce?''

"I wanted the affair to end. I told my wife so, and she agreed. She promised that if I would forgive her and resume our marriage, she'd make certain that she was never alone with the man again.''

"And she's kept her word?''

"Yes. After a rather difficult few months, we managed to put the whole episode behind us and carry on. We've never spoken of it since. I had no idea that Barbara knew,'' he repeated.

"Do you think it's possible that Adrienne confided in her mother?''

Calder shook his head. "I doubt that Adrienne has confided anything to her mother since she was five years old. I don't know how Barbara found out, but it wasn't through my wife. She probably just guessed. She's a very keen observer.''

"Does Leigh know about it?''

"Absolutely not. The family has a long-established habit of protecting Leigh from anything upsetting. And in those early years she was completely besotted with Stefan.

Knowledge of his unfaithfulness, especially with her sister… It would have killed her.''

"Was Stefan unfaithful with other women?''

"I have no idea,'' Calder said, his face cold. "I don't involve myself in that kind of gossip.''

Jackie nodded. "I wish I could get a handle on Leigh and Stefan's marriage,'' she said. "I can't seem to form any kind of reliable picture of their relationship. The image keeps changing depending on who's talking to me.''

"All marriages are like that to some extent,'' the lawyer said. "A marriage is a very private country, you know. Only the inhabitants can really know what goes on within its borders.''

She thought about Harlan Calder's own relationship, his beautiful brash young wife and the depth of a love that could survive her betrayal.

Jackie felt suddenly wistful, and very much alone.

"You realize,'' he went on carefully, "that I expect anything discussed between us today to remain confidential. I've only told you all this in hopes that a better knowledge of the family situation might help you to find Michael.''

"Of course.'' Jackie took the photograph of Paul Arnussen from her notebook and handed it across the desk. "Have you ever seen this man, Mr. Calder?''

He studied the picture, then shook his head. "I don't think so.''

Jackie returned the photograph to her book, stood up and reached across the desk to shake Calder's hand. "Thank you,'' she said. "You've been very helpful.''

He came out from behind the desk and walked with her to the door. "If there's anything else I can do, don't hesitate to let me know.''

"Thanks.'' Jackie opened the door and started down the

paneled corridor, then turned around. "As I told your wife this morning, Mr. Calder, we need all the help we can get."

Stefan Panesivic was packing. Jackie stood in the foyer of his apartment and looked at the piles of boxes, the mounds of books and assorted belongings.

He moved back to the center of the room and began tossing books into a cardboard box. It was a job he'd apparently been occupied with when she rang from the lobby.

"I'm making some changes in my life," he said abruptly. "I have to do something. I'm going out of my mind with worry."

Jackie watched him in concern. Stefan's handsome face was haggard. Even his body seemed thinner, as if he'd lost weight, including muscle, since she'd first spoken with him. "Where are you moving?"

"I'm looking for a house. This stuff is going into storage until I find the right place."

"Isn't that a bit out of sequence?" Jackie asked.

He glanced at a book, leafing quickly though the pages, then grimaced and threw it into the box along with the others. "What do you mean?"

"Isn't it customary to find the new place and then move?"

"They have a tenant for the apartment. When I told them I wasn't prepared to sign another lease, the manager asked if I could vacate by the middle of the month."

"So you're looking for a house?"

"Michael's going to need more space than this. He needs a fenced yard to play in and a room of his own."

"Michael?" she asked, startled.

Stefan dropped another armful of books into the box, then looked up at her. "He's coming back, Detective, even though it's becoming rather obvious that you can't find him. I'm going to go out and start looking on my own. I plan to find my son. And when I do, I'm keeping him. Leigh's certainly demonstrated that she's not fit to have custody."

"Stefan, you told me your marriage was perfect in the beginning, then it went bad. Was it because you lost interest?"

Stefan gave her a sharp glance. "Aren't you getting a little beyond the scope of your investigation, Detective?"

"The solution to any case lies in the relationships between the people involved. And your marriage is at the center of everything."

"How could it be? My marriage doesn't exist. Maybe it never did."

"What do you mean?"

"Maybe it was all a romantic fiction in Leigh's mind. She was very young, and not an experienced woman. She thought we'd wander off into the sunset together and live happily ever after. She knew so little about life."

"Did her naiveté start to bore you?"

His jaw set and he turned away. Jackie could see that she wasn't going to get any further with this line of questioning.

"Why was Leigh afraid of you?" she asked.

"I don't believe she was afraid of me. I never laid a hand on her."

"I don't mean physically. She wasn't allowing you access to Michael, so you had to go to court and fight to see him. What made her afraid you were going to abduct him?"

"Probably her mother. I'm sure it was something that Barbara Mellon stirred up, just to set Leigh against me. The woman's always hated me."

Jackie considered this. "You think it was Barbara's idea

to deny you access and charge that you were an abduction threat?''

"I wouldn't doubt it. The whole thing sounds more like Barbara's style. Leigh's never been a vindictive woman, but the rest of the Mellons like to play hardball.''

He left the room and came back with a stack of tissue paper, which he used to wrap a collection of Japanese netsukes from one of the bookshelves. Jackie watched while he stored the figurines away in one corner of the box.

Finally she took the photograph of Paul Arnussen from her notebook and carried it across the room, holding it out for Stefan's inspection. "Have you by any chance remembered where you saw this man?''

He glanced at the picture, then at Jackie. "Why do you keep asking about him?''

"Because it might be important.''

He sighed and ran a hand though his hair again, then concentrated on the photograph. "Isn't this the man you brought to my parents' farm the other day? Your so-called psychic.''

"Yes, it is. But you thought you recognized him before that day. When I showed you the picture, you said he looked vaguely familiar.''

He moved closer and gave her a probing look. "What's going on, Detective?''

"Do you remember seeing him anywhere else?''

"Not that I can recall. I must have been mistaken.''

"All right.'' She put the snapshot and notebook away in her bag. "If you remember anything, could you give me a call?''

Stefan took her arm and stared down at her, his eyes blazing with anger. "Quit screwing around, Detective,'' he said softly. "Go out there and find my son. I'm running out of patience. If this goes on much longer, I can't be held accountable for my actions."

20

Jackie awoke from a troubled sleep and lay in the morning stillness, trying to recall her dream. She couldn't recapture the images, except that Paul Arnussen was somehow involved.

Gradually she became aware of a noise that carried faintly through the silence of the apartment. Alex was sobbing in her bed on the couch, unsuccessfully trying to muffle the heartbreaking sounds in her pillow.

Jackie lay tensely in her own bed, looking at the open door. She was actually a little relieved to hear the girl crying. Until now, Alex had exhibited a degree of composure that was unnatural and troubling, considering what she'd been through. Although Jackie had been expecting some kind of emotional breakdown, she still didn't know what to do about it.

Instinct told her not to go into the living room and take the girl in her arms. She knew that Alex didn't want to be comforted. She wanted to endure, to impress Jackie with her strength.

Jackie waited until the sobbing stopped and she heard Alex climb out of bed, come down the hall to use the bathroom and then go to the kitchen. After Alex was clear of the bathroom, Jackie hurried through her own daily routine of showering and dressing.

Still in her stocking feet, she padded out to the kitchen filled with the delicious aroma of fresh-brewed coffee.

Alex looked up and smiled wanly, then went on placing pots of jam and honey on the table, lining them up next to the boxes of cereal.

She wore a pair of Jackie's denim cutoffs, a baggy cotton shirt and socks, and had her hair tied back in a ponytail. Her face was pale but calm, and all traces of her recent tears had been scrubbed away.

Jackie seated herself and took a slice of buttered toast from her plate, then reached for the strawberry jam. "So, what are you doing today?" she asked.

"Cleaning the cupboards. I'm going to take every single thing out of every cabinet, wash down all the shelves and then arrange stuff neatly."

Jackie grimaced and took a sip of coffee. "I hate to think of you wasting a beautiful summer day on a job like that. Why can't you go down to the park and hang around smoking and being obnoxious like other kids?"

"I like housework. If I get time, I'm going to wash the windows, too. And next week I'm cleaning out the storage closet."

Jackie thought about those heartbroken sobs and felt a deep wave of sadness. "Honey," she said gently, "you know I love having you here. But no matter how good you are or how hard you work, I can't keep you indefinitely. We have to find you a proper home."

"Why? I won't cause you any problems, Jackie. I promise."

"But it's no kind of life for you. You need a normal home. You need company for more than half an hour a day, and people around to talk with, and some stable surroundings."

"This is fine," Alex said earnestly. "Honest it is. Pretty

soon the summer will be over and I'll be back in school, and then I'll be busy all day long.''

Jackie gave up for the moment and ate her breakfast. By the time she left the apartment, Alex was already squatting on the kitchen floor, emptying the cabinets under the sink.

On the way to work, Jackie frowned at the morning traffic and wondered what to do with her houseguest. None of the standard police solutions for young runaways seemed appropriate for Alex, a beautiful, brainy, sweet-natured child who couldn't go home.

She parked at the substation and attended the daily briefing session, where an air of palpable tension between Michelson and Wardlow made everybody uncomfortable. The two of them had evidently had an argument recently. Both were still edgy and curt.

But then, everybody was feeling edgy these days. Their failure to make any progress in the Panesivic case was getting to them. To make things worse, Michelson handed around copies of an editorial from one of the local newspapers, attacking the police for their ''fumbling ineptitude'' in the investigation and their ''cavalier lack of interest'' when a child's life was at stake.

Jackie read the article in grim silence, wondering if the Mellon family was behind it. When the briefing ended, she gathered together her shoulder bag and files, coordinated schedules with Wardlow and left the office, heading across town to the South Hill.

It appeared the Mellons had indeed come home last night as Adrienne had said. The intercom buzzer was answered at once and the gate swung open. Jackie drove up and parked, then hurried to the front door where Monica waited to admit her to the foyer.

''How was Kalispell?'' Jackie asked casually. ''The lake must be beautiful this time of year.''

Monica gave her a level inscrutable glance. "We were all far too upset to enjoy the lake," she said in her softly accented voice. "Mrs. Mellon is practically beside herself with worry."

She turned and walked off, motioning for Jackie to follow her through the luxurious rooms. They arrived in the room with the windows, but Barbara Mellon wasn't working at her loom on this balmy Friday morning. She sat by a window in a beige silk dressing gown with a coffee mug balanced in her lap, and gazed out at the trailing leaves of a willow tree near the greenhouse.

Monica left Jackie at the door and gave her a significant warning look, then vanished down the hallway. Jackie stepped into the room.

"Good morning, Mrs. Mellon," she said. "How are you today?"

Barbara looked up sharply, almost spilling her coffee. Jackie was shocked by the change in the woman. During the few days since they'd last talked, Barbara Mellon seemed to have aged about twenty years. Her face was drawn and pale, her eyes heavily shadowed with fatigue.

This was, without a doubt, the face of a person going through almost unendurable anguish. Jackie felt an impulsive flood of sympathy.

"I'm so sorry," she murmured. "I wish we could find him, too. Your suffering must be unbearable."

"It is," Barbara whispered. "I'm sure you're doing your best, Detective. It's all just…just so hard."

Her voice caught, and Jackie was afraid the woman was going to start crying. But Barbara regained control of herself with a visible effort, then set the coffee mug on a nearby table and gripped her hands tightly together in her lap.

"Alden is probably suffering more than I am," she said,

looking through the windows again. Jackie could see the distant figure moving amongst the flower beds behind the greenhouse. "He can't understand, you see. He doesn't know why Michael can't be here, and I don't know what to tell him."

All the pointed questions Jackie had planned to ask seemed to vanish from her mind. She couldn't believe the woman was faking this kind of emotion. And in the light of Barbara Mellon's agony, it seemed callous to interrogate her about the abrupt trip to Kalispell, about Paul Arnussen or her relationship with her former son-in-law.

"You seem very upset," Jackie ventured at last, sitting in a chair next to her hostess. "You didn't feel this way at first, Mrs. Mellon. You were convinced that Stefan had abducted Michael, and your grandson was probably safe."

"I know I was. But Stefan's still…he's still here, you see, and you haven't found Michael. I've begun to believe I was wrong about Stefan's being the abductor." Barbara turned to Jackie, her face tragic. "And the alternative is…simply unthinkable."

Jackie looked down at her notebook, wondering if Barbara Mellon had ever before suffered so profoundly. Apparently her love for her little grandson went deeper than her feelings for either of her daughters.

Or perhaps the stresses of life and her husband's illness were finally mellowing the woman, making her vulnerable like everybody else.

Jackie took the picture of Paul Arnussen from her notebook and handed it to Barbara. "Have you ever seen this man?"

Barbara took the photograph, clearly grateful for the distraction, and studied it carefully. "No," she said at last. "I've never seen him."

Her burst of energy faded. She turned back to the window again, and her shoulders began to quiver under the silk of her dressing gown. Jackie pulled her chair closer and put a hand on the woman's arm. They sat together quietly, watching as the lawn sprinklers sent bright rainbows cascading into the summer air.

Outside in her car, Jackie gripped the wheel and tried to decide what to do next. She drove out through the wrought-iron gates of the property and watched in the rearview mirror as they drifted shut behind her. Then she pulled over to the curb and opened her notebook, frowning.

The words of that newspaper editorial kept ringing inside her head. *Fumbling ineptitude, cavalier lack of interest...*

Was that really the way the public saw the police? Didn't they have any concept of the hours that were being logged, the dozens of people who were sacrificing their holidays and upsetting family plans, the other cases that were being backed up, all in an effort to find this missing child? Apparently not, Jackie thought bitterly. She closed the notebook and sat tapping her fingers on the wheel, thinking.

Right from the start, instinct had told her that the key to the abduction lay somewhere within the two families, and that Paul Arnussen was probably also involved. But the more she investigated, the less sure she was about anything.

And over it all was the maddening sense that she was missing something vitally important. As the days went on with no sign of Michael's whereabouts, the impression strengthened, taunting her from the shadowy region just beyond her conscious mind. Sometimes the frustration was so intense she almost screamed.

At last she shook her head, put the car in gear and pulled off down the shaded avenue, intending to take the street that ran past Helen Philps's house because it was the shortest way back to the north side.

But when she turned the corner and glanced down the street, Jackie's hands froze on the wheel and her heart began to pound noisily.

Paul Arnussen's dark blue truck was parked in front of the Philps' home.

Jackie edged forward, then pulled into a spot at the curb under a spreading elm, about half a block away from Arnussen's truck. She got out her notebook and checked the license plate to confirm the identity of the vehicle, then put on her sunglasses and settled back to wait.

After about fifteen minutes, Arnussen came striding down the walk and paused at the back of his truck to open the tailgate. He wasn't looking at Jackie's car, but she slid low enough in the seat that her head wouldn't be clearly visible through the shadows if he happened to turn around.

Arnussen was dressed for work in jeans and heavy lace-up boots, with a denim shirt and the faded baseball cap he always wore. He leaned inside the truck to adjust some of the tools, then closed the tailgate and glanced around.

His eyes rested for a moment on the unmarked police car down the street, but there was no flicker of recognition. At last he rounded the truck to the driver's side, got in and drove off.

After he was gone, Jackie drove forward and parked in the spot he'd just vacated, wondering how to handle this situation. Especially when she hadn't the slightest idea what Arnussen's presence here meant.

She removed her sunglasses and tossed them onto the dashboard, took her notebook and started up the walk, deciding at the last minute to go round to the back where she knew the kitchen door was.

The backyard was as pleasant as she'd remembered. The bronze weather vane turned lazily in the breeze, masses of flowers glowed on fences and trellises, and the lawn was damp and fragrant from a recent watering. Helen worked in the garden, wearing her big straw hat and a pair of baggy shorts that revealed slim freckled legs. She was tying tomato plants with twine to some stakes.

"Hello," Jackie called, shading her eyes with her hand as she peered into the sunny garden. "How are you today, Ms. Philps?"

Helen got up and stripped off her gardening gloves, then came through the rows of plants to meet Jackie at the back door. "Good morning, Detective. Please—call me Helen," she said. "It's such a lovely day, isn't it?" she said.

But her expression belied the cheerfulness of her words. Helen Philps looked as miserable as most of the other people involved in the case. Her delicate freckled face was taut and strained, almost frightened-looking, and her eyes were heavily ringed with dark shadows.

She pulled off the straw hat, allowing her long plait of hair to tumble down her back. "The curse of redheads," she said to Jackie. "If I don't wear a hat all the time, I turn into a boiled lobster."

Jackie nodded sympathetically.

"Have you found out anything about Michael?" Helen asked.

"We're making some progress," Jackie said. "Could we go inside for a minute?"

"Of course. I'll make some lemonade."

"I don't need any refreshments." Jackie followed her into the kitchen. "I only have a few questions to ask you. Please don't go to any trouble."

Helen didn't argue, just paused to wash her hands at the sink, then sat down opposite Jackie at the wooden table.

"When I arrived here a few minutes ago," Jackie said, "a man was just leaving. Did you talk with him?"

"Mr. Arnussen, you mean?"

"Yes." Jackie took out the photograph. "Last time I was here, I showed you this picture. You had a feeling you recognized the man, but you didn't recall his name."

Helen examined the photograph in obvious surprise. "It's the same man," she said, glancing up at Jackie. "I'd forgotten all about this." She studied the picture again.

"Why was he here today, Helen?"

"He's going to fix the roof. He came by a couple of days ago and told me there was a lot of wear on the shingles, and he'd like to quote for the job."

"So you hired him, just like that?"

"Of course not. He gave me the names of some other people in the neighborhood that he's worked for. They're mostly friends and acquaintances of ours, so I didn't mind calling a few of them up to see what kind of work the man does. Everybody gave him glowing references. His price was fair, and those old shingles really do need to be replaced. I finally contracted with him this morning to do the work."

Jackie made some notes. "When does he begin?"

"Tomorrow."

"He's starting this big project on a Saturday morning?"

Helen nodded. "He said he didn't mind working through the weekend because after this job, he's going to take a long holiday."

"I see."

Helen looked up again, clearly startled by the grim tone in Jackie's voice.

Before either of them could speak, the doorbell rang. Helen jumped a little in her chair and looked at the clock.

"That must be the paperboy," she said. "He always comes by to collect on a— Damn, I don't have any change unless I..." She pushed the chair back, looking distracted. "Could you excuse me for a minute, Detective?"

"No problem," Jackie said. "I'll wait here and update my notes."

While she was working at the kitchen table, Grace Philps wandered into the kitchen. The old lady wore a flowered cotton dress and cardigan and a pair of leather moccasins. She headed for the fridge, shuffling across the hardwood floor, then stopped when she saw Jackie.

"You're the policewoman," she said.

"Yes, I am."

"Beg pardon?"

Jackie introduced herself loudly and the old woman nodded.

"Do you still have your gun?" Grace asked, leaning closer. Jackie could smell the faint tang of a medicated cream, mixed with some kind of perfume.

She drew back her blazer to reveal the side holster. Grace Philps peered at the handle of the gun in fascination, then gave a satisfied nod.

"I wish you'd shoot him," she muttered, glancing over her shoulder at the door. "You should just shoot him like a bad dog."

"Shoot who, Mrs. Philps?"

Jackie heard the sound of running footsteps on the stairs. Helen had apparently gone upstairs to find some money for the paperboy.

"That man," Grace said in a hoarse whisper. "He was here again, you know."

"The man who's going to fix the roof?"

"He's a bad man," Grace went on. "It's not right that he comes here after dark and slips into her room. It's a sin, and she knows it."

Jackie's head began to spin. "That man comes here at night?"

"Bad things are happening." The old woman's face

crumpled, and tears coursed slowly down her wrinkled cheeks. "I'm afraid."

"Let's go for a ride in my car," Jackie suggested. "We can talk about what's bothering you."

"No!" The old woman cringed in alarm, then glared at her. "I don't want to talk to you about anything."

"But if you—"

"No!" Grace shouted, her face turning pink with anger.

Jackie dug into one of her jacket pockets and took out a business card. She looked furtively down the hall, then pressed the card into Grace's veined hand and leaned close to the ear with the hearing aid.

"If anything frightens you, call me at that number and I'll come right away," she said distinctly. "Do you understand?"

The old woman nodded and gripped the card, staring vacantly at Jackie.

"Even if you just want to talk with me," Jackie went on, feeling a little desperate as she heard Helen's quick footsteps approaching from the foyer. "You'll call me, won't you, Mrs. Philps?"

"Mama?" Helen asked sharply. "What are you doing out here? I thought you were still watching your game show."

"That show is stupid," Grace said, her expression turning sulky. "They're all stupid. I was hungry," she added, "and there's never any decent food in this house."

Helen's face tightened with impatience. She sighed and went to the fridge. While her back was turned, Grace slid the card into the pocket of her cardigan.

Jackie watched the two women arguing in their big, old-fashioned kitchen. She stared at Grace's fluffy white head, wondering if the old woman was delusional. It was certainly hard to believe that Paul Arnussen was slipping into this house at night to make love to Helen Philps.

But then, she told herself wearily, a lot of things about this case were hard to believe.

21

Saturday morning, Jackie arrived early at the office and got herself a cup of coffee. She sat down at her desk and began to page through her files with concentrated attention, trying to memorize every detail, to make sense of all the conflicting stories she'd heard.

"Eleven days," Wardlow muttered, sliding into his chair.

"Hmm?" Jackie frowned as she studied one of Leigh Mellon's statements.

"It's been eleven consecutive days, Kaminsky, since we've had a day off."

"And more than a week since Michael went missing," Jackie said. "How are you doing?"

He gave her a bitter smile. "Professionally or personally?"

Jackie leaned back and stretched her arms over her head. "Both, I guess."

"Well, my home life sure isn't getting any better. I hardly see my wife anymore."

"And you still haven't really talked to her?"

"Hell, I wouldn't know what to say, even if I could ever find more than a couple of minutes to spend with her."

"Brian—"

"And this goddamn case," he went on, glaring at his desk. "It's making me crazy. The leads have started to dry up, but now everybody's yelling and demanding immediate results. The press, the guys from downtown, even Michelson's been getting on my back.''

''I can see the tension between you two,'' Jackie said. ''What's the problem?''

Wardlow made a curt gesture and switched on his computer.

''It's not easy for him, or for the lieutenants, either, you know,'' Jackie said after a brief silence. ''They're the ones who have to take all the heat from higher up.''

''That doesn't mean Michelson has to—''

''Jackie?'' Alice closed the door behind her and crossed the squad room briskly. ''I've got some phone messages for you.''

''Okay.'' Jackie reached for the sheaf of telephone slips. ''Thanks, Alice.''

She glanced at the calls, none of which seemed pressing. One of them was simply a number and a note that read, ''Please call back.''

''What's this, Alice?'' Jackie said. But the secretary was already gone.

Jackie put the messages at the corner of her desk, took out her calling card and dialed a number in Los Angeles.

As usual, Lorna McPhee answered on the first ring. ''Don't you ever take a day off?'' Jackie asked.

''And I suppose you're at home right now, wearing a bathrobe and eating chocolates,'' Lorna scoffed.

Jackie laughed, then sobered. ''Have you visited my grandmother?''

''I went by on Thursday. They're all fine.''

''Really?''

''As well as can be expected, I guess,'' the social worker said. ''Joey's got half a dozen old cars dumped in the weeds out back. He says he's been stripping them for parts.''

"Are they hot?'' Jackie asked in alarm.

"I didn't probe, honey. They're in full view, so it's probably legal. At least semilegal.''

"What about Carmelo?''

"He's back home and looking for work, but not too hard. He and your grandmother were playing cribbage for a nickel a point. She'd won almost four dollars off him by the time I got there.''

"How's she feeling?''

"A little shaky, but okay. She's not getting any younger, Jackie. When she goes on one of these benders, it takes a real toll.''

Jackie felt an anxious twist of guilt. "I should move her out here, Lorna. I should—''

"You shouldn't do anything of the sort,'' the social worker said. "You can't change her. She has to do it for herself.''

"But she's going to kill herself.''

"Then that's her choice. You've made the offer and she's refused. You have to leave it there. The ball's in her court, not yours.''

"Did she...did Gram say anything about me?'' Jackie asked wistfully. "Last time we talked, she was really angry with me.''

"No, sweetie,'' Lorna said, her voice suddenly gentle. "She didn't say anything.''

Jackie was silent for a moment. "I wanted to talk with you about something else, too, Lorna,'' she said at last.

"Go ahead. I'm listening.''

Jackie told her about Alex, how she'd found the girl and called her mother, and her concern about what to do next.

"So what's the situation at the moment?'' Lorna asked.

"Like I said. She's staying at my place, and I'm still trying to decide what to do with her. She seems calm and cheerful, but I'm sure she's really bent out of shape. The poor kid's been through hell."

"She needs counseling, or at least someone who can get her to talk about what's happened."

"I know," Jackie said. "But I've hardly had time to say more than hello and goodbye. She spends the whole day alone, slaving in my apartment like a housemaid. It's not right, Lorna."

"Well, you can't send her home. It's out of the question. She'd be back on the street in twenty-four hours. I've seen too many cases like this."

"But I can't keep her at my place, Lorna. There's only one bedroom in my apartment, so she's sleeping on the couch. It's an impossible situation."

"You know the alternatives as well as I do, Jackie. You work with these kids all the time."

"Group homes, foster care, that sort of thing?"

"They're not all bad, you know. A hell of a lot better than the alternative," Lorna added grimly.

"I know, but Alex is..." Jackie thought about the girl's shy humor, her gentleness and talent, her touching eagerness to do anything that might ensure her a home and some security. "Oh, God. I just want her to have a normal home like other kids, the sort of thing she deserves. Failing that, I was wondering if you could make any suggestions."

"Like what?"

"Well, I'm sure her mother would pay for her to go to a private school somewhere, if it was the only way to get rid of her."

"But where would she go on holidays?" Lorna asked. "You can't make a life out of an institution."

"I know." Jackie twisted the phone cord around her fingers.

"I'll check into a few things and call you back as soon as I can, okay?" Lorna said. "Maybe we can find something for your girl."

"Thanks," Jackie said gratefully. "You're an angel, Lorna."

"I certainly am."

Jackie laughed at the placid tone of her friend's voice. They said their goodbyes and she hung up, feeling somewhat cheered.

She returned to her handful of telephone messages, leaving the nameless one until last.

When she dialed the number, a woman picked up the phone after the fourth ring.

"Hello?" the woman said, sounding breathless and annoyed.

"Helen?" Jackie asked in confusion.

"Who is this?"

"It's Detective Kaminsky. Did you call me about something?"

"Of course not," Helen Philps said. "Why would I be calling you?"

"But I thought..." Jackie looked at the slip of yellow paper and then remembered giving her card to old Grace Philps.

"There must be some kind of mix-up. Look," Helen added hastily, "I'm sorry to be so rude, but I really can't talk now. I'm late for an appointment. I was just going out the door when the telephone rang, and I have to be home within an hour because Mr. Arnussen is coming over to start working on the roof."

"That's all right," Jackie said. "Sorry to bother you."

"But why did you call me?" Helen asked, her voice suddenly wary.

"I made a really stupid mistake," Jackie lied freely. "I just realized it. I was making some calls from a list, and I must have dialed your number, instead of the one below it. I'm sorry I bothered you."

"No problem," Helen said, sounding relieved. "Let me know if there's anything I can do to help. I should be home in about an hour."

"Sorry," Jackie repeated. "Go and keep your appointment. I'll talk to you soon."

She hung up and went back to her paperwork, forcing herself to wait twenty minutes to make sure Helen would be well away from the house. Finally she called the number again, praying Grace Philps could hear well enough to recognize the ringing of the telephone.

She was ready to give up and drive over to the house, when a quavery voice finally answered.

"Grace, is that you?" Jackie said. "It's Detective Kaminsky, returning your call."

"I'm afraid," the old woman said without preamble. "I want you to come here."

She obviously had no trouble hearing Jackie's voice. The telephone must be equipped with some kind of amplifying device, making it possible for Grace to carry on a normal conversation despite her hearing loss.

"I'll come right away." Jackie cupped the receiver against her shoulder and began to gather the files.

"Not today," Grace said. "Don't come today. She's going to be home soon."

"When can I talk to you?"

"Tomorrow. She always goes to church on Sunday morning. She'll be gone for a long time."

"But if you're afraid, Grace—"

"Not today," the old woman said firmly. "She teaches Sunday school and sings in the choir. She leaves the house at nine-thirty and doesn't get home until after twelve. Come in the morning." She paused. "I have things to tell you about her," she added darkly. "Terrible things."

Again Jackie wondered if the woman was senile, or if these accusations were simply part of Grace Philps's apparently ongoing feud with her daughter.

"I'll be there," she promised. "I'll come as soon as I can after nine-thirty."

"Good. I'll be waiting." Grace hung up without another word.

Jackie replaced the receiver and looked at her partner. "Did you find out anything about the Philps family?"

"Like what?" He opened a file.

"I don't know. Background, money problems, anything like that?"

"Not much." He consulted a sheet of paper in the file. "You said the baby-sitter didn't have much relevance in this case."

"I know. But now I'm not so sure." Jackie told him about Grace's call and her hints of "terrible things."

Wardlow shrugged. "The father was an industrialist, one of the city's upstanding citizens. He died about twenty years ago and left a good-size fortune, which the mother and daughter have been living on ever since. No sign of any money problems. In fact, Helen Philps still donates two thousand dollars every year to the local fine-arts society. There's nothing more on file about them, except that a few of the neighbors told me they felt sorry for poor Helen, being stuck in that house with her mother all her life. They all thought the old lady was getting senile."

Jackie sighed. "It sounds like another dead end, doesn't it?"

She switched on her computer and began to organize files while her partner worked next to her in silence.

On Saturday afternoon, clouds massed along the horizon, dark and brooding. By eleven-thirty it was raining, a cold slashing downpour that thundered on the worn shingles of the old house and overflowed the gutters in muddy waterfalls.

Helen Philps lay sleepless in her bed, listening to the mournful wail of the wind around the eaves and the spatter of raindrops against her window. She watched the red numbers on the digital clock, her hands clenched nervously under the covers.

Ten minutes before midnight she slipped out of bed, pulled on her bathrobe and slippers and crept from the room, pausing in the hallway to listen at her mother's door.

There was no sound from Grace's room. Helen pushed softly on the door and peered inside.

A dim glow from the hall light illuminated the massive four-poster bed with its knitted coverlet. Grace Philps's body was so slight she was barely visible in the big bed. The old woman snored lightly, her mouth agape, false teeth grinning in a jar of water on the bedside table.

Helen closed the door and stood on the worn Turkish hall runner, hugging her arms.

At last she descended the curving staircase, clutching the polished oak banister, and ran through the silent house to the back entry. She opened the door on the stroke of midnight.

He was waiting on the back steps, smelling of rain and warm maleness, his shoulders glistening with bright drops of moisture. She drew him inside and brushed the rain from his coat, then pulled him into her arms, kissing him hungrily.

"Oh, God," she whispered, touching his hair, his face, his chest and thighs, stroking him with urgent desire. "You feel so good. I've been practically dying, waiting for you."

He returned the kisses, gripping her masses of loosened hair, then forcing her mouth open and probing deeply with his tongue as he drew her bathrobe aside to fondle her breasts.

Helen gasped and swayed against him. She reached down hungrily to caress the swelling hardness at his crotch. "I want you," she whispered against his wet cheek. "I want you right now."

He laughed softly and pulled her along the hallway toward the stairs. They went up to her room, hugging and grasping, stumbling against each other in their eagerness.

"Be quiet," Helen whispered. "She wakes up so easily now."

"Didn't you give her something?"

"I was afraid to. It's been making her so cranky. Yesterday she…"

They went into Helen's room and closed the door. He unfastened the bathrobe, pulled it from her shoulders and looked down at her, his face darkly shadowed in the glow from the bedside lamp.

"What did she do?" he asked, reaching inside the lace of her nightgown to touch her nipples, stroking them slowly with his fingertips until Helen was shuddering with pleasure.

"She's been…threatening to talk to the policewoman."

His hand stilled and his face grew hard, almost frightening. "Kaminsky, you mean?"

Helen grasped his hand, rubbing it urgently against her breast. "I made sure they weren't alone together. Mama didn't say anything."

"What could she say?" he asked. "The old lady doesn't

know anything, does she? I thought you told me you've been careful.''

He pulled away and went to stand by the window. Helen hurried over to him, drowning in anxiety, and grasped his arm. She could feel the hard bulge of muscle under his shirt.

''You're so beautiful,'' she whispered, kissing his sleeve, running her lips along his shoulder to the warm hollow of his neck. ''Such a beautiful man.''

He didn't respond, just stood and gazed angrily out the window, his jaw working. ''Does she know anything?'' he repeated.

''Of course not. She doesn't even know about you. I've been so careful, darling. I promise I've been careful.''

''You're sure?''

''I'm positive. Please, don't be so cruel to me. You know how much I love you.''

He relented and drew her into his arms, holding her with the powerful, almost brutal grasp that she loved. After a moment he released her and allowed her to undress him, standing quietly while she slipped the shirt back over his shoulders, then unfastened his jeans and pulled them down.

He stepped out of the jeans and stood in front of her, arrogant in his male beauty. She drew his undershorts slowly over his ankles, kneeling before him in ardent worship.

''Oh,'' she whispered, gazing up at him while he watched with an inscrutable expression. ''Oh, look at you, my darling. So marvelous...''

Tenderly, reverently, she took him in her hands, then into her mouth, loving the way he trembled and shuddered under her caress. Helen burrowed against him, breathing in the scent of him, tasting the silky warmth of his skin.

Finally he swept her into his arms and carried her to the

bed, tossing her down on her back and thrusting himself on top of her. She clutched at him, moaning.

"You're a strange little woman," he said in amusement. "You like it rough, don't you?"

She dug her fingernails into his shoulders and whimpered with joy while he battered at her, hurting her. The pain was necessary because it carried her outside herself into a wild savage place where she could be the person she'd always wanted to be, free of everything but feeling.

At last, sated, they collapsed against the pillows and lay together in a sweaty tangle of arms and legs.

"You're really something," he whispered, his eyes gleaming in the darkness. "You're amazing. I'm going to miss you."

Helen stiffened and lifted herself on one elbow. "What do you mean?"

"I can't take you with me," he said quietly. "You know that."

"But you said—"

"We've been through all this before," he muttered. "Don't make me angry."

She was terrified of his displeasure, and the kind of controlled viciousness she'd seen from him a few times in the past. But she was even more afraid of losing him.

"I want to go with you," she said, whimpering in her anxiety. "You said you were going to arrange things so I could go, too. Please, *please* don't leave me. I'll die if you leave me."

He rolled onto his back and stared at the ceiling, his face tight with annoyance.

"I won't be a problem for you," she went on. "I won't do anything to upset you ever. Just let me go with you and I'll do anything you say. You know how much help I've been," she pleaded, terrified of the anger she felt growing in him, but unable to stop herself. "I've done everything you asked, haven't I? You know I've done everything you wanted. You know I have." Her voice rose, quivering.

"You're being hysterical," he said coldly. "It's out of the question. You can't come with me now, and you know it. Maybe later when it's all over, I'll come back for you."

He got out of the bed and crossed to the window, picking up his jeans and pulling them on.

Helen watched him in alarm, then stumbled from the bed and knelt in front of him on the hardwood floor, naked and shivering.

He pulled away with an impatient gesture as she tried to grasp his legs. "Please," she said, sobbing. "Please, darling…"

Even in the darkness she could see the look of distaste on his face. She licked her lips and stared up at him. "I'll tell," she whispered. "If you leave me, I'll tell everything."

He stiffened and paused in the act of zipping his jeans, suddenly still. "What did you say?"

"I'll talk to the police," she said rashly. Tears streamed down her cheeks. "I'll tell them what you did."

He grasped a handful of her hair and pulled her to him. "Listen, bitch," he muttered, bending closer. "You won't tell *anything*. Do you hear me?"

She whimpered, still on her knees. "You're hurting me." She tried to shake her head free. "Stop. Please stop."

His eyes glittered. "You won't say anything."

He gave her head another savage wrench and she screamed in pain.

Suddenly she could feel him relax his grip and turn away. The door to the hallway was open. Silhouetted against the hall light stood Grace Philps, thin and trembling in a flannel nightgown, her hair a fluffy halo of white.

"What is it?" she asked, her voice quivering. "Helen, what's going on in here?"

Grace peered at the man's bare shoulders and her daughter's huddled naked body.

He moved across the room toward her, and she glared at him. "Get out of here," she said sharply. "Get away from me."

But he continued to advance. Grace's defiance faded into uncertainty, then fear.

His tall body blocked the old woman from Helen's view. The last she saw of her mother was Grace's frantic clutching hands as she huddled against the door frame.

22

Toward dawn the rain slowed to a steady drizzle, gray and cold in the Sunday-morning stillness of the city. Jackie had a leisurely breakfast with Alex, who planned to spend the day tidying the living room and arranging the CDs in alphabetical order. It was so cozy and pleasant in the apartment that Jackie had to exert considerable effort to tear herself away and drive across town for her appointment with Grace Philps.

Just after nine-thirty, she drove down the back alley and parked the police vehicle out of sight behind the Philps house. She opened the car door and pulled on her old denim jacket, hunching her shoulders against the chilly dampness.

Then she let herself in through the back gate and started up the walk toward the house, glancing briefly at the neat bundles of wooden shingles that Paul Arnussen had stacked along the side of the garage.

On the back porch she paused and looked at the door. It was slightly ajar, standing open to the kitchen. Apparently Helen had left through the back on her way to church. Jackie rang the doorbell and stood looking over her shoulder at the curtains of mist that fell across the flowers and shrubs.

She tried the bell again without success, finally pushed the door open wider and stepped inside. She paused by the kitchen table and listened for any sound. Nothing. The house seemed empty, desolate.

Jackie stood uncertainly, wondering what to do. At last she moved down the hall and through the rooms on the lower floor, calling loudly.

Still there was no sign of Grace Philps. Jackie checked her watch and frowned. Nine-thirty, the old woman had insisted, sounding very definite. But it was now edging toward nine forty-five.

Jackie stood in the foyer at the bottom of the stairs, gazing upward. The house remained utterly still. She could hear the ticking of an antique grandfather clock in the hall behind her, the soft hiss of rain against leaded-glass windows.

"Grace?" she called again, looking up the stairs. "Are you there?"

The silence was oppressive, almost menacing. Jackie began to climb the steps, then stopped and reached under her jacket to take out her gun. When she reached the top of the stairs she gripped the carved newel post, peered down the hallway. She froze.

One of the doors stood open and a woman's bare feet and legs were sprawled into the hallway on the Turkish floor runner.

Jackie cocked her gun and hurried down the hallway. She stepped over the woman's feet and leaped square into the doorway.

"Oh, God," she whispered, lowering the gun and fighting waves of nausea. "Oh, God."

Grace Philps lay on the floor, eyes wide and staring, head lolling at a grotesque angle. Her flannel nightgown was rucked up around her thighs. She looked like a wretched little white kitten, killed in a fit of rage and tossed carelessly aside.

Her daughter was on the bed. Helen Philps looked as if she'd been strangled, but before she died she must have fought hard enough to incur some serious damage. Her hair was a wild tangle and her face was a ghastly bluish-white, covered with congealed welts of blood. Helen's tongue protruded from her mouth, swollen and hideous, and her throat was livid with bruises. Her naked body sprawled across the covers, brutally exposed.

Jackie's first urge was a compassionate desire to toss a blanket over the woman, but she knew better than to touch anything.

Instead, she raised her gun and moved back into the hallway, then began to edge her way cautiously along the corridor, pushing doors open and peering into each room in turn.

When she was satisfied that there was nobody else, living or dead, on the upper floors, she descended the stairs and looked through the other rooms. She opened a wooden door at the end of a corridor near the kitchen, and saw that it led downstairs to a dark basement.

Jackie closed the door again and stood by the kitchen table for a moment, breathing deeply to compose herself. She set down the gun, reached into her shoulder bag and took out her cell phone, dialing Wardlow. He was supposed to be at the men's shelter downtown questioning another possible witness, an acquaintance of Waldemar Koziak who occasionally slept at the shelter.

Wardlow had promised to carry his phone, ready to provide instant backup if Jackie needed help.

She waited tensely, listening to the empty ringing at the other end. There was no answer. Jackie swore fiercely under her breath and tried his number again. At last she abandoned the effort and dialed the downtown station.

Struggling to control her voice, she gave her location to

the receptionist, described the scene briefly and requested immediate assistance, then put the phone away, her hands shaking.

Suddenly she heard a breath of sound, a soft muffled thump from somewhere beneath her feet. Jackie whirled, her gun drawn, and stared at the basement door. She'd noticed the windows set into the foundation at ground level. The killer could be down there right now, preparing to climb through one of those windows and make his escape as Jackie waited for backup to arrive. Precious moments were ticking away while she stood here doing nothing...

She took a few more deep breaths and removed a small powerful flashlight from her bag, slipping it into a jacket pocket. Then she raised her gun again and opened the basement door. She began to edge downward, wary and alert, holding the gun in front of her with two hands.

Musty silence closed around her as she descended the steps. The only sound was the pattering of rain on the ground outside the small windows, and the soft gurgle of water as it flowed from the downspouts.

At the bottom of the stairs she stopped and let her eyes adjust to the weird half light that filtered through dirty windowpanes set into the foundation above her head. The basement walls were constructed of fieldstone and cinder block, sagging and frosted with a sulfurous white patina of age. Junk was stacked everywhere. Old cans and bottles littered the floor, along with bulging cardboard boxes secured with twine and scraps of lumber from ancient renovation projects.

In addition to the modern furnace, a huge boiler stood along one of the inner walls, lurking in the shadows like a many-armed monster, its pipes trailing tattered strips of insulation.

There appeared to be another room behind the boiler,

partially concealed by a heavy beam and a half wall of old planks.

The place was eerily quiet, but Jackie had the feeling that someone was waiting and watching. All her senses were heightened, alert with primal fear. She could almost smell the presence of danger hidden nearby, hear the heartbeat of a predator lurking in the shadows.

She picked her way though the clutter on the floor, conscious of the creaking weight of the old house above her, and of that grisly scene in the bedroom on the second floor.

"Police," she called, trying to keep her voice steady. "Come out with your hands up. Come into the center of the room where I can see you."

The silence pressed against her. Rain drummed on the windowpanes and splattered into the muddy flower beds above her head. In a faint ray of light from one of the smeared windows, she could see a black spider on the basement wall, working its way across the tattered lace of a cobweb. Sweat trickled down her neck and under her collar.

"Come out," she repeated.

Slowly she moved around the boiler toward the half wall and the darkened room beyond it. She shifted the gun to one hand and took out her flashlight, playing it over the wall and a stack of wooden crates in the middle of the floor.

Jackie paused, suddenly tense. There was something odd about that pile of boxes. Everything else in the basement was covered with a thick layer of dust, but the crates looked clean and bare, as if they'd just been moved recently.

She checked the room again, then began to pull and kick the wooden crates aside, working awkwardly with her left hand while she held the gun in her right.

Suddenly she paused.

"What the hell?" She stared at the floor.

A wooden framework about three feet square was set into

the concrete. The hatch contained a trapdoor of stained splintering planks, fitted with a recessed metal loop.

Jackie bent and tugged on the handle. The trapdoor lifted on well-oiled hinges to reveal a gaping cavern with wooden steps descending from the edge of the framework.

She knelt cautiously and shone her flashlight into the hole. It was an ancient round cistern, about ten feet in diameter and eight feet deep, installed, no doubt, when the house was built to drain rainwater from the roof and store it for future use. The primitive plumbing was long since disconnected, but a dangling length of pipe at the top of the cistern had once been attached to the rear downspout outside the house. Near the floor was the outflow pipe that would have led to a hand pump on the kitchen counter.

Jackie held her gun out stiffly and shone her flashlight around the cavernous interior.

The walls had been freshly coated with thick foam insulation in a creamy blue color, like the sky on a hot summer day. The bottom was carpeted and fitted with an oval braided rug. On the carpet stood a little daybed covered with a thick quilt and blanket, a miniature rocking chair stacked with a pile of children's storybooks, a covered white plastic commode and a shelf filled with toys.

"Jesus," she whispered, looking down at the little bed, the chair and commode and piles of toys.

Apart from this, the cistern was empty. Jackie scrambled to her feet and continued to shine the flashlight into the depths.

Something startled her, another breath of sound, the whisper of a presence.

She looked up sharply, pocketed the flashlight and held the gun with both hands in front of her again.

Then she began to move slowly forward, staring at a far corner of the room where a shadowed alcove was partly concealed behind the projecting wall of old planks. She could see a fuse box fitted on one wall of the alcove, along with a rusted electrical panel and a heavy tangle of wiring.

"Come out of there," she commanded.

There was no response. Jackie crouched and edged forward. Her eyes were beginning to adjust to the dim light in the basement. She could actually distinguish the shape of a figure behind the tangle of old wiring, a human body flattened against the wall.

"I know you're there," she said with an icy calm that belied the racing of her heart. "And I have a gun pointed straight at you. Come forward a few steps and then stop. Keep your hands in front of you where I can see them."

The figure moved. It ducked under the twisted wiring, stepped forward out of the alcove and stood facing her.

Jackie gasped when she recognized Paul Arnussen. He was bareheaded, wearing a denim jacket and jeans. He stopped near the edge of the cistern and looked at her, his face calm, expressionless.

"Get down on your knees," she said. "Put your hands on top of your head."

He stood without moving, still watching her.

"Do it!"

"You won't shoot me, Jackie," he said. "I'll bet you couldn't pull that trigger to save your life."

"That's where you're wrong, Mr. Arnussen," she told him coldly, keeping the gun extended. "Get down on your knees."

"Have you ever shot anybody?"

"On your knees!"

He obeyed silently, kneeling on the cracked concrete floor and putting his hands on top of his head while he continued to look up at her with that cold, inscrutable gaze.

"You have the right to remain silent." Jackie moved

toward him, holding the gun on him. "If you give up the right to remain silent, anything you say can and will be used against you. You have the right to have an attorney present while being questioned. If you wish to—"

"Are you arresting me?"

"Yes, I am." She finished reciting his rights, then reached into the pouch at her belt, keeping her gun directed at him with her free hand while she fumbled to extract the handcuffs.

"What for? Why am I under arrest?"

"Unlawful trespass, for starters. Later we'll talk about murder." She moved around behind him, pulling his arms back and snapping the handcuffs around his wrists. "Get up."

"Murder?" He got to his feet and twisted his head to stare at her. "What are you talking about?"

"I think you know what I'm talking about. Where's Michael Panesivic?"

"I have no idea."

"You might as well tell me," she said. "Your game's all over."

With his arms pinioned behind him, Arnussen jerked an elbow toward the cistern. "I don't know where little Michael is now, but I'd guess he's been in that hole for a while. Wouldn't you?"

"I'm asking the questions, Arnussen. Tell me what you've done with the boy."

They heard the sound of doors opening overhead, of voices and heavy footsteps. "Police!" a man called. "Is anybody here?"

"Downstairs," Jackie shouted back, limp with relief. "In the basement!"

A pair of uniformed officers clattered down the steps and

came through the other room to find Jackie standing near the empty cistern, still holding Arnussen at gunpoint.

"He was hiding in the alcove over there when I came into the basement." She gestured toward the shadowed corner. "There are two bodies in a bedroom up on the second floor."

"Two bodies?" Arnussen jerked his head, looking from Jackie to the other officers. "What are you talking about? What bodies?"

She ignored him. "And this," she told the two policemen, pointing down at the cistern, "is the place where Michael Panesivic has been hidden for the past week."

The younger officer stared at her in confusion, then edged nearer to peer into the dark cavern. "Is the kid still down there?"

"No. But I'm sure Mr. Arnussen can tell us where to find him."

The other officer moved forward and put a hand on Arnussen's shoulder. "Have you read him his rights, Detective?"

"Yes," Jackie said. "But you'd better do it again before you take him away."

She watched as the two officers escorted Arnussen out of the basement. He was taller than either of them, lithe and powerful-looking even with his hands pinioned behind his back.

When they were gone and Jackie was alone in the shadows, her hands began to shake and her whole body was gripped by convulsive spasms. She put the gun down and sat on one of the crates, breathing in deep ragged gulps until the pounding of her heart subsided.

Finally she shoved the gun back into its holster and took another look at the empty cistern, then climbed the stairs to the kitchen.

Several uniformed officers and a couple of homicide detectives were already on the scene, unpacking cameras and fingerprint equipment.

Through the kitchen window she could see Arnussen's broad shoulders and the faded blue denim of his jacket, dark with rain, as the officers marched him to a police cruiser at the edge of the property. One of them opened a rear door and put his hand out to protect Arnussen's head as he climbed in. Moments later the car drove away.

Jackie drew a panel of curtain aside, leaning forward to watch it vanish down the rainy street. She turned to gather her bag and notebook from the table.

"Good work, Detective." One of the homicide men paused in the doorway. "I understand you found the bodies and made the arrest."

"He was hiding in the basement."

"It took a lot of guts to go down there alone," the older detective said, his voice warm with admiration. "You're a good cop, Kaminsky."

She nodded wearily. "I guess you need a statement from me, don't you? I haven't had a chance to make any notes yet."

He gave her a keen glance. "Why don't you step outside for a bit of fresh air?" he said softly. "We can talk in a few minutes."

She smiled her gratitude and walked through the kitchen into the backyard. The flowers nodded under the drizzle of rain, and the lawn glistened like a carpet of emeralds. A breeze sprang up, making the brass weather vane on the old stable rotate gently. It gleamed with moisture.

Jackie looked up in shocked disbelief, wondering how she could have failed to notice this before, back when Paul

Arnussen was talking about seeing a chicken in his psychic vision.

The weather vane was a big brass rooster, proud and erect, with golden feathers sculpted around its body.

23

"Where the hell were you?" Jackie asked in a low furious voice. She glanced over her shoulder at the partly open door of Michelson's office, then turned back to glare at her partner, sprawled miserably behind his desk.

It was early on Monday, more than twenty hours since she'd arrested Paul Arnussen in the musty basement of Helen Philps's house, but Jackie still hadn't fully recovered from the shock and horror of finding those bodies and coming upon the man in the shadows.

In fact, as reaction began to set in, she felt even less in control of her emotions.

And her frustration was increased by the fact that, in spite of the arrest of Paul Arnussen and the discovery of Michael's hiding place, their investigation had come to a virtual standstill while the Major Crimes division conducted an initial probe of the murders.

There was even some question about whether Jackie's team would be able to continue with the child-abduction case. Michelson had cautioned the office by telephone on Sunday afternoon not to do anything further until new assignments were allocated.

"Wardlow," she said to her partner, "I was alone in that goddamn house with two bodies upstairs and a murderer hiding in the basement, and I couldn't raise you on the telephone. How do you suppose I felt?"

He dropped his head into his hands and rubbed his temples. "I'm sorry."

"Sorry! You'd better have a good excuse, dammit. I should report you to Michelson for failure to provide backup."

He raised his head, looking haggard. "Please don't do that."

"Why shouldn't I?"

"Because I need this job. I've worked so hard. I don't want to get a disciplinary letter in my file and be busted back to traffic patrol. I swear to you, Jackie, nothing like this is ever going to happen again."

"Where were you? You were supposed to be downtown, carrying your phone with you."

"I know."

"So where were you?"

"I was heading down to the men's shelter when I saw a car. It was a white Chevy convertible. I turned and started following it."

"Why?"

"Because Sarah was in the car. She was with a guy."

"Your wife?" Jackie asked.

"My wife," he echoed bitterly.

"So what happened?"

"I followed them out to one of the hotels on the freeway. They got out of the car and took a suitcase from the trunk, then went inside to register. I confronted them in the lobby while they were waiting for the elevator. But I guess in the heat of the moment I must have left my cell phone out in the car. I'm really sorry, Jackie."

She watched him, fascinated. "How, exactly, do you confront somebody in a situation like that?"

"Hell, you'd have been proud of me," Wardlow said bitterly. "I was cool as a cucumber. I said hello to Sarah, then introduced myself to the guy as her husband. I even shook his hand and made some small talk about the weather.''

"My God, Brian."

"And then, Sarah—"

"Detective Kaminsky, Wardlow," Michelson called from his doorway. "Could you two come in here, please?"

Jackie and her partner exchanged glances, then filed into the office and sat down. Michelson shut the door and seated himself behind the desk, regarding them coldly.

"Well, I just heard the whole story about what happened yesterday," he said at last. "Kaminsky, you're a goddamn idiot."

Her eyes widened. "Me? Why?"

"Going down into that basement in an empty house at a fresh crime scene without backup. What kind of damnfool stunt was that?"

"It was the appropriate procedure for that situation, sergeant, right out of the police manual," Jackie said. "In fact, the quote is, 'An officer arriving at the scene of a crime is expected to make every reasonable effort to apprehend the suspect or suspects before they are able to flee the scene. Apprehension always takes precedence over initial investigation, except in a case where injured parties may require the officer's immediate attention.'"

"I see. And what's the operative word in that whole passage?"

Jackie looked down at her hands.

"The word is *reasonable,* Kaminsky. Why didn't you wait for backup?" Michelson's weary eyes shifted to her partner. "And you, Wardlow. Where the hell were you while Kaminsky was out there being a hero?"

Wardlow shifted in the chair.

"Brian was on assignment downtown to interview a possible witness," Jackie said. "We were both carrying cell phones along with our police radios. I knew I had backup arriving within minutes, so I didn't feel it was excessively dangerous to check the basement on my own. Besides, I certainly didn't want to risk letting somebody climb out through one of those little windows while I hung around upstairs waiting for backup to arrive."

She could feel Wardlow relax beside her. He tossed Jackie a quick smile of gratitude, which she ignored.

Michelson looked at the files on his desk. "Well," he said at last, "we've got two investigations now, a child-abduction and a double homicide, obviously connected. The homicide belongs to the downtown guys, but apparently we still have the abduction. We need to decide what direction we're taking."

"If we still have the case, can we go down and talk to Arnussen?" Jackie said.

"Arnussen isn't talking. He spent the night in a detention cell, cold as ice, hasn't said a word to anybody."

"Has he called a lawyer?"

"Like I told you, he hasn't talked to anybody. He just sits on his bunk and stares at the wall."

Jackie pictured Paul Arnussen, caged and defiant in his jail cell. For some reason the image upset her. She felt no triumph, only sadness.

"What do we know so far?" Wardlow asked.

Michelson consulted his notes again.

"The urine in the potty was probably less than a day old. We can assume the kid was alive as late as last night."

"But he's not alive anymore," Jackie said in a low voice. "Not a chance."

"Why not?" Wardlow asked.

"It's classic in child-abduction cases," Michelson told him. "If the child gets a good look at his abductor, or if he has to be moved from an initial hiding place, he's almost always killed. I agree with Kaminsky. There's not much chance poor little Michael survived the night.''

"Do you think he'd have been able to identify Arnussen?" Wardlow asked. "We don't even have a scenario yet for this abduction, do we?"

"We're working on a couple of theories. Arnussen could have known Helen Philps for a long time and had an ongoing sexual relationship with her. Her body showed evidence of recent intercourse. So maybe he wanted a little boy, and she was able to provide both the kid and the hiding place. Sort of a gift to please her lover, you might say. The cistern was soundproof, too, so he could enjoy himself down there without anybody hearing the kid's screams.''

"My God," Wardlow whispered, appalled.

"And Helen could easily have done the snatch from the mall,'' Jackie said. "Michael knew her so well. She was his regular babysitter.''

"What's the other scenario?" Wardlow asked.

Michelson popped a couple of antacid tablets into his mouth and nodded at Jackie. "Tell him, Kaminsky. I read your notes.''

"I think maybe Helen Philps was coming unglued from the relentless pressure of caring for her mother,'' Jackie began. "I know from my own observation that Grace could be pretty difficult. Maybe Helen envied Leigh Mellon and wanted the little boy all for herself. Or maybe she was planning, after a while, to use him to raise some money for her future, since her mother controlled the cash flow. She could even have decided to hit the Mellon family for a huge ransom so she could escape from her mother.''

Michelson looked skeptical. "So where does Arnussen fit in?"

"He was having a sexual relationship with her, and

found out what she was doing. He's not deaf like Grace was, so maybe he heard Michael's screams when he visited Helen at night. He was afraid she was getting unstable and might hurt the boy, but he didn't want to be involved for fear of being named an accessory. Instead, he pretended to be psychic and dropped hints to me about chickens and basements, hoping I'd make the connection with the brass weather vane and go down into the basement of the house to investigate, the way we did out at the Panesivic farm.''

"That's all very neat," Michelson said. "Except that the kid's vanished again and we also have these two murdered women."

"Have they established a cause of death?" Wardlow asked.

"The old woman's neck was wrung. In fact, her head was practically twisted right off. The man must be damned powerful. And the daughter was strangled, but she put up a pretty good fight before she died. The medical examiner tentatively fixes the time of death as midnight, give or take a few hours."

"Arnussen had no marks on his face or hands," Jackie said thoughtfully.

Michelson gave her a keen glance. "You've seen him, Jackie. And you knew Helen Philps. Is it likely that she could put a mark on that guy, no matter how hard she fought?"

"Explain exactly what happened at the crime scene," Wardlow said.

"Sequence, you mean?" Michelson peered at them over the rims of his glasses, then went back to his notes. "The bodies were found in the daughter's room. The homicide guys assume that she and Arnussen are involved in some noisy sex, or maybe he's already busy trying to kill her.

The old lady wanders in to see what's going on. What you might call a fatal mistake," he added grimly.

"So they're saying that Arnussen killed both women around midnight, took Michael out of the basement and killed him, too, then drove away and disposed of the body?" Jackie asked.

"In all likelihood. The neighbors are being questioned to see if anybody noticed a vehicle arriving or leaving during the night."

"Then why did he come back on Sunday morning to the scene of the crime? Wouldn't that be a really idiotic thing to do, especially when he couldn't even be sure the bodies hadn't been discovered yet?"

"He had a perfect excuse to be there," Michelson argued. "He was working on the roof. The theory is that he left behind some kind of incriminating evidence and came back as soon as he could to remove it. But he sure didn't figure on Kaminsky coming downstairs and catching him red-handed."

"I still want to find Michael. We have to check every place that's ever been involved with Paul Arnussen," Jackie said. "We certainly have enough grounds now to obtain a warrant for the landlady's house and her outbuildings. Also, we should send a couple of teams to look through that canyon north of the city where he likes to go hiking."

"There's a lot of brush and rugged country out there," Michelson agreed, making a note on his file. "Not a bad place to dump a body. Particularly a small one."

"When do we tell the boy's families about these murders?" Jackie asked.

"We can't sit on it much longer. Twenty-four hours is pushing our limit. The media's been all over us, but police communications have been confined to cell phones and we've kept a lid on the murders…so far. Captain Alvarez was hoping we could get a statement out of Arnussen before we approached the families with this, but the bastard's not talking.''

''Well, we need to—''

The phone rang. ''Yeah?'' Michelson said curtly, picking up the receiver.

He listened for a moment, then hung up and turned to the two detectives. ''On your horses, kids,'' he said. ''Arnussen's ready to talk, but he wants you to be there, Kaminsky. In fact, he's refusing to start until you're in the room.''

''So what are you going to do?'' Jackie asked as she wove expertly through the busy Monday-morning traffic, heading for the downtown police station where Arnussen was being held.

''About what?''

''About your marriage. About Sarah and this man and…everything,'' Jackie finished lamely. ''Are you going to talk to her?''

''It's too late for talking.'' Wardlow stared out the passenger window. All Jackie could see was his profile and the freckles standing out darkly against his pale skin. ''I packed my stuff and moved out last night.''

''Oh, Brian,'' she murmured. ''I'm sorry. Where did you go?''

''To my brother's house. I'm sleeping on a foldout couch in his family room.''

''Are you going to start looking for a place?''

''I can't stay at my brother's house for long.'' He gave her a haggard smile. ''When I'm in bed, my little nephew climbs onto my stomach and sits there to play video games. It's pretty uncomfortable.''

Jackie gave him a brief answering smile. She was encouraged to hear him making a joke, no matter how feeble.

"Hey," he said. "And there's always your foldout couch, right?"

"Sorry," she said dryly. "It's already occupied. Brian..."

"Yeah?"

Jackie pulled into the parking lot, tossed her sunglasses on top of the dashboard and gathered her supplies from the back seat. "Do you think Michael's dead?"

"Why not ask your friend Arnussen?" Wardlow said with an angry grimace of distaste. "After all, he's the man who knows."

Jackie nodded and walked with him into the police station. They made their way along busy corridors to an interrogation room and peered through the panel of one-way glass.

Paul Arnussen sat with his callused hands folded quietly on the table. Across from him were Dave Kellerman and Ozzie Leiter, the detective team assigned to the Philps' double homicide.

Jackie knocked, then eased the door open a crack.

"It's Kaminsky and Wardlow," she said when Kellerman turned to look at the door. "Okay for us to come in?"

"Yep." Kellerman lifted an arm wearily. "We've been waiting for you."

Jackie and her partner closed the door behind them and took seats at either end of the table. She glanced at Paul Arnussen, shocked by his appearance.

He still wore the jeans and plaid shirt she'd arrested him in the previous morning. The blond hair was rumpled, and his face looked drawn. His jaw was covered in heavy stubble. The dark eyes flicked toward Jackie briefly as she sat down. Then he turned and stared at the opposite wall again, above the heads of the two homicide detectives.

For some reason, Jackie thought of the calendar in his tidy little basement suite, the wild horses galloping into the sunset with their manes and tails streaming....

"Well, she's here, Mr. Arnussen," Detective Leiter said. "Can we start now?"

Arnussen nodded, his expression remote.

"And you are fully aware that you have the right to have an attorney present while you give your statement, and that you do not have to make a statement if you choose otherwise?"

"I'm aware of my rights. I knowingly waive my right to silence and to the presence of an attorney while being questioned."

Although the room was being monitored on closed-circuit television, Kellerman put a small tape recorder on the table and leaned forward to speak into it, recording the time, date and circumstances of the interview.

"First question," Leiter began. "What were you doing in that basement, Mr. Arnussen?"

The prisoner looked up abruptly. "I want to answer questions from Detective Kaminsky. I told you that."

"We'll make a little deal with you, okay? Detective Kellerman and myself, we're investigating a few different aspects of the case," Leiter said smoothly. "If you'll answer just a couple of questions for us, then we'll turn the rest of the interview over to Detective Kaminsky. All right?"

Arnussen's gaze moved slowly from one face to another, weighing and measuring.

Finally he nodded again. "All right."

"So what were you doing in the basement?"

"I was looking around. I wanted to see what was down there."

"Why?"

"I guess I suspected something."

"Like what?"

Arnussen glanced over at Jackie but refused to answer.

Detective Kellerman leaned forward and gave the prisoner an engaging smile. "Why did you kill Helen Philps and her mother, Mr. Arnussen?"

"I didn't kill anybody. I'd only met Miss Philps once, and I didn't know her mother."

"So what were you doing in their basement?"

"I told you. I was looking for something."

"What were you looking for, Mr. Arnussen?"

"The cistern," Arnussen said. "I was looking for the cistern."

"Why?"

Arnussen glanced over at Jackie again. "Do you remember when we drove by the house that day?"

She nodded. "Yes," she said aloud for the tape recorder. "I remember."

"Well, something about that house jogged my mind a bit. I don't know why. I just thought it looked…interesting."

"Interesting, Mr. Arnussen? In what way?" Leiter smiled at him across the table.

Arnussen ignored the man and went on speaking to Jackie. "I noticed the roof was pretty badly worn in places, and I needed a job after I finished the veranda, so I figured that might be a good chance to get inside and have a closer look at the house. I went over the next day and asked her if she wanted to consider having her roof replaced."

"Helen Philps?" Kellerman asked. "Is that who you spoke to?"

"Yes."

"And you'd never seen her before that?"

"The woman was a complete stranger to me."

"What did she say when you asked her about replacing the roof?"

"She said she'd check with some of the other people in the neighborhood that I'd worked for and then call me back."

"And did she?"

"Yes. She called that same night."

"Would you like anything to drink, Mr. Arnussen?" Leiter asked solicitously. "Maybe a cigarette?"

"I don't smoke."

"Coffee, then?"

Arnussen made an impatient gesture. "Let's just get this over with, all right?"

"Sure, Mr. Arnussen," Kellerman said softly. "What happened after she called and told you she wanted the work done?"

"I drove by on Friday morning and checked the house, then wrote up an estimate. We agreed on a price and I went back Friday afternoon with a contract for her to sign."

"That's true," Jackie said. "I saw his truck leaving the Philps house on Friday afternoon when I arrived there to talk with Helen."

Arnussen cast her another expressionless glance.

"Did you see Ms. Philps again after signing the contract?" Leiter picked up the questioning.

"Briefly. I delivered the roofing supplies on Saturday afternoon. She came out to talk with me for a minute."

"What time was that?"

"I don't remember. Probably about two."

"What did she say?"

"Not much. She seemed kind of tense. I remember asking her if I could go inside the house and check the electrical supply to make sure there was enough power for my equipment.''

''What did she say?''

''She refused.''

''Helen Philps wouldn't let you into the house?''

''No, she wouldn't.''

''Why not?''

''She said something about disturbing her mother while she was having her nap. But I couldn't see how it would bother Mrs. Philps if I went downstairs to look at the electrical supply.''

''So what did you do next?''

''I wanted more than ever to get into that basement. Especially after I saw the backyard of her house.''

''Why, Mr. Arnussen? What was so significant about the Philps' backyard?''

He looked fully at Jackie. ''When I was behind the house unloading my bundles of roof shingles, I saw the weather vane. Did you notice it?''

She nodded slowly.

''What about the weather vane, Paul?'' Kellerman asked him.

''I'd...seen it before. I knew it was related to the little boy who'd been kidnapped. And I still had a strong feeling he was below ground. I wanted to get into the basement and look around.''

The homicide detectives exchanged a glance. ''This was one of your paranormal visions, I assume?'' Leiter asked with a benign expression. ''Detective Kaminsky tells us you're something of a psychic.''

''I'm not a psychic. I just...sometimes I know things. But I don't like to talk about it.''

''So you'd never approached the police before with one of your...psychic visions?''

"No." Arnussen looked around the table grimly. "And I doubt I ever will again."

"Have you ever killed anyone else?" Leiter asked quietly. "Like a little girl in Billings or a small boy over in Boise, for instance?"

Arnussen stared at the man, turning pale beneath his tan. "What the hell are you talking about?"

"Let's leave that alone for now." Kellerman leaned forward. "You wanted to get inside the Philps' basement, right?"

"Yes, I did."

"So what did you do about it?"

"Nothing. I went home and decided to sleep on it. I thought I'd go back on Sunday, and if the feeling was still strong, maybe I'd call Detective Kaminsky and tell her about the weather vane, and suggest that she check out the basement."

"But you didn't."

"No. I went over on Sunday morning after the rain to make sure none of the shingles were standing in water. When I went up to the house, the back door was open. On impulse, I decided to see if I could get inside without being seen."

"Let's get this straight, Mr. Arnussen. You dropped by a client's house on a rainy Sunday morning and decided to do a little breaking and entering just out of curiosity?"

"I knew she wouldn't let me into the basement. I had to see what was down there. I figured that if anybody caught me in the house, I could always say I just needed to have a quick look at the wiring, but nobody answered my knock."

"In other words, you were planning to lie."

"That's right," Arnussen said coldly. "I was planning

to lie. With a little kid's life at stake, I thought it was justified."

Kellerman made a note on his pad. "So what did you do next?"

"I pushed on the open door and looked inside. Nobody was in the kitchen, so I decided it was probably safe to slip into the house."

"And you'd never been inside that house before?"

"Only in the kitchen. We sat at the kitchen table to sign the roofing contract."

"How did you know where to find the basement?"

"I've worked on a lot of these old houses. They're all pretty similar. I had a fair idea that the door at one end of the kitchen would open to the basement."

"You never went upstairs?"

"Of course not. I didn't want anybody to see me. I tiptoed through the kitchen and downstairs to the basement."

"What did you see when you got there?"

"A lot of junk. A furnace, and an old coal-fired boiler that had been converted to natural gas. Some wooden crates stacked in the middle of the floor."

"When you arrived, were the crates piled in the same way that Detective Kaminsky found them when she went downstairs?"

"Pretty much. After I heard her walking around upstairs, I replaced the crates where I'd found them, then went over and hid in the corner by the electrical panel."

"Let's back up a little bit, Mr. Arnussen." Leiter glanced down at his notes. "What made you move the crates in the first place? If you'd never been in the house before and you didn't know any of these people, how did you happen to guess that there was an empty cistern hidden under the floor?"

"I told you, I've been inside a lot of those old houses.

I work on them all the time. It's a dry climate and they didn't have municipal plumbing at the turn of the century. I'd estimate that at least a quarter of the houses on the South Hill originally had some kind of under-floor cistern.''

Jackie watched his face closely, trying to see beyond the hard lines, the blunt slanted cheekbones and enigmatic dark gaze, the heavy golden stubble on his jaw.

"So you pulled the crates away and looked inside the cistern,'' Kellerman prompted.

"Yes. And I saw just what I'd expected.''

"What was that?''

"I saw a little room underground. I knew the boy had been hidden down there.''

"What were you planning to do about it?''

"I wasn't sure. I knew I had to tell Detective Kaminsky, but I didn't know how to go about it.''

"Why not just call and tell her?''

"I didn't have any permission to be down there. Besides, she already suspected me of the kidnapping. I was trying to figure out how I could let her know about the cistern without making myself look even guiltier in her mind.''

"So would it be fair to say, Mr. Arnussen, that you were a lot more concerned about yourself and your own safety than you were about little Michael?''

"Not at all. I knew I hadn't taken him. But if the police were convinced I had, they'd stop looking for the real kidnapper. I knew the boy was in danger. I didn't know what to do.''

"What did you decide?''

"I didn't have time to decide anything. Before I could leave, Detective Kaminsky came into the house. I hid in the corner, hoping she'd go away without seeing me. But—'' he flicked another glance in Jackie's direction "—she didn't.''

"Why did you kill Helen Philps, Mr. Arnussen?"

"I didn't kill her."

"Were you lovers?"

"I told you, I'd never seen her before I went over to talk to her about the roof."

"They found semen in her body." Kellerman's voice was suddenly hard and blunt. "We're having it tested. You won't be able to get away with this, you know. We'll have you nailed as soon as the tests come back, so you might as well go ahead and tell us what happened."

"I never touched the woman."

"Let's go over your activities and movements on Saturday night, shall we?"

"I want to talk to Detective Kaminsky," Arnussen said. "I won't answer any more questions from you until I've talked to her."

Leiter and Kellerman leaned close together, conferring briefly. Kellerman turned to Jackie. "Go ahead, Detective."

Jackie was sitting at Arnussen's right elbow. She looked directly at him. "Did you put Michael Panesivic down in that cistern, Mr. Arnussen?"

"No, I didn't. You know I didn't."

Jackie met his gaze with unwilling fascination. All at once she felt herself being tugged and pulled, drawn deep inside his mind. The sensation was unsettling, almost terrifying.

"Do you know where he is now?"

"If I knew, I'd tell you. But I think…"

She leaned closer to him, mesmerized by his dark compelling stare.

All her training and natural caution, even her rational thought processes, deserted her. She was conscious of nothing but the power of the man's personality.

He was trying to tell her something. It was a message of reassurance, passing directly from his mind to hers. At first she felt comforted, even happy, though she knew her feelings were a bizarre response to what was happening in this room. But along with the warmth came a sense of urgency that was almost paralyzing in its intensity.

Jackie stared into his eyes, shaken by unfamiliar emotions as she struggled to comprehend the message he was trying to give her.

"Tell me. You're seeing something," she whispered. "I know you are."

Jackie was vaguely conscious of Wardlow's embarrassment, of Kellerman's derisive grin and the skeptical look on Leiter's face, but she ignored the other police officers.

"Yes," Arnussen said.

Jackie clenched her hands. "What do you see?"

His face altered subtly and took on a troubled faraway expression. Even his voice changed, growing softer, almost husky.

"He's sitting on a bed, holding his stuffed yellow duck. He's terrified, crying. The poor little guy. Somebody's packing a suitcase."

The room was utterly silent. Jackie picked up her pen and gripped it so tightly her fingers ached. "He's alive?" she whispered. "Michael's still alive?"

Arnussen's face hardened, and his eyes focused again. He nodded tightly, all the gentleness gone.

"Hurry," he said to Jackie. "You have to hurry. There's not much time."

"Look, Mr. Arnussen—" Kellerman began.

Jackie made a curt gesture, silencing the other detective.

"Where should I go, Paul?" she asked. "I don't know where to go."

"That farm," he said. "Go out there."

"What farm?"

"The one we were at, with little horses in the meadow and onions hanging from the roof beams."

"Is Michael there?"

"No." He settled back in the chair and ran a shaking hand through his hair, looking even paler and more exhausted than before. "No, he's not there, but it's a place to start. If you go there, you'll find out what to do next."

"Christ, this is insane," Leiter said angrily. "It's the craziest thing I ever heard. You expect us to believe that you actually—"

"Don't you understand?" Arnussen had turned away from Jackie and was looking at the policemen across the table. "I don't give a damn what you believe. It doesn't matter. All that matters is finding the little boy, and there's no time left."

He reached out and gripped Jackie's hand, holding it tightly.

"Go!" he said.

She nodded mutely, got up and ran out of the room while the other three officers sat around the table, watching her in stunned silence.

24

While Jackie was driving out to the Panesivic farm, the fitful sun vanished behind a heavy bank of clouds. The sky darkened and rain began to fall again, hissing on the windshield and splattering into the puddles at the side of the road.

For the first time, there was nobody in the garden when she arrived at the farm. She parked the police car and made her way through the sodden yard, heading up the walk toward the back door.

Miroslav answered Jackie's knock, his eyes widening in surprise and fear when he recognized her. He reached for her hand with automatic politeness, then gripped it tightly. His face was tense behind the flowing silver mustache.

"No," she said, answering his unspoken question. "I just wanted to see how you're doing."

Miroslav relaxed and squeezed her hand gratefully, then released it.

"Come in. Come and say hello to Mama." He watched while Jackie kicked off her shoes and put them on a mat near the door.

Ivana was in the kitchen, bending to lift a tray of cookies from the oven. She straightened and wiped a strand of hair back from her forehead, then stared at Jackie. Her eyes darted to her husband in agonized appeal.

"No news, Mama," he said gently, crossing the room to

take her in his arms. "The detective just stopped by to see us for a little while. I think maybe she wants some of your cookies."

Ivana gulped back a sob and burrowed into her husband's arms, holding him tightly. Jackie felt like an intruder as she witnessed their love and suffering.

She turned away and saw little Deborah sitting gravely in a corner on the floor, watching her with wide dark eyes.

"Hi, honey," Jackie said. She crossed the room and knelt beside the little girl. "What are you doing this morning?"

"I'm making a house. See? My grandpa's helping me build it."

Several large cardboard boxes were piled in a corner of the kitchen, held together with packing tape. Deborah clutched a box of broad-tipped felt markers, which she was using to draw wavering uneven squares on the outside of the boxes.

"What are those?" Jackie asked.

"Windows. There's lots of windows. And this is the front door."

"I see." Jackie smiled at the neatly trimmed flap of cardboard with a thumbtack serving as the doorknob. She bent to look at a row of pink and yellow blobs along the base of the largest box.

"What are those colored things?"

"Flowers," Deborah said. "There's a garden beside the house."

"That's very pretty. Who lives inside the house?"

"My kitty. See?"

Beaming with pleasure, Deborah opened the little flap of cardboard and held it back. Jackie peered into the shadows, where the long-suffering black kitten lay on a towel at the far side of the box. He looked up, his yellow eyes gleaming faintly in the darkness.

She thought of Paul Arnussen crouched in the darkened corner of the old basement while the women's murdered bodies lay upstairs.

Jackie shivered briefly at the memory. "He looks very comfortable," she said, touching the child's smooth hair. "It must be nice and cozy for him to be inside his house on such a rainy day."

"Do you know where Michael is?" Deborah asked.

Jackie looked down at her in surprise.

Deborah frowned in concentration and marked a few more windows on the outside of her box. "Grandpa says Michael got lost, but you and your friends are helping us to find him."

"Do you miss him?" Jackie asked, her heart aching.

Deborah nodded and her eyes welled with tears. "I want to play with Michael. I want him to see my kitty's house."

"Come, Deborah." Ivana lifted the little girl into her arms. "Come and have some milk and cookies."

"Is the lady having cookies, too?"

"Of course she is. And she's having a nice hot cup of Bavarian chocolate with whipped cream."

Jackie opened her mouth to protest, then stopped when she saw Ivana's face.

The woman was suffering terribly. She looked thinner, and her fine dark eyes were shadowed with sleeplessness and fear. The only way Ivana Panesivic could survive this nightmare was by submerging her feelings in a constant tide of feeding and nurturing others.

Again Jackie thought about that musty basement, about the hole in the floor with its child-size furniture and the two murdered women on the upper floor, and the ominous connection between them and little Michael.

She wondered how Ivana Panesivic was going to endure that knowledge. Jackie knew that these grandparents had to be told before they read about the murders in the newspaper, no matter what the police brass ordered. Even Michelson believed that the media were going to break the story about Helen Philps and her mother before the end of the day.

Her intention was to take Miroslav aside before she left the farm and tell him what had happened at the Philps house, then allow him to choose his own way of giving the news to Ivana.

Stefan Panesivic would have to be told the story this morning, as well, along with Leigh Mellon and her family, and all of them would have to know about the cistern under the basement floor...

"Thank you," she said automatically, seating herself at the big kitchen table and accepting the mug of hot chocolate with its lavish mound of whipped cream. "This looks delicious."

Deborah sat opposite her in a wooden high chair, looking longingly at the plate of warm cookies that her grandmother placed on the table.

Jackie smiled. "You're a lucky little girl, getting to come out here and visit your grandma and grandpa," she said. "I wish I could stay all day."

"Deborah stays with us for a long time now." Ivana paused by the little girl's high chair and stroked her glossy head. "She stays with Grandma for almost two weeks while her mommy and daddy are gone. Don't you, sweetheart?"

"Really? Where are her parents?"

"Zan and Mila are flying overseas today." Miroslav stirred his hot chocolate. "I hope there will be no problem at the airport, with all this cloud and rain." He looked at his watch, then smiled at Ivana. "Their plane leaves in half an hour, Mama. They fly direct to London, then on to Zagreb.''

Jackie lifted her cup, frowning. "But I thought..."

Alarm bells began to ring inside her head.

"They were planning to take Deborah with them," Ivana said. "But they decided at the last minute that the trip would be too much for her. Zan brought her to the farm last night to spend the holiday with us."

Jackie's mouth went dry and her throat tightened as she stared at the older couple.

Suddenly, with blinding clarity, she recalled the elusive detail she'd been struggling for more than a week to remember.

"My God," she whispered, shaken and terrified.

She pushed the chair back and jumped to her feet. "I...I'm sorry. Please excuse me, Ivana. I have to run."

She stepped into her shoes and left the house, still muttering apologies as she hurried out into the rain.

Miroslav and Ivana stood together in the doorway, partly obscured by the flowing mist, while Jackie got into her car, wheeled around in the yard and sped out onto the road, water spraying from her tires.

She fumbled for the cellular phone, her mind a crazy jumble of thoughts and memories. She recalled Zan Panesivic sitting with her on the shaded veranda, telling her about their planned trip to Croatia, how they intended to take Deborah and show her off to Mila's relatives around Dubrovnik.

That memory had lodged just below Jackie's conscious mind, nagging and haunting her ever since. Because, of course, it was all clear to her now. She could see the whole plan and how it was done. The mystery, in fact, was that it had taken her so long to understand.

Jackie punched one of the speed-dial buttons on her phone. "Alice," she said. "Where's Brian?"

"He's still downtown."

"Get hold of him and have him stand by the phone. I'm probably going to need him in a few minutes. And contact the radio room for me, okay? Ask them to send a couple of officers to the airport. Any car that's in the neighborhood."

"Okay. Anything else?"

"Yes. Look up the number for the administration office at the airport. Hurry, Alice. I need it right away."

When she got the number, Jackie disconnected the first call and dialed again, gripping the phone with one hand while she drove. The country road was almost deserted. She pushed the speedometer up over seventy miles an hour, then eighty, careering through the mist and rain.

"I'd like to speak to John Shephard," she said when her call was answered at the airport. "It's an urgent police matter. Tell him Detective Kaminsky is calling."

She clutched the phone, praying Shephard was at his desk. He was a senior executive at the airport, and she'd helped his teenage son out of a serious scrape a year or two earlier.

"Jackie?" he said. "What's up?"

"Thank God you're there." Jackie reached the main road, paused to let a truck pass and then headed west toward the freeway. "I'm on my way over. I need to know about the next flight scheduled for London. I'm hoping it's been delayed."

There was a silence while he consulted the schedule of departures. "United Airlines. It's on time, leaving at eleven forty-five."

She glanced at her watch, and her heart began to pound. "Jesus. That's just a few minutes from now."

She pulled onto the freeway and stepped down hard on the accelerator, slipping in and out of the driving lanes. As a precaution, she turned on her siren and slapped the cherry onto the roof, where it flashed brightly in the rain.

"Check the passenger list on your computer, John. Is there a Zan and Mila Panesivic on board?"

"Yes," he said after another brief silence. "Traveling with their daughter."

"Can you stop the plane?"

She left the freeway at the second exit and started up a secondary road, racing toward the airport.

"Come on, Jackie," he said. "You know better than that."

"Can't you just give me a couple of minutes?" she pleaded. "Find some excuse to delay the takeoff."

"There's no way I can do that. Not even for you, kid. Boarding is completed and the plane's been cleared for takeoff. It leaves here in—" he paused "—six minutes, Jackie."

"Shit," she muttered, gripping the wheel and tramping down harder on the gas pedal.

If only the police had the kind of sweeping powers everybody thought they did! But Jackie couldn't stop this plane. In fact, without more evidence, she might even have trouble arranging for law-enforcement officials to intercept the flight in London.

"Look, I'm hanging up, John. I'll be pulling into the front of the terminal in about three or four minutes. Clear a path for me at the entry and be ready to tell me what gate I need."

"Will do."

She tossed the phone onto the seat and concentrated on her driving. The bulk of the airport terminal loomed out of the mist, its towers sending fitful beams of light into the rainy sky.

Jackie stopped at the terminal entrance, slammed the car door and ran inside. Shephard was waiting at the front entry.

"Gate twenty-six," he said as she dashed by him. "You've got two minutes."

She sprinted for the distant row of departure gates, flashing her badge at the customs officials and security personnel, passed the boarding desk and ran down the long covered tunnel to the plane.

The steward was closing the door when she arrived. "Police," she gasped. "I need to board the plane. Give me just a couple of minutes, okay?"

He stood aside in surprise and let her pass. Jackie stepped into the curtained first-class section and paused for a moment to catch her breath while the passengers looked up at her curiously. Then she made her way through the small cabin and drew the curtain aside, scanning the main section of the plane.

She spotted Zan Panesivic at once, tall and sturdy, sitting next to his wife. The seat beside them was empty.

Jackie stared at the vacant seat, feeling confusion and crushing disappointment. But when she moved down the aisle, a few steps closer, her pulse quickened.

Mila Panesivic held a small child in her arms, wrapped in a blanket and snuggled close against her body.

25

Zan Panesivic put an arm around his wife's shoulders. Mila held the blanket-wrapped bundle closer to her and stared at Jackie in startled defiance.

"Get up quietly and come off the plane with me," Jackie said softly, leaning close to them. "Let's not a make big scene, all right?"

The senior flight attendant hurried along the aisle from the rear galley, stiff with disapproval.

"Ma'am," she told Jackie, "I'm afraid you're going to have to leave the cabin immediately. We've already been cleared for takeoff."

Jackie palmed her badge, keeping it out of sight of the other passengers. "These people are coming with me," she said. "We'll be out of your way in just a minute."

"You can't pull us off this flight," Mila protested. "You have no right!"

"You, on the other hand, are an American citizen and have all kinds of rights." Jackie gave her a grim smile. "Do you want me to read them to you in front of everybody, Mila? You have the right to remain silent. You—"

Mila's face paled. "You're arresting us?"

"I certainly intend to."

The flight attendant moved closer to Jackie, casting a nervous glance at the front of the plane. "Please, Officer, could you just—"

"What are you planning to charge us with?" Mila asked.

"Kidnapping, for starters. I'll probably be able to think of a few more as we go along."

"This is my daughter." Mila held the blanket-wrapped child closer to her. "Deborah's passport has been cleared through American customs. We're leaving for Europe to visit relatives."

Jackie shook her head. "I have to admire your guts, Mila. But I just drove here from the farm about twenty minutes ago. Your daughter's sitting on the kitchen floor, eating cookies and building a cardboard house for her kitten."

Zan's broad shoulders slumped in defeat. He levered himself out of the seat and opened the overhead compartment to take out their flight bags while Mila watched him sullenly.

"Come on, Mila," he said. "We're making everybody wait."

She got out of the seat, still clutching the child, and made her way down the aisle, holding her head high and looking straight ahead.

"We can't do anything about their checked baggage," the flight attendant told Jackie. "It's too late to have it removed."

"That's okay. We'll make arrangements to get it shipped back. Thanks for your patience."

They left the plane and walked in silence down the deserted tunnel.

"Just a minute." Jackie stopped them when they were halfway down the corridor.

She moved close to Mila who drew away stubbornly, then yielded and allowed Jackie to lift a corner of the blanket.

Michael Panesivic slept deeply in his aunt's arms, cheeks

flushed, forehead damp with moisture. Bronze curls were plastered around his face. He was a handsome child, and appeared healthy in spite of the nightmare he'd been through.

Jackie looked at his face for a long time, then swallowed hard and turned away.

"Okay," she said curtly. "Go ahead. I'm right behind you."

John Shephard waited for them at the boarding gate, but nobody else noticed their arrival or watched with any particular interest as they made their way through the terminal to his office.

As they walked, Jackie looked at the warm bundle in Mila's arms and felt a strange kind of emptiness. This should be a moment of blazing triumph. The entire police team had worked so hard. But all she could really think about was how close they'd come to losing.

Just a few more minutes, literally, and Michael would have been gone forever. Only luck had saved this boy's family from a lifetime of agonized loss.

Luck and Paul Arnussen, she reminded herself.

She followed the little group into John Shephard's office.

"I've got some soda and fruit juice in the bar fridge," he told Jackie. "Anything else you need, just buzz my secretary."

"Thanks." Jackie stood by the door. "A few other police officers will be arriving soon if they're not here already," she told him. "Could you have them come up and wait out here in the corridor so they're handy when I want them? And I'll need to use your phone, if that's all right."

"Anything you say, Jackie."

She watched him leave, then closed the door behind him and regarded the couple in the office. Mila had placed Michael on a padded leather couch where he slept deeply under the blanket with his stuffed duck.

"Is he sick?" Jackie asked. "Why is he still sleeping so late in the morning?"

Mila's face set and she refused to answer.

"We gave him a sedative," Zan said. "We thought it would be easier for him on such a long flight."

"And safer for you," Jackie said coldly, "if he wasn't talking to people and telling them his real name, right?"

Zan looked down at his feet.

"So how did it happen?" Jackie asked. "One of you trailed Leigh while the other one grabbed Michael from the toy store?"

"No!" Zan said. "It wasn't us. We had no idea where Michael was. We were as upset as everybody else when he disappeared, and the whole time he was gone."

"We were sure the Mellons had taken him," Mila said, speaking up at last. "We felt just awful for Stefan and for the grandparents."

"So how did you happen to have him on that plane with you? You're telling me it wasn't planned? That it just sort of happened?"

Mila and her husband exchanged frightened glances, then turned back to Jackie.

"In a way it did," Mila said. "Our plan was always to take Deborah on this trip. We even bought her some new outfits, and some toys to keep her happy on the plane. And then yesterday…"

"It was late in the afternoon." Zan picked up the story. "Stefan came to us and said he was in big trouble. He said he had Michael, but he had to get him out of the country right away. Everybody knew we were leaving for Croatia the next day. Stefan asked if we could take Michael on Deborah's passport."

Jackie nodded thoughtfully. This, of course, was the very detail that had escaped her for so long, tantalizing her constantly just below the conscious level of her thoughts.

The two Panesivic children looked quite a bit alike. They both had brown eyes and golden brown hair. At three years of age, there wasn't much difference in facial structure between a boy and girl. And no customs official was going to check the sexual identity of a child traveling with its parents.

"What did you say when he asked you that?"

"I didn't want any part of it," Zan said.

Jackie looked into his guileless blue eyes and found that she believed him.

"I knew how illegal it was," Zan went on. "But Stefan seemed really desperate. He said if we didn't do this one thing for him, he'd never see his child again."

"He told us he was desperate," Mila added. "He said the Mellons were trying to get him in trouble with the police by accusing him of a serious crime, and we had to get Michael out while we had this opportunity. He said Michael would be safe as soon as the airplane lifted off American soil. He promised he'd join us in Zagreb in just a few days." She looked at her husband, then back at Jackie. "But Zan didn't want any part of it. We argued and fought for hours. Finally I convinced him to go along with Stefan's plan for the sake of the family."

Jackie watched them for a moment, weighing and considering. "Did Stefan tell you what kind of trouble he was in?" she asked.

"There wasn't time to go into any details. We had to make all the arrangements, get Deborah out to her grandparents without making them suspicious, all kinds of things."

"So you don't know where Michael's been hidden for the past ten days?"

"We don't know anything about it," Zan said. "We didn't ask, and Stefan didn't tell us."

Again Jackie found herself believing him.

Stefan had manipulated these people, just as he manipulated everybody. He'd played on their sympathies and their powerful sense of family unity, as well as Mila's hatred of the Mellons, to complete his whole macabre scheme. No doubt it had been Stefan's plan right from the start to substitute his son for Deborah on the flight to Croatia.

And he'd come within a whisper of getting away with it....

"Michael was in an empty cistern underneath the basement floor at his baby-sitter's house," Jackie told them. "For over a week, this little boy was kept in a hole in the ground like an animal."

Zan and Mila looked in alarm at the child's drowsy face, and the soft yellow toy cuddled close against his cheek.

"Late on Saturday night, the baby-sitter and her mother were both murdered when the boy was removed from the cistern," Jackie went on. "Stefan told you he was in trouble. He didn't exaggerate. He's probably guilty of a double homicide."

The shock and horror on Mila's and Zan's faces were clearly genuine.

Zan's eyes filled with tears. "Poor Mama," he whispered, his expression stricken. "This is going to kill my parents. It's just going to kill them."

Mila stared down at her hands while Jackie picked up the telephone and dialed the downtown station, asking to speak with Wardlow.

"What's up?" he said, coming to the phone immediately. "I've been sitting here waiting for your call."

"I need you to contact Michelson and get some things under way."

"Like what?"

"First we have to locate Leigh Mellon," she said. "Tell Michelson I have some good news for her. Try Adrienne Calder's house and Leigh's parents, or Harlan Calder's office if you can't get hold of her anywhere else. Have her go over to the substation and tell her I'll meet her there as soon as I can."

"You said it was good news?"

"Really good news. The best." Jackie smiled at the sleeping boy. "And, Brian..."

"Yeah?"

"Tell Leiter and Kellerman that Stefan Panesivic is probably their man. His old address is on the computer, along with the place he was moving to. Tell them we'll have to work fast, because he's booked on a flight to Europe in the next day or so, maybe even later today. In fact, they'd better start checking all the nearby airports."

"Okay. Hey, Kaminsky?"

"Yes?"

"Kellerman just got a report back from the FBI. Arnussen's fingerprints have been checked through every computer in the country. He's clean as a whistle. Never even had a speeding ticket, as far as we can tell."

Jackie was surprised by the warm flood of happiness she felt.

"I know that," she said softly. "I should have known right from the beginning. Hurry, Brian. Report all this to Michelson for me, and then get busy. Tell him I'll try to be back in the office within an hour or two."

"Good work, Kaminsky. You're the best."

"Thanks, partner." She hung up and walked out into the

hallway, where a pair of uniformed patrol officers sat waiting on a leather bench.

"There are two people in this room," she said. "I want them booked as accessories to a child abduction."

The police officers moved into the office where Zan and Mila slouched in their chairs, silent and miserable.

"What about the kid?" one of the policeman asked, gesturing at the sleeping child. "Should we take him down to the station?"

"No way." Jackie lifted the small boy into her arms. "I plan to look after this fellow myself. I don't want to let him out of my sight until I hand him over to his mother."

The rain was falling in gentle whispers over the city when Jackie parked in the lot at the substation. She got out of the car and leaned into the back seat to free Michael who still slept deeply, strapped beneath a couple of seat belts.

She lifted the small wrapped form into her arms, making sure that his stuffed duck was held in place by the blanket, and carried him into the station.

Alice Polson got up from her desk and hurried across the reception area, her plump face wet with tears. She followed Jackie down the hall to an alcove that contained an old couch and a vending machine.

"Oh, the little darling. Is he all right?" she asked, pulling the blanket away to look at the boy's red cheeks.

"They gave him some kind of sedative," Jackie said. "But he seems to be breathing all right."

She looked thoughtfully at Michael's closed eyes and soft pursed lips.

"Alice," she said, "could you look up his pediatrician in the file? Call and ask if it's possible for the doctor to come over here right away. I don't want to send this kid home without having him checked out, but I'm not anxious to haul him all over the city, either.''

"Okay. I'll call right now.''

"Is his mother on her way?''

"I don't think so.'' Alice paused in the hallway. "They haven't been able to find her.''

"What?'' Jackie asked in alarm. "Why not?''

"Sergeant Michelson will tell you. He's waiting for you in his office.''

Alice returned to stroke the boy's cheek again with a gentle lingering hand, then hurried back to her desk.

Jackie carried her burden through the squad room into Michelson's office. She placed Michael on a vinyl bench near the bookcases and sat next to him.

"Good work, Jackie.'' The sergeant's broad face was wreathed with smiles. He got up and came over to examine the child, leaning down to touch the boy's tousled curls. "I didn't think we'd ever see this little fellow again.''

"Neither did I.'' She looked at Michael's flushed face. "Where's his mother, Sarge?''

"Apparently she went for a drive with her sister. Wardlow's bringing the brother-in-law over to talk with you.''

"Okay. What else is happening?''

"The media broke the story about the Philps women a few minutes ago. They're calling it a brutal homicide, and playing up the connection to the missing boy.''

"They haven't been told anything about the cistern, have they?''

"Not a word. But we can't count on the information not being leaked,'' Michelson said grimly. "I hope we're able to get hold of the mother before that happens.''

"Have they picked up Stefan Panesivic?''

"Not yet, but the FBI is working with us and the highway patrol's been put on alert in all the neighboring states. He won't get away from us."

"I hope not." Jackie looked up as Wardlow came into the office, accompanied by Harlan Calder.

The lawyer stood looking down at his nephew. His eyes glistened and he brushed at them without self-consciousness, then reached out to touch Michael's face, drawing the back of his hand softly across the child's rounded cheek. Jackie watched him, deeply moved.

He turned to Jackie and said with simple sincerity, "Thank you, Detective Kaminsky."

"It wasn't just me," she told him. "It was a lot of people working together. And," she added honestly, "a pretty hefty dose of luck, too."

"We can't get hold of Leigh," Wardlow told Jackie. "She's out of town for the afternoon."

"Where?"

"Adrienne was getting worried about her," Calder said. "Leigh's been sinking deeper and deeper into depression. Adrienne thought it might help to get away from the city and go for a long drive. They were heading for Idaho, planning to be home around four o'clock."

Jackie glanced at her watch. "That's still almost two hours from now. Can't you reach them somehow?"

Calder shook his head. "Adrienne hates car phones. We'll just have to wait until they get back."

"And hope they aren't listening to their car radio," Michelson added.

"Why?" Calder looked at the three police officers. "What's on the radio?"

Briefly Michelson told him about the murders, about the cistern under the basement floor of Helen Philps's house and the hunt currently under way for Stefan Panesivic.

"My God," the lawyer said, looking shaken. He sank

into the nearest chair and passed a hand over his face, then looked at Jackie.

She met his gaze steadily, knowing what he was thinking.

This man's wife, the woman he adored, had had an affair with Stefan Panesivic. She'd slept with a man capable of two brutal, cold-blooded murders, as well as the abduction and concealment of a little child.

Jackie gave him a brief, sympathetic glance. He shook his head, still looking dazed and uncertain, then turned to the sergeant. "Will they be able to find him before he gets away?"

"We hope so." The phone buzzed. Michelson picked it up, said a few words and put down the receiver. "The doctor's here."

"That was fast," Jackie said in surprise.

"Apparently he works in a neighborhood clinic just a few blocks away. Alice said he was pretty excited when she told him the news. He dropped everything and came right over."

A tall young man entered the office, wearing jeans and a tweed sports coat and carrying a black leather bag. He glanced at the others in the room and muttered a greeting, then hurried over to the child lying on the vinyl bench.

"Well, well," he murmured, drawing back the blanket. "It's our Michael, all right. It's really him."

He opened his bag to take out a stethoscope and blood-pressure cuff, unbuttoned the boy's shirt and listened to his chest, then examined his eyes and ears.

"This little fellow's been pretty deeply sedated," the doctor said at last. "And I'd say he's lost some weight, too. He's probably been kept drugged most of the time since he's been gone."

Jackie thought about the dark airless hole in the basement

floor and the need to keep a small boy quiet while he was imprisoned. Even so, Grace Philps had suspected that "terrible things" were happening in that house.

Suddenly Jackie realized that Michael had probably been right under her feet, the first time she stopped to talk with Helen Philps. They'd sat in the kitchen eating date squares, and all the time—

"Is he going to be all right?" Michelson asked.

"I think so." The doctor continued with his examination. "There are no other signs of abuse. He might be a little nauseated when he wakes up, and he'll certainly be hungry for a few days, but there shouldn't be any lasting harm."

"What about his emotional state?"

"That's a whole different problem. We'll just have to deal with it as we go along, I suppose."

"Can we release him to his mother?"

"Oh, absolutely." The young doctor looked up with a smile. "That's going to be the best therapy for both of them."

He rearranged the child's clothes, drew the blanket up around his shoulders and left the office.

Michelson's phone rang again. He spoke briefly and hung up, looking at Jackie and Wardlow with grim satisfaction.

"The highway patrol picked up Stefan Panesivic in his Mercedes about fifty miles west of the city. He was heading for Seattle where he was booked on a flight to Paris tonight at seven o'clock."

Jackie sagged in her chair, almost sick with relief. "Oh, thank God," she whispered.

"They're taking him to the downtown station." Michelson glanced at Wardlow. "You'd better get down there, Detective. The patrol officers indicate that he's ready to give a statement."

Wardlow sprang to his feet, then paused. "What about Kaminsky?"

She smiled at him and patted Michael's leg. "I'm baby-sitting. Besides, Panesivic belongs to Leiter and Kellerman, now. They only need one of us down there to monitor his statement. Go ahead, Brian. You can call me here if they want me for anything."

He nodded gratefully and hurried toward the door, then paused to drop an awkward hand on Jackie's shoulder.

For the first time, she noticed that her partner looked a little better today. Wardlow was still shaken, but he seemed more confident, not quite so beaten.

People were amazing, Jackie thought. They had incredible resilience, and a seemingly endless capacity to adjust when reality was staring them in the face. All it took was time.

And a lot of courage, she reminded herself. Life took so much courage....

"Brian?" she asked.

"Yes?" He stopped in the doorway and looked back at her.

"I know they're releasing Paul Arnussen from custody, but if by any chance he hasn't left the station yet, could you tell him..."

She paused, conscious of the two policemen watching her curiously.

"Nothing," she said awkwardly. "It was nothing."

Michelson got to his feet. "I want to have a word with Detective Wardlow," he told Jackie and the lawyer. "I'll be back in a few minutes."

When the door closed behind the sergeant, Harlan Calder turned to Jackie. "Stefan's a complete monster," he murmured. "I never liked him, but I certainly didn't suspect him of something like this."

"Neither did I. It would have saved everybody a lot of suffering if I'd seen through him right from the beginning." Jackie looked down at the sleeping child. "Leigh tried to tell me, but I wasn't listening."

They were silent for a moment.

"The poor woman. No wonder she tried to arrange for her own abduction of Michael," Jackie went on. "She must have been practically out of her mind, worrying about what Stefan was likely to do."

Calder stood up and cleared his throat. "When Adrienne and Leigh get home, I'll call you right away."

"Thank you," Jackie said. "I'll be waiting."

He crossed the room to look down at Michael. "Will he be all right until his mother gets back? If you prefer, I could take him with me."

She smiled. "I'm happy to look after him for a couple of hours. Believe me, it's a whole lot better than looking *for* him."

Calder reached out to shake her hand. "Thank you again, Detective Kaminsky. On behalf of all the family, thank you from the bottom of our hearts."

She got up and followed him into the hall, then hesitated.

"Mr. Calder," she said on impulse, "will you and Adrienne be home tonight?"

"Absolutely. It's going to be an evening of celebration at our house."

"Do you think it would be all right if I dropped in for a few minutes? I want to talk with both of you about something."

"Related to the case, you mean?"

"Just a…a sort of loose end I want to tie up," Jackie told him.

"Of course. We'll be happy to cooperate any way we can."

"Around, say, eight o'clock? Would that be all right with you?"

"Certainly. We'll be expecting you."

"Thank you."

Jackie watched his spare erect form and balding head until he disappeared around a corner. Then she went back inside and sprawled wearily on the vinyl bench next to Michael.

All at once she was so drained and utterly exhausted that it seemed like an effort to breathe. She rested her hand on the boy's little shoe and leaned back, closing her eyes.

26

Adrienne peered through the windshield at the rain, now turning from a drizzle to a slashing downpour again as they neared the city.

"Sorry about this weather, honey," she said. "I thought we'd go for a nice drive in the country and see some scenery, but all you've been able to look at is the windshield wipers. What a rotten day."

Leigh was slumped in the passenger seat, gazing through the rain-smeared window. "It's all right. I don't care about the scenery. It was nice to get away for a while."

"Honest?" Adrienne gripped the wheel. "Do you feel a little better?"

Leigh nodded listlessly, hugging the teddy bear in her arms. "You know, I wish we didn't have to go back. I honestly don't know if I can take another day of waiting and waiting for the phone to ring and knowing it never will. I just can't take it."

"Come on, don't be like that." Adrienne squinted at a semitrailer that loomed out of the mist. "It's been only a little more than a week, Leigh. They could find him anytime. Maybe Jackie found him today while we were gone."

Leigh sighed and closed her eyes, letting her head drop back against the soft leather seat.

Adrienne felt a quick stab of concern. "Are you sure about this?" she asked.

"What?"

"About going home alone. Wouldn't you rather stay at my place for a few more days?"

Leigh shook her head without opening her eyes. "It's time for me to go home. I have to start dealing with my life again, Rennie. I can't keep hiding in your house forever. I've been there six days already."

"Nobody's counting, Leigh," Adrienne said quietly. "You're on your summer holidays, and it's not going to matter one bit if you stay with me for another week or so. Harlan and I are worried about you being all alone."

"I'll be fine. You've both been wonderful, but it's time for me to go back home and start trying to make it on my own."

"Maybe you could go over and visit with Mother and Monica for a few days, and help Daddy with his orchids. Wouldn't that be nice?"

Leigh rolled her head on the seat again. "Mother's in worse shape than I am. We wouldn't do each other any good."

Adrienne gave up the argument, but she continued to cast concerned glances at her sister's white face and trembling hands.

The outskirts of the city began to appear, gray and ghostly in the ceaseless rain.

"Well, almost home," Adrienne announced with forced cheerfulness. "I told Harlan we'd be back by four o'clock, and we're going to be right on time. Do you want to stop at my place for anything?"

"I don't think so. There's not much there except my robe and a toothbrush, and you can drop them off tomorrow. I just want to go home."

Adrienne opened her mouth to argue again, then thought better of it. Reluctantly she headed north and made her way through the wet streets to park in front of Leigh's green-and-white house.

"Want me to come in for a cup of coffee? I can call Harlan and let him know where we are."

Leigh smiled and touched her sister's arm. "I think I'd rather be alone, Rennie. You do understand, don't you? I really appreciate everything you've done for me," Leigh added with a tremulous smile.

"Oh, sweetie…" Adrienne hugged her. They clung together until Leigh pulled away.

"I'll call you," she promised, gathering up her handbag and Michael's teddy bear and reaching for the door handle. "I'll probably give you a call later in the evening. Thanks for the ride."

"You're welcome." Adrienne watched her get out of the car. "Leigh, are you sure…"

"I'm sure." Leigh paused in the open door and forced another smile. "Thanks again." She ran up the walk to the house, fumbling for her key.

Adrienne watched until her sister was safely inside the door, then shifted her car into gear and headed off into the rain.

For the first few minutes, the pain was almost unbearable. It suffocated Leigh, filled her head and her lungs so there was no room for thought or breath. All she could do was stand perfectly still in the empty house and try not to break, to explode and fly off into a million pieces.

Gradually she became accustomed to the silence and was able to move slowly around the house. She made herself a cup of coffee, watered the plants that had been neglected while she was at Adrienne's, touched her books and ornaments, reached out wistfully to stroke the cross-stitch upholstery on the dining-room chairs she'd always loved.

Finally she steeled herself to climb the stairs, still carrying Michael's teddy bear, and went inside her own bedroom. It was neat and empty in the weird half-light. Rain streamed down the windowpanes, making the room seem cavelike.

Leigh hung her sweater in the closet, took off her jeans and slipped into a jogging suit. She brushed her hair and pulled it back into a ponytail, staring at the hollow-eyed stranger in the mirror.

At last she forced herself to go down the hall to Michael's room. She sat on his little bed, holding the teddy bear. Her tears began to fall again, welling up from a place so deep within her she could never find its source, a dark and endless pit of sorrow.

Her arms yearned to hold her son, ached with an actual physical pain that made her grip her arms convulsively around the stuffed toy. She got up and rummaged in a drawer for one of Michael's cuddly blanket sleepers. Working quickly, almost frantically, she wrapped the sleeper around the teddy bear and zipped it up, then held the toy close to her, burying her face in the soft fleece of its shoulder.

"Oh, Michael," she sobbed. "Michael, darling..."

In the distance she heard something, a harsh sound that echoed through the house. She raised her face and rubbed at the tears, listening. The sound came again, and she realized that a telephone was ringing somewhere.

Leigh put the stuffed toy down on Michael's bed and padded along the hall to her own room, searching for the ringing telephone as if she was in a stranger's house.

"Hello?" she said at last.

"Leigh? It's Detective Kaminsky. We've got him. I'm—"

"What?" Leigh gripped the phone.

"We've got him. Michael." The policewoman's voice was distant, choppy. The connection was lousy. "Look, I'm in my car, heading for your house. I'll be there in a few minutes, okay?"

Leigh felt such a surge of excitement she couldn't speak. Had she heard correctly? They really had Michael?

Jackie was saying something else but Leigh couldn't make it out over the static on the line. She shook the receiver in frustration.

"Jackie!" she shouted.

But the line was dead.

Leigh hung up and ran downstairs. By the time she reached the living room she was shaking so hard she could barely walk. She stood at the window to wait.

The police cruiser pulled up and parked. Jackie Kaminsky got out, wearing a long hooded raincoat over her slacks, and hurried around to the back seat. She opened the rear door of the car and lifted something in her arms.

Leigh's eyes widened. She rubbed frantically at the condensed moisture on the inside of the windowpane, then leaned forward to stare again, her heart pounding.

The policewoman was carrying a small bundle wrapped in a blanket.

She was carrying a child.

Leigh screamed and ran to the front door, wrenched it open and stumbled into the rain.

Jackie smiled at her from under the hood of her coat, and Leigh couldn't tell if it was rain or teardrops on the woman's face.

"I've brought him home," Jackie told her simply. "I've brought Michael home."

Leigh pressed close to her and drew the blanket aside, whimpering when she saw her son's face.

"Oh, my baby," she whispered, reaching out to touch his cheek. "Oh, darling…"

"Let's get in out of this rain, okay?" Jackie said. "You're going to get soaked."

Inside the house, Jackie handed the little boy over and Leigh stared down at him in wonder.

"How on earth..." She turned to Jackie, who stripped off her dripping raincoat and stood in the hallway, smiling.

"Where did you find him?"

Jackie told her about the cistern under Helen Philps's house, and Stefan's plot to hide the boy until he could be smuggled out of the country.

Leigh listened and tried to concentrate. But it was too wonderful to hold Michael in her arms, to feast her eyes on his face and feel the sweet weight of his little body.

She understood that there was going to be more to the story, upsetting and terrible things that she would have to hear eventually.

Jackie would tell her everything later, when she could bear to hear it. Right now she only wanted to sit here in the old rocking chair, to kiss Michael and breathe in his drowsy fragrance, the warmth of his skin.

"Why is he so sleepy?" she asked, frowning as she pulled the blanket aside to examine his body. She stroked his arms and legs, touched his fingers, squeezed his feet.

"They gave him a powerful sedative before they got on the plane. It's beginning to wear off," Jackie said. "For the past half hour he's started waking every few minutes and asking where he is."

"Oh, Michael..."

The little boy had long dark eyelashes that lay on his round cheeks like fans. His eyelashes began to flutter, and lifted slowly. He stared up at Leigh with big dark eyes that looked vague at first, then startled and disbelieving.

"Mommy?" he said in wonder, his voice husky. "Mommy?"

Leigh sobbed aloud in joy. "Yes, it's Mommy," she said through her tears. "It's Mommy, and I'm holding on to you just as tight as anything. I'm never, ever letting go of you again, my darling."

The little boy continued to watch her for a moment, then twisted in her embrace and scrambled upward. He threw his arms around his mother's neck and clung to her fiercely, his small body shaking. Leigh held him and rubbed his back, murmuring against his hair as she rocked him.

Jackie stood watching them for a moment. Finally she rummaged in her pocket for a tissue, blew her nose and vanished down the hallway. Leigh could hear her working in the kitchen, filling the teakettle and getting out the cups. From time to time Jackie broke into happy little snatches of song that drifted warmly down the hall from the kitchen.

Leigh smiled and continued to rock dreamily, caressing her son and holding him tight in her arms.

The effort to put dinner on the table every night was clearly straining Alex's ingenuity, as well as her culinary skills. Tonight she'd prepared a bowl of macaroni and cheese studded with chopped wieners. She served the makeshift casserole with a grimace and a murmured apology.

"It looks great," Jackie said. "I love macaroni and cheese."

Alex smiled hesitantly and took off her apron, seating herself in the opposite chair.

Jackie cast a concerned glance at the girl's pale face. "What did you do all day?" she asked. "I know it's been raining, but did you get outside at all?"

"There was a break in the rain for a little while this

afternoon, so Tiffany and I walked over to the park. She likes to play on the swings.''

"Why was Carmen at home today?"

"She always has Monday off," Alex said patiently. "The salon's closed on Mondays."

"Is it just Monday?" Jackie shook her head. "I keep forgetting what day of the week it is."

"Carmen says we should visit them after dinner tonight. Tony's bringing over some new kind of board game."

"That sounds like fun, but you'll have to go by yourself, Alex. I've got an appointment." Jackie checked her watch. "In fact, I'm going to have to rush or I'll be late."

The girl's face twisted with disappointment. "Are you still working? I thought after you found the little boy, you'd be able to take some time off."

"I work most of the time, honey." Jackie looked at her steadily. "I told you that. In fact, I'm going to be busier than ever for the rest of the week. A lot of other things have been piling up while I've been working on this case."

Alex toyed with her meal, picking out the bits of meat and stacking them neatly at the side of her plate. She'd only put the wiener in the casserole for Jackie. "Don't you *ever* take holidays?"

"I get four weeks a year. In fact, I'm thinking maybe I'll take about ten days off, starting next week."

Alex brightened. "Hey, that'll be fun. Maybe we can—"

Jackie reached out and touched the girl's hand. "I have to fly to Los Angeles, Alex," she said gently. "I go down there every year to make sure my grandmother's all right."

Alex looked at her plate, then forced herself to smile. "Well, I'll stay here and water the plants for you," she said brightly. "You won't have to worry about a thing."

Jackie's heart ached for the girl, but she didn't say anything more about the upcoming holiday. Instead she hurried through her meal, then changed into jeans and a sweatshirt and drove across the city to the Calders'.

The couple were spending a quiet evening together in their family room, reading and listening to music. Harlan met Jackie at the door and ushered her into the cozy room where Adrienne was curled on a love seat by the fireplace.

When Jackie came in, Adrienne got up and hurried across the room to hug her tightly. Jackie submitted to the embrace and patted the woman's slim back, startled by this open display of emotion. She drew away and looked at Adrienne's flushed cheeks and reddened eyes.

"My goodness," she said with a teasing smile. "If I didn't know better, I'd swear you've been crying."

Adrienne clutched her arm and led her toward the couch. "It's just so damned wonderful. Leigh's in seventh heaven. Simply ecstatic. It chokes me up whenever I think about it."

"Have you been over there?"

Adrienne shook her head. "Michael's still pretty groggy, and he feels a little sick from all the drugs. Leigh wants to be alone with him tonight, but tomorrow evening there's a big celebration over at Mother's house. Monica's already started baking."

"I'm happy for all of you." Jackie sat on the couch and stretched her legs wearily. "I really am."

"Can I get you a drink, Jackie?" Harlan asked.

"I'd love a drink. White wine, please, if you have it."

"Chablis or chardonnay?"

Jackie grinned. "Just white. Whatever you've got."

He smiled back and left the room.

"Do you think it's dawned on Leigh yet?" Jackie asked. "The reality of what actually happened to Michael, I mean?"

Adrienne sobered and shook her head. "Not yet. God, what a nightmare."

"I can hardly stand to think about it myself. The poor little boy. Grace Philps tried to warn me that something was going on in that house, but she seemed so rambling and confused that I didn't understand."

"Stefan has always been so…" Adrienne stared moodily at the fire. "I can understand how the poor woman got involved with him."

"He gave a detailed confession this afternoon," Jackie said. "The whole plot was really cold-blooded. He said he needed Helen's cooperation if his plan was going to work, so he deliberately targeted her months ago."

"And seduced her, you mean?"

"He went over after Leigh stopped allowing him access to Michael and begged Helen to let him see the boy. She took pity on him and started letting him come to the house while Leigh was working. After that, apparently, it was a small step to convince Helen that he should be the one to have custody."

"But how did he get her to cooperate with the kidnapping?"

"Well, for one thing," Jackie said, "he started making love to her. The poor woman was completely besotted with him. Then he promised to take her away to live with him in Europe. Helen was anxious to dump the responsibility of caring for her mother and she didn't want to lose Stefan, so he had no problem getting her to do anything he wanted."

"Then why did he kill her?"

"When Stefan broke the news that he wasn't taking her away with him, after all, Helen became hysterical and threatened to tell the police about the kidnapping. Stefan said he simply had no choice. It's as if killing those two women meant no more to him than disposing of a couple of nuisance rodents.''

Adrienne looked down at her hands, shuddering. ''Harlan told you, didn't he?'' she whispered.

''About what?'' Jackie asked cautiously.

''About me and Stefan. Don't try to look innocent, because I know he did. The poor man loves me so much it's impossible for him to hide anything from me.''

Jackie stared at the leaping flames on the hearth, wondering what to say.

''I don't mind if he told you,'' Adrienne went on, hugging her knees moodily. ''I know you won't tell anybody. God, I can't imagine how I could have been such a fool, except that the man has some kind of overwhelming animal magnetism. And I was so unhappy about not having a baby. It's like I went temporarily insane, Jackie. I hate myself whenever I think about it.''

Her mouth began to tremble, and her head drooped.

Jackie put an arm around her shoulders. ''But you told your husband, and then you ended the affair, right? Anybody can make a mistake. God knows, you're only human.''

Adrienne shook her head. ''You're really something, Kaminsky,'' she muttered. ''You know that?''

Jackie drew away and smiled at Harlan who appeared in the doorway with a bottle and a tray of brimming wine goblets.

''Thank you,'' she said, accepting one of the glasses. She looked around wistfully at the comfortable room, the bright flames and the two people who looked so relaxed and comfortable in their home. ''This is really nice.''

Adrienne handed her a yellow ceramic bowl. ''Here,'' she said. ''Have some popcorn. Harlan just made it a few minutes before you came.''

Jackie took a handful of popcorn, listening to the music. "I've always loved the flute passage in this piece," she said dreamily. "Listen, isn't that beautiful?"

Adrienne burst into laughter. "I adore this woman," she told her husband. "I really do."

"Well, that's good," Jackie said. "Because I have to ask both of you a favor. It's something that's important to me."

"Go ahead," Harlan said. "We'll be delighted to help you with anything we can."

Jackie shook her head ruefully. "You might not be so quick to say that once you hear what it is."

Adrienne munched popcorn and leaned forward to sip her wine. "Go on," she said. "We're all ears."

While they listened in growing bewilderment, Jackie told them the story of Alexandra Gerard. She left nothing out, from their first meeting on the downtown street corner to her discovery of the girl's identity, her call to Alex's mother and the girl's touching effort to be the perfect houseguest so Jackie wouldn't send her away.

When Jackie recounted her conversation with Alex's mother, Adrienne clenched her hands tightly and her face twisted in pain. Harlan cast a concerned glance at his wife.

"So that's where it stands," Jackie said at last. "Next week I'm going away for a few days, flying to L.A. to visit my family. I can't afford to take Alex with me, but I can't leave her alone in the apartment, either. She spends far too much time alone as it is."

"Do you want her to stay with us while you're gone?" Harlan asked.

"Actually," Jackie told them quietly, "I want you to become her legal guardians."

Adrienne's eyes widened in shock. "Her *guardians?*

Come on, Jackie. What do I know about raising a teenager?''

"You were a teenager yourself," Jackie told her, "and
a pretty difficult one, too. You remember how it felt, don't
you?''

"I certainly remember how it felt to have my mother
being more concerned about her own life than anything
going on with mine," Adrienne said grimly.

"I know. That's why I think you can identify. Alex is
such a darling," Jackie told them earnestly, turning to look
at Harlan. "She's quiet and sweet, and she never complains
about anything. She tries so hard to be good. It just breaks
your heart.''

"But she's been through such hell," Adrienne said. "All
that niceness is probably just self-preservation. The nega-
tive stuff has got to come out sooner or later. She should
probably be in therapy right now, talking to somebody
about how she feels and about everything that's happened
to her.''

"See?" Jackie said. "You already know how to do
this.''

Adrienne turned desperately to her husband, who
watched her with a calm steady gaze.

"Come on, Harlan," she pleaded. "Surely you don't
think we could ever—"

"I think you'd be wonderful," he told his wife. "I think
you could do a world of good for this poor girl.''

Adrienne lifted her hands, then let them drop helplessly
into her lap. "I always wanted a child," she muttered. "I
wasn't thinking about becoming a surrogate mother to a
runaway teenager.''

The others watched as emotions played across her face.

"You'd have to help me, Harlan," she said at last.
"You'd need to be home a lot more often for meals, and

I'd want you here in the evening, too. We'd have to start being a real family, having barbecues and going out for drives and weekends at the lake..."

"Nothing could please me more," Harlan said simply. "I love the idea of going on family outings."

"I'm outnumbered," Adrienne said plaintively. "This is a damned conspiracy, that's what it is."

Jackie laughed and squeezed her hand. "I'll bring her over tomorrow on my way to work," she said. "Look for us early in the morning."

Adrienne paled. "Do I have to do anything to get ready? God, Jackie, I don't know if—"

"Be yourself, that's all. I think you and Alex will get along just fine."

"I guess we should think about filing for guardianship, or at least foster-home status," Harlan said.

"Just treat her like a houseguest for now," Jackie said. "See how you get along. If it works out, you can take care of the legal stuff down the road. She'll have to be registered for school in the fall, and that sort of thing, but I'll give you the numbers of a whole lot of people in Social Services who can help out when you need them. Let's take it one step at a time."

Adrienne gripped her hands together nervously. "I can't believe I'm doing this," she said in a small voice. "I just can't believe it."

Jackie patted her shoulder. "Don't worry. You'll be great."

27

In the week after Alex moved in with the Calders, Jackie spent every evening at the office, working to clear her desk. She closed some files, made dozens of phone calls and tried hard to wind up loose ends on other cases.

Then she booked off ten working days and left on the weekend, planning to spend most of the vacation time in Los Angeles with her grandmother.

Instead, she found herself taking an early flight back to Spokane after just six days in California, gloomily contemplating the prospect of another entire week with nothing to do but stare at the walls in her apartment.

It was Monday, her first morning back at home. She wandered around aimlessly in the sunshine for a couple of hours, then drove over to the substation to see what was happening. The squad room was even busier than usual, but her desk was clean and bare except for a couple of telephone messages.

Jackie picked them up and studied them in growing alarm. Both messages were from Adrienne Calder, who was trying urgently to get in contact with her.

She dialed the Calder number, and Adrienne answered on the second ring.

"Adrienne? It's Jackie Kaminsky. What's up?"

"Jackie! We didn't expect you back so soon. I just left those phone messages on the chance you might call in."

"Well, I was planning to stay longer in L.A., but things...didn't work out."

"Jackie..."

"Yes?"

"Could you come over tonight? I really need to talk with you."

The woman sounded distraught. Jackie's heart sank. "Is there a problem with Alex?"

"You might say that."

"Oh, no. What's happening? I hope she hasn't run away again."

"Look, we'll talk later, okay? I was hoping you might be able to come for dinner. There's going to be some family here, too."

"Sure," Jackie said. "I'd like that. What time, Adrienne?"

"About six, if that's not too early. We'll be out back by the pool. Wear shorts and bring your swimsuit if you like."

"Okay. Goodbye, Adrienne." While Jackie was staring at the phone, Wardlow strolled in from Michelson's office with his hands full of files. He stood looking at her in surprise.

"Hey, what's this? I thought you were supposed to be gone for another week."

"I'm still on holidays. I just got back to the city a little early, that's all."

"Why? Weren't you enjoying the California sun?"

Jackie toyed idly with the computer keyboard. "It was okay."

"You had another fight with your grandmother, didn't you?"

She grimaced and turned away. Wardlow moved nearer to drop a sympathetic hand on her shoulder.

Jackie composed herself and gave him a wan smile. "So

what's happening with you? You're certainly looking better."

"I've got a little apartment downtown. Just moved in yesterday. I'm doing okay."

"You're not so upset anymore?"

He looked down at the files in his hand. "I guess I'm starting to accept the fact that Sarah never loved me. I kept hoping things would change, but people don't change, Kaminsky. No matter how much we want them to, they stay the same."

"I suppose you're right. What a bleak prospect." Jackie twisted the cord on her telephone. "What else is happening? Here at work, I mean."

"All kinds of stuff. The usual rash of hot-weather crimes. We've been really busy."

"What about the Panesivic case?"

"Stefan's bail was denied. He's been moved to a prison downstate while he waits for trial. His lawyer's got him pleading guilty to the abduction, but not guilty to the murders."

"Why?" Jackie asked in surprise. "We've got him nailed, Brian. There's DNA, a valid confession, the whole works. How can he possibly plead not guilty?"

"He's arguing temporary insanity, because Helen Philps was trying to keep him from having Michael. He claims his son matters more to him than anything in the world, so when Helen threatened to expose the kidnapping, he went out of his mind for a few minutes and lost control of his actions."

"No kidding. Well, I guess we'll have to wait and see what a jury thinks of that argument. What about Zan and Mila?"

"They're still free on bail, cooperating fully with the

investigation, so their charges will probably be reduced. They might just get probation.''

"That's good.''

"Good?'' he echoed in surprise.

"I wouldn't want Miroslav and Ivana to lose their whole family over this," Jackie said. "They're probably suffering enough as it is. And I'm satisfied that Zan and Mila weren't involved in any of the planning. They just got swept up into Stefan's craziness. Like a lot of other people," she added, thinking about Leigh Mellon, about Adrienne and Harlan Calder, about Helen Philps and her mother…

"I think you're right," Wardlow said. "The man's a real master at playing on people's weaknesses.''

Jackie began to toy with the phone cord again, and cleared her throat awkwardly. "What about Paul Arnussen?'' she asked.

"What about him?''

"Have you seen him since he was released?''

Wardlow shook his head. "Actually I stopped by his place a few nights ago. I was off duty and looking for company, and I figured he might want to go out for a beer or something. But he was gone.''

"Gone?''

"The landlady said he wasn't there anymore. I got the impression she was pretty upset about it and blamed the police. She sure wasn't very cordial. Practically slammed the door in my face.''

"I wonder where he went?''

"Nobody seems to know." Wardlow grinned briefly. "I guess he probably just packed up his tools and wandered off to some other town where they need a psychic carpenter.''

Jackie stared at her desktop. Finally she shook her head

and got up. "Well," she said, "I'd better get busy enjoying this holiday. See you next Monday, Brian."

He punched her arm gently. "Buck up, Kaminsky. Life isn't all bad."

"I know. It's just lonely, that's all. Look after yourself, okay?"

When Adrienne said "some family" would be present for dinner, Jackie hadn't realized that the whole group was invited.

She walked through the back gate and around the yard to the pool, carrying a bottle of wine, and was met by an astonishing sight.

Harlan Calder had a gas barbecue, flanked by a table laden with food, set up on the deck. He wore a yachting cap and red gingham apron and was grilling steaks, assisted by Monica who watched the cooking process with quiet vigilance.

Jackie had never seen the Mellons' housekeeper in anything but her neat gray uniform and apron. Tonight, though, Monica wore a pair of brilliant orange cotton slacks, a yellow print blouse and a wide-brimmed straw hat with a bunch of scarlet carnations tucked into the band.

Barbara Mellon sat under one of the umbrellas in a long khaki skirt and plaid shirt, rolling a box of yarn placidly into bundles. Her husband was beside her on another folding chair, smiling as he watched the children.

Alex, looking sun-browned and healthy in denim cutoffs, her hair pulled neatly back into a French braid, played on the deck with Michael. The little boy appeared fully recovered from his ordeal. He was dressed in nothing but a baggy swimsuit, and his small body was tanned golden. He raced around on the tiles, shouting with laughter as Alex tossed a beach ball to him.

Adrienne and Leigh moved between the house and the barbecue carrying trays of utensils and covered plates heaped with food.

Leigh was the first to see the new arrival. She dumped her plate on the table and ran to hug Jackie.

"I'm so glad you could come. Look, everybody, Jackie's here!"

A chorus of voices greeted her. Even Alden Mellon looked up and gave Jackie a smile of extraordinary sweetness, then turned to watch his grandson again.

"Come here, Jackie," Barbara called, patting a chair next to her. "Come and sit by me."

Jackie deposited her wine bottle on the table, smiled at the others and crossed the deck to sit under the umbrella with the elder Mellons.

Barbara leaned over to pat her knee. "I didn't get a chance to thank you," she said. "Our family owes you a debt of gratitude that we can never repay."

Jackie shrugged, feeling awkward. "I was just doing my job, Mrs. Mellon."

The older woman looked at Michael's sturdy little body as he ran after the ball. Her eyes misted briefly with tears. "We can never repay you," she repeated.

Alden leaned forward and smiled. "I brought you some of my nicest orchids," he said shyly. "They're in the refrigerator."

"Thank you," Jackie said, truly touched. "That's very nice of you."

She got up along with the others to fill a plate with food. The group sat around the pool, engaged in lively conversation as they ate. There was much teasing, which Harlan Calder endured with patient good humor, about his abilities as a cook.

Alex came by, holding Michael by the hand, and leaned

down to give Jackie a hug. "Hi," she murmured. "How was Los Angeles?"

"Hot and polluted. I'm glad to be home. How are you, honey?"

Alex smiled radiantly. "I'm fine." She bent to whisper in Jackie's ear. "I love it here. It's great."

She swept Michael into her arms and hurried away. The little boy giggled and squirmed as Alex carried him to an open cabana by the pool and pulled a red T-shirt over his head. Jackie watched the two children, feeling puzzled. Whatever the problem was that Adrienne had hinted at, it seemed Alex wasn't aware of it.

Maybe Adrienne just found the responsibility too much of a burden. If so, Alex would have to move again. Jackie sighed, then turned when Leigh dragged a lawn chair over and settled next to her.

"I wanted to chat for a bit before everybody else starts to monopolize you," the blond woman said with a smile. "I'm so grateful to you, Jackie."

"Hey, don't start again. I feel really uncomfortable when people say things like that."

Especially, Jackie thought, since it was Paul Arnussen who deserved most of the credit.

If it hadn't been for the unassuming carpenter with his rare gift, little Michael Panesivic would be lost in a foreign country by now. His father would be there with him, and two brutal murders would likely have gone unpunished.

Considering the political unrest in the former Yugoslavia, bureaucratic efforts to extradite Stefan Panesivic and recover Leigh's son from Croatia would probably have been stonewalled for years, if not forever.

Jackie shivered and gripped her hands together in her lap, appalled once more by how close they'd come to losing everything.

Leigh misinterpreted the shiver. "Are you cold, Jackie?" she asked at once. "Would you like me to get a sweater for you?"

"I'm fine, thanks. How's Michael?"

Leigh smiled fondly, watching her son. "He's almost back to normal. He still has bad dreams sometimes, and he can't bear to be separated from me yet even at night, but he seems all right otherwise."

"How will he cope when you have to leave him and go back to school in the fall?"

"I've decided to quit teaching for a couple of years. I'll go back after he's in school, when we'll be away from home for the same hours."

"Can you afford that? Isn't it—" Jackie stopped in embarrassment.

Leigh Mellon came from one of the wealthiest families in the state. She could afford anything she chose. But Jackie had always gotten the impression that Leigh wanted to be independent.

"Actually," Leigh told her with a smile, "I have another job. It doesn't pay as well, but it's something Michael and I can do together."

"What's that?"

"We're going to be helping Miroslav and Ivana out at their farm. I've hired on as a general farm laborer, Jackie. Michael and I will drive out there every day and help with whatever they're doing, and in return they'll give us lots of good farm cooking and a small wage I can use to pay the mortgage. We're all very happy about it."

Jackie patted the woman's slender hand. "You're a nice person, Leigh."

"So are you, Jackie Kaminsky."

There was a brief awkward silence.

"How are they?" Jackie said at last, thinking about Stefan's parents. "Has it been awful for them?"

"Pretty rough. But they grew up in a culture that knows how to deal with tragedy. They believe that family is more important than anything, and that people have to carry on with their lives no matter what happens. Ivana was so happy I wasn't going to abandon them and she'd still be able to see Michael all the time."

"How do they feel about Stefan?"

"Well, as you'd expect. They despise what he's done, but they still love him. They'll never give up on him. Ivana will probably go faithfully to visit Stefan every month, for as many years as he stays in jail."

"I should have believed you right at the beginning when you told me he was a monster. But he always seemed so..."

"I know what he's like. He can fool anybody. You mustn't blame yourself."

Jackie looked at her curiously. "Will you take Michael to see him?"

Leigh bit her lip. "I don't think I could bear it," she murmured. "Not when I keep picturing what he did to those poor women." She paused. "But I'll probably let Miroslav and Ivana take him after the trial is over. It means the world for Stefan to see Michael. It would be cruel of me to forbid it, now that he's..." She didn't complete her sentence.

Jackie gave her a hug. "How about Zan and Mila?" she asked. "What's your relationship with them?"

"I believe Zan was caught up in something totally against his nature. I don't hold any of this against him." Leigh's face hardened briefly. "It's going to take longer for me to forgive Mila, but Ivana will probably win both of us over eventually."

"I'm so glad you haven't abandoned that whole side of the family. It's a rich heritage for Michael. Family is precious," Jackie added, looking down at the rippling water of the pool. "We can't afford to throw away the people who love us. God knows, the world has few enough of them as it is."

"Mommy!" Michael called from the cabana. "Alex says it's bedtime. You have to come and read me a story. Come on, Mommy!" He was clinging to Alex with one hand and gesturing impatiently to Leigh with the other.

Leigh smiled and got to her feet, then bent to drop a kiss on Jackie's cheek. "Thanks again," she whispered.

As soon as her sister was gone, Adrienne settled into the vacant chair. She looked trim and attractive in madras shorts and a long-sleeved cotton shirt tied into a knot at her slender midriff.

"You're so damned popular I can hardly get you alone for a second," she complained.

"So what's the problem?" Jackie asked. "Why did you want to talk with me?"

Adrienne grinned, and looked so much like her old self that Jackie felt briefly reassured.

"Look, Kaminsky, if you're going to hang out in these upper-crust circles, I have to teach you the art of meaningless chatter. First, you ask me how I've been."

"How have you been, Adrienne?"

"Just fine, darling. And you?"

"I've been okay."

"Now you tell me how good I look."

"Those shorts are simply divine," Jackie said, getting into the spirit of things. "You know, the little black lines in the plaid are exactly the same color as the pupils of your eyes."

Adrienne chuckled. "I love you, Kaminsky. I really do. How was your trip?"

"It was depressing." Jackie dropped the banter. "It reminded me vividly of all the reasons I wanted to run away when I was fourteen. I don't know why I keep going back."

"I'm sorry, kid."

"So what's the problem with Alex? Why did you leave those phone messages?"

Both of them looked at the girl, who spoke briefly to Harlan and disappeared into the house.

"She looks happy," Jackie ventured when Adrienne said nothing. "And she told me that she loves it here."

"I know she does. She's positively blooming." Adrienne rubbed at the wicker on the arm of her chair. "Not that we haven't had a few bad times. She's broken down twice since she arrived and cried practically all night long. Harlan and I took turns holding her and letting her talk. She seems more at peace now, but the poor kid's been through a living nightmare, Jackie."

"That's why I'm wondering... It would be so hard for her to move again when she's just gotten settled here and begun to trust you."

Adrienne gave her a sharp glance. "Why would Alex move away from here?"

"But," Jackie said in confusion, "didn't you tell me there was a problem?"

"Yes, but it's not with Alex. The problem is with me."

"Tell me," Jackie said.

Hidden patio lights began to flicker on, illuminating the shrubbery and the rippling water. Adrienne stared broodingly at the pool.

"I'm so goddamn scared, Jackie," she said at last.

"Why?"

"What if we lose her? What if her mother comes back

and takes her away? I couldn't bear it, you know. I already love the girl so much I'd die if we lost her. So would Harlan.''

Jackie relaxed and expelled a long sigh of relief. ''That's not going to happen. No chance at all. You can quit worrying.''

''But I keep reading all the time about these people who look after kids for years and then lose them to the natural parents.''

''Those are little kids, Adrienne. Three-year-olds like Michael. Alex is fourteen, certainly mature enough to decide where she wants to live. No judge in the world is going to order her back to Seattle if she chooses to stay with you.''

''Really?''

''Of course. Look, Harlan must know all this.''

''He told me pretty much the same thing, but Harlan's specialty is corporate law. He doesn't know anything about child-custody cases. I wanted to hear it from you.''

''Well, now you've heard it. Nobody's going to take Alex away as long as all of you are happy with the situation. End of story.''

She cast a sidelong glance at Adrienne, who still looked troubled.

Alex came out of the house with a leather case and sat cross-legged on the deck of the pool near Harlan's barbecue. In response to a word from him, she opened the case and took out a silver flute, fitted it together and began to play ''Danny Boy.''

The group around the pool listened in pleasure. Patio lights shimmered on the girl's tanned skin and smooth golden head, and the music drifted softly in the warm evening air.

''She's going to leave, anyway,'' Adrienne said in a

small choked voice. "We've got her registered in the ninth grade this fall. Soon she'll be finished high school and heading off to college."

"So?"

"So we'll be alone again, and what do I do then?" Adrienne asked in despair. "After I've had the experience of this girl filling my life, what will I do when she leaves?"

"You'll take another one," Jackie said calmly. "There are thousands of girls like Alex, you know. And you and Harlan have room in your hearts and in your home for more than just one of them."

"But do you really think I can…"

"Of course you can," Jackie said. "Look, when you're ready and Alex's room is empty, I promise I'll have somebody else waiting to move in. In fact, I may have two or three of them if you're getting really skilled at being a mother."

Adrienne considered this in blank astonishment.

Then she rested her head against the cushions and began to laugh, with amusement so genuine and infectious that the others around the pool turned to them with warm puzzled smiles.

28

Jackie left the party early, when the twilight began to deepen and stars glittered brightly overhead. She drove through the streets to her apartment, watching a summer moon drift above the hills.

The moon had been high and full a week ago, but was now faded to a pale whisper of light. After she parked the car and wandered upstairs, she could still see the narrow crescent as it floated beyond the window, looking sad and diminished.

Jackie moved listlessly around the empty rooms, picking things up and setting them down again, trying to think of something to hold her melancholy thoughts at bay.

It was too early to go to bed, but she didn't feel like going out again for a walk or a drive. Briefly she considered visiting Carmen, then abandoned the idea. Tony was probably there.

At last she switched on the television set and clicked through the channels until she found a wildlife documentary. This one was about the private lives of tigers. The big animals lay sprawled in the shade of a banyan tree, licking each other with lazy tongues.

Jackie sat cross-legged on the couch and gripped a cushion in her lap as she watched. The camera left the group under the tree and moved to a mating couple hidden in tall grass.

The male batted at the female with a heavy paw and mounted her, growling deep in his throat. She lay submissively under his muscular body, her eyes half-closed. The big tiger bit her neck to hold her in place, then released his grip and caressed her with surprising tenderness. She writhed in pleasure, kneading her paws in the grass, and twisted her head to gaze at him while his body moved and thrust against hers.

Restlessly Jackie tossed the cushion aside and got up, heading for the kitchen. She made a bowl of popcorn and spent some time wiping a counter and cleaning a sink that were already spotless.

At last she carried the popcorn back to the living room, hoping the mating scene was over.

Just as she was settling on the couch again, her intercom buzzed. Surprised, she answered it. Who on earth…?

It was Paul Arnussen, asking if he could come up. Numb with astonishment, she pressed the entry button.

Moments later she opened the door.

"Hi," he said gravely. "Is it too late for a visit?"

"No. I was just—" she stood aside in confusion, holding the door "—watching television."

"And eating popcorn, right?" He smiled down at her. "I can smell it."

"Yes." She felt as awkward as a teenager, speechless with shock and some other emotion she was afraid to analyze.

God, he looked good. He wore clean faded jeans, a white shirt and a soft leather jacket. He was bareheaded, and his smooth blond hair gleamed like silk under the foyer light.

"What are you watching on television?" he asked.

"Tigers."

"I like tigers. They're so beautiful."

"They look…they remind me of you."

He was clearly startled. "Why?"

She stared down at the floor, scarlet with embarrassment. What an idiotic thing to say. He must think—

"Are you sure I'm not coming at a bad time, Jackie?"

"No. No, now's a good time."

She led the way into the living room and indicated a big overstuffed armchair, then hurried to the kitchen for another bowl.

Arnussen watched while she filled the second bowl, dividing the popcorn.

On the television, a female tiger was teaching her two cubs to stalk game. The three of them slipped noiselessly through the scattered brush, following a herd of antelope.

"I thought you were gone." Jackie sat on the couch with her legs folded under her.

"Why?"

"Brian stopped by one night to invite you out for a beer. Your landlady said you were gone. We thought you'd moved away."

He shook his head. "I haven't moved anywhere. I just took a couple of weeks off and went shopping."

"For what?"

"My ranch. I was looking at some places over in Idaho and Montana."

"Really?" she asked in surprise.

"Oh, I won't be buying for a while. It'll take me about three more years to save enough for a down payment, but I still like to go and look." He smiled again. "Dreams are what keep us going, aren't they?"

"I guess they are." Jackie munched popcorn and stole another glance at him.

She still couldn't believe how good he looked.

The man was comfortable and relaxed in her apartment. Paul Arnussen had such innate power that his surroundings always seemed to break up and reassemble themselves around him, making him the natural center of any space he occupied.

"You were gone, too," he said. "I called the station a couple of times, but they told me you were going to be away for two weeks. I didn't really expect to find you at home tonight."

"I went to California to see my grandmother."

"And came home early?"

"I...wasn't enjoying my visit very much."

"Why not?"

She found herself telling him all about her family, about her cousins and her grandmother and the emptiness of the relationship.

He listened gravely, watching her face.

"I always go down there feeling so anxious to see her." Jackie looked at the sliver of moon beyond the window. "And after a while I realize that she's just going through the motions. She's waiting for me to leave so she can get on with her life."

"But you keep struggling to make the relationship something it isn't."

"I know. It's crazy, but I can't seem to give up, even when she's cruel to me. I guess I have the feeling that I need to salvage something from my childhood because I...don't have much of anything else. In an emotional sense, I mean. It hurts a lot." She glanced at him and tried to smile. "This will probably surprise you, but I'm not actually as tough as I pretend to be."

"I've known that from the beginning, Jackie."

She saw that he did know; saw, too, the compassion in his face, the gentleness of his mouth, and wondered how she could ever have suspected this man of doing anything cruel.

He leaned back in the chair and began to talk, telling her about his travels, about the ranches he'd been looking at and his dreams for the future. While he spoke, she could see vistas of cloudless sky and wide horizons, of animals and sunshine and a waving sea of grass.

Jackie sighed. "It all sounds so beautiful. I can hardly imagine a world like that."

"I'll take you for a drive tomorrow if you like. You've still got some time off, right?"

"A whole week."

"Let's go over to Montana. You can see where I grew up and meet some of my friends."

"I'd really enjoy that, Paul."

The barriers were gone between them, all the natural constraints of policewoman and suspect. She felt so open, and very, very vulnerable.

That tense dangerous edge of suspicion had protected her from her feelings before. Now, however, she longed to touch his face and stroke his hair and feel his arms around her.

"Look at that," he said, watching the television. "The little antelope's getting away, Jackie. Your tigers aren't going to eat tonight unless they improve their hunting skills."

"How does it work?" she asked abruptly.

"What?"

"Your psychic gift. Can you call it up at will?"

He shook his head, looking uncomfortable. "Not at all. It comes and goes, and I have no control over it."

"I don't understand."

He frowned thoughtfully as he searched for words.

"It's like, say, switching through your car-radio channels on a summer evening. You know how all of a sudden some distant station will come in loud and clear for a few minutes, then fade away?"

Jackie nodded.

"Well, it's sort of like that. The flashes don't happen more than once or twice a year, and only when somebody's in pain or distress. I usually don't know what it's about, so I try to ignore it."

"But with Michael, you couldn't ignore it."

He shuddered and looked at the television set. "Lord, it was awful. The poor little kid."

"He's fine now, thanks to you."

Jackie told him about her evening, spending some time letting him know what had happened to everybody involved in the case.

Arnussen listened quietly and asked a few questions, watching her with thoughtful dark eyes.

While they talked, her loneliness eased and vanished, slipped away into the summer night. She was left with a warm sense of friendship and trust that filled her with a sort of trembling joy.

He continued to look at her intently for a moment, then set his bowl of popcorn aside, got up and moved close to her. "I'm going to do something I've wanted to do ever since the first time I saw you," he said.

"What's that?"

In reply, he bent and swept her into his arms, then sat on the couch, holding her. The man was amazingly strong. His arms felt like bands of steel around her body.

"I'm going to kiss you, Detective. If I do, will you promise not to arrest me?"

"I can't promise," she murmured against his neck. He smelled of after-shave and sunshine, of warm cotton and leather and clean maleness. "I guess you'll just have to try it and find out."

Then his mouth was on hers, taking her breath away. For a man who was so hard and muscular, his lips were surprisingly soft. They moved gently on hers, seeking and tender.

The kiss went on for a long time, and Jackie was drowning in the pleasure of it, wanting it to go on forever. But at last she drew away and looked up at him with a misty smile.

"You're one hell of a kisser," she whispered.

"So are you, Detective. I think I've been waiting all my life for you. And when I finally found you, what happened? You threw me in jail."

"Don't remind me."

He laughed and cuddled her tenderly in his arms. Together they turned to watch the television set as the tigers sprawled under the banyans again.

"They look so contented, don't they?" he murmured against her cheek, his voice husky. "Just a big happy family."

"You know, that's all I've ever really wanted," Jackie said. "To be part of a family, have somebody who cared about me."

"Me, too." He drew away to smile at her. "It's hell being lonely. But it's not easy for tigers to find their mates. It can take a long, long time."

She nestled in his arms, drew his head down and kissed him again.

The sun dropped lower behind the banyan tree, and its slanted light gilded the branches with bright fingers of gold. In the shadows, the tigers moved closer together and slept peacefully while darkness gathered around them.

Turn the page for a preview of
Jackie Kaminsky's next exciting case

SECOND THOUGHTS

by

Margot Dalton

coming early in 1998

only from

MIRA Books

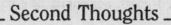

Second Thoughts

Detective Jackie Kaminsky sat at the kitchen table across from Maribel Lewis, who fumbled in her pocket for a cigarette package and a lighter. Jackie's partner, Brian Wardlow, had taken the two children out of the kitchen and was questioning them on the glassed-in front porch.

"I quit smoking almost six months ago," Maribel said. "But with all this going on..." She flicked the top of the lighter with shaking hands.

Jackie looked down at the picture—now encased in a clear plastic envelope—that had been left in Maribel's kitchen by whoever had broken in last night. It was an explicitly sexual scene—a voluptuous woman in shredded garments kneeling before a naked man with a huge thrusting phallus. The heads of the couple had been obliterated, covered by smiling faces cut from photographs and pasted neatly into place. The rest of the paper was spattered with dark red stains that looked like blood.

"You say the man in this cut-out photograph is your son, Mrs. Lewis?" Jackie asked, opening her notebook.

"Yes. His name is Stanley Lewis."

"Age?"

"Thirty-four."

"And where does he live?"

"He has an apartment out in the Valley. He works at a feed mill east of the city."

She gave addresses and phone numbers, and Jackie wrote them down. "When would be the best time to contact him?"

"Evening, I guess. Sometimes he's home in the evening."

"Okay. And the woman?"

Maribel took a long, hungry drag on her cigarette. "That's Stanley's ex-wife, Christine."

"Gordie's mother?" Jackie said, beginning to put it all together.

"Yes. She lives in a basement suite a couple of blocks from here. Gordie and Desiree live with her. She works at a ranch out by Rearden, training horses."

"How long has she been divorced from your son?"

"About eight months. They were married for twelve years. They met on the rodeo circuit. Stanley used to be a champion rodeo cowboy back in his early days." Maribel blew out a plume of smoke, her eyes narrowed. "He met Christine when she was just a girl, and she chased him and got herself pregnant. They were married when she was eighteen. Gordie was born a few months later."

"So Christine's about thirty years old?"

"That's right." Maribel's lip curled briefly. She tapped her cigarette against the ashtray.

"You don't like her at all, do you?" Jackie asked casually.

"No, I don't. When she was living in this house—"

"She lived in your house?"

"Yes. After they were married, it was hard for Stanley to make a home when he was gone so much on the rodeo circuit, and they had the baby and Desiree to look after, besides. So I let them stay here. They took over a couple of rooms on the second floor, and we had a small kitchen put in up there.''

Jackie looked thoughtfully at her notes. "But both of them moved away after the divorce?''

"I couldn't possibly have that woman in my house. And Stanley didn't want to stay here after they broke up, so I lost my son, too. I hardly ever see him anymore," Maribel added, her voice breaking.

"When Christine left, she took the kids with her, too?''

"They didn't want to go. They wanted to stay with me, but she wouldn't let them.''

"Even Desiree? She's Christine's sister, isn't she?''

"Yes, but Desiree hates Christine as much as I do. She's just a young girl, but she knows well enough what that woman is.''

"I see." Jackie glanced up. "Could you show me the anonymous letter you received, Mrs. Lewis?''

The older woman's head jerked back and two spots of color appeared in her cheeks again. "No!" she whispered. "No, it's too awful.''

"I think you should let me see it," Jackie said patiently. "I don't want to alarm you, but if you've had a threatening letter and somebody's broken in to your home, you might be in danger, especially when you're living here all alone. I really think we should check out the letter.''

"Gordie and Desiree will stay with me at night whenever I want them to," Maribel said stubbornly. "I won't be alone.''

"I thought you were working at night.''

"Yesterday was my last graveyard shift for a couple of months. I'll be on straight afternoons now until June.''

"Don't you think you should consider the welfare of the children?" Jackie said. "If there's any possibility of danger…''

Maribel stared down at her cigarette for a moment, then got up abruptly and left the room. She came back carrying a plain white business envelope—gingerly, as if she couldn't bear to touch it—and tossed it onto the table in front of Jackie.

The postmark bore a date about a month old, and the address was printed by computer.

Jackie sighed and put her plastic gloves back on. Modern technology was a great boon to anonymous letter writers. They no longer had to cut words and letters out of magazines and paste them onto sheets of paper to avoid detection. Even with the most sophisticated lab equipment, it was virtually impossible to identify a laser printout and trace it back to a specific computer.

She glanced at the other woman. ''Have you handled this a lot?''

Maribel shook her head. ''Just once. I opened and read it, then put the thing away. I couldn't stand to look at it again.''

''I'm surprised you didn't throw it out.''

''Other things were happening. I thought it might be best to hang on to the letter, just in case I…'' Her voice trailed off.

Jackie opened the envelope and eased the letter out. It was a single printed sheet, plain and featureless except for a neat little star hand-drawn in a lower corner. She began to read.

Dear Bitch
You are a nasty and cruel person, and you think people don't know about your sins but they do. You are being watched. That money you stole has not been forgotten, or the way you whored after another woman's husband. And you dare to judge others! The Divine

One is not mocked. You will be the first to die. You will drown in your own tainted blood.

There was no closing or signature. Jackie folded the letter and slid it into the evidence folder along with the envelope. She looked up at Maribel Lewis, who was lighting another cigarette.

"What's this about stolen money?" Jackie asked.

Maribel took a drag on the cigarette, avoiding Jackie's eyes. "It was years and years ago. I worked at a bank downtown, and I...took some money."

"Why?"

"Stanley was eighteen, just finished high school. He wanted to go to university. My husband had been dead for years, and I couldn't possibly afford the expense of college. I did it for Stanley."

"How much money?"

Maribel licked her lips nervously. "About twenty thousand dollars. I took it gradually over a year or so. When they found out, the manager said they wouldn't press charges if I paid it all back. But most of the money was already gone, so I had to mortgage the house. After a while I got another job, out at the nursing home, and I've been paying off that mortgage ever since."

"I see. How many people would know about this?"

"Just some of the family, and the management at the bank. It was all kept very quiet. That's why this letter..."

She bit her lip and blinked back tears.

"And the part about somebody else's husband?"

Maribel's flush spread down onto her neck. "It happened about the same time as...as the problem with the money. He lived across town and worked at the same bank. They moved away more than fifteen years ago."

"His name?"

"Tony Manari. I have no idea where he's living now. He patched things up with his wife and they moved away. I haven't seen or heard from him since, but somebody told me that his wife died of breast cancer about five years ago."

Jackie nodded thoughtfully. "So these two old secrets of yours…they wouldn't likely be known or remembered by anybody except family members?"

"I can't think who else would know."

"What else has happened to alarm you?"

Maribel hesitated. "Sometimes I have the feeling that somebody's watching me," she said at last. "Peeking in the windows and so on. But whenever I go check, there's nobody there."

"When did all this start, Mrs. Lewis? You told me things were happening when the letter came, and that's why you hung on to it. Did you feel you were being watched back then?"

"It's been going on for a long time. Ever since the divorce, when Stanley left and I sent Christine away."

"And that was last year?"

Maribel nodded. "In the summer. It's that woman," she said darkly, the cigarette trembling in her hands. "I just know it is. She took my son away, and now she wants to humiliate me and scare me to death."

Jackie sat in the passenger seat while Wardlow drove back to the substation. She looked down at the plastic evidence case, frowning. "This is really an ugly one. Did you get any information out of the kids, Brian?"

"Not much. That Desiree is some piece of work, isn' she?"

"Pretty strange, all right. Did she tell you anything a all?"

He shook his head. "Just answered in monosyllables and stared out the window. It was like talking to a ghost. The girl's barely human."

"She looked human enough when she was watching Joel Morgan."

Wardlow grinned. "You noticed that, too?"

"It was pretty obvious. Naked, breathless lust, and the poor guy didn't even notice her."

"I don't blame him. Why would any boy be interested in spooky Desiree?"

"Did Gordie tell you anything?"

"He talked a lot more than Desiree, but he's got nothing to tell, really. He's just a scared little fat kid."

"What did he say about his mother?"

Wardlow shrugged. "He seems to care about her a lot more than Desiree does. Christine Lewis trains horses for a living. She left early this morning to haul a couple of mares over to a ranch in Montana and won't get back until tomorrow night."

"And his father?"

"Gordie seems pretty neutral about his father. Apparently Stanley isn't in the picture much anymore. He promises to come over and take Gordie out on weekends, but he's either too late to do anything or else he doesn't show up at all. And the father and mother still fight a lot."

"What do they fight about?"

"The kid didn't say."

Jackie looked down at the picture again. Suddenly she held the plastic case up to the light and squinted at it.

"What?" Wardlow glanced away from the traffic to watch her.

"There's a little symbol here in the corner. I didn't notice it because it's drawn right onto the picture, down in the shadows by the guy's foot."

"A symbol?"

"It's a little star, just like the one on the anonymous letter."

"Aha!" Wardlow said darkly. "The plot thickens."

"You're not taking any of this very seriously, are you?" Jackie asked.

"Not a bit. I think it's a bunch of childish pranks. Probably just our sweet little Desiree, getting her kicks."

"But there's blood on this picture. Where do you think it came from?"

Wardlow pulled up behind the Northwest Substation, which was a fully operational division of the Spokane Police Department, located a few miles north of the main downtown station. "My bet is that she pricked her thumb and squeezed some blood onto that picture just to make it look really scary."

"But what's the motivation? Desiree's supposed to care about Maribel. Apparently it's her sister that she hates."

"That kid doesn't have feelings for anybody, as far as I can see," Wardlow said. "Except maybe some intense hots for the neighbor boy, who doesn't even know she's alive."

"Well, I'm not so sure. I don't believe this is just childish mischief."

"What do you think it is?" he asked.

"I don't know, but I've got a really bad feeling about all this, Brian. It seems so…twisted. Full of hatred."

"No kidding." He raised his eyebrows in surprise. "You're really concerned?"

"I can feel it in my bones." Jackie stared down moodily at the grainy pornographic images. "Somebody's going to get hurt."

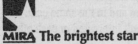

If this poignant and
heartfelt story by

MARGOT DALTON

made a great FIRST IMPRESSION,
here's your chance to receive another great read
from this bestselling author and MIRA® Books:

| #66047 | TANGLED LIVES | $5.50 U.S. ☐ |
| | | $5.99 CAN. ☐ |

(limited quantities available on certain titles)

TOTAL AMOUNT	$
POSTAGE & HANDLING	$
($1.00 for one book, 50¢ for each additional)	
APPLICABLE TAXES*	$ _____
TOTAL PAYABLE	$ _____
(check or money order—please do not send cash)	

To order, complete this form and send it, along with a check or money
order for the total above, payable to MIRA Books, to: **In the U.S.:** 3010
Walden Avenue, P.O. Box 9077, Buffalo, NY 14269-9077; **In Canada:**
P.O. Box 636, Fort Erie, Ontario, L2A 5X3.

Name: _____

Address: _____ City: _____

State/Prov.: _____ Zip/Postal Code: _____

*New York residents remit applicable sales taxes.
Canadian residents remit applicable GST and provincial taxes.

MIRA

Look us up on-line at: http://www.romance.net

MMDBL1